A Kiss from Maddalena

A Kiss from Maddalena

Christopher Castellani

LARGE PRINT

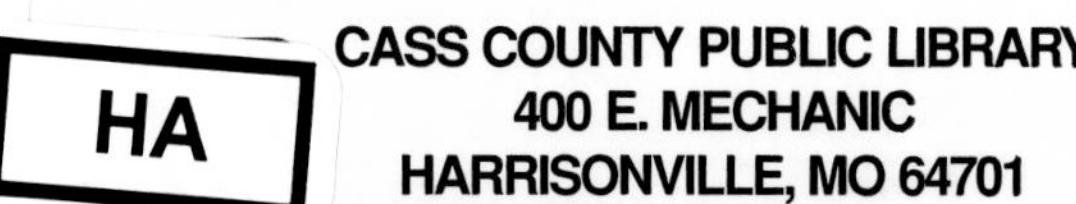

This large print edition published in 2003 by
RB Large Print
A division of Recorded Books
A Haights Cross Communications Company
270 Skipjack Road
Prince Frederick, MD 20678

First published by Algonquin Books, 2003

This book is a work of fiction. Names, characters, places, and incidents are products of the author's imagination or are used fictitiously. Any resemblance to actual events or locales or persons, living or dead, is entirely coincidental.

Publisher's Cataloging In Publication Data
(Prepared by Donohue Group, Inc.)

Castellani, Christopher, 1972-
A kiss from Maddalena / Christopher Castellani.

p. ; cm.

ISBN: 1–4025–6542–9

1. World War, 1939-1945—Italy—Fiction. 2. Large type books. 3. Italy—History—German occupation, 1943-1945—Fiction. 4. Historical fiction. 5. Love stories. 6. War stories. I. Title.

PS3603.A875 K5 2003b
813/.6

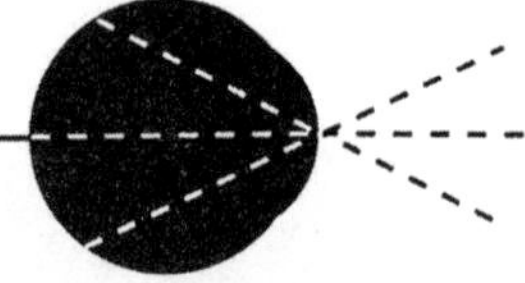

This Large Print Book carries the Seal of Approval of N.A.V.H.

For my parents,
Vincenzo Castellani
and
Lidia Marcelli Castellani,
who lived in this world
and inspired these stories

This book is my love letter to you.

When the evening fades in the fountains,
my town has a bewildered color.

I am far away, I recall its frogs,
the moon, the sad chirping of the crickets,

Rosario is playing, getting hoarse in the meadows:
I am dead at the song of the bells.

Stranger, when you see me slowly fly through
the plain,
don't be afraid: I am a spirit of love

returning from far away to his town.

—Pier Paolo Pasolini

There is nothing more difficult in this world than to achieve a marriage exactly the way you want it.

—Italo Svevo, *Zeno's Conscience*

PROLOGUE

September 1945

Dr. Fabiano pressed the buzzer three times, then let himself in. He climbed the stairs slowly. In the front room he found Concetta Leone sitting on the couch, chewing her nails and staring at nothing. By this time the old woman had lost most of her hair and was more than half crazy.

"My son found a shirt," the doctor said. He explained that his boy had been playing on the slope of the gorge, where he shouldn't have, adventuring like boys do. He'd spotted the shirt near the river, wedged between two rocks. The front of it was crusted with blood, which had dried in the shape of a giant tooth. The boy had brought it home, and now his father had brought it to Concetta.

Dr. Fabiano stood beside her, held up the shirt, and turned it twice around. He pointed to the torn sleeve and the blood and the frayed threads of the collar.

"Tell me, Signora," he said, lowering his voice. "Does this belong to your son?"

She took the shirt with both hands and held it to her nose. She smelled the armpits and handed it back. "No," she said. "*Grazie*, but no. This isn't Vito's. Do you want a glass of wine?"

The doctor's face was serious. "Guglierma Lunga told me she saw Vito in a shirt with a torn sleeve this summer," he said. "She felt sorry for him, she said, because his father was the best tailor in three towns but too far away to mend it. Everyone I talk to remembers it the same."

"What does everyone know?" Concetta said. "Is everyone his mother?" She looked toward the kitchen. "I have some chestnuts. Do you want chestnuts?"

He sat on an arm of the couch. He folded the shirt in half and set it on the floor, then took her hand in his. "Do you get enough to eat, here by yourself?" he asked.

"Of course!" she said. "What kind of question is that?" She took her hand away and put it on her lap. "I can get you chestnuts. I can even get you veal. Which do you want? I can send Vito to the woods or to the butcher. It depends how hungry you are." She tried to stand.

"No, no," said Dr. Fabiano. "I'm not here for food. Tell me: Do you know where Vito is? Right now?"

"Right now?" She repeated. "*Scusi* for one second." She called out, "Vito!"

No one moved. Birds flew across the front window and flashed shadows on the wall.

"He's probably at the Piccinelli store," she said. "It's getting close, you know. The wedding. The sooner the better, if you ask me. If you had to pick the most beautiful girl in the village, Dr. Fabiano, wouldn't you say Maddalena Piccinelli?" She fingered the small gold crucifix hanging from her necklace. "You have no daughters, do you? Only sons?"

He nodded. "Do you see Vito anywhere here?" he asked. "Do you talk to him?"

"There's no one else," she said. "Nobody comes. Guglierma's a *strega*, a witch! And my head, Doctor! The inside, it feels thick. And so dark! Vito makes it light. He sings the old songs and tells me about his life. He loves his mother." She rubbed her head behind her ear. "My daughters don't write anymore. America keeps them too busy to write even once a month?"

"I'm sorry, Signora," said the doctor. "Really, I am. Life hasn't been good to you. Everybody remembers that, too. But I have to tell you: No one in Santa Cecilia has seen your son in more than a week, not since Maddalena—" He stopped. "We thought he might have run away, but now that my boy's found this—"

"It's lamb you want, then?" she said.

He took a deep breath. He leaned over, picked up the shirt, and again held it in front of Concetta's face.

She narrowed her eyes at it, then looked at him. "It's dirty," she said. "You want me to wash it?"

"This is Vito's shirt," Dr. Fabiano said. "There's no doubt, Signora. Don Martino in Broccostella saw him in it, blood and all. He hurt himself. On purpose." He lowered his voice. "He's dead."

Concetta threw her head back, laughing. "Really?" she said. "You should stay for some wine, Doctor. When Vito comes home, you can tell him that yourself."

THE BIKE

May 1943

CHAPTER 1

From the air, the village of Santa Cecilia appears in the shape of a woman lying down. If you'd been a pilot flying over it—on your way to Germany or Africa or some other place to drop bombs—you'd have noticed how the main road forms a kind of spine leading to a round piazza, where green trees fan out like hair over the hills, and four narrow roads grow into limbs at both ends. One of the woman's arms cradles a cluster of white stone houses; the other stretches lazily into fields, in a way that suggests she is resting. Her legs straddle farms and orchards and a few scattered vineyards. She bends her knee at a curve just before an olive grove. If you'd been a pilot—young, maybe, one of the thousands of boys soaring over every week—you'd have had a woman's figure on your mind anyway, and you'd have longed to land in this place, to hide with her from Hitler and Russia and the *passo romano*, and to lose yourself in the parts of her body you can only see up close.

If you had come early on this spring afternoon, you'd have found Maddalena Piccinelli, not yet a woman but close enough, standing on the terrace above her family's store. This is as high above her village as a girl can expect to get, and many years will go by before someone describes its shape to her. Today, though, she watches something much more interesting: Vito Leone, a boy she's grown up with, celebrating the first victory of his life. All winter he'd talked big about building a bicycle from scraps he found lying around three towns, and no one believed he could do it, not even his own crazy mother. But now here he came, pedaling it up the main street of Santa Cecilia for all to admire.

"Free rides!" he shouted. "Come to the olive grove for free rides!"

Maddalena rested her forearms on the iron railing. Vito wobbled toward her on a heap of rattling metal that seemed about to burst. He'd painted every inch of it bright silver, from the handlebars to the rubber tires. The front wheel was nearly twice the size of the back, but the two did turn together, and Vito did flash the proudest of smiles when he noticed her.

"You're coming, right?" he asked without stopping.

"Depends," she said.

"I made this for you," he said. "Believe me or not. It'll go to waste if you don't come." Still he rode past her toward the spring and the upper half of the village, toward the twenty other girls her age. "Free rides!" he started again.

Shutters smacked open against the fronts of

houses. Fiorella Puzo, three doors down, sat up from her place on the roof, where she was taking a sunbath. She climbed into her bedroom window and in seconds emerged fully dressed on the street, smoothing her skirt and rushing toward the olive grove.

He must have made it just for her, too, thought Maddalena.

She had turned sixteen that month, almost two full years after Vito, but they were in the same grade. For a boy, he'd never had much luck. He was short for his age, and skinny in the arms. No hair grew on his face. He had a long and oval head like a peanut, a shape that Maddalena, from her seat behind him in school, found more comical than ugly. He was always spilling ink on his fingers, then forgetting and rubbing it on his temples when he got nervous. He told long, complicated jokes, sometimes funny ones, and once someone laughed no one could stop him from telling another. Other than that he was like most boys, best at standing around for hours in his pressed white shirt, smoking and whistling at girls. At least now he had the bike to show for his time.

Maddalena went inside to grab her shawl. It was too warm for it, but the pinks and blues matched the flower pattern on her dress, and she liked that she had to hold it clasped at her neck to keep it on. It made her look more dignified than if she let her arms swing loose at her sides. She'd learned from her mother, who'd grown up in Rome and seen real operas, that even though Santa Cecilia was a tiny village at the top of a mountain, it was still a stage where the world could see her.

You could never mistake Maddalena, the youngest, for one of her sisters. Yes, she had the same full lips, and the same nose, a bit too long and slightly rounded at the tip. Like the older Piccinelli girls, she was tall, with slim legs and hips just broad enough to catch the fall of her dress. But no Piccinelli, as far back as anyone could remember, had hair like hers—the color of straw, with streaks of white blond. It both thrilled and embarrassed her, and so conflicted was she about it that in public she wore the long curls pulled tightly back, secured with a handful of pins. She arranged it this way now, and washed her face with the kettle water, still warm from the morning coffee.

She found her sister Carolina in the dining room where she'd left her, sitting on the long table and digging under her toenails with a twig. "Well?" Carolina said. "How's it look?"

"No worse than that," said Maddalena, pointing to the pile of fuzz she'd cleaned from between her toes. "But it works. You have to admire him a little."

"Not too much," said Carolina. "When he builds a car or a tank, then maybe."

"A bike isn't hard?"

"He'll make like it was harder than it was, that's for sure," Carolina said. "I know him. He'll show us his scars." She jumped down from the table and brushed the mess she'd made onto the floor. "I'm riding first," she said, "before the thing cracks in two."

Carolina was Vito's age and slightly taller than Maddalena, with wider shoulders and more womanly breasts. She wore her hair long, styling it only when her mother ordered her. She had dark eyes that dared you to step closer. Vito was a little bit scared of her, and sometimes Maddalena was, too.

"Fiorella's already halfway there," Maddalena said.

"Fiorella's always halfway there."

They ran down the marble steps out of the house. Their two older sisters, Celestina and Teresa, twins, stood huddled with a few of their friends against the front wall of the store. They'd turned twenty this Christmas, and since then had had no time for the teenaged sisters they called "pretty babies." If she had wanted to be laughed at, Maddalena would have asked them to come along.

They ran past Guglierma Lunga, sitting as always on the crumbling steps outside her house, hungry for gossip. They waved without a *buongiorno*, afraid the old lady would make them stop and talk and sit through some horrible prediction about a girl getting killed on a homemade bike. They passed the butcher's house, their dead Zio Anzio's, the barber's, and the empty *tabaccheria*. When they turned the corner and saw the crowd at the olive grove, they slowed down.

There must have been fifteen girls in a circle around Vito, pulling at his shirt and begging. Fiorella knelt at his feet. Vito held his arms out in front of him, fanning them slowly up and down like Mussolini.

"Quiet!" he said, with a big grin. "*Pazzi!* You're all nuts." He spun around slowly. "I'm changing my mind as I speak."

"Changing your mind?" said Carolina, pushing through the pack of her groaning friends. "No way in the world!"

"I slave all winter," Vito said, "and everyone makes fun of me, especially you girls. Then I show up and everyone's my best friend? I don't think so. There has to be a price."

Maddalena took her place beside Luciana Campini, just a year older but already promised to Vito's best friend, Buccio. Buccio sat on the grass a few yards from the group, guarding the bike. Paying little attention to Vito, he straightened the spokes and polished the frame with a rag. Maddalena watched him. The muscles in his arms pulsed as he rubbed the metal tire guard until it shone. In two months, he'd turn eighteen and get sent to fight the Russians. He'd end up like her brothers Maurizio and Giacomo, who'd left for the front more than five years ago, and who'd stopped sending letters or telegrams ten months later. There was a time when Maddalena believed they'd make it home with all the other boys the village no longer heard from. Now when she thought of them, their faces glowed in her mind like the pictures of saints on funeral cards. They lived and breathed somewhere, but in another world. Lately she caught herself thinking of Buccio and Vito this way, too, though Buccio still had until June and Vito three months after that.

"You asked us to come here, Vito," Carolina was saying. "We were at home minding our own business. You can't take back your offer now."

"Did I know what animals you'd be?" he said. "No, I didn't." He folded his arms and thought a moment. Everyone was quiet. "I'll tell you this." He looked to both sides, the way he did in school when he was trying to cheat. "You can each have a free ride, but only"—he checked again—"only if you kiss me first."

"That doesn't sound free to me," Carolina said.

"Take it or leave it," Vito said, shrugging. "To me it's the same. I ask only for a little kiss. A little kiss isn't much for all my hard work."

"I agree," Luciana said. She broke from the circle and bounded toward Vito. She clasped her hands behind her back and leaned in toward his chest. She brushed the underside of his chin with her lips, as if she were sucking up spilled wine.

The girls howled.

Luciana turned around and held out her arms. "It wasn't so bad," she said. She winked at Carolina. Then, to Vito: "I'm first now, right?"

"New rule," said Vito. "The kiss must be on the lips, or a long one on the cheek."

"Do I have to do it again?" Luciana asked.

Buccio, the *fidanzato*, suddenly appeared beside her. Vito looked at him. "Next time," he said.

"I don't mind," said Luciana.

"I think once was enough," Buccio said.

"I'm still first, though?" Luciana asked Vito, not embarrassed at all.

"Yes, yes," he said. "But not until I show you all how to use the bike." He turned to the crowd and spoke louder. "This is a special vehicle, you know, with special brakes and a special seat. I fashioned it in the cold winter months, sealed it with my own blood."

He pointed to the cuts on his fingers.

"*Gesù mio*," said Carolina, and smiled at her sister.

"Listen to me," Vito said. "I'll give you all a lesson, a group lesson, one only. You watch me the first time and then Luciana will ride, and while she's on it we can do more kissing. No time to waste. Follow me!"

He broke through the pack and brushed Maddalena's shoulder as he passed. She still held her shawl to her neck, though her armpits were sweating. Leave it to a boy, she thought, to take something fun and make it dirty and complicated. Leave it to Vito Leone to finally do something right, then mess it up with his big silly talk. She wasn't about to throw away her first kiss for this boy, or risk her father's or brother's finding out—not for ten rides down the hill. I only kiss people who deserve it, she told herself and, as she watched the girls fight to form a line behind Vito, decided this was what she would say when he asked her to pay his price. It was a good answer; it would stop him cold; it would get a good laugh.

Vito marched through the olive grove like an invader. He led everyone down the main road, which became a steep and broad hill, perfect for bike rides. The hill split the grove in half, dividing it into two regions the girls named East and West Olive. One of the boys was always arguing that what the girls called West Olive was really East, or, worse, that East was really South or North. But Maddalena thought it sounded right the way it was, and that it was bad luck to change names after all these years.

Boys gathered in the gorge and the woods behind the spring, but the olive grove had been girl country since their *nonni* were young. Girls made up plays here, practiced dance routines, and performed shows for each other on the stage in West Olive, which was really just a mound of grass. This was where Maddalena did her famous imitations of Guglierma Lunga, Caldostano the drunk, and other misfits of the village. Fiorella sang Christmas songs whatever the season, and Luciana told long, sexy stories about German soldiers without blushing, but Maddalena always got the loudest applause.

In the far corner of West Olive, the trees stood so close together that the leaves made a second sky. Girls sat in circles under it and complained about their mothers. They gossiped about whoever showed up late or left early. When the army trucks swallowed up their brothers and boyfriends and young fathers, they came here to forget or cry or admit *I'm glad he's gone*. After they turned twenty, they found somewhere else to talk—they got married, or they leaned against the front walls of stores and acted smart—but until then, the olive grove was the center of their world.

The road flattened at the bottom of the hill, by the sign that announced the exit from Santa Cecilia on one side and the entrance on the other. If Vito kept walking out of the village, he'd lead them all to Avezzano in an hour, Rome in a day. Instead he propped the bike against the sign and waited for the girls to pay attention.

The Santa Ceciliese took pride in this road Vito now commanded. They celebrated it like a saint, all because one day three years ago a radio announcer told them it was one of the widest in Italy. It was so wide, in fact, this road that seemed so little, that the government made it a main artery for German tanks to drive south through the country. The announcer had listed all the towns the tanks would pass through, and when the words Santa Cecilia left his lips, Maddalena swore that Hitler himself could hear the cheers. Like everyone else, she'd hoped that soldiers coming through would mean money for the town and the store, but soon she came to fear these men. She avoided listening to the one o'clock news, afraid to hear stories of the approaching war front, of untrained sons and fathers and husbands becoming an Italian army overnight, of Axis planes getting shot down over cities as close as Naples. Twice a day, when the tanks rumbled through the town, she found herself unable to breathe. While the ground shook, the chandeliers swayed, and the slow parade of blond soldiers shouted and lifted their guns in the air, she waited for the world to end. Then the planes would come, screaming overhead by the thousands, and she'd run to find and grab onto her mother until they passed.

"I'm next," Carolina said. She bumped Maddalena with her hip. "You awake? I'm after Luciana. Don't even try to get ahead of me."

"Don't worry," Maddalena said. She folded her arms. "I'm not interested."

"There's nothing to be scared of," Carolina said.

"Who said I was scared?"

"Listen," Carolina whispered. "I talked to Luciana." She cupped one hand behind Maddalena's ear and whispered into it. "She told me that kissing Vito was like rubbing her lips against a peach. She said his skin is softer than a girl's."

Maddalena laughed. "Still."

"What's so funny?" Vito said, smiling at them. "Are you telling jokes, Signorina Piccinelli?"

"Mind your own business," Carolina said. She pinched Maddalena's arm and turned to the crowd. "Can everyone shut up, please? I want to ride this jalopy before I'm fifty, and Vito still needs to play teacher for us."

"*Grazie*," said Vito. He gripped the bike and wheeled it to the center of the circle. "First I should tell you how I made this."

"We don't care!" Carolina said. "We only care if it works."

"That's what I'm trying to explain," Vito said. "Listen. One day, Buccio and I skipped school. We found a barn, way in the middle of nowhere, in the fields outside Broccostella. In the barn was this bike, smashed up in three big pieces, like it was hit by a tank or something, and maybe it was. The chain was rusted, and it was missing this half of the frame." He pointed to the bar between the seat and the back wheel. It was thicker than the other pieces. "And the front wheel, and one side of the handlebars, and the seat, all missing." He stopped. "And the brakes didn't work."

"It was a pile of shit," Buccio said.

"It was," said Vito. "I told Buccio, 'Watch me turn this pile of shit into gold,' and I did. I looked everywhere for pieces to fill it in. The frame here and the handlebars are both from an old stove my father kept under the house. The front wheel I found in the graveyard, no air in it at all. I blew into it myself through a little hole, then sealed it with glue. I banged out the rest of the body to straighten it, and fit the new wheel on the front. I filled all the holes in the metal and the rubber with the glue, and soaked the chain in grease. All I had left was the seat, and I have to say that took me a long time. Finally I got a chunk of wood, and carved it until it fit inside the hole in the frame. I wrapped the top part in rags, because of the splinters, and to make it easier on the *culo*." He slapped his behind. "But still, it's not very comfortable. That much I admit."

"And what happened to the brakes?" Luciana asked.

"That's the important part," Vito said. He held up one finger the way their teacher, Signora Grasso, did. "That's the part I have to show you." He eased himself onto the seat and started pedaling up the hill. He couldn't just walk it like a normal person. He weaved and strained until he reached the top, and when he turned around, his face was flushed. "I recommend you girls walk up when it's your turn," he said.

Carolina rolled her eyes.

"Now watch me, and when it's your turn, do what I do," Vito called down. "When I hit the grass at the bottom of the hill, I'm going to turn the handlebars as hard as I can to the left, to get the speed out. Then, I'll let go and hop off the bike. Just hop off, like a rabbit. Not too high, or you'll kill yourself. Don't try to stop with your feet or you'll trip. And don't worry about the ground; me and Buccio and Marco and everybody spent all yesterday cleaning the stones out of the grass. Understand?"

"It's a death machine," Maddalena said.

"I'm still going," said Carolina.

They watched him. The bike popped and jumped over the rocky hill so roughly that Vito's cheeks jiggled. His eyes got wide and scared, and his shirt flew up, flashing his pale, sunken stomach. When he reached the grass, he turned fast, released his grip from the handlebars, and launched himself into the air. He landed safely on his back, rolled a few times, then came up all smiles. He wiped dirt from his hands with a few hard slaps. The bike, still in one piece, lay upturned a few yards from him, its back wheel spinning.

Luciana ran and flipped it right side up. "I got it," she said. "I watched really close. Here I go." She ran it up the hill and barely turned around before she hopped on the seat, screamed "Ouch!" and headed down. She flew toward them and, midway, lifted her hands high and waved. Vito crawled out of the way when she turned, expertly, at the last possible second, onto the patch of grass. Then she tumbled off the bike. "No problem!" she said, and exhaled all the air from her lungs. "You're next, Carolina."

Carolina gave Vito a quick peck on the cheek, then rode. After her, Fiorella. Then a girl named Silvia who showed up from Broccostella with her cousin. Then Ada Lupo, the dentist's daughter, and Nunzia Vattilana, Buccio's sloe-eyed sister. No one seemed to mind giving Vito what he wanted. Eventually, after every girl had had a turn, he came for Maddalena.

"Well?" he said. He lowered his voice. "You remember what I told you today? Who I made this for?" He leaned in and tilted his right cheek upward. "Do I have the honor?"

It rolled off her tongue perfectly, like a prayer: "I only kiss people who deserve it," she said, loud enough for everyone to hear. As soon as she said it, she turned and, feeling triumphant, climbed the hill on foot.

The crowd howled again, this time in her honor. She walked slowly so some of the girls—Carolina, at least—could catch up, but halfway up the hill she found she was walking alone. She heard Luciana say, "Me again then! *Me!*" and one of the boys whine, "When's our chance?" but there were no shadows or crunching footsteps behind her. No one called out, "Stop, Maddalena! Come back!" As she walked toward her house, she closed her eyes and wished for the rush of wind against her face, for the sudden plunge, for the shawl she was sweating under to unclasp and float off her shoulders into the air.

One by one that spring, every girl in the village—even Maddalena's older sisters Teresa and Celestina—pressed her lips to Vito Leone's hairless cheek. Again and again Vito asked Maddalena if she'd changed her mind, and again and again she repeated that same answer.

"Am I that terrible?" Vito would ask.

"Maybe," she'd say.

It wasn't him, though, not after a while. It was a matter of pride, but she couldn't let him know that. Instead she recited for him the story of Saint Cecilia. She was a real person a thousand years ago, she reminded him, who let herself suffocate from smoke and get struck with an ax rather than submit to the soldiers pounding at her front door. They were trying to get her to deny God, but Cecilia wouldn't let anyone force her to do what she didn't want to do. And neither would Maddalena, no matter how small that something was.

"You'd rather get struck with an ax than kiss me," was Vito's response.

"That's not what I said."

"I must be that terrible," he said.

All that spring Maddalena watched Vito get more expensive. He charged two kisses to get from the olive grove to the church, and one on the lips to ride the length of all three village streets. Sometime near the end of May, just as school was ending for the summer, Luciana kept the bike overnight, and everyone wondered what she'd had to pay for that.

"Two on the cheek," she said.

They were huddled in a circle in the cool darkness of the olive grove, all of them who mattered: Maddalena, Carolina, Fiorella, Ada Lupo, Clara Marcelli, and Luciana.

"That's it?"

"Well, then a real one on the lips," Luciana said. "With this!" She stuck out her tongue.

"So elegant," said Carolina.

"Does Buccio know?" Maddalena asked. She sat half in, half out of the circle, stretching her legs and pulling up grass with her toes.

"It was *for* Buccio," Luciana said, waving her away. "No, I didn't tell him. Why should I? I did it for both of us. We snuck out of the house in the middle of the night and rode the bike out to that barn, where they found it. I sat on the handlebars the whole way, with Buccio driving like a maniac. It was freezing."

They looked at her.

"What?" she said, as if she did this every night.

"You slept there?" asked Ada. "Together?"

"If you have to know," Luciana said, "then no. We didn't sleep very much." She rubbed her arms as though she were still cold and blinked. To Maddalena she said, "Don't stare at me like that."

"I'm not staring," said Maddalena, though she was.

"Buccio's already eighteen. By the end of the month, maybe sooner, he'll be in Russia." She kept her head down. "We're engaged, more than engaged, really. I cook for both families every night. We might even get married before he leaves. What are we waiting for? When he comes home in a box?"

Slowly Maddalena rubbed the middle of her forehead, then under her chin, then both shoulders—a long, stealthy sign of the cross.

Luciana noticed. "This one!" she said. "God was the last thing I thought of." She searched the other girls' faces. "What if I get pregnant? What if my clothes get dirty? What if my father finds us? How will I look at myself the next day? That's what I worried about. God will come later, I guess."

"Maddalena would worry about all of it," Fiorella said. "She can't even kiss Vito Leone on the cheek. I think that says it all. Doesn't it, girls?"

"It's fine with me," said Ada. "I mean, one girl less means more rides for us, right? But really, Maddalena, when are you going to grow up?"

"She's right," said Fiorella. "It's over in one second. You just smash your lips really tight together and let them touch his cheek. You don't even feel anything."

"It's not about the kiss," Maddalena started to say, but Luciana interrupted her.

"How are we talking about Maddalena," she asked, "after what I just told you?" She'd pulled her hair back over her ears and kept smoothing it with her palms. "Don't you want to know how I feel? How it felt? How it is with Buccio and me now?"

Carolina shrugged. "I'm not biting my nails waiting for the story," she said.

"I am," said Fiorella.

"Me, too," said Ada.

Though Maddalena was the youngest of them by only a year, today it felt more like ten. For months she'd been making a big deal about one kiss, and here was Luciana, spreading her legs in a dark barn for a boy she hadn't married yet. And why didn't it impress Carolina? What had she done with boys already; what had any of them done? Maddalena hated having brought God into the group, like a child, when Luciana already had so much else to worry about.

"Buccio was nervous, too," she was saying.

Maddalena didn't want to listen, not if Luciana was going to make herself sound like a *puttana*. But if she got up and left, they might never ask her back.

"He kept asking if I was all right, even though all we did for the first few hours was sit next to each other on the hay, not talking." She smiled, and now instead of keeping her head down, she looked out over the heads of the girls in front of her. "We kept most of our clothes on at first, it was so cold. Then we warmed up. I can't say too much. All of a sudden it was happening, and Buccio moved very fast, and I was holding my breath, and the pain was so bad at first I got tears in my eyes, and I almost told him to stop, but if you could have seen his face, so sweet and still nervous, you wouldn't have wanted him to think he was hurting you, either."

"I don't know about that," said Carolina.

"Well," said Luciana, "I do." She sat back on her hands and let her hair fall in front of her face, all confidence now. "And when it was over—it didn't last very long, maybe five minutes?—we put our clothes back on, and we were both shaking, and he lay down next to me and put his arm over my chest, and I was about to fall asleep, but he started whispering to me this long story about his Zio Salvatore in Pescara, who lived on a boat, who had all these tattoos and scars on his body, whose wife died a year after they got married, and how Zio Salvatore pushed him off the back of his boat once for no reason, then laughed and laughed for the first time in years, even after he found out Buccio had smacked his leg on the motor and could barely swim anyway; I had no idea why he was telling me this, and I don't think he knew either, but I liked hearing his voice. Then he started kissing me again, and we kissed and kissed, and then it started again right before we had to ride back, and this time"—she brushed the hair from her eyes—"it didn't hurt that much at all."

Fiorella had her collar pulled up over her nose and held it there.

"You're probably pregnant right now," Carolina said. "You should get married the minute you wake up tomorrow."

"You don't get pregnant the first time," said Luciana. "That's what Buccio's brother told him. And even the second time there's less of a chance."

"Well, you know more than I do," Carolina said, standing up. "Congratulations to you. Honestly. We'll have to start calling you *signora*."

Luciana didn't answer. Ada whispered something in her ear.

When they broke through the olive trees onto the road, Maddalena asked, "Do you believe her?"

"Half of it, maybe," Carolina said. "The part about Buccio's uncle I believe, and the cut leg. But we'll see. Watch if she starts getting fat. I mean, fatter."

Maddalena laughed. She took Carolina's hand in hers. Music was coming from the Al Di Là Café, and she wondered if there were soldiers inside. The owner, who'd closed up and moved to the coast after the war started, once held dances there, on the flagstone patio under strings of white lights, where bands from as far away as Florence came to play. The men wore suits; the women, pale-colored dresses that fanned out above their knees when they twirled. Kids danced and ran jumping among them for hours, then fell asleep on folding chairs set up around the floor. Now sometimes the German soldiers used the café as a free hotel, sleeping there overnight when they passed through. When the rooms filled up, they knocked on the doors of the houses next door and kicked out whoever lived there. They forced them to the street with guns, and sometimes the families ended up on the floor of the grocery.

"I miss the dances," Maddalena said.

"I miss ricotta," said Carolina.

"I miss the old Luciana." This was one of

their games—listing all the things the war had taken away.

"I miss eggplant. How did the Nazis scare off eggplant?"

"I miss having the village to ourselves."

"I don't know," Carolina said. She was always the first to interrupt the game. "I like the soldiers. They stop looking so mean if you smile at them a little. Ask Fiorella."

It was almost dark. They were nearing their house. "What do you mean?"

"Nothing," said Carolina.

"No, what?"

"I'm just making things up."

Later that night, they lay alongside each other on the bed. There was a cool breeze, but the air stayed warm enough for them not to need covers. Teresa and Celestina slept beside them, Celestina snoring as always.

Maddalena reached her arm over Carolina's chest and pulled her closer. "Tomorrow," she said, "if the weather's nice, I want to make a deal for the bike."

"Really?" Carolina asked. She flipped around to face her and propped herself up on her elbow. "Why now, all of a sudden?"

Maddalena thought a moment. "I don't know."

"Well, I'm surprised," Carolina said. "Believe me, I don't want Vito to think he beat you—I don't want to see the satisfaction on his face—but there's no reason you should miss the one fun thing in Santa Cecilia just because he made it."

"You have to do the talking," said Maddalena. "I still won't kiss him, but I thought maybe I could cook him some *fritelli*, use that as a trade. That, or something else fair."

"He doesn't want food," Carolina said, laughing. "You don't hear his heart break every time you say he doesn't deserve you." She took a curl of Maddalena's hair between her fingers. "It's hard to believe, but maybe he's smart enough to see how special you are."

That Carolina believed this, that she more than once and without jealousy called Maddalena's hair and eyes a blessing from God, amazed her. If she were Carolina, she would hate this Maddalena and everyone who fussed over her. Instead, Carolina adored her. She treated her like a church statue: too sacred and precious to disturb. She trusted only herself and Maddalena and made everyone else work to get along with her. No one disliked Carolina, as far as Maddalena knew—but no one rushed to throw his arms around her, either. Only Maddalena saw her many sides and, though they sometimes confused her, loved them all.

"I was thinking about when we were kids," Carolina said, "How Vito used to push you off the dance floor at the Al Di Là. Do you remember? You couldn't be there for two seconds before he'd run out and knock you over. He didn't do that to anybody else."

"He did that to everyone," Maddalena said, but, when she thought back, maybe he didn't. He used to make her so angry. Teresa would be trying to teach her the tango, and Vito would come stomping between them, making her lose her place. She'd even tripped over his leg once and torn her dress.

"Crazy must run in his family," Carolina said. "You almost have to feel sorry for him."

CHAPTER 2

Vito lay face up on his bed, hoping the rain would keep Buccio from coming to his door as he did most mornings at nine. He couldn't look at that face anymore, that giddy, grinning, satisfied face, without wanting to smack it, without thinking, He's made love to a woman and I have not.

He regretted ever telling Buccio about his feelings for Maddalena Piccinelli. That was Christmas night six months ago. They'd finished off the last of the wine, and the sun was coming up. Vito had been losing at cards for six hours and was grateful to be playing an easier game: the one where they compared the size and shape and overall beauty of each girl in the village. They'd played this before, many times, but this night they decided to be thorough: to go house by house, north to south, and youngest to oldest if there were sisters. Vito had been struck again and again by Buccio's bad taste—how he'd go straight for the chest, hardly bothering with the legs and face at all. This was how he'd ended up with Luciana, who was bursting out of her dresses, but who also had a smashed-looking nose, crooked lips, and not a single curve below the waist.

When the game had reached the Piccinelli house, Vito announced what he always announced: that Maddalena was by far the most beautiful girl in the village.

"She's got a pretty face, yes," Buccio said. "Maybe the prettiest. But she still looks like a kid. When her body changes, then we'll know for sure."

Vito had remembered watching Maddalena and her friends one day in the olive grove. He'd stood at a distance behind a tree. Maddalena stood out from the circle of ordinary, black-haired girls. They slouched and picked their teeth and interrupted each other with nonsense, talking just to fill the air around them. But Maddalena kept her back straight, her hands at her neck, and waited her turn to speak. She saved up what she wanted to say, then said it clearly. As she spoke, she slipped off one shoe and rubbed her bare foot up and down her calf.

The memory had made Vito drunker. "I think—no, I'm sure. I'm sure I'm in love with Maddalena Piccinelli," he told Buccio.

"I'm sure I'm in love with her, too," Buccio said. "You and me and everyone else. It's easy to be in love with the youngest. They're not as complicated. I'm telling you, wait two years."

"No," Vito said. "I mean, I'm really in love with her. Husband kind of love."

This time Buccio laughed, a full, open-mouthed laugh that showed his Chianti-stained teeth. "Husband kind of love!" he repeated. "Good luck, *vaglio*."

"Someone has to marry her."

"You'd have better luck with Carolina," Buccio said. "She's still a Piccinelli, but the father won't be so picky with her."

"I don't want second-best."

"Once you're in the family, you never know what arrangement you can make." Buccio's eyes widened. "My zio in Pescara married one woman just to keep porking her cousin. Every man that age has at least two women on the side, and if their wives know, they look the other way."

Vito didn't want an arrangement, not six months ago and not today. Shouldn't the hours he'd slaved on that bike count for something? He locked his hands behind his head and listened to the rain, remembering what he told Buccio weeks later, during another drunken round of *scopa*, which he was losing badly. Wives were like cards, he'd tried to explain. Some were aces and others just fives, not terrible but not great, either.

He'd held up the five of cups in one hand and the ace of swords in the other, to demonstrate. "The two young Piccinellis," he'd said. "The goal of life is to avoid the fives. A five will stay a five, no matter how long you sit at the table scratching your head. You can stall all you want, but she'll never turn into an ace or a *settebello*. If she changes at all, she gets worse. More than that, you can't hold the five against your chest and play the ace, like your zio. Sooner or later, trouble gets you."

"I was lucky," Buccio said. He plucked the card from Vito's right hand and fanned it against his cheek. "I got an ace right away."

"Sure you did," Vito said, though in his eyes Luciana came closer to the other card. Buccio hadn't even tried for someone better. "But I won't get stuck with this." He flicked his five onto the table. "I'd rather be alone forever than put up with a wife like Carolina."

"Girls should come marked," Buccio said, laughing. "Then you'd know who was what right away."

"I'd rather not play at all—I'd rather quit—than lose with a five," Vito said. He brushed the breadcrumbs from the table into his hand and popped them in his mouth. "That's what my father did. Lose."

Buccio didn't say anything.

"You think I shouldn't talk like that," Vito said. "But it's true."

"I don't think anything," said Buccio. "I don't live with your mother. I'm just here to play *scopa*." He shuffled the cards.

"If I had Maddalena Piccinelli, I wouldn't have to run off anywhere, not ever. I'd live in Santa Cecilia until the day I died. I'd walk through the streets singing."

"You're more romantic than Luciana," Buccio

said. He fished through the deck and held up the two of swords. "Maybe this is you." He laughed. "The ugliest girl in Italy."

With that Vito jumped up and chased him around the table, into and out of his bedroom, and down and up the front stairs, finally tackling him in the living room. They wrestled on the cold stone floor until Buccio held up his hands in surrender. "I take it back!" he said. "You're a beautiful boy, Vito Leone! You'll have to fight off Maddalena with a stick!"

That was the old Buccio. The new one acted so tough he'd never give up a fight. He wore his tightest shirts and was letting his beard grow. Vito waited for him to buzz his door, but what he really wanted was for Maddalena to take his place, to walk through the rain to his house. She'd come to him alone. They'd face each other at the bottom of the steps, shuffling their feet, unsure how close to stand. Her face would be wet and shiny under her umbrella, her deep brown eyes desperate to speak. She'd take off her jacket, and her dress would be soaked through in patches on her chest and shoulders. She'd be shy, keep her head down, and stumble through explaining her visit. "I'll get you a towel to dry off," he'd say, and invite her upstairs to sit down, but instead of accepting his offer she'd look up and say, "I'm sorry." Without warning she'd press her cool lips against his cheek, their hands still joined, and say, "You deserve this." Her eyes would close. She'd go for his mouth.

Vito believed the war would never touch them. God liked to play games, but He'd always protected Vito when it mattered. Vito was sure He'd end the fighting before October 28, his eighteenth birthday; whether a day or a month in advance he didn't care, as long as it meant he could stay in Santa Cecilia and marry Maddalena Piccinelli. Yes, he thought, as he listened to the rain, the war would end by October, and by Christmas he'd have a job in the Piccinelli store as a handyman or a fixer of leaks or a shipment fetcher, maybe even as the man behind the counter. He'd stay for dinner a few nights a week and drink sambuca at the table with Aristide and however many sons made it back from Russia. He'd tell his jokes and play cards past midnight. He'd stumble home to Maddalena, who'd be waiting for him in his house, the one his father left him. His pride would never let him take a room in the Piccinelli house. Every night in this bed, he'd drape his arm over his wife's undressed body and pull her closer; he'd slide down and give the curve of her hip a hundred kisses.

In the middle of this lovemaking, the church bell rang. At the tenth strike, Vito sat up: alone, mouth dry, neck sore, stomach hollow, thanking God for at least sparing him Buccio's chubby face. But this was only more of God's teasing. He'd also sent what sounded like the worst storm in months, making the olive grove too muddy for rides. On Vito's dresser sat his father's most recent letter from Philadelphia: one page of complaints about the weather and the noisy city, another page of lies about how much he missed them, a third to explain that he couldn't send a check because "the world, my son, is in the sewer." He signed his letters "Massimo." Vito knew he should write back, but what could he say? *We're still alive. Hope you are, too. Next time, try harder for the money.*

A full day inside was more exhausting than a bike ride to Rome. It meant wandering in and out of the five dark rooms, light-headed and hungry. It meant sweaty naps and staring into the mirror and playing with himself, all to avoid housework. Vito knew he should scrub the kettle. He should sweep the ashes from the fire and clean the thin layer of dust and hair that covered every surface. He should set out a few pots and save some rainwater for washing clothes. These jobs took his mother hours each, but he could finish them all in a half a morning. What was wrong with him? He should talk to her. He should try to make her feel less afraid.

He hadn't even made it out of bed yet, and already he felt guilty.

Concetta Leone got worse every week, even after Dr. Fabiano assured her she was as healthy as Hitler. She saw "zigzags" in her eyes, she said; they gave her headaches and made her want to throw up. She swayed like a drunk when she walked, one palm always pressed against her temple, and fell asleep wherever she landed: couch, bed, floor, or street. Sometimes she woke up screaming, convinced she was on fire. Her friends, who came by in packs of five the year her husband left, came less and less often. Sometimes Guglierma Lunga visited, but mostly to yell in her face that she still had exactly eighteen years and four months to live, so she might as well suffer through them like a normal woman.

She ate very little, though she insisted on walking to the Piccinelli store every morning to find something to cook for Vito. For years she'd been so plump that Massimo called her his *salsiccina*; now her blouses hung from the bones in her shoulders, and the veins in her legs had dried up blue just under her skin. Sometimes she misbuttoned her clothes, and Vito would find her walking to the store with her underwear showing through the gaps.

Dr. Fabiano had told him to be patient, that his mother's sickness would never kill her. "She has a plant in her head," he'd explained the last time he'd come over, almost two months ago now. The doctor was a short man, with a little head round and bald as a bocce ball. He'd sat on the couch, calmly polishing his tiny black-rimmed glasses. "Not a real plant, of course. An imaginary one. It starts small, then grows thick leaves and crowds the skull and sucks all the air out of her brain. It makes her thinking muddy. I don't know why, but right now your mother wants to take care of this plant; she wants to water it and make sure it stays healthy. But she'll get tired of this soon. She'll see it's not real; she'll see how ugly it is. She'll start to hate it, and think about all the time she wasted on it. The hate will make it dry up and die, and then, like that"—he snapped his fingers—"her head will clear, and all the life the plant was taking will rush back to her. How beautiful it will be for both of you! I've seen it happen many times. I've been in the room when it's happened! Never in this village, but in my wife's town." He tweaked Vito's nose with his thumb and forefinger. "Don't worry, son. I have seen it. The trick is to not let the plant grow back."

Vito had believed him—what choice did he have?—and tried to explain it to his mother.

"I understand," she'd said, cupping his cheek with her palm. "When I was a girl, before I got married, I used to feel so light, even though I was like this." She held her arms out wide and smiled. "But maybe this is how it goes, at the end. God makes you want to die, and then He gives you what you want."

Outside, in the sun, on his bike, with Maddalena and the others, Vito could escape her. Inside, staring up at the cracked stone ceiling and the watermarks, listening to the tree branches smack against his window, his mind played tricks on him. He'd smell the thick cuts of beef and roasted pig she cooked just last winter, before the war made meat scarce. He'd hear her voice, singing. Slowly he'd walk to the kitchen, sure it couldn't be true but still hoping to see the fat, clapping mother of his childhood, the woman who'd sweep his eight-year-old body into her arms the moment he walked through the door, as if he'd won a prize just for being alive. Instead he'd find this other mother—the one abandoned, as good as widowed, the one of the war and the terrifying plant—slumped in the corner by the fire, her legs spread in front of her, her bare feet black with soot.

He got up to check on her. He slipped on the clothes he'd worn yesterday, a white undershirt and a grass-stained pair of shorts, from the pile beside his bed. He found her lying on her back on the couch, a damp towel over her forehead. A rosary was laced into her folded fingers. Her eyes were closed, the skin around them a bruised pink. He knelt in front of her and leaned in to make sure she was breathing. Her chest barely moved, but a thin breath of air did pass between her cracked lips. She looked peaceful, untouched by whatever cursed her, content as Saint Rita, who was preserved forever in a glass case in her church at the top of the next mountain.

"Are you hungry?" she asked suddenly.

Vito drew back onto his ankles. "You could warn me when you're awake," he said. "No, I'm not hungry."

"You don't have to lie," she said, moving only her lips. She kept her eyes closed. "You're not starving, though? You can stand up, walk around?"

"Of course," Vito said.

"Good." She breathed deeply. "What do we have in the house?"

"Not much," he said. "A handful of pasta. Three potatoes. Some garlic."

"More than enough," she said. She pinched a rosary bead between her thumb and middle finger. She had two conversations going at all times: one with Vito and one with God. "Go out, then. Have fun. Tell Buccio I'm praying for him."

"He didn't come today," Vito said. "And I'm not going out. There's a big storm. You don't hear it?"

She opened her eyes. The whites were filled with little red spokes. "You're staying here with me?" she asked.

"Inside, yes," Vito said. "At least until the rain stops."

She lifted herself, Vito supporting her as she sat back against the thick wooden arm of the sofa. He could feel each knobby bone in her spine, tightly bound but fragile as a string of pearls. "It's like a holiday," she said, as she arranged a pillow behind her.

"If you say so," Vito said. He sat cross-legged on the floor. "We don't have to talk for long if you're too tired, you know, but it might make you feel better."

"It does," she said. "I can feel it already. Most of the time I try not to move, just lie still and pray, and that does good. But talking out loud helps, too. I think the more air I breathe, the better for me."

"Could be." He didn't want to go back and forth about what made her sick; it never came to anything. "So, what should we talk about?" he said. He gave her a sweet smile. "The weather I mentioned. Gossip I don't have. School?" He clapped his hands together and forced a laugh. "We shouldn't talk about school."

"How long until it's over?" she asked.

He waited a moment. "It's been over for weeks."

Her face reddened. "I'm sorry," she said. "I knew that; I wasn't thinking."

"It's all right," he said. "But wait until you hear what Signora Grasso had the nerve to tell me on the last day," he said. "This will make you laugh for real. She stopped me outside the room and grabbed my arm really tight. She looked me right in the face and said, 'Vito Leone!' Very dramatic. 'Yes, Signora,' I said, very polite. 'I have news for you,' she said. 'There's no juice left in that brain of yours. You're used up.' Then she knocked on my forehead with her knuckle. 'Tell your mother to find you a job,' she said. 'You've learned as much as you can from here.' What do you think of that?"

"I think she's crazy," she said.

"She is! That's what happens when you teach for four hundred years."

"You've got plenty of juice."

"I know it!" Vito said. "But if I don't have to go back, I won't go back. What good is it, anyway?"

School had never helped Vito's father. He

learned everything about tailoring from his Zio Gabriello: how to measure and cut, and add and subtract. If you knew that much, you could make a living. You needed school for a government job, but Vito told his mother he didn't want a government job. He didn't want to move out of Santa Cecilia.

"There's nothing out there you can't find here," she said.

"That's the truth," Vito said. "You know, even if Babbo asked us, I still wouldn't go to Philadelphia."

"He won't ask," she said.

"But even so. Everything I want is here. I'm not going anywhere, not ever."

His mother turned her face away, toward the front window, and threaded her rosary through her fingers.

"What?"

She shook her head. "I can't even think about it."

"You don't want me here forever?" He sat up on his knees. He was trying to joke. "I get in your way? I make a mess and eat too much and cost you money?"

"They'll come for you sooner or later," she said. "Then what will happen?" She turned to him. "How will I survive without you? Me alone in here, you out there—I can't do it."

"You won't have to," Vito said. "I'm luckier than that, Mamma. I've had you praying for me since the war started, haven't I? In October we'll be dancing, not fighting."

If his father were here, he'd never let him say this. He was young enough to fight in the war himself, and he would have dragged Vito along with him, made him enlist early, and gotten them both shot in the head.

"Listen," Vito said. "Listen to what a beautiful life I have."

He told her what he charged for his bike rides, and how quickly the girls lined up to pay. He described the excitement on their faces, how, for the few minutes they spent on his creation, they had no worries: They weren't hungry; their brothers and fathers weren't missing; the village was safe.

"You don't have to tell me that," his mother said. "A boy as smart and handsome as you, with a village full of girls? I told everybody from the beginning: The girl who marries my son will be the luckiest wife in Italy! But you can't make a living selling kisses."

"I know that."

"If they come for you, Vito, you won't have a choice. But maybe they'll send you to a place that's not so bad, where you can do your duty but still be careful. Don't some soldiers go to France? Or stay in Italy? If people start shooting, you can hide behind a tree. And when it's over, you can come back here, and the state will take care of you, give you enough money to live on for the rest of your life. They do that, you know."

The Leones didn't have a radio. Concetta didn't hear what happened to soldiers. It was one big show to her: Boys put on uniforms and marched in rows and hoped a bomb didn't land on them.

"I told you," Vito said, "no one's coming for me, and I already have a job." He hadn't planned to tell her about Maddalena, but he wanted to give her peace. She spoke more clearly now than she had in months; her body didn't shake so much under the blankets; there was color in her face. Surely the little hope he'd already given her had caused this. "I have my eye on one girl," he said. "And once I marry her, I'll work in the Piccinelli store. I ask you, is there a better living in Santa Cecilia?"

"Carolina Piccinelli?" she said. She raised her eyebrows. "Talk sense. She's pretty enough, but a donkey would be easier to live with."

"Not her," said Vito. He drew a circle in the floor dust with his fingers. "Maddalena," he said. "The blonde. The youngest." His mother was now the second person he had told, and the moment the words left his lips they sounded less impossible.

She grew quiet again, and lowered her eyes. She'd never learned how to hide her feelings.

"Now what? She's not good enough?"

"If you ask her, she's better than everyone," his mother said. "She walks around like God's great angel."

"You don't even know her," Vito said.

"I talk to her father," she said.

"And he likes me!" Vito said. "When I walk into

the store, he runs to help me. He trips over his feet, he hurries so much. And I never leave the place without a free piece of candy from his sleeve. 'You're a good kid, Vito,' he told me once. When the father likes you, you can take your pick from the daughters. And I pick her."

"He talked to me about you already," she said. "I don't believe a word of what he said, but if you really have this idea, you have to know what he really thinks."

"What could he say bad about me?" Vito said.

"I was in the store," she began. Her voice was strained and dry, and Vito knew he should get her water. Instead he folded his arms. "He was yelling at the son who stayed. I forget his name—"

"Claudio," Vito said.

"Claudio, yes. Claudio slammed the door in his father's face, and Aristide started talking out loud to himself. 'It's the mothers who make the boys,' he was saying. 'Am I right, Concetta?' I didn't realize he was talking to me. I didn't want him to think I was listening, but I was. So I pretended. 'What did you say?' I said, 'I didn't hear you.'

" 'I just told my boy he had to go to Civitavecchia next week for business. And he said yes, very sweetly, he would go. But now he's walking upstairs to ask his mother if it's true, does he really have to go. He's as angry as the devil, the way I used to be when I had to help my own father.'

"He looked so tired, Vito, like I've never seen

before, like he was sick of life. 'That's just boys trying to get out of work,' I said to him."

"What's this have to do with me?" Vito asked. This was why he never talked to her. Not only did her stories make no sense; she never got them over with fast enough.

"You have to listen," she said. "Aristide told me why his sons are men and my son is not. That has to do with both you and me."

"I'm not a man?" Vito said.

"Listen," she repeated. "He told me, 'Claudio will go upstairs and complain, but his mother won't put up with it,' he said. 'She won't say "I'll ask your father if you have to go for sure" or "Maybe you can go some other time, when it's not so rainy." No. She'll say "If Babbo says you go, you go."' That's the only way a son learns respect, he said. A mother should tell him that no matter what his father says, right or wrong, he should listen. If the mother doesn't do that for her son, if she tries to play the sweetheart, he doesn't turn out right. He gets spoiled and starts sleeping all the time. He marries a lazy woman. 'You're playing the sweetheart too much, Concetta Leone,' he told me, 'and that's why Vito's less of a man than he could be. That's why the war will be the best thing for him.'"

"You don't believe that," said Vito. "He's crazier than Signora Grasso."

"'Sons are not their mothers' husbands, never,' he told me. Word for word I remember that."

"He's trying to make trouble," said Vito. "I don't know why, but he is. You should see how good he is to me. He puts his arms around me like a son."

"'Don't let Vito sweet-talk you,' he told me," Concetta said. I was barely listening to him. "'You don't need your son to take care of you. You're healthy enough, and he's not a nurse.' I said nothing and paid for my potatoes and walked out. My skin was burning, I was so angry. I wanted to come home and tell you, so you could know what the great Aristide Piccinelli thinks, but you were out somewhere. And by the time you came home I couldn't bring myself to do it."

Vito stood up, brushing dust from his legs. "You didn't defend me?" he said. "You just went along with it? What kind of mother does that make you?"

"A terrible one," she said. "That much I know." She spoke more slowly, and there were tears in her eyes.

"Don't start that," Vito said. "What you should have said was that I'm just as much of a man as Claudio or Buccio or even Babbo. Aristide Piccinelli will see that soon, and you should see that already. So stop crying." He walked over to the window and stared down at the brown puddles forming in the road. "What am I supposed to do, not take care of you when you're sick?"

"Forget about me," she said. "That's what he wants you to do. Why not, he thinks, she's half-dead anyway. And when the time comes, you're supposed to let the war take you. His son gets to stay home, but mine has to go."

"That's right," Vito said. "What's the difference between me and Claudio? Isn't he staying home to protect his family?"

"You're right."

"If the trucks come for me, I'll hide in this house, just like Claudio's hiding in his. You'll tell them I ran away. No one will know the truth, only Maddalena. By then she'll trust me. Then I'll stay in my room until I'm eighty if I have to, and she'll take care of me."

"I hope she will," she said.

"She will, Mamma," Vito said.

"You're not a nurse," she said. "You're a good son," she said. "As good as Claudio. A good son stays with his mother." She straightened her back and looked at him. What was left of her gray hair stuck up behind her in a kind of crown. "If the trucks come, Vito, I'll do what you tell me. I'll lie for you. I'll be very good."

CHAPTER 3

After their mother told them the news, Maddalena and Carolina quickly finished their lunches and rushed to the house of Fiorella Puzo. They found her on her bed, her face full of tears, her left hand wrapped in a thick white ball of gauze that lay on her lap like a giant egg.

"Who'll marry me now?" Fiorella asked. Luciana sat on a rocking chair beside her, shaking her head. Ada and Clara and the rest of the girls elbowed for space on the floor. Fiorella's mother knitted in a chair by the door, letting in visitors a few at a time.

Two weeks ago, Fiorella explained, she'd ridden too fast on Vito's bike and turned too wide, and when she fell she jammed her left hand into a rock the boys must have missed when they'd cleared the field. The rock sliced a gash into her palm and smashed her middle and ring fingers. She immediately shoved her hand in her dress pocket and didn't tell anyone, afraid she'd never get another turn on the bike. She hid it for as long as she could, using her right hand to cook and wash clothes as usual, and faking a cold to justify the handkerchief she carried in the left. She'd hoped it would heal itself. Then the infection came and not only turned her fingers purple but swelled them to double their size. Her mother finally noticed yesterday afternoon, dragged Fiorella into a carriage, and through the rain drove her to the better doctors in Avezzano.

But it was too late, the doctor said. He gave her a needle for the pain. Then he cut off her middle finger, halfway up the bone where it bent the first time, and left a rounded little stump. After that he removed the entire ring finger, leaving nothing.

Carolina and Luciana begged her to show them.

"Never," Fiorella said, shaking her head so hard that an earring flew off. She covered the gauze with her good hand. "I'll never come out of this room," she added. She sobbed and shut her eyes. "Why would I?"

Her life is over, Maddalena thought. With all the choices men had, who'd pick a cripple? She walked over, sat beside Fiorella on the bed, and lay her head on her shoulder. Her hair was greasy, her neck and the side of her face sticky with tears and sweat. This was the girl who wanted a husband more than she wanted to breathe, who was so jealous when Luciana got engaged that she offered to pay Guglierma Lunga to put a curse on her. "Nothing serious," she'd told her, "just to scare Buccio away." But instead of taking the money, the old woman told everyone what Fiorella had tried to do.

"God will take care of you," Maddalena said quietly, knowing no other way to comfort her. Secretly she worried that Fiorella would end up alone, like her Zia Zabrina, stranded on a farm somewhere whispering to goats. Left for Saint Anthony, people said of girls who never married.

"It's very nice to think that," Fiorella said. "But God won't give me babies. I'm not the Virgin Mary."

"Maddalena's right," said Carolina. "But I think God would want you to hide your hand in your pocket for a little longer." She had a wicked smile on her face.

"What are you talking about?" Luciana asked.

"None of us noticed Fiorella's hand when it was broken, did we?" said Carolina.

They shook their heads.

"So you could hide it from a man, too. They're not looking at your hands, anyway. After you get married, when there's nothing he can do, that's when you show him."

"And what about the wedding?" asked Luciana. "Where's he going to put the ring? Her nose?"

Carolina thought a minute. Fiorella gripped Maddalena's leg as she waited for the answer. "She'll wear gloves," Carolina finally said, "and stuff the fingers with clay."

"That could work!" Fiorella said. Her eyes hopeful, she searched each girl's face.

"You take the gloves *off* when the man puts the ring on," said Signora Puzo, bitterly, from across the room. "Stop talking nonsense. My daughter won't have to trick anyone to marry her."

Nobody said anything. Eventually, Signora Puzo left her post at the door and Carolina convinced Fiorella that hiding her left hand might just work after all. "Mothers think it's easier than it is," she said. "They don't believe in games. They all think their daughters are good enough to pick and choose. Then they make you wait and wait your whole life, and by then the man you end up with isn't worth the mud on his shoes."

"I hope one of you is right," said Fiorella.

She drifted off to sleep soon after, with Maddalena's head still on her shoulder. As the girls left the room, Ada whispered, "She'll be fine."

"Of course she will," said Carolina.

"Absolutely," Luciana said.

Still, as they walked to the olive grove without her, Ada started calling Fiorella *La Nubile*, the single one. It had a nice sound to it, they decided: "Fiorella La Nubile," like a song about a girl with an apple cart. Maddalena laughed along with this image, but worried that the name would stick, and that the curse Fiorella had once wished on Luciana had now come back to doom her.

They found Vito waiting for them at the top of the hill. From this distance, about six houses away, he looked to Maddalena more like a boy than a young man months away from the army. He'd tucked his shirt too far in on one side of his slouching body, which made the other ride up and show his bony hip. His ears stuck out from his head. As Buccio circled him on the bike, he kept looking down and scratching his nose.

As the girls came closer, Vito changed. He stood up straight and lifted his head high and held his hands stiff at his sides like a soldier. "Don't let Fiorella's mistake stop you," he said, with a commanding face. "It's a sad story, but you can avoid it for yourselves. If you follow the rules, you see, nothing bad happens. When you try to get away with too much, that's when you ruin your life."

"Thank you for the speech," said Carolina. "I'm much smarter now."

It was windy, the sky one flat, gray cloud. The dirt road, usually a pale golden color not unlike Maddalena's hair, was still wet and brown. Most of the mud puddles from yesterday's storm had dried, though, and before Maddalena knew it Ada had stepped forward. She kissed Vito sloppily, half on the lips, half on the cheek, and everyone headed down the hill to watch her. The damp grass licked Maddalena's toes as she walked through it, and she imagined her skirt stained from a tumble on the ground. "Maybe this is the wrong day," she said to Carolina.

"It's today or never," she said. "Tomorrow you'll have a different excuse." She ran ahead and fell in line beside Vito.

Buccio and Luciana lagged behind, their arms

linked. No respectable girl, engaged or not, would walk this close to a boy down the main street of the village, in sight of everyone. But here, for a few brief moments, the slope of the hill hid them from the houses behind, and they were high enough to see who came toward them from the other direction.

Carolina had her arm wrapped around Vito's shoulders. She patted him on the back and rubbed up and down. She threw her head back and laughed. When they reached the bottom of the hill, she turned and gave her sister a big wink.

Maddalena's face was burning. What had Vito said to make her laugh?

"He wants to see your impression of Guglierma Lunga," Carolina whispered to her as the girls settled into their places in West Olive.

"What?" Maddalena asked. She noticed Vito leaning against the entrance sign. He raised his eyebrows at her and smiled. "That's all?"

"Well, he wanted a private show, just the two of you, but I told him no chance. We'll all be there."

"It seems like too much and not enough at the same time," said Maddalena.

"That's Vito," said Carolina. "It's enough, don't worry. He knows his luck's run out, so he's taking what he can get."

Vito's price was easier than even Carolina knew. The other girls hated it when the boys overheard them, but Maddalena secretly wanted someone else to hear how well she imitated voices. She didn't do many shows anymore, not since Vito's bike took over their time, and she missed the applause and the "How did you do that?" look on the girls' faces. She'd even been practicing some new riddles and predictions she'd heard from Guglierma herself.

"I'll do it," she said to Carolina.

"I already told him you would," she said.

Maddalena had to wait through seven full rides before her turn. She avoided Vito's eyes, and whenever she sensed him inching closer she stopped the conversation she was in and found another circle of girls to talk to. After everyone got at least one ride, the cycle was about to start again. The sun, which had been breaking steadily through the clouds since they left Fiorella, was now close to setting, and there was only time for one or two more rides. Ada rushed to claim her place, but Vito interrupted. "I have a special announcement," he said, picking up the bike with one hand. He carried it over to where Maddalena stood, and dropped it in front of her. "It seems I'm still not worthy of her kiss, but the very stubborn Maddalena Piccinelli has finally agreed to a fair price for my hard work."

"I don't believe it!" Luciana said. She held her arms up to God. "But what price does she get? Does it go for us, too?"

"Not unless you can do impressions," said Vito. "Soon I'll be joining you in West Olive to hear the famous impersonation of Guglierma Lunga, something no boy in the history of the world has ever heard. Am I right, Maddalena?"

She nodded.

"Big deal," said Ada. "That's all it takes? Think up a few riddles and make fun of an old lady?"

"If you were great at something," said Carolina, "maybe you'd get a special price, too."

"I don't care," Ada said. "As long as she hurries. I'm next, and I want another turn before it's too dark."

"Fine," Maddalena said. She removed her shawl and handed it to Carolina, feeling the cool rush of wind against the skin just above her breasts, where her blouse was cut in a crisscross pattern. She grabbed the handlebars and tried to push the bike up the hill, still avoiding Vito's face. But he held it by the back tire.

"Not so fast, Signorina," he said. He took a handkerchief from his back pocket, snapped it in the air, and laid it on the seat. "For comfort." He patted it with his hand, and stepped away with a short hop meant to be elegant. Instead he slipped on the slick dirt and almost landed on his *culo*. When he got his balance back, he said, "You can go now," and bowed.

"*Grazie*," Maddalena said.

"I never got a cushion," said Ada.

"Remember," Vito said, and grabbed the bike again. "Don't turn too fast, but not too slow, either." The advice didn't help her much, but she did finally meet his eyes to thank him for it.

They were black, ordinary eyes, without a trace of color, and set back a little in his head. More kind than not. When she nodded, he released his hold.

"Hurry up!" said Ada.

Maddalena walked the bike slowly up the hill, inspecting the frame for cracks, taking every bit of her time for herself. At the top she turned the bike around, smoothed out the creases in the handkerchief, and sat on the hard seat, looking first at the sunset between the mountain peaks, then down to her friends waiting with their hands on their hips. She sat there a long minute, sensing at her age what most girls don't learn until too late: that these moments before the plunge are the delicious ones, that whatever comes next will surely disappoint. She tried to shake the thought, but it stuck and got her mind spinning. She hated how impossible she made it to enjoy even the simplest things, that she looked at them from their darkest sides first. She saw Carolina grinning up at her now and found her so achingly beautiful that she seemed fragile. Someday a man will fall for her, Maddalena thought, and she'll beg him to take her away. There was Luciana beside her, already a widow; there was Vito, a pile of bones crushed under a Russian tank; here was this happy village, flattened by bombs and burning.

"Sometime today please, *piccolina!*" Ada yelled up to her.

"Take as long as you want," Vito said.

Finally, Maddalena started pedaling and felt the

bike rattle against the rocky ground. The wind blew through her hair, and before she knew it, she was flying fast down the hill. She felt suspended in the air, as if she'd just been lifted above the world and was watching it shrink beneath her. She wanted to touch the gold clouds, to wrap their soft fabric around her like a scarf.

Too soon she came upon the crowd, who'd formed their usual pack in the middle of the road. She was supposed to turn now—*Svelta! Svelta!*—into the patch of grass to their left and let Ada have her second turn of the day, but at that moment Maddalena decided she couldn't let this ride end so quickly. She'd waited too long. She kept the wheels pointed straight ahead.

"Turn, Madda-*le!*" the girls yelled. "*Turn!*" as she glided directly at them, then parted their bodies into two staggering lines.

"You're supposed to stop!" Ada called after her.

She zoomed fast down the dirt road, past the entrance sign, out of the limits of the village. The road grew narrower and rockier, surrounded on both sides by small ditches and fat, bristly bushes. Then came a long tunnel of trees, where the branches high above the road reached across and grabbed each other so tightly that no light could break through. The dirt was dry and gray, and the jagged rocks beneath her threatened to puncture the tires, or her skin if she fell. But she was able to avoid the holes and rocks with only a little effort, as if she'd been riding bikes for years. She pedaled hard and swung the handle-bars quickly from side to side, kicking up dust and hitting bumps that lifted her from the seat and sent Vito's handkerchief fluttering into the wind. She turned to watch it land on a branch.

When she'd gone too far, she lowered her body over the crossbar and dragged her feet on the ground. Though she was less than a half mile beyond the Santa Cecilia line, it seemed like another country. She slid calmly off the bike, careful not to tear her skirt.

She sat on a patch of grass and caught her breath. She heard the crunch of the pack of girls and boys marching toward her, kicking up dusty gray clouds. Vito was first, running far ahead, alone. His expression wasn't angry, though he didn't say a word. The rest of them skipped and made loud whooping noises, excited to leave the village, if just for a little while. Buccio carried Luciana on his back, and she nibbled on his earlobe from behind.

Vito headed straight for Maddalena, offered his hand, and lifted her from the ground. They stood face to face for what felt like a long time, though it was only a few moments.

"Let me help you," he said, and pulled from his pocket the handkerchief she'd lost on the way. He spit into it, then took both of Maddalena's dusty hands in his. He rubbed her fingers with the cloth and wiped away the dirt.

She was breathing hard. Carolina and the others were almost upon them now, though they couldn't see him touching her. Maddalena felt the texture of Vito's hands through the fabric. They were hard and grainy, like her brothers' after using the ax—not smooth, not delicate, as she'd expected. "Ow," she said, when he squeezed too tightly, and her mind suddenly told her, Vito Leone has strong hands. They didn't fit the rest of him, the shirt he'd tucked in wrong, the face blushing like a girl's.

The woods became quiet. Everyone gathered in a whispering circle around them, the girls with their arms crossed. When Maddalena saw Carolina's angry face, she immediately unlocked her fingers from Vito's and ran to her. She wiped her hands on her sister's dress. Carolina would do the talking now. She'd tease Vito and scare him away. She wouldn't tell him what Maddalena wished she could: *You feel different than you look.*

"Listen, Valentino," Carolina began. "I kept my mouth shut when you got romantic with the bike seat, but this is too much."

"What did I do?" he asked, turning his palms up.

"It's not what you did," said Carolina. "It's this idea you have. I couldn't see it more clearly if you wrote it on your forehead. If you think you can make my sister your *fidanzata*, you're more stupid than I thought."

"Excuse me," he said, laughing, "but it's not possible to be that stupid."

"Play games with me all you want," said Carolina, "but not with her. She's too young for all this anyway."

"She's only a year younger than you," Luciana said.

"Almost two years," Carolina said. "Get it right. And I don't care." She pulled Maddalena closer and turned to Vito. "You picked well, Vito, I'll give you that. But you picked wrong."

"I don't see what you're so upset about," Vito said. "Your sister is beautiful. It's not a crime to talk to a beautiful girl, to make sure she's comfortable. Is it, Buccio?"

Buccio just rubbed his chin.

"Maybe you should ask Claudio about it," said Carolina. "Or my father. Or maybe I should tell them how you've been making all the girls kiss you."

"You wouldn't!" Ada said. "You'll ruin it for everybody!"

"For him more than us," Carolina said. "I can make my own bike. How hard can it be?"

"*Disgraziata*," he said, under his breath.

"What was that?" said Carolina. She stepped closer, pulling Maddalena along. "Do you have something to say?"

Her feet stirred up dust, which hung in the air like fog. Buccio slapped Vito's thigh. Vito shifted his gaze from Carolina's and searched Maddalena's face, the first time he'd looked directly at her since they separated. She couldn't go against Carolina, not out loud, not after the way she'd fought for her, but she needed to send him some sort of message. So she bit the corner of her lip and flashed him a quick smile she hoped he could read, one meant to calm him and apologize and warn him not to push.

"I don't mean any harm, Signorina," he said. He held his palms out to keep her back. "I'm sorry you think I do. All I want is to see your sister's imitations, that's all. Honestly."

He was either a coward or a master at reading faces, Maddalena thought. If he was a coward, he was the same Vito Leone she'd known for sixteen years. If he was the other, he'd changed into someone new, and it had been a long time since she'd met someone new in Santa Cecilia.

CHAPTER 4

Early in life, Vito learned that people could disappear. He used to stand on his toes in his living room and peek through the bars of the crib where his Nonna Evelina, his mother's mother, slept. No bigger than a child, she lay curled on her side, dressed always in the same pale pink nightgown embroidered with angels. Hair sprouted from her chin and above her lips, tough gray bristles she'd scratch and pluck with her fingernails. She never spoke. Every once in a while she'd open her watery eyes and stare for a minute before fading. She had lived like this since long before Vito was born, and for six years after that. Then one October morning, just before he turned seven, she and her crib and her sour smell were gone, and in their place stood a large wooden chest of drawers.

Vito remembered looking for traces of his nonna in this chest: the angel gown, her little white slippers, the thick gold rings she wore on four of her bony fingers. Instead he found it packed with rolls of fabric for his father's tailoring business. There were wool and tweed from England in the highest drawers, French silk and paisley in the center, and all colors of Italian cotton and linen at the bottom.

Five years later, just before he left for America, Vito's father emptied this chest and stuffed the material into large leather suitcases. Vito watched him from the doorway of his bedroom. Massimo Leone was a big man and solid, but he was precise with his hands. He fit the bundles snugly into the bags, dragged them to the top of the staircase, and stood there, resting a moment against the wall. He wiped his sweaty face and the back of his neck with a handkerchief. He wore his hair long in the back, like a vagabond.

"Are you going somewhere?" Vito had asked him.

Massimo was startled. "Where did you come from?"

Vito shrugged.

"Your sisters and I are going on a trip. For a few weeks." He squatted and waved his son over. "Your job is to stay here and take care of Mamma. Can you do that?"

He shrugged again. "I think so."

"Good," Massimo said. They had to leave right away, he explained; he had a chance to do big business in Rome. Sandra and Silvia were older and hadn't seen anything of the world, so they were coming along. "Besides," he added, "can you imagine if I took one and not the other?"

They hadn't stayed for lunch. Concetta silently wrapped bread and cheese in wax paper and tucked them into her daughters' purses. Vito and his father loaded the carriage in the noon heat, arranging and rearranging the bags until they fit.

"You don't carry one of these yet, do you?" his father asked him, holding up his handkerchief.

"No."

"Take this one, then," he said, and tucked the square white cloth into the front pocket of his shirt. He bent down to look in Vito's eyes. "Don't worry," he said. "One day I'll take you to Rome, too."

When the time came, Massimo had to pull Sandra and Silvia away from their mother. He dragged them to the carriage, slammed the door, and ran around the other side. Concetta buried her face in Vito's chest and screamed. As the coach pulled away, the girls leaned out the window and blew kisses, stomping their feet and crying, which kept scaring the donkey.

"Enough!" Massimo yelled, and they stopped.

None of this had scared Vito. The women got this way whenever they left each other. He'd stood at the side of the road, smoothing his mother's hair from the top of her head to her shoulders, until the carriage turned left at the piazza toward Frosinone.

The handkerchief was Vito's father's last gift meant only for him. Over the next seven years he'd sent checks and photographs and letters, but those were for him and his mother. Until she got sick, Concetta took care of all the money. Now that it was Vito's job and the war had started, the letters came less often, and most of the time without checks. His father still wrote his letters as if he were just about to finish his short trip and head home.

Strange that Vito's mind should go to his babbo and his nonnina now, he thought, as he sat under a tree in West Olive, waiting for Maddalena to perform. It was a Wednesday, six days from her first bike ride, six days since he'd felt the soft skin beneath her muddy fingers and caught the flicker of the smile he sensed was just for him. He found it hard to think of either her or Buccio without older memories crowding them out. Maybe it was because he hadn't been in Buccio's house two nights ago, when the officers showed up and threw him his uniform. He'd seen his father's carriage return empty; he'd seen his nonnina's crib rolled into another house by Dr. Fabiano; but he hadn't seen Buccio's face as the soldiers pulled the heavy curtain across the back of the truck. The almost full carton of cigarettes Vito had saved for him he'd have to smoke himself. He wouldn't share them with Marco Ceccarelli or Toto Volpe, the other seventeen-year-olds. Vito had never liked them much, anyway, and besides, they had each other.

The girls were late. Vito took out one of the cigarettes, lit it, closed his eyes, and held the smoke in his lungs as long as he could. He said a prayer for Buccio and cursed himself for the mornings he'd dreaded his friend's knock at his front door. When Vito opened his eyes, he told himself, Maddalena would be there, and she'd make him forget. But she wasn't.

It was almost a quarter past five, nearly an hour after the time they'd agreed on, before the girls burst through the thick trees at the other end of West Olive. Carolina led. Behind her, Fiorella, her mangled hand in the pocket of her dress, wrapped her other arm around the grieving Luciana's waist. Luciana's head hung low, her hair covering her face. She swayed from side to side, her arms clutching her stomach. Maddalena walked far behind with the younger girls. There were maybe ten of them altogether.

He looked up when Carolina's shadow covered him.

"Here she is," she said. Her arms were folded across her large breasts, and she ticked her head toward her sister. "It won't last long, so you should pay attention." She turned around and joined the others at the left side of the stage—that lump of worn grass too shy to be a hill.

"Do you feel safe over there?" Vito called through his hands, making a show of the distance the girls kept from him. They'd tucked their skirts under their knees and sat upright in a cluster around Luciana.

"Mind your own business," Fiorella said.

Maddalena rose from the pack. She leaned over and kissed Luciana on the top of her head and took her place at the highest point on the mound. The girls clapped, and Vito followed their lead.

He recognized her dress from church. It had fancy ribbons at the shoulders and fell below her knees. It started at the neck and hugged her arms and waist tightly, which outlined the shape of her body. Her curves weren't as obvious as Carolina's, but they melted Vito just the same. In a few years, he thought, there was no telling how she'd look; she'd lose the baby softness in her cheeks, but her lips would stay full. As he kissed her, she'd take down her hair and let it fall against his face.

She lifted her arms to begin, and they stuck there, stiff, in the sunlight. She closed her eyes. Every inch of her body—her elbows and knees and the tilt of her head—settled into the transformation. A breeze bent the tree branches into each other, releasing the leathery scent of olives.

Her eyes flashed open. "I see the end!" she said. She fell to her knees and hugged herself tight. "A man burned, a woman frozen, the pigs with their snouts cut off!" She rolled onto her side, twitching her left eye. The girls giggled. Even Luciana managed a thin smile. The real Guglierma's left eye fluttered constantly, like the wing of a moth.

"Beware!" said Maddalena. "Beware of the five eggs and the man with the soft feet!"

"She sounds just like her," Vito said.

"Shh!" hissed one of the girls.

"Guglierma!" Carolina said. "My name is

Eleanora Vattilana." Everyone grew quiet. This was Buccio's mother's name.

"Yes, my dear," said Maddalena, tenderly.

Luciana gave Carolina a confused stare, her smile gone.

"Can you tell me, please," Carolina went on, "what will happen to my son in the war?"

Maddalena stood up, kissed the air three times in a circle, then swiveled her head from left to right. She fell back down and rolled onto her stomach, spread her arms and legs into a large X, and rested her cheek against the grass, facing them. "Your son will return with a snail in his ear," she finally said, "and that will be his only pain. Thank for this the God who brought you light and happiness and eternal salvation, and of course thank Guglierma, who saved you years of worry."

She blew a small kiss to Luciana.

"Guglierma!" said Vito. "Let me ask you, woman of God, what do you see in the future for me?"

"You're not allowed to ask questions," Carolina said.

"Let him be, *ragazza*," Maddalena said. Still on the ground, she made a fist and pressed it against her forehead. She stayed like that for so long that Vito wondered if she'd fallen asleep.

"You don't have to answer, Guglierma," Carolina said.

"Don't rush me," Maddalena said. She sat up on her knees, set her hands on her hips, and threw her head back. "I'm waiting for the angels to tell me."

"Take your time," said Fiorella, very serious. "They can be stubborn."

When Maddalena finally turned her face to Vito, it was with the same smile she'd given him six days before. He was sure of it: the girlish pout as she bit the corner of her lip, that shy bending of her chin into her neck, the eyes locked on his. It had stopped him cold and convinced him not to kick dirt at Carolina Piccinelli. It had told him, in the moment it lasted, *I'm on your side.*

"You won't grow up," Maddalena said, her lips pursed.

This was her vision of his life.

"The years will pass and the war will end," she said, "but you will not get old." She raised her voice to a squeak and pinched her thumb and forefinger together in front of her one open eye, the way Guglierma did when she saw something clearly. "I see you running through a green field. I see you laughing, chasing a dog, everyone around you with white beards and crooked legs, with canes! But you are still young, still as much a boy as today, forever. That is what I see for you; it is here in front of my face."

"What does it mean?" asked Fiorella. She looked over at Vito curiously, as if she'd just seen him for the first time.

"How do I know?" said Maddalena. "But I can tell you, it seems like a beautiful future to me."

Vito watched as best he could as she did more impressions. He smiled and laughed in the right places, but in his mind he turned over Maddalena's prediction again and again. That was how she saw him? As a little boy? Of course it was. What else had he shown her? She liked him that way now, but in a few years, when she herself grew up, she'd have to like him as a man.

"*Finito!*" he heard someone say, and applause erupted from the girls. Vito looked up. Maddalena lay on the ground, her face turned away from him. He'd missed the finale.

"You got a good show, Vito," said Carolina, from across the theater. "Worth maybe ten bike trips!"

He nodded and rubbed his arms. His feet felt sweaty in his sandals—hadn't Maddalena said that, too, something about soft feet? What did it mean? Was he going crazy?

He wanted her to stand so he could ask her what she meant. He would be brave; he would make a proposition. But she kept still. When the others crowded around Luciana, he walked quickly up to Maddalena and squatted beside her, his forearms on his knees.

"Signorina," he whispered.

She opened her eyes.

"Will you—" He stopped. His question seemed suddenly too much and too little to ask, but he had to say something. "Will you meet with me . . . alone?"

"Hey!" This was Carolina's voice. She was walking toward them. "What are you saying, Valentino?"

He looked at Maddalena.

"Yes," she said quickly. "I will. But I'm never alone."

Vito jumped up. He stepped back from her. He stood tall at the edge of the stage, snapped his feet together, and stuck out his chest. He bared his teeth. In his arms he held an invisible rifle and aimed it at the charging sister. *"Hefegingschwanzinnichts!"* he yelled. He spat at the grass, but it landed on his foot.

"Idiot," said Carolina, stopped in her path in front of him. "Who are you supposed to be?"

"I am Herr Eckhart," Vito said, "friend of the Fascists. You see, I can do impressions, too." Maddalena's small laugh drove him to march over to a tree and snap off a long branch. He studied it a moment, twirled it in his right hand, then, in one quick motion, lunged with it toward Carolina.

She screamed.

"Raus!" he grunted at her as he chased her away from Maddalena, up the hill in wide circles, then across the road, then in wider circles until she fell in exhaustion. He went for Fiorella and Ada next, tickling the backs of their necks with the leafy end of the branch. The girls ran as fast as they could, tumbling and using their hands to push off the ground, but they couldn't outrun him. He left Luciana alone, until she said, "What about me?"

and he ran her down toward the exit sign. He repeated, louder each time, *"Raus! Raus!"* a word the German soldiers used when a villager got in their way.

After he'd scattered every girl but Maddalena far enough across the olive grove and given Carolina one more chase, he stopped, beat his breast, and screamed *"Gibzenyockafult!"* into the sky. He had run out of breath. The girls lay on the grass before him, faces flushed, chests heaving. He ran to Maddalena.

He fell to his knees and crawled toward her. "I make you laugh," he said when he reached her.

"You do." She propped her head up with her hand but kept her eyes down.

"I got rid of them," he said, "so I could be alone with you." Their faces were so close, he could see the color rise in her cheeks, spreading like sunlight over her skin. "Did you like that?"

She nodded. "We'll both get in trouble." She plucked blades of grass and flicked them away.

"I don't care."

Her eyes met his. "I should," she said. "But I don't. Not this minute, at least."

He wanted to say a thousand things, to make sure she knew all he felt for her, that she wasn't this new idea he had. But he didn't have time for the whole story—how beautiful she was, how much more special than the others, how honored he was when she spoke kindly to him. He searched his mind for the few words that could mean everything, but what came out was, "I loved your show."

She sat up quickly, a fake, goofy smile on her face. She started waving to someone behind him.

It was Carolina, of course, staggering toward them from the top of the hill.

"Doesn't she ever get tired?" Vito asked.

"She's a general," said Maddalena, still waving. "She never quits."

"Tell her there's no war here," said Vito.

"I won't tell her anything," Maddalena said. "No one can know. If you want to see me, come to the store on Tuesday, at four. Tuesday's the day I work. It's usually empty then, but bring money to buy something, in case you see customers or my father."

If he moved his body forward just a few inches, their lips would touch.

She lay back down on the grass. "Now get out of here before she kills you," she said.

Vito jumped up and ran backward up the hill, mouthing "Tuesday" to Maddalena and blowing her kiss after kiss. He stretched his arms out wide to hold, if just for a moment, this new world: the girl at his feet, the trembling trees, the stage, the perfect sky.

When he turned around and just missed slamming into Carolina, it was all he could do not to laugh. She looked so serious, he wanted to tickle her. Instead he pointed to his bike, propped against the entrance sign across the field, and said to the entire olive grove, "Ride it all day if you want! Any of you! It's really free now!"

Not until he passed the Piccinelli store itself did he calculate that today, Wednesday, was as far from Tuesday as a day could be. It was another of God's games, he thought, to make him wait six more days for something he'd wanted his entire life. He headed instinctively for Buccio's house, ready to brag and tell him how wrong he was, but when he got there, the curtains were drawn and the gate was closed. Through the windows he heard women crying.

CHAPTER 5

To have a chance with a girl like Maddalena Piccinelli, you had to be handsome or rich. To win her, you'd better be both. Vito Leone, licking his fingertips and dabbing back his hair, knew he was neither. Buccio had told him as much, and the mirror confirmed the rest: his face as soft as a baby's, his eyes too sunken, his chest so bony and narrow he could use it to wash clothes. And though he and his mother did have some money saved, it was nothing to wave under the noses of Aristide and Chiara Piccinelli—unless he wanted them to laugh.

He was one of three young men left in Santa Cecilia, and still his chances were slim. He was thinking this as he stood at one end of the main street, at five minutes to four on the first afternoon he was to meet Maddalena alone. He reminded himself that she had agreed to this meeting, and that in the past few weeks she'd sent more than one unexpected signal; but that all seemed unreliable, the passing interest of a child with a new toy.

At the moment the church bell struck four, Vito started down the road. He looked behind him and up at the windows of the houses, to make sure no one was watching. Then he pulled out his father's handkerchief, lifted up his good blue shirt, and wiped the sweat from his armpits. He didn't smell yet, but that would change if he didn't keep dry.

He went to wipe his forehead and realized he had only this one cloth, now damp. "*Stronzo!*" he said aloud. He stepped off the road, picked a leaf from a tree in front of the store, and used that for his forehead.

He stood before the entrance for a moment and caught his breath. He'd prepared a joke, one he'd come up with himself. He went over it again: the setup, the buildup, the punch line. "You won't grow up," Maddalena had predicted, but he wondered if maybe that was what she wanted for herself. For a while, he thought, she'd treat him nicely, like a friend, the way girls treat the family horse; but soon, after he sneaked into her heart with jokes and dances and crazy made-up songs, she'd suddenly see him as a man. He wasn't exactly sure how that last part would work, except that by that time they'd actually be old—over twenty, at least, marrying age—and they'd be used to each other, and there'd be nothing else to do but tell the priest.

He pushed open the door and saw her at the front counter, her head bent over a gigantic black book, a pencil in her hand. When she turned to him, her eyes seemed glassy and afraid. She had what looked like a pimple above her lip, a pink blotch that she immediately scratched. She smiled, and the blotch blended into her skin.

"Is anyone here?" Vito mouthed, moving his hands in a wide circle.

She shook her head. "Go to the back," she whispered, and pointed the eraser end of the pencil toward the dingy room behind the aisles, where fruit boxes and extra newspapers and buckets were stored. "I'll meet you in a second."

Vito walked between two rows of barrels, each of which held small white mounds of salt and sugar and flour. The only full barrels contained nuts, chestnuts and almonds and pignoli, piled high and overflowing onto the floor. Nut trees grew like weeds in Santa Cecilia; Vito had eaten so many walnuts this year that just their smell made him sick.

All over Italy there must have been villages overrun with pigs and chickens; in Vito's it was nuts and olives. He imagined that the Piccinellis must eat like human beings, that they had plenty of animals hidden in the back, and probably more in a shed somewhere on the other side of the mountain. Aristide must kill one a week for their nightly feasts. They didn't eat as Vito did, in a chair next to his mother's bed, his plate in his lap, watching the dust hang in the window light. Claudio and his father talked about the business; the girls in their aprons handed plates back and forth from the kitchen. Uncles and cousins and neighbors stopped by for cake and espresso on the terrace—all while

Vito sat at his window, his mother asleep beside him under six blankets.

It was like a grotto, here in the back of the store; the walls rounded, and the farther Vito walked, the lower they sloped. A tiny window, blackened with soot and barred with two iron slats, faced the main street. Vito drew a line in the soot with his finger, then quickly wiped it on the side of a box. But the slick and grainy dirt left a film no matter how hard he cleaned it, and now he'd have to keep Maddalena from noticing it.

He stood beside some mops and waited.

He listened for her movements. The church bell struck the quarter-hour. He tried to keep standing tall, but his shoulders, pressed against the concrete, hurt his back. She must have gotten scared or nervous and sneaked upstairs. No, she'd run to find Carolina, who had her platoon of girls ready to poke fun at him. The angry sister had masterminded this trick, this cruel trick, all to humiliate him. Even Marco and Toto—even his mother and Dr. Fabiano—knew. If this were true, Vito decided, he'd never let a single one of them ride his bike ever again. He'd stop speaking to all of them. For the rest of his life, every time he rode by them he'd spit on them; they'd call him the Spitter of Santa Cecilia, and what would it matter—

"Hello," Maddalena said.

She appeared in front of him, in a green dress

with white buttons down the front. Her hair was pulled back, as always, but a strand had escaped and fallen in a curl behind her ear. She held her hands behind her.

"Fiora mia," Vito said. He hadn't planned to call her this. He stepped forward to greet her. As he'd do for any woman, aunt or sister, he kissed first her left cheek, then her right, before stepping back. "I thought you ran away."

"I had to finish my work," she said. "Every Tuesday I record receipts in the ledger. I keep track of who's buying what, and how much people are trading."

"That's an important job," Vito said.

"That's what everyone says," she said. "But Papà doesn't write a receipt half the time. And when he does remember, he scribbles it and the numbers are hard to read, so I don't know what to put down."

"Really?" Vito asked.

"I shouldn't have told you that," she said. "Now everyone will know, and they'll take advantage." She looked behind her. "Why did I say anything?" She narrowed her eyes and bit at her thumbnail.

"I won't tell anybody," Vito said. He reached out and cupped her elbow with his palm. She shifted her feet, and he took it away. "Honestly. And anyway, how would I say I found out?"

"That's true," she said, and smiled. She looked behind her again, then at him, then the ground. "We don't have much longer," she said.

"Much longer? I just got here."

She kept her eyes on her shoes. She stood an arm's length from him, across a deep crack in the concrete floor. "I didn't finish my work," she said guiltily, as if explaining it to her father. "I couldn't concentrate."

"Because of me?" Vito asked.

She nodded.

He took her right hand and led her a few steps farther back to a corner of the grotto, where he'd cleared some space. "So much junk back here," he said.

"My brothers' job," said Maddalena. "My older brothers. No one's cleaned this room since they left. Mamma says it's bad luck to do their work, that it means we don't believe they'll come back to do it themselves."

"And when they do get back?" Vito said. "Instead of a glass of wine and a steak, she'll hand them a mop and rag and say, 'Well, it's about time'?"

Maddalena laughed. "That sounds like her," she said.

"You're beautiful when you laugh," Vito said. "You're beautiful always, but especially when you laugh. I want you to laugh all the time."

"Nobody laughs all the time," she said.

"Nobody's with me all the time."

From overhead came the sound of planes, and Maddalena's back stiffened. Someone passed by the window, but she didn't seem to notice. "It's okay," he said. "Nothing to be scared of. Listen to this joke I have for you."

"Is it long?" she asked immediately. "I should be with my family. If this is a raid—"

"It's not a raid," Vito said. "And the joke's not long. As soon as it's over, you can go. I mean, I'll go, if that's what you want."

"No," said Maddalena. "What I mean is, the longer you stay, the more of a chance that someone will find us. And people might come in here to be safe."

"I understand," Vito said. "And if they do?"

"I don't know," she said. "Run? Or hide back here until I can get you."

"I meant, if they find us, what happens then? Is the world going to end?"

"I'm not allowed to talk to you alone," she said. "To any boy. You should know that." She had to speak louder over the roaring planes, now directly overhead. Her voice was shaking, and Vito wished he hadn't asked. "My mother would slap me in the face, and never let me see you again. My father wouldn't let you in here anymore, not even if you were starving."

"Okay," Vito said. "I'm sorry. It's all right." They were leaning against the same wall now, facing each other. Her face, a few inches from his, had lost its color; he could feel her breath on his cheek.

"Tell your joke," she said. "Hurry."

He closed his eyes. "There are these two

compari," he said, "Older guys, best friends, in a tiny village, say, Broccostella. Not Santa Cecilia, of course."

"Did you make this up yourself?" she interrupted.

"Not this one," Vito lied, in case she didn't like it. "My Zio Gabriello told it to me a long time ago. I was going to tell it to the others, but I saved it for you. It's about a bike."

She rolled her eyes, but not mockingly. "My family's sick of your bike," she said. "Claudio, not my sisters. He said if any of us mentions it again he'll take it and throw it in the gorge. He said it's not ladylike for us to ride it all over the place, screaming."

"He should talk to Luciana about ladylike," Vito said.

This made her blush and cover her grin.

"One of these *compari,* then," said Vito, encouraged, "we'll call him Claudio. Just for fun. Claudio and—" He thought for a moment. "His best friend, Vito the Second."

The sounds of the planes faded into a hum, and Maddalena breathed easier. She took her hand from her mouth and laid it on his hip.

"Vito the Second has a bicycle, you see, the only one in the village. He bought it brand new, paid a lot of money for it. He's single, and loves it like a wife: polishes the chrome, paints designs on it, stores it under a blanket in his bedroom so it won't get dirty or cold or lonely."

"Sounds like someone I know," said Maddalena.

"I'm not that bad!" he said. "I don't cover it up. Anyway, Claudio has a real wife—we'll call her Antonietta, I don't know why—and Antonietta is sick in bed and needs medicine from Avezzano. She needs it bad, and there are no cars and no horses to get there. The only way for Claudio to get to Avezzano on time is to borrow Vito the Second's bike."

"Oh no."

"But Vito never loans his bike to anyone—not his father or his brother and certainly not his friends. He hardly rides it himself, he's so scared of getting it dirty. But Claudio has no choice. He walks to Vito the Second's house, and on the way he imagines how the conversation will go. He plays both parts in his head. 'Please please please,' he hears himself beg. 'I'll do anything for you, Vito! I'll pay money; I'll let you beat me at bocce; I'll find you a woman. Anything.' And he sees his friend shake his head and stroke the handlebars and say, 'No way.'"

"Okay."

"Claudio imagines how upset he'll be when Vito says no, how the blood will boil in his heart, how he'll throw things around the room. He thinks, 'I'll finally tell that Vito how selfish he is, how he doesn't care for anyone but himself and his stupid bike while my wife is home suffering.'"

Though Maddalena kept her hand on his hip and her eyes on him, Vito felt this joke was going on too long. Closer up, the pink blotch on her face was nothing more than a blemish, not a pimple, not a rash. He wanted to kiss it, then to move from there to her lips, and for her to take one step closer to him so their bodies would touch at every point. He wanted to feel her legs between his, her breasts against his chest, and her tongue warm in his mouth. He was ready for this, his first time, and the sooner his silly joke was over, the more time they'd have for love.

"So Claudio gets to Vito the Second's house," Vito said, "and knocks on the door, the angry conversation still playing in his head. 'Please let me borrow your bike,' he says to himself, practicing. He waits and waits, and soon Vito the Second comes to the window, happy to see him. *'Compa!'* he calls down. 'What a nice surprise! What can I do for you?'

" 'I'll tell you what you can do,' Claudio says. He steps out in the street and shakes his fist at him. *'Vaffanculo,'* he says, 'you and your goddamned bike!' Then he goes home."

She hadn't flinched at the bad word, but she hadn't laughed, either. Instead she gave a polite smile, as if waiting for more.

"That's it," Vito said. "That's the joke."

"Oh!" Her hand flew to her mouth again. She leaned forward a little and grinned, making fake *ha-ha-ha* noises from the back of her throat. "That's really funny, Vito."

"Zio Gabriello," he said, waving his hand. "His humor's not for everyone. Claudio, you see, by the time he got to Vito the Second's, he'd already—"

"I understood," Maddalena said. "It's very funny. Believe me. When I think about it later, I'm sure I'll laugh really hard. Maybe I'll tell it to Carolina." She patted Vito's chest with her palm, then left it there. He stood on his tiptoes and kissed the top of her head. Her hair smelled like apples. She relaxed and let her head fall against his shoulder, though she kept the rest of her body from touching his.

They stood there for a minute or two, tensely, until someone pushed through the front door. Maddalena ran down the far aisle without looking back, and came up behind the counter. Vito slid over to the aisle near the door, near the rows of barrels.

"*Buongiorno*, Signora Lunga," he heard Maddalena say, too loudly to seem normal. "What can I get for you?"

As Guglierma showed Maddalena the artichoke she came to trade, telling her how fresh it was and how delicious it would taste roasted with a little garlic and oil, Vito sneaked out of the store. His joke had failed. He'd sweated too much. He'd forgotten to hide in the corner and wait for her to rescue him.

But she let him come the next four Tuesdays all the same, even as the store got busier and there was a greater chance of getting caught. It amazed him. And on the fifth Tuesday, when Maddalena Piccinelli finally kissed him in their Grotto—nervously at first, then slowly, with tenderness and something close to joy—Vito Leone believed his luck had changed.

THE TANK

CHAPTER 6

Every night, Maddalena asked God to forgive her for her many sins. She'd grown brave, kissing Vito first on the chin and cheek only, then the mouth; she danced close to him across the floor of the Grotto and let him hold her from behind, with his arms across her chest. These were not only sins, but promises she wanted to be sure she could keep. They told him yes, I'll be your wife someday soon, tell your mother, tell the priest, tell everyone. Instead she gave him a hundred good reasons to keep their romance secret: she was too young for a *fidanzato*; her older sisters weren't married yet; her brothers were still missing. The biggest reason: If the village learned she was meeting a boy alone in the back room of a store, they'd brand her a *puttana* no better than Luciana. She'd disgrace her family. She polished these reasons well, and every week she vowed to stop letting Vito into the store. But then Tuesday would come and she'd find herself in the Grotto again, standing with him between the broom and the bucket of wash-cloths. He'd be barefoot, in a shirt with the sleeves rolled up and shorts too big for him. He'd unfold his arms and hold them out for her to step into, calling her *stella, sogno, diamante*—his star, his dream, his diamond. Every week some new, beautiful thing.

While Maddalena spent that summer of Tuesdays in 1943 kissing Vito Leone, the Allies were busy bombing Sicily. Eleven thousand Italian soldiers had surrendered the forgotten island of Pantelleria a month before, and now Naples and the rest of the south were in danger. When news like this came over the radio, Maddalena asked whoever was around her to help make sense of it. Did this mean the war was headed north, straight up the road to their village? How long would it take? How could people want to hurt this beautiful country? The men—her father, Claudio, Vito—always gave her answers meant to calm her; they told her not to worry, that their gut trusted the Germans to protect them as well as they were protecting Giacomo and Maurizio in Russia. Her father explained that the Germans had adopted Italy the way a family adopts a slow child, and would never let anyone harm her. The women's answers, of course, were full of doom. Instead of eventual peace, her mother and Celestina and Signora Puzo described obliterated villages, pregnant women hung from trees, the Earth dividing and mountains tumbling over themselves. The truth, of course, lay in some third sex somewhere, but Maddalena had no knowledge of that sort. Her life was a constant switching from trust in the men to belief in the women, from a childlike calm to a terror that seized her suddenly and held her for hours until she switched back.

To quiet her mind, she'd rest her head against Vito's chest. She'd hear his heart beat deep within and make a hollow sound, like the drop of a church kneeler. The rhythm steadied her. She'd listen for the door, for Claudio's or her father's footsteps on the stairs, but mostly she'd forget for a while who and where she was. She'd imagine herself ten years older, a wife and mother; her parents laughing at one of Vito's jokes; the fighting over; her brothers and Buccio and the other men crowding the Al Di Là, sweet-talking her sisters and friends.

Vito treated this war as if it were a fly he could swat away. He told her over and over that nothing—not the army or his father or the law itself—could make him leave her or Santa Cecilia. The planes were nothing more to him than angry birds. If Claudio was allowed to hide, Vito had said to her, then he, too, should be allowed. Maddalena hadn't disagreed with him to his face, but she knew the one important difference between her brother and Vito: Claudio *wanted* to fight. It had all happened this way: Years ago, her father had thought of a number, and whichever son came closest to it had to stay in the village and protect the family in case something happened to him. Claudio had lost. Everyone in the village knew how brave he was: They'd seen him in the street, making his thumb and forefinger into a gun and aiming it at invisible Russians coming at him. Everyone said he stayed home out of duty, but they wouldn't be able to say the same about Vito. What would they say about the girl who married him?

Instead of worrying about his eighteenth birthday, now less than two months away, Vito spent his time convincing Maddalena to meet him more than once a week. They agreed. The best place was behind the butcher shop, near the spring, where they couldn't be seen from the road. She'd volunteer to fetch water, a chore that took a while and didn't require a chaperone, then sneak behind the shop just before getting in line. If the pots in her kitchen happened to be full at the time and day they'd settled on, she'd either dump the water out a back window or take a long, stomach-bloating drink.

On one of these new meeting days, a late Wednesday afternoon in early September, Maddalena set her two dented copper pots on the grass behind the butcher shop, leaned against the back wall, and waited for Vito. He was late. She took off her shawl to cool her shoulders on the stone and stood listening to the women at the spring fight for their places in line: the screechy voices, the scuff of shoes on the dirt as they pushed forward, the constant clanging of pots. This noise—"the music of Santa Cecilia," Carolina called it—was loudest near dinnertime, but it never let up, not even in the middle of the night or the dead hours of the afternoon *riposo*.

Just as Maddalena was about to give up on Vito, she peeked around the corner of the wall to find him leading his mother to the back of the line. The old woman moved like a cripple, with a cane in one hand and her other arm clutching her son's waist. She had a rag tied around her head. Maddalena hadn't seen her up close in months, but with just a quick glance across a hundred feet of tree branches, she could tell she was much worse than Vito had described.

He steadied his mother behind Luciana Campini and looked in Maddalena's direction. He cupped one hand around her ear and spoke into it, then placed the other on her cheek to pull her closer. It was at that moment—the moment Vito's hand touched his mother's face—that Maddalena first heard the grinding of a car engine. No one in the street seemed to notice. Then she smelled the exhaust and heard honking and something like very loud radio static coming toward the piazza.

"Italy has surrendered!" came a deep voice from the hill behind the spring. "Mussolini is deposed! Italy has joined the Allies!"

Maddalena watched the crowd as the honking grew louder and closer and pots crashed to the ground. The women ran in all directions. Luciana, looking stricken, stood as frozen as a statue. Water rushed over Vito's bare feet and he jumped up as if it had bitten him. Maddalena gripped the corner of the wall and waited for the talking car to appear. She'd seen it a few times before: after the bombing of Sicily and, just two months ago, the arrest of Mussolini. The government couldn't wait to announce bad news; they liked to make a parade of it and scare everyone to death.

Some of the women cut in line as the fat black car parted the crowd. "The retreat has begun!" the car boomed through the two round speakers that stuck out like gigantic ears from its back windows. Guglierma Lunga, standing next to one, was knocked to the ground by the force of its shouting "Hitler's army is retreating!"

Vito pulled his mother to his chest to shield her. Maddalena hooked her shawl around her shoulders and, unthinking, ran toward them, leaving her pots on the grass. The piazza was full of people. Doors swung open, spilling out families in packs. They stood in front of their houses, shading their eyes and staring up the main street at the car. Some ran toward it. Some hugged each other and jumped up and down. Signore Volpe, the loudest Fascist, shook his head slowly back and forth, looking at the ground. Dr. Fabiano, whose wife, Frieda, was from Berlin, patted him on the back.

Maddalena didn't understand the news the car was belching out, a string of garbled Italian and what must have been German. To whom had Italy surrendered? Was the war over? Vito saw her running toward him, and held out his hand. "Are you okay, Maddalena?" he called out.

"Yes," she said. "You?"

Luciana was watching them. Maddalena looked

from her to Vito, then at Concetta, her head still buried in Vito's chest. When she noticed Claudio across the crowd in the other direction, she turned and ran to him.

"Maddalena!" she heard Vito call.

"No one outside after six o'clock," the car announced. "During the retreat, anyone outside after six will be arrested. Go home! Now! The curfew begins now!"

The crowd groaned and banged on the hood and windows. Someone yelled, "The Germans are everywhere! What will they do to us?" but the car didn't answer any questions. It sped up. It pushed past them and knocked old Ganzo, the carpenter and mail deliverer, out of its way. It continued down the main street, past the Piccinelli store, where Chiara stood with the twins and Carolina. It headed south toward the olive grove and Broccostella, and when it turned the corner it began again, "Italy has surrendered!"

A group of old men had formed a circle around Claudio, puffing on cigarettes and arguing. Claudio pressed his palms together as though he were praying and shook them at one of the men. "Without Mussolini, who are we?" he was saying. "What is Italy? The world laughs at us! It laughed before Mussolini, and it laughs now. But when he was in power—"

"Il Duce murdered my son," said one of the old men, who must have been from another town, since Maddalena didn't recognize him. He flicked his cigarette down and smashed it with his shoe. "Bring my Menotti back and let them laugh at him all they want. But bring him back."

"Your son didn't die for nothing," Claudio said. He stepped closer to the man. "He helped make this a better country, a world-class country. He saw that we're more than this." He pointed to the crowd, to one of Fiorella's aunts pulling on her hair and screaming, to the children running barefoot in circles. By now the farmers, who tended the fields farther down the mountain, were making their way to the piazza. The old men of the Moravia family walked with their arms around each other, drying their tears and blowing their noses into their sleeves. They wore hats and suspenders and black boots; their skin was wrinkled and sunburned. "Look at them. Do they even know what they're crying about? What do they understand? These people can't find their own town on a map. Half the men in this village can't read or write, can barely tell you what year it is, and it's the same all over the country, one illiterate *paese* after another stuck on top of mountains, afraid to look down. That's what Mussolini was trying to change." When he finally noticed Maddalena, he pulled her into the circle. "Our two brothers are fighting in Russia right now," he told the man. "If I could take their place, I would. Wouldn't I, Maddalena?"

"You would," she said, half listening to him, half looking for Vito and Luciana in the crowd.

"I would take your son's place if I could," he said

to the man. “That’s how much it’s worth to me.”

“That’s very easy to say,” said the man. He started to walk off, his hands in his pockets. “My wife is waiting at home, probably scared out of her mind. This old Italy you talk about was fine with her.”

When he got far enough away, Claudio turned to Maddalena. “It’s people like him who made this happen.”

“I’m so confused,” said Maddalena. “What does it mean?”

“Perfect example!” Claudio said, laughing. The men grunted on their cigarettes, and Claudio lit one for himself. “Don’t you hear the news with us every day?” he asked her. He shook out a match. “Aren’t you in the room?”

“She’s dreaming of husbands,” said one of the men, who turned out to be one of Buccio’s uncles, Signore Vattilana. “‘A hundred men dead,’ the radio says, and she thinks, ‘a hundred chances gone.’”

“That’s not true, Signore,” she said, as politely as she could. She wanted to say, what do *you* know about me? But she was with Claudio, the policeman of respect.

“Maddalena’s too young for that,” Claudio said. “No, what it means, *cicciottina*,”—he pinched her cheek—“is that we’ve switched sides. The Germans used to be our friends, and the Americans our enemies. Now it’s the opposite. The problem is: There are more Germans in this country than

Americans right now, whether we want them or not. All those tanks we let through here the past few years? They're coming back, and this time they'll run us over. They're ready to fight *us* now."

"The car said they were retreating," said Maddalena. "Doesn't that mean they're going back where they came from?"

"Yes," said Claudio. "But they want Italy for themselves. And if they can't have it, they'll make sure no one else gets it. They'll destroy it."

"This place?" Maddalena said. She held her hand over her mouth and squinted to keep back tears.

"Only the Fascists are lucky," said Signore Vattilana. "Dr. Fabiano, Matteo Volpe. They should put a black shirt outside their windows so the Germans know who their friends are and don't burn their houses down. You know what? We should all do that. We should all pretend to be Fascists. Tell your father, Claudio."

Claudio narrowed his eyes at him. "Watch your mouth," he said.

"No harm!" said Signore Vattilana. He stepped back and threw up his hands. "No harm!"

The group stopped talking.

"What?" Maddalena asked.

"Your father's thrilled about this," said Signore Drago. He had a soft voice, with a whistle in the *s*s. "He hates Mussolini."

"He does?" asked Maddalena. "Did I know that?"

"I don't know," said Claudio, "but you're a girl. And you don't pay attention. So you might have known it five minutes ago and forgot."

They laughed and laughed, and Signore Vattilana lit another cigarette for Claudio as a way to make peace. Out of the corner of her eye Maddalena noticed Vito walking his mother slowly back up the street toward their house. She didn't realize she was staring at them.

"That's another lucky one," said Signore Vattilana, nodding toward Vito. "My nephew's somewhere in Russia, fighting one of those animals with his hands, and this boy gets to sit pretty for the next ten years."

"What do you mean?" Maddalena asked. She turned to Claudio. "He doesn't have to go anymore?"

He shook his head. "Not unless he wants to," he said. "Everything's the opposite from before," he said. "If the Germans don't kill them first, our soldiers are coming home. Maurizio, Giacomo, Buccio, everyone."

"It's over, then," said Maddalena. Her heart was pounding, in joy for her brothers, in confusion over Vito. What would she do now that he wasn't leaving after all?

"You didn't hear your brother say 'if,' Signorina?" said Signore Drago.

Claudio was looking at her. Though people were still wailing, and the toothless farmers now formed a circle and kicked their legs in a victory dance, everything seemed quiet. It was as if she could hear the trees breathing or the water hissing over the rocks in the gorge a hundred feet below.

"Are you all right?" Claudio asked her.

She nodded.

"It's not over," he said. "Not even a little bit. Anything can happen. In ten minutes, it could all change again. But we'll be fine, don't worry."

"I have to go home," Maddalena said, and broke from the circle.

She ran toward her house, swerving around the donkeys and carriages and dancers. She'd hand her sins over to Carolina—the kissing, the promises, the sneaking around. She'd beg her to fix it all before everyone in Santa Cecilia found out and made her keep her word. If she were brave enough, she'd tell Carolina the sin she'd been keeping even from God: that sometimes she felt grateful for the draft, and counted on it for the certainty that, no matter what, Vito would be gone by November. Yes, she always knew she'd miss him and dreaded the thought of watching him go. But she also dreaded the burden of saying to the world "I choose him," and longed to be free of it. Only the most wicked of girls were this confused, she thought. What had made Cecilia a saint was that she knew her mind so well, so absolutely, that she'd rather die than change it. Maddalena was no saint, and, as she approached her house, it seemed everyone could see it on her face.

⋆ ⋆ ⋆

There had been a breeze all that day, but by eight o'clock the air was still. The three streets of Santa Cecilia were empty, the stores closed. The old men sat on their terraces and yelled to one another across the main road. The two Drago brothers, who lived side by side in the houses facing the Piccinellis', played cards through their open windows. Maddalena could never remember their names. When it got too dark to see, the bald brother, the one who'd spoken to her that day, accused the bushy-haired one of cheating, and then the bald one called the bushy-haired's son a *bastardo*, and soon men were leaning out of the windows of five houses, arguing and throwing pebbles at one another.

Maddalena sat in the kitchen, quickly peeling potatoes for a dinner that the announcement of the surrender made two hours late. She hadn't yet been able to get Carolina alone. The women worked busily around her. Carolina snapped the ends off the *fagiolini;* Teresa stirred the soup; Celestina stopped stacking plates to complain that her friend Lorena always seemed to have a new dress; Chiara pulled the bones from a boiled chicken; Claudio and Aristide huddled in the corner with the muttering radio, talking low.

"We have news," Claudio finally said, loud enough to interrupt Celestina. He switched off the radio. "And you all have to listen. As far as we know, the German tanks will travel mostly at night. That's the reason for the curfew. But no one knows what they'll do. They might just roll through, like they did when they came, so they can get back to Germany faster, but they might not."

"What else could they do?" asked Teresa.

"Shoot us," Carolina said, without turning around. "Is that enough?"

"They won't shoot us," their father said. "Not if we stay inside. Not if we don't bother them. They don't care enough about us to get out of their tanks."

"That's not true," Carolina said. She turned to face him. "They hate us. They hate every Italian, and I don't blame them. We let them down."

"Are you crazy?" Claudio said. "Who have you been talking to? If the Germans—"

"*Zitto!*" Aristide said. "We don't have time for this. Carolina, shut up about what you don't understand. Your brother follows the news. You don't."

"'One of the only roads in all of Italy wide enough for tanks,'" she said, trilling her *r* like the radio announcer's. "We were so proud of our stupid road! It's probably not even true. I bet there are plenty of roads this wide."

"It was like a parade when they came before," Celestina said. "Those big machines, and the men in their uniforms standing so straight, so serious. It was so pretty! Even the guns!"

"It won't be pretty this time," said Aristide. "And you won't be watching it. Listen to me. When the tanks come, I want everybody in the back of the house. Stay in the girls' bedroom until I tell you it's safe to come out." He reached down and tugged on Maddalena's chin. "Are you listening, *piccolina*?"

"Yes," Maddalena said. "I'm trying to." Her hands were shaking, and she had to focus on the knife to keep from slicing a finger.

"You're not scared, are you?" Aristide asked. "There's nothing to be scared of if you do what we say."

"I'm not scared," she lied. It wasn't only Vito in danger now, but everyone she knew. At any minute, even as they slept, a tank could smash into their house, if that's what tanks did, and kill them. No one could protect her. "It's not so bad to have to stay inside for a while. We can make it like a party."

"That's right," said Chiara. "I want all my children around me."

Hours later came the first rumble, as Teresa was spooning out the soup. It was past ten o'clock. They looked at one another, grabbed their bowls, stood up, and followed Claudio to the back. Celestina switched off the lights. Aristide closed the door once everyone was in the bedroom. The girls took their places on the bed: Carolina and Maddalena on one side, their mother and sisters on the other. Claudio and Aristide stood in the corner. Aristide paced back and forth, his bowl shaking in his hands.

"I spilled broth all over myself," said Celestina.

Aristide threw his bowl at the ground, where it broke into thick chunks. Maddalena flinched, and Chiara immediately reached down and gathered up the terra-cotta pieces coated with chicken broth and little *quadretti* of pasta. “Keep eating,” she said. “Don’t waste this food.” She took a small votive from her apron pocket. “I may light a candle, Aristide?”

“Yes,” he said. “They can’t see it from the back.”

They waited together in the dark bedroom, silent, the votive glowing and casting thin shadows on the wall. The familiar thunder came closer, and the floors began to tremble—first in a low hum, then stronger, as if about to crack. The dressing table slid forward and turned in an arc, but the wardrobe, which held all the girls’ dresses and scarves and, under her pink-and-blue shawl, Maddalena’s collection of romance books, didn’t move. From outside came long, fading whistles and the sound of breaking glass, and a popping noise like gunshots that grew louder. From across the village, in the direction of the olive grove, they could hear screaming. Celestina and Teresa started to cry.

“Quiet!” said Claudio. “They’re right in front now.”

The room filled with smoke that smelled like burned hair, and Maddalena started coughing. Carolina lifted her blouse up to her nose to breathe and rubbed Maddalena’s back.

Soon the tanks' steel cranking slowed. Men were yelling in what Maddalena guessed was German, but it sounded more like grunts. Then the voices stopped, and for a few seconds the house was quiet. She inhaled deeply without coughing and raised her head. She looked at her family, a circle of ghosts in the half light. Only Teresa was eating. Her father stood with his shoulders pressed against the back window; Claudio scratched the length of his arm and smiled weakly at her.

Then came an explosion, and the sound of glass shattering in the front room of the house. The bed jumped out from the wall, and Maddalena fell from it with her mother and sisters. She covered her head and screamed.

"Quiet!" came her father's voice. "You're safe. Don't let them hear you!"

Maddalena lay on the ground, thinking, This is the end of my life. She grabbed Carolina's arm and gripped it as tightly as she could. She imagined Vito's house, far down the branch off the main road: Did that make it safer or more dangerous? She pictured him hiding under his bed with his mother, keeping her safe, as Claudio and her father were trying to do for her.

"It's just stones," Claudio finally said, after more breaking glass. "That's all it is."

"Something exploded," Teresa said. "That wasn't a stone."

"My house!" cried Chiara from the other side of the bed. "My beautiful house!"

"We didn't blow up," Carolina said.

They heard footsteps crunching in the streets. A sour-smelling smoke filled the room. Soon the rumbling faded, and after the ground had been calm for a while, Aristide stood up.

"Everyone's all right?" he said. "Maddalena?"

"She's fine," said Carolina.

Chiara crawled around the bed and pressed Maddalena to her chest. "*Cara mia,*" she said, and rocked her. The candle still flickered in the middle of the room.

"Let's see the damage," said Aristide. He opened the door to the hallway, letting in a fog of gray light.

"Stop!" Celestina said. "How do you know they're gone?"

"They're gone," he said. "For now. But not for long." He turned toward them, his face barely visible, and stopped. "I didn't think it would be so bad at first. If it's this bad now—"

"We'll have to do this every night," said Carolina. "And every day we'll have to clean up—not only our house, but everyone else's. Some party, Maddalena."

"Will you shut up?" said Claudio. "Once and for all?"

The men led the file into the smoky hallway, Maddalena following with her arms outstretched and her hands brushing the walls to guide her. Though she'd walked these few feet between her bedroom and the dining room every day of her life, she felt now as if she were exploring an unknown cave.

Aristide stopped when he reached the front room. "*Dio mio!*"

His family fanned out behind him and stopped in front of the table. Outside their house, people were screaming for help, and a woman was crying and calling out "Fulvio!" for one of the Drago brothers.

The mound of chicken lay untouched on its platter in the middle of the table, but a rock had shattered the dishes on the men's side and knocked over their wine glasses. The women's settings were undisturbed. A few of the heavy wooden chairs had toppled, and the portrait of Chiara, painted when she was Signorina Fabbri of Rome, that had hung on the wall had landed faceup on the floor.

All five front windows were shattered. In three of them, the glass had fallen completely through, making clean, square openings. The others were cracked in spiderweb patterns, with holes in the center big enough for birds to fly through. Aristide walked over the rocks and shards to the window and looked out.

He raised his arms and formed his hands into fists. "*Bastardi!*"

Beside him, Claudio lowered his head.

"What is it?" Maddalena asked. Chiara tried to hold her and her sisters back behind the table, but Carolina broke through. Maddalena followed. Teresa and Celestina didn't move. Aristide and

Claudio ran out of the room and down the front steps.

The roof and front of Fulvio Drago's house were now a pile of stones. The side walls remained but had nothing to hold up between them. Maddalena stared at it, thinking, This is a bomb, this is what they mean by a bomb. It had ripped open a block of stone and brought down three floors of windows and terraces she'd seen every day. She'd watched planes fly overhead on their way to some other part of the world, and she'd been told that when they got there, they'd drop enough bombs to turn ten Santa Cecilias into hills of rubble. She hadn't known that tanks had bombs, too, or that they could do this.

"They blew up Signore Fulvio's house, Mamma," Carolina said.

Chiara started to cry but didn't come forward.

"Keep her away," Carolina said to the twins. "You shouldn't look, either, Maddalena."

But Maddalena stayed. She watched people run back and forth in front of the house, climb up and down the mountain of stones with their torches, and gather in the back corner, in what used to be the dining room. The people—mostly men, their faces hard to see—formed a circle; some squatted; some lifted blocks of stone and heaved them to the other side of the room, for what seemed like no reason. The rest, including the two Piccinelli men, just looked on, obscuring her view.

"Someone's dead," Carolina whispered.

"Don't say that," said Maddalena, but soon the

circle parted, and a man appeared with a body slung over his shoulder. He carried it slowly over the mounds of rock, holding its legs close to his chest, following another man who led with a torch. When they reached the street, the bearer, the bald Signore Drago, laid the body of his bushy-haired cheating brother on the lap of Signora Evelina Drago, who waited by the firelight.

"Fulvio!" She bent over her husband, then screamed his name for three villages to hear. The crowd stood around her with their hands in their pockets.

"It's not us," Carolina said. "It could have been, but it's not." She turned from the window and bent to scoop up the stones from the dining room floor. She held them in the folds of her dress, then dumped them out the back window. Maddalena scraped the leftover food from the plates and cleared the table.

An hour later, when the rumbling began again, Aristide and Claudio came running up the stairs, and all the women hid under the bed. Their bodies were pressed together, shaking and reaching to hold one another.

"We make it through tonight," said Aristide, breathing hard, as he closed the door, "and then we leave as soon as we can." His voice came in whispers from all around the room. "We'll pack everything, and as soon as we finish, we move. We'll be lucky if the house is here when we get back."

"Where are we supposed to go?" said Carolina. "We have nowhere."

"We have the farm," said Claudio.

The grinding of the tanks shook the floors again, and Maddalena could barely hear their voices over the noise. She remembered well her Zia Zabrina's few sad acres near Teramo, but she'd never thought of that place as a farm, certainly not a Piccinelli farm, though of course that's what it was. Zabrina had inherited it from Nonno Piccinelli and let it rot into nothing more than rows of dying vineyards and dry rocky fields.

Carolina tried to speak, but Aristide interrupted. "There are no arguments. No choice. Every family in the village is leaving. If you want to end up like Fulvio Drago, you stay here. If you don't, you get as far away from the main road of Santa Cecilia as you can."

Maddalena held on to the leg of her bed and closed her eyes. At any moment, a tank could crash through the front of her house; a bomb could drop on the roof; a line of German soldiers could break in and shoot them all dead. She had her family around her, and whatever happened to her happened to them, too.

When the line of tanks had passed and Maddalena could breathe easier, she asked, "Is every road in danger, or just ours?"

"Mostly ours, I think," Claudio said. "But you can't tell. That's why everyone's getting out."

"How can we leave here?" Chiara said. She stood

and walked to the moonlit back window, her hair still pinned into a ball on top of her head, her elbows protruding from where her arms crossed her chest. "How can we live at Zabrina's, in the middle of nowhere in that filthy house? How will Giacomo and Maurizio find us? They'll think we're dead, and if there's no one to tell them—"

"Don't talk like that," Aristide said.

"I'll talk how I want," said Chiara. "I'm not human anymore. You tell me we have to leave our house before our sons come back to us. I won't be human until I see them—"

Aristide stomped his foot hard, and she stopped. "That's enough," he said. "They've passed now. I'll go see what we can take from the store." He turned to his children. "The rest of you, pack. Only what you can carry. If you hear more tanks, come back to this room. Sleep if you can. Either way, we leave as soon as the sun comes up."

After just an hour, they'd filled their set of leather suitcases with clothing and photographs. Aristide and Claudio packed leftover food into burlap sacks. Teresa and Celestina wrapped sheets around whatever was left and tied them into bundles. Chiara stood motionless at the window, her tall body like a scarecrow against the outside world. Across the street, unseen by the Piccinellis, Evelina Drago gave over her husband's body to Dr. Fabiano, who settled him onto a stretcher, closed his eyes, and helped carry him off. Two doors down, Fiorella La Nubile took the jar that held her severed fingers and stuffed it into a traveling bag. On the other side of the village, Luciana Campini lay on her bed, terrified, screaming into a pillow she'd pulled over her face.

When the work was done, and Teresa and Celestina were sleeping soundly and fully clothed on their bed, Maddalena led Carolina out of the bedroom and down the back steps. It was past midnight, and no tanks had come for almost two hours.

"Your hands are sweaty," said Carolina.

They sat side by side on the steps. Carolina squinted in the candlelight. "Look at you," she said, and wiped Maddalena's forehead with the sleeve of her dress. "Are you that scared?"

"Yes," Maddalena said. "I don't know what to do. I can't leave here. Not tonight. Not without saying good-bye."

"What are you talking about?" Carolina asked. "Say good-bye to who? We're all here."

"To Vito Leone," said Maddalena. She lowered her eyes. "I'm in love with him."

CHAPTER 7

"What we need is a radio," Vito said. He walked hunched over across the living room, sweeping shards of glass into a pile near his father's bureau. He kept his back below the empty windows. The streets were quiet now, but at every sudden rush of footsteps, every name wailed from some other part of the village, Vito had dropped to his knees and covered his head. Then he'd thought of Maddalena, of the danger on the main road, and waited for his hands to stop shaking before resuming his work.

"They must have warned us," he said. "How are we supposed to know anything without a radio? How are we supposed to protect each other?"

His mother didn't answer. She sat under a blanket behind the sofa, her back against the wall and her hands folded around her rosary. She muttered prayers, bobbing her head to the rhythm of the repetitions. Vito had barricaded them both behind the sofa when the first tanks came through, five hours earlier. They'd wrapped their arms around each other and pressed their bodies close, waiting for the splashes of gunfire and the angry soldiers to reach them. Through it all, Vito had needed to hear his mother's voice. For the first time in as long as he could remember, he'd wanted her to tell him stories of her childhood in Santa Cecilia or of his father. He'd even begged her to describe the zigzags in her eyes or the pain in her legs or how scared she became at night alone in her bed. Instead she kept muttering those prayers. He'd told her again and again that he no longer had to go to the war, trying to cheer her up; he said, "I've been released from prison, Mamma," and she smiled and patted his knee. He'd told her about his secret meetings with Maddalena—about the Grotto, the butcher shop, that first touch in the tunnel of trees near Broccostella—and she'd gripped the beads more tightly. "You have to ask God to keep her safe," he told her. "Do you hear me?"

After a while, he gave up. It occurred to him that he needed a radio, and maybe a gun and a better hiding place, not a mother. After a long stretch of silence outside, he dragged her from the living room to her bed. The room had grown cold as the breeze blew in through the missing casements, and now even he was shivering.

"I'll go to Dr. Fabiano's as soon as the sun comes up," he said, as he pulled the covers up to her chin. "He'll know where I can get a radio."

He set the plate of *lupini* he'd fixed her for dinner on her nightstand in case she got hungry in the morning. Though these flavorless beans, her favorite, grew like weeds in the village, Vito had stuffed handfuls of them in his pocket last week as he waited for Maddalena in the store. He'd soaked them for the past five days in the river, then boiled them, sprinkled them with salt, and arranged them with sprigs of rosemary. It had seemed like nothing at the time, but now—alive in his house, rubbing his hands to keep warm, the world exploding outside—he felt what a luxury it had been to walk lazily down the aisles of the store, to steal beans for his mother, to look up and find that Maddalena had been watching him.

Concetta was stirring. "Guglierma had a vision," she said.

Vito turned around. "When it's time to sleep," he said, thinking she was dreaming, "this is when you talk?" But when he saw the tears in her eyes, he softened. "You're awake, Mamma?"

"A month ago she warned me," she said, still with her eyes closed and muttering prayers between her words. "And she was right! 'Don't get comfortable,' she said. 'Don't forget that Vito's alone in the world, with no one to take care of him.' "

"You take care of me," Vito said. "Look at me." He held his arms above his head. "I'm not missing anything. You know not to listen to her. It makes me angry. It sets you back—"

"The saints have forgotten your name," Concetta continued. "That's what she said. They drew her a picture of you, and what they drew was an empty face: no nose, no mouth, no eyes, just skin. All this outside, it means she's right. You're in danger!" Then her voice broke, and she had to hold her chest to keep from sobbing.

"*Gesù mio*," said Vito. He knelt beside her bed and held her head in his hands. "She makes no sense," he tried to explain. "The war's over for me. It's the opposite of what she said." He stroked her hair, but she wasn't listening. Her body was shaking. Guglierma had sent her somewhere far away again, and there was no way of knowing when or if she'd come back. "Nothing will happen to me," he told her, but she couldn't hear him.

CHAPTER 8

The candle had burned down to a stub, and still Carolina kept talking. Every minute Maddalena listened to her repeat all the reasons not to love Vito—reasons Maddalena herself had said out loud to him many times—was another minute she'd wasted.

"So I was just thinking," Carolina was saying, "if it were up to me—which of course it never is—I wouldn't run off to some farm in the middle of nowhere. I'd take whatever I needed from here and move somewhere interesting: Morocco or Argentina, even Greece. I'd never let anyone scare me onto some nowhere farm just so I could come back to this nowhere village." She leaned back on the stair. "Mamma hates this place as much as I do. More, I think. You're the only one who loves it, who thinks it's heaven on Earth. Mamma hates it because it's not a city, but I hate it because of the people. Don't you ever get tired of them, Maddalena? Don't you wonder who lives in other places? If they think or feel, or eat and drink, differently from you? I wonder all the time. How's Vito going to show you any of that? And sometimes I think: If something terrible happened to one of the girls in this village, say Ada or Luciana or Fiorella, or even me—this may be terrible to say—or if we'd never lived at all, what would the world have lost? We talk the same and gossip and make the same jokes, and one day we'll marry the same kind of man. If you took our heads off and put them on different bodies, no one would know the difference."

"You don't really believe that," said Maddalena.

"Except I do," she said. "I'm not talking so much about how we look on the outside, though that's mostly true, too. I'm talking about the inside, our brains. I don't want to end up like Mamma, stuck in six little rooms with a villa's worth of furniture. Teresa and Celestina are halfway there, but we don't have to be. You were born special, Maddalena; no one could mistake you for anyone else. You don't believe it now—you look at Vito and think 'Yes, that's enough for me'; but one day you'll stop thinking that. I wasn't born special. I have to make myself. The day I figure out how to do that—what a beautiful day that'll be."

"I wouldn't trade you for anyone," Maddalena said. "I bet you could stay here, just you, and face an army of Germans." She put her hand on her shoulder. "Let's go to sleep now." She looked at the door. "I won't go and see Vito. I'll write him a letter like you want me to."

"Those Germans wouldn't even touch me," said Carolina. "Everyone's terrified of them, of what they'd do to an Italian girl, but let me tell you something: They don't want anything from us that an Italian man wouldn't take in a second."

"They say German men are barbarians," Maddalena said. "Let's go to sleep."

Carolina laughed at her, a full laugh from the throat, the way the twins did when they made fun of her. "First of all, I'm not tired. Second of all, Maddalena, all men are barbarians. Every one of them, even our brothers and Babbo. Even Vito the Romantic. When you sneak out of this house later, when you think I'm asleep, remember that." Here she stopped smiling and made her voice more serious. "Don't let him trick you into anything because you're leaving."

"Is that what you're worried about?" Maddalena asked. "That's why I'm still here?" She wanted to push Carolina aside and rush through the door to Vito's. "What kind of girl do you think I am? I didn't have to tell you about him. I could have gone on my own—"

"You're not the only one with secrets, you know. Or some great romance."

"I never said I was."

Carolina got up and stood against the door. She folded her arms. "Listen to me," she said. "I'll tell you one more thing, and then I'll let you go."

"Then please hurry up."

"I was with Fiorella a few months ago, when she still had all her fingers. We were walking to the olive grove. It was during the *riposo*, and we were going to sleep on the grass together. This is before your big love affair. Anyway, this German soldier—he had blond hair, short, and was wearing his uniform—came up to us and tried to make conversation. This was when they used to sleep overnight."

Maddalena nodded.

"He moved his hands all over the place like an Italian, trying to signal the words, but we couldn't understand him. I think he was telling a joke, and it was probably dirty. He had the face of someone funny, though, a handsome face, not hard or angry. His soldier friends were watching from the balcony of Al Di Là, smoking cigarettes and pointing at us. Then all of a sudden our soldier stopped talking and stuck out his arms and started dancing with nobody, right there, around and around in the street, singing "*valtz! valtz!*" I started laughing, it was so sweet, so unexpected. Fiorella kept saying, 'Let's go,' and pulling my sleeve. Instead I held out my hand and let him take it."

"In the middle of the road?" Maddalena said. "Nobody saw you?"

"You look like Fiorella now," she said. "She had her mouth open like this." She made an O with her lips. "I didn't care who saw me. What did it matter? I knew how to waltz—Celestina taught me—and I was counting steps. That's all they dance in Germany, you know, the waltz and that's it. And this boy, as soon as he touched my hands and put his arms around my back, he moved so smoothly that I could've danced with him forever. I remember what Mamma told me once, what she'll tell you when you're old enough to talk to boys—"

"I'm that age now."

Carolina waved her away. "'If you want to know how a man will treat you,' Mamma told me, 'let him dance with you. When he's dancing he shows you who he is on the inside, even if he doesn't want to.' And I saw this goodness in him, Maddalena, this man I barely knew, who hadn't said a word I understood. And before I knew it I was letting him follow us to the olive grove, and he and I were dancing some more, in private, in East Olive under the trees. I made Fiorella wait outside to listen in case I needed help, but it was just the two of us in the shade. Pretty soon we got too tired to dance, and I let him kiss me."

Maddalena looked at her. "What's wrong with you?" she said. "This German is good enough for you, but not Vito for me?"

"You don't know my point yet," said Carolina. She took Maddalena's hands and looked down at them, avoiding her eyes. She dropped her whisper even lower. "I understand Luciana now. I know how she felt, how it feels, how she could let Buccio do that to her. I had to run out of the olive grove because—I almost couldn't stop myself. I won't let that happen to you. Not with Vito. Not with anyone. You have to promise me you won't ruin your life."

"I told you you don't have to worry," Maddalena said. "I only want to say good-bye to him! Just tell him we're leaving, so he doesn't worry. That's all. Can't you understand that? We only have a few hours left together, Carolina. Please. Let me go."

"First you have to promise me," she said.

"I promise," said Maddalena. There were tears in her eyes now. "I can't leave without making sure he's safe."

Though it was now completely dark, Maddalena sensed that Carolina was staring at her. Thinking. Then she moved aside and unlatched the door, and Maddalena reached out to thank her. She left her in the doorway. But when she got outside and found her footing on the grass, she couldn't shake the feeling that she was being followed.

CHAPTER 9

To get to Vito's unseen, Maddalena cut through the woods behind the houses on her street. She followed a narrow ductlike path, muddy and worn from years of people's sneaking around. To her left, the mountain rose and blocked out the moon; to her right, rows of picked-through gardens and the homes of her neighbors, some already abandoned. It was as quiet in Santa Cecilia as she'd ever heard it, the only sounds her own breathing and the thrashing of her legs through the tall, wet grass. In the morning, in just a few hours, she'd have to find some way to explain the welts surely blooming on her calves.

She kept her head down and her gaze focused on the path. Her eyes had not yet adjusted to this new darkness, grayed by the faint moonlight, softer than the blackness of the stairway she'd just left. When she collided with washing pinned to a line, she spun around and screamed and tore it off, thinking Carolina had come to stop her. Then she stood still a moment, steadied her breathing, and stared down at the man's white shirt she'd almost torn in half. She picked it up, wrapped it around her head and shoulders like a nun's wimple, tying the sleeves under her chin.

She looked in both directions on Vito's empty street. At one end, the spring burbled in the piazza; in the middle was his house; at the other stood the church and the wall that faced the gorge. Beyond that, the road bent around the mountain toward Luciana's, and it was impossible to see whether anyone was coming.

Maddalena waited a moment before running across. She was not only breaking the curfew but risking her life, and she still hadn't come up with the words to tell Vito she was leaving.

She tapped the buzzer at his house, then hid behind the side wall. She didn't worry about waking his mother, who, from what Vito told her, wouldn't remember anything an hour after it happened. She worried more that she'd be seen by someone who liked to talk.

Soon came footsteps on the stairs and the slow creak of the door. Maddalena craned her head around the side of the wall and saw Vito's head and elbow peeking out from behind it.

"Vito," she whispered.

He turned toward her.

"It's me."

He stepped out into the street in a white undershirt and long pants. When he recognized her, he scratched his chest and the back of his neck and said, "Maddalena? What are you doing here? Are you crazy?"

"I don't know," she said. She unwrapped the shirt from her head and tied it around her waist. "I had to see you."

"You shouldn't be outside," he said.

"Let me in, then," she said. "It's cold. And I can't stay long."

"Of course," he said. "Come." She took his hand and followed him up the stairs. He took slow, careful steps. "We have to be quiet," he said.

The inside was small and dusty and smelled of chamomile. It was the first time Maddalena had been in his house. The furniture in the front room, a long sofa and dresser, three armchairs, a dining table, was crammed so close together, and in such a jumble, that she feared she'd knock it all down if she bumped against one piece. When Vito didn't turn on any lights, she wondered if they had electricity.

The table, with two chairs on either side, jutted into the middle of the room. She leaned carefully against it and gripped the edge with both hands. Vito stood in front of her and held her at the waist.

"*Angelina*," he said, and kissed her. "You're safe."

She nodded.

"And your family?"

"Everyone," she said. "But Fulvio Drago—a bomb hit his house, and he died. The house is a pile of rocks."

"No!" said Vito, and pulled her closer. He

stroked her hair. "Nothing touched your house?"

She shook her head.

"It's a miracle," he said. "I told my mother tonight: God is smiling down on us. I believe that, even with this craziness. I haven't been wrong yet."

"Vito," she said. Her cheek was pressed against his chest, and she felt relieved not to look at him. "I have to tell you something." She told him about her aunt's farm near Teramo, that she and her family were leaving in the morning and would live there until the war ended for real. She talked rapidly so he wouldn't interrupt. It wasn't only them, she explained, but most of the village. Everyone was packing tonight and getting off the main road. "You have to leave, too," she said. "It's not safe anymore, even this far down. I came to say good-bye. I couldn't leave without seeing you."

He pulled away and covered his face. Then he slammed his fist on the table, rattling dishes and glasses across the room. "I'm sorry," he said, and grabbed her again. He kissed the top of her head. "I should have known. I had it too good, right? For a few hours I had you and I was free of the war. I let myself believe it. And now—it's like I go from one prison to another. Why do I bother to thank God for anything, Maddalena, if He just takes it away again?"

Maddalena didn't know what to say, so she said nothing.

"God will keep you safe," he said. "He wouldn't

hurt you. He wouldn't do that to me. I believe that. But you don't know what I heard today." He let her go and stepped toward the front of the room. He couldn't stand still.

Maddalena, her eyes adjusted now, watched him walk along the row of windows. "What?" she said.

He picked bits of glass out of the panes and flicked them into the street. "Ten Italians for every German," he said. "Dr. Fabiano told me. Every time the Allies kill a German soldier, the Germans kill ten Italians. Not just soldiers, either. Girls and babies and grandmothers." He turned to her. "Where am I supposed to hide, Maddalena? My mother can't get out of bed. We're stuck in this house. No one thinks to check on us or help us; they pack up and they go and they don't ask us, and we have no more family in Italy. She thinks every noise is a German come to kill us. If my voice wakes her up now, she'll start screaming. When I'll try to tell her we're safe, she won't hear me."

"Why are you telling me this?" Maddalena said. "I'm not scared enough?"

"I don't know," he said. "You make me want to jump in front of the tanks. Do you understand that? I can't hear that you're leaving. I wish you'd never told me. I wish I could have gone to your house tomorrow and found a note from you, so you wouldn't have to listen to me or see me like this."

"Don't say that," she said.

"Maybe I do want to scare you a little," he said.

He faced the road again, his back to her. "If I scare you, maybe you'll think of my life sometimes, for just a little while, when you're safe on your zia's farm. Maybe you'll think of my mother's legs that don't work, that won't let us leave here. Of her sleeping twenty hours a day and not recognizing me when she wakes up. I want you to think of me, Maddalena, with you not here anymore. Because what if you forget, and you come back and I'm—" He ran his palm up and down the air where the windowpanes had been. "I can't even cover these up or they'll know someone's inside."

What Maddalena felt for Vito had started out as pity—for his skinny arms, now shivering in the cold night air, for his father who forgot him and his mother who embarrassed him. She'd felt sorry for him in school, for the ink on his temples and the way Signora Grasso picked on him when he stuttered through his wrong answers. She'd believed her mother and Carolina when they'd told her he wasn't good enough. But now how much better could he be, this man who'd jump in front of tanks for her? If she explained it to her mother this way, and made her father and Claudio believe it, how could they not find it beautiful, too?

She moved toward Vito, her arms limp at her sides. They'd danced together across the stone floors of the Grotto, and if her mother was right, he'd shown her then how he'd treat her for the rest of their lives; he'd make her laugh and forget that no music was playing and change the steps the moment she got bored.

She pulled him away from the window, took his hands, and locked their fingers together. She parted his lips with her tongue, tasting wine and chamomile and something like soap. "You've talked a lot," she said. "Now let me talk. Let me say it out loud for the first time: I love you. I won't forget you. The miracle is, you're not going to Russia. You'll hide here instead, and keep your mother safe, and I'll live at the farm, and when the war's over, we'll be together again. And at the farm—" she stopped here, not sure about this next promise, the more difficult one, but willing to make it anyway. "I'll tell my parents about you, about how good you are. I'll prepare them."

Vito fell to his knees, hugged her tightly around the waist, then quickly stood up. "I'm sorry," he said. "I shouldn't have said—I'm just—I want to believe you."

"Then do," she said. This was falling in love, she told herself. She was making it happen. You saw something about to be taken away from you, and in that moment you saw how much it was worth. She'd sneaked out of her house in the middle of the night, broken the law, and betrayed her parents to come here, and that had to mean something. God had to recognize it and remember.

"I'll write to you," he said. "No. I'll wait until you write to me and tell me I can write to you."

"Yes," she said. "Until then, stay here. Don't

leave the house. Don't make yourself a *bravone* and try to fight anyone. Don't go outside at night, even if it's quiet, even if you're sure no one's there."

Vito pulled her closer, kissed her on the mouth, then guided her between the tables and dresser to the sofa. He took the white shirt from around her waist, spread it like a blanket on the cushions, and lay along the inside. She lay beside him with her back to him, keeping one foot on the floor. He kissed the back of her neck, the curve of her shoulders.

"You can stay another hour?" he asked.

"An hour and a half, maybe," she said. "That's all. If we see light outside, it's too late."

After a while, he slipped his hand under her dress. She tensed but didn't stop him. He reached around to her breasts.

He turned her onto her back and lifted her leg from the floor. He kissed the inside of her thigh and knee. When he got to her calf he asked, "What happened here?" and held her foot at his shoulder.

She explained about the scratchy grasses, and in a second he'd gone and returned, carrying a jar. He opened it, dipped his fingers in, and rubbed the liquid over the welts on her skin.

"What is that?" she asked. Her head felt too heavy to raise from the cushion.

"Olive oil."

He treated both her legs, then rubbed them with a little salt and blew on them until they cooled. The itching stopped.

"My mother used to do this for me," he said. "She used to say, 'If it doesn't work, at least you'll taste good.'"

She laughed. "It's working."

He started to take off his shirt, hesitantly, as if waiting for her to stop him. She reached up and ran her finger along the hairless rows of bones, one by one, not sure what else to do. Every time she moved down to the next row, he arched his back.

"I want to make love to you," he said.

"*O Dio!*" she said immediately, and pushed herself up. "No, Vito. *O Dio*, that's not what this means."

"Wait," he said. He held her still, a big smile on his face. "I said 'I want to,' not 'I will.' Don't be nervous." He laid two fingers gently on her lips. "My mother's in the next room. How much can we do?"

She relaxed a little but covered her breasts with her arms. She looked up at him, thinking Carolina had almost been right.

"I wish you could see yourself," Vito said. He closed his eyes and shook his head. "You would think, 'If I were him, I wouldn't be able to stop.'"

"I'm not Luciana," she said.

"And I'm not Buccio," he said. "I'm much better-looking."

"You are," she said. "And better than that: You're still here."

They heard footsteps, someone running on the

road. He squeezed her arm, and they stayed quiet until the sound faded.

"There are people outside," she said. "I can't stay here." She started to sit up.

"We still have time," he said. "Whoever that was is gone. No one's awake yet. You'll stay unless we hear tanks or the sun starts to break; then I'll let you go right away. I promise. I'll walk you back, whatever happens."

She thought a moment. "All right," she said.

"Good," he said. "We don't have much time." He pulled the straps of her blouse down from her shoulders. "I don't want to waste any of it."

"I don't, either."

"You love me," Vito said, as if he'd just started to believe it. "So let's keep loving each other, okay? For a half hour more, we won't think of anything else."

CHAPTER 10

"Your legs," said Vito, as Maddalena stepped onto the path.

He'd heated water in the kettle, taken off her sandals, and washed her feet before he'd let her leave his house. He'd wiped off the oil and salt with a hot towel. Now she trudged again through the mud and wet leaves, and at the end of her trip there would be no one who'd take care of her the way he had.

"Do you hear that?" she said, paying no attention. She stopped and grabbed his elbow.

He heard crickets and her breathing and the wind in the trees. "No," he said. But then, suddenly, he did: from far off, a high-pitched but muted whimpering, continuous, like an underwater siren.

"It's coming from down the street," Maddalena said. "I've never heard that sound in my life."

"I'm sure it's nothing," Vito said. "What you should worry about is your legs, after all the work I did. Let me carry you."

"Something's wrong," she said. "Very wrong. That's someone crying. I can tell."

He listened again. "It's an animal, probably," he said. "Someone left his pig behind and now it's hungry, that's all. Tomorrow I'll have it for dinner."

"I'm not joking," she said.

The path was too narrow for two, so Vito walked behind her, holding her hand over her shoulder. He took short, heavy steps, wanting to make this as slow as a funeral procession: the labored shuffling, the hours it took to cross the village. If only he could drag out time like that; if only he could delay the moment when he'd have to return Maddalena to the people he'd taken her from. But it was past three in the morning, and their time was up.

The drowned siren kept on, rising and falling like music. When they reached the Castellanis', the now empty house next door to the Piccinellis, Maddalena stopped again, this time so suddenly that Vito stumbled into her.

"I'm telling you, it's nothing," he said.

"Shh," she said. "Don't move." Her body grew stiff, and she clenched her fingers into a fist in his hand. She reached back, lowered his head to her shoulder, and whispered, "There's someone behind my house."

He squinted at a figure leaning face forward against the back wall. He recognized it right away. "It's Carolina," he said. "Isn't it?" She'd crossed her arms between her forehead and the wall, as if she were resting or thinking hard.

"It is for sure?" said Maddalena. She took one

careful step forward to get a better look, and a twig cracked under her feet. "I knew she'd wait for me," she said, and let out a long breath. "She's going to kill me for staying so long."

"At least it's not your father," he said. "For once I'm happy to see her."

Carolina finally noticed them, then came slowly toward them like a sleepwalker. When she reached them, they could see that her face looked swollen and the ends of her hair stuck to her face.

"What happened?" Maddalena asked. "Are you all right?"

She shook her head and buried it in Maddalena's chest.

"What is it? Is it someone in our family?"

Carolina was shaking. "Luciana," she managed to say. "She's dead."

"What?"

Vito covered his face with his hands, and thought immediately of Buccio. He'd come home safe from the front, he'd march into town in his uniform and a big silly grin, to learn the war had killed his *fidanzata* just for sitting in her house. "You have to be quiet," he said to Maddalena. "No one can find us here."

They ignored him. "How did it happen?" Maddalena asked. "A bomb, like the Dragos?"

Carolina wiped her eyes. She gathered herself and looked from Vito to Maddalena, then back again. "She was pregnant," she said. "Your friend Buccio got her pregnant, then left her alone. A doctor from Frosinone had to come. So he came, and tore her open."

Maddalena sank to her knees.

"This happened tonight?" Vito asked. Carolina nodded. "They had to do it tonight? In the middle of all this? They had to rush?"

"The doctor was coming tonight anyway," Carolina said. She knelt on the ground in front of Maddalena and held her in her arms. "They planned it a week ago, before anybody knew about a surrender. Luciana told only me. And I promised I'd be with her, to make sure she was all right, but by the time I got there, she was dead. I was wasting my time with you, Maddalena, trying to warn you without telling you everything. You think today was all about you, but there are other people in this world." She spoke calmly now, like a doctor herself, as if she were talking about someone in a book and not someone they'd both seen every day of their lives, someone who'd ridden Vito's bike and complained and made fun of him and loved his best friend.

"They wouldn't let me see her face," Carolina went on, now on her knees beside Maddalena, mumbling into her folded hands. "Her bed was soaked with blood. They covered her with a sheet. The doctor ran off like a thief."

Again Vito thought of Buccio, of the day he'd come back to Santa Cecilia. He'd run up to the door of the Campini house and find only her parents. Before he understood, her father would punch him in the face and drag him through the streets, and people would rush to their balconies to watch.

"She's better off, Maddalena," Vito said, the only way he knew to comfort her. "She'd be disgraced. She was already disgraced. She'd have had to move away."

"For once Vito's right," Carolina said. "I wouldn't lie about that."

"Who knows?" Vito said. He looked up. The light was breaking through the trees. "She could be with Buccio now. God might have brought them together, taken them at the same time."

"She's too young to understand this," Carolina said.

"I'm not," Maddalena said. She looked up at them. "I understand better than the two of you. God punished her."

"Don't say that," Vito said.

Maddalena turned her face away. "Luciana made a big mistake," she said, "and God taught her a lesson. You know I'm right, Carolina. You tried to tell me that yourself."

"Try to keep your voice down," Vito said. "Everyone's waking up."

"I don't care," said Maddalena. "This isn't a big enough reason to scream in your backyard?"

"Tell her she's wrong, Carolina," Vito said. "Nobody punished Luciana."

Carolina looked at him. "She's not wrong, Vito," she said.

"We wouldn't do what Luciana did," Vito said. "We haven't. We won't. But Maddalena and me, we're together now, whether you like it or not. Don't let her think God will punish her for that. She'll believe you if you tell her."

Carolina bit her thumbnail. "But she will be punished," she said, in that same careless, infuriating voice. Vito wanted to smack her. "I don't want it to happen, Vito. You think I do, but I don't."

He shook his head. Did she know how new Maddalena's love for him was, how easily she could undo it?

"God punishes everyone," Carolina went on, "one way or another." She took Maddalena in her arms and laid her head on her shoulder. "He'll get all three of us, sooner or later."

THE CARRIAGE

CHAPTER 11

The morning of September 9, the day after the surrender, the Piccinellis packed their carriage with clothes, blankets, photographs, jewelry, and all the food in the store. They saved room only for Aristide, who was to drive the carriage as quickly as he could to his sister's farm, empty it, then turn back to meet his family, who had started out on foot at the same time. Some Santa Cecilia families could escape to relatives just a few miles from the village, but the Piccinellis had to cross the width of Italy if they wanted to stay safe together. None of Aristide's nearby sisters had room, and what remained of Chiara's family, two uncles, a spiteful sister, lived in the heart of Rome, a city lying belly-up and waiting to be squeezed to death.

Zabrina Piccinelli lived in the Abruzzi countryside outside the small town of Frattoli, east of the city of Teramo, at the foot of an unnamed mountain so tall that the top of it disappeared into the clouds. To the west of this mountain stood the rest of the Gran Sasso range, far to the east the Adriatic Sea. On the slope of Zabrina's mountain lay the remains of the family vineyard, planted on the first warm day of the twentieth century by Aristide's father, now ten years dead. The farm bordered this vineyard on its southern side, as if holding it against the mountain.

When the Piccinellis' carriage crested a hill and all this came clearly into view, they'd been traveling four days: two on foot and two the easy way. Even this far from the main roads, they could move only during daylight. They spent their evenings and nights sleeping on leaves in the woods, rationing water and the nuts, bread, and cheese they carried in bundled sheets. No one talked about Luciana, though the news had spread all over the village by morning. But as she walked over the dusty roads or tried to sleep or sat crowded into the carriage between her sisters, Maddalena could think of little else. She'd see the blood on Luciana's sheets, her face as cold and empty as her nonna's had been in the casket, Luciana's mother slumped in the corner of her bedroom, wailing loud enough to be heard twenty houses away; then Maddalena would see herself, lying half naked on Vito's couch, his tongue on her belly and breasts—and to breathe she'd have to shut her eyes hard and block the pictures out. She tried to imagine Luciana alive: that first kiss she'd broken through the circle to give Vito's chin, the dark eyes, the fast talking. She couldn't be dead. She was right now begging her father to steal a horse and carriage so she wouldn't ruin her feet in the escape.

Then Maddalena would remember the truth: God had reached down and dragged Luciana off somewhere to suffer. And unless she paid attention to the warning, He'd do the same to her. All the trouble in her world, she realized, had started with her sneaking around and lying. Now she had to stop that; she had to be as good and honest as she'd always been and live her life God's way and listen to her parents. It had been good enough for her mother and all the women before her.

When Claudio saw what was left of the family vineyards—the thin, black, burnt-looking vines hanging off more than ten rows of wood posts—he said, "Did a bomb hit here?"

"No," said Aristide. "It didn't."

"We can fix it," Claudio said. "That's what we'll do while we're here, Babbo. You and I, we'll bring the Piccinelli vineyards back from the dead."

"I don't think so," he said. "You can't make up for all those years."

It was early afternoon, the sky blue-purple and cloudless. Though they seemed to be climbing closer to the sun the past four days, the air kept getting colder and thinner. No matter how close to her mother she huddled, Maddalena couldn't keep warm.

"Why can't we work on the vineyard?" Claudio kept insisting. "The girls will help, right?"

They looked at him blankly.

"Well then, there has to be someone around who

can help," he continued. "Doesn't Zia Zabrina know anyone?"

"You talk this way now," Aristide said, his hand on Claudio's shoulder, "but wait until you see how hard it is. I don't have much faith in you for work." He shook his head. "Politics maybe, business yes, but not work with your hands. Your brothers could have done this, but not you."

They neared the gate to the farm. "How can Zia Zabrina live here all by herself?" Teresa asked. "What does she do all day?"

"She doesn't clean, that's for sure," Chiara whispered to Maddalena. "I can promise you she hasn't mopped the floors twice since we were here last."

Eight years, half Maddalena's life, had gone by since she'd been here. Zia Zabrina had had a barn full of animals then, each with a name, and whenever you passed by one she made you say *buongiorno* to it as if it were a fieldworker. Maddalena and Carolina had taken turns interviewing the goat—Topolo, Zabrina's favorite—about his many girlfriends. At night, the animals made crying noises.

Maddalena smiled at her mother. "Maybe she taught Topolo how to sweep," she said.

"Who else does she have to talk to?"

Chiara was like Carolina. When she didn't like someone, she couldn't hide it even when she tried. She'd tell Maddalena terrible things about people they knew, even relatives, and Maddalena would keep the news to herself. She wanted to have secrets that only she and her mother shared. She'd always wanted her mother to be her closest friend. Only the two of them knew about the girlfriends Nonno Piccinelli had in every village between Santa Cecilia and the vineyard, and that they were the real reason for all his trips back and forth. They knew which families their priest, Don Paolo, liked and which he didn't care about, no matter how much money they gave. They knew Signora Puzo chewed on her toenails and that all the Lupo men drank. Once, before Vito had finished his bike, her mother had told her, "Concetta Leone has troubles down here," and pointed between her legs.

"What kind of problems?" Maddalena had asked.

"Nothing you'll ever have," she'd said. "It makes her do too much of everything: cry too much, talk too much, eat, drink, fall in love, everything too much. It makes her head all wrong."

Maddalena had forgotten about the too-much disease, but it came back to her now with the memories of Topolo and Zia Zabrina alone and friendless on her farm with no friends.

Finally, after a rainy night and a morning of riding soaked and shivering in the carriage, Aristide stopped the carriage in the yard of Zia Zabrina's white stone house. It was half the size of the Santa Cecilia house and only one story. It had a large, square porch in front, surrounded by an iron fence covered in weeds. Drapes hung in one of the two front windows.

Immediately the door swung open and out came Zia Zabrina, her arms above her head, lunging for Claudio, grabbing him by his ears and pulling his face against hers. She kissed his forehead and his lips and the tip of his nose and gripped him around the back in a hug so tight he had trouble pushing her away.

"I'm not the only one here," he said.

"*Mia famiglia!*" cried Zia Zabrina. She went for Maddalena next, then the twins and Carolina, then Chiara. "Welcome, welcome to my home," she said. "You've been away for so long I'm sure you don't recognize me. I looked more like this, remember?" She pulled her skin back at the cheeks to smooth out the wrinkles. "Try to think of me like I was then."

She was twice as skinny as Maddalena remembered, with big eyes and brown teeth, her hair half done up in a bun and half spilling on to her shoulders. When she wasn't talking, she squeezed her lips together into a little pink heart.

She took Claudio by the wrist and led him into the front hallway. "Come in, please," she said. "No sleeping outside anymore. You remember this house? Sit, sit! Rest your bodies. Zia Zabrina never has company." She sat down next to her brother and patted his stomach. "I have a pig in the back, Aristide. How long since you've had pork?"

“We’re not starving,” he said. “We were eating fine in the village.”

“Don’t be such an old man,” she said. “I know you’re not poor. I also know you haven’t had pork the way I make it for a long time. I’ve been waiting for you all for a week. I saw families walking by during the day, and I asked them, ‘Do you know Aristide Piccinelli?’ Everyone said no. I sat every day on the porch, waiting for someone I recognized from Santa Cecilia, though I don’t know anybody anymore. Then came my brother in our old carriage, like a dream!” On the table a hollowed-out rock overflowed with cigarette butts. She gripped it with both hands, as if to keep warm.

“And here we are,” Carolina said. “For the rest of our lives, maybe.”

“If I’m lucky!” said Zia Zabrina. She jumped up and walked to the boiling kettle, still clutching the ashtray, little black ashes floating behind her.

Maddalena looked around the kitchen, noticing the dusty marble mantles and the cracked pots and the little weeds growing through the windowsills.

“When you’re alone too much,” Zia Zabrina said from across the room, “this is what happens to you: You smoke until there’s no more cigarettes in all of Italy, and then you welcome a war if it brings your family together.”

Maddalena watched her. She moved clumsily, as if she’d never cooked before, still holding that ashtray in her left hand as she tried to spoon gnocchi out of the boiling water and drop them into a pot of sauce.

"Let me help you," Teresa said, but Zia Zabrina waved her away.

Later she went out the back door and returned with the pig on a large terra-cotta tray. There were onions and tomatoes and bitter greens on a platter, all fresh from somewhere, all a miracle after three days of nuts and cheese. The food tasted so good, no one complained that everything—the pasta, the meat, the vegetables, even the wine—was flecked with bits of ash.

There was more work to do at the farm than in Santa Cecilia, even though they had a smaller house to clean and one extra woman. It was hard to count Zia Zabrina as extra, though, since she spent most of her time tending the animals. She'd start out helping with the week's cooking every Sunday, but got too exhausted by the hours it took and the amount of food that had to be prepared, having cooked only for one person for the last twenty years. Aristide and Claudio worked on what was left of the fields, weeding and turning the dirt, hoping the little care they offered would make it fertile. Claudio brought cuttings from the grapevines into the house and stared at them; he sliced them down the middle, held them up to the light, and said, "Hmm."

"Did you figure something out?" Maddalena would ask.

"Not yet."

Mornings, Claudio waited on the road, asking travelers how to save a vineyard. Every few days someone offered to take a look, but as they got closer to the crop they shook their heads, and some even laughed.

The road brought many families Maddalena recognized, children and grandfathers and widows singing and carrying all they had, looking for a safe place to wait out the war. Though they were usually headed north, away from Santa Cecilia, Maddalena knew she could give a friendly looking woman a few lire and ask her to take a letter and post it to Vito in the next town. She'd seen her father mail letters to his other sisters this way, despite his lack of faith that this government system still worked. "My words will end up in the dirt somewhere," he'd say.

Maddalena had been composing a letter to Vito in her head since the moment she left the village. She wanted Carolina's help to find the right words, but not only was her sister turning into some kind of animal—climbing up and down the muddy mountain every chance she got, getting sweaty and refusing to wash her clothes—Maddalena wasn't sure she could trust her. They hardly spoke anymore. Carolina ate her meals half asleep and spoke only when asked a direct question. As soon as she finished her food, she either ran outside or lay facedown for hours on the bed. Many times Maddalena tried to talk with her about Luciana, to try to make sense of what had happened to her, but Carolina just looked at her blankly. "I never lived in Santa Cecilia," she told her. "I don't know that girl."

Unlike in the village, where she always had a chaperone or someone checking on her every half hour in the store, Maddalena spent most of her time at Zia Zabrina's alone. When the morning cleaning was done, she'd hike lazily up the side of the mountain and wander among the dead and dying grapevines. She wrote Vito imaginary letters about it, describing all she saw and her sense that time and the world had stopped for a while, and before they knew it, it would start again with them together. She pictured the vineyards as they must have looked forty years ago: the thick leaves making a jungle out of the mountainside; her nonno bent under the vines, plucking the fat fruit from the stems, digging his toes in the dirt. Her father must have stood beside him, a young boy filling the baskets, his fingers sticky with juice.

Through one corner of the vineyard ran a small creek full of flat slippery rocks. Maddalena liked to balance herself on them and pose with her arms out for an invisible audience. The creek, Zia Zabrina had told them, had once been enough water for the grapes, the farm, the house, and the wash, but over the last twenty years it had thinned to a trickle. Moss lined its banks and covered the rocks in a thick carpet. It was the only place Maddalena felt protected. She loved the damp smell the vineyard still held even though the roots were dried up and the leaves brown; that once she stepped a few yards up and away from the house to the mountainside, the animal stink faded; that instead of the stink she smelled rain and fruit and the faint trace of olives.

It was a Tuesday in mid-October when the Allies crossed the Volturno River and began the push north toward Mignano and the central Apennines. Maddalena heard the news with her family on the one o'clock broadcast the next day, when Italy declared war on Germany and officially sided with the British and Americans. The Piccinellis had brought the radio with them from Santa Cecilia and set it like a statue on a small table. Aristide had his chair pulled up close to listen, his hands folded under his chin. Claudio sat beside him on the floor. In the kitchen, Zia Zabrina swirled sauce around her brother's plate with a ladle to make it appear fuller. The rest of the women stood in the doorway of what had been the dining room but was now called the radio room.

Maddalena leaned against the wall, her eyes closed, longing to be back in the olive grove before the surrender, sitting on the grass in the fancy dress Carolina made fun of, their circle of friends around them. Instead she was in a strange room far from home, listening to a radio announcer's voice, deep and rushed and too beautiful for news, praying he'd say "The war is over! You can go home now!"

"Kesselring and the German troops have been

pushed back to the Lazio border," the announcer said. The microphone crackled. "For the British Fifth and the American Thirty-sixth Armies," he continued, "Rome glows like a jewel on the other side of the mountains."

"He's a poet," Claudio said.

The front was now less than a hundred miles from Rome. The Germans—and whichever Italians would stay on their side, though neither the newsman nor anyone in the Piccinelli family seemed sure who they were—began retreating to the tops of the mountains. They looked down on the coming troops and fired at them as they mobilized and climbed. "The German wall around Lazio is shrinking and showing its cracks," said the announcer. "The eyes of the Allies are burning as they gaze upon the Eternal City."

"I think he's drunk," said Claudio.

"How close is the Volturno to us?" Maddalena asked.

"Very far, *carina*," said her father.

"They won't come all the way out here," said Zia Zabrina, from the other side of the kitchen. "Don't worry. The Abruzzese don't matter to anyone."

"I don't care where they go," Chiara said. "I don't care if they run over every house in Abruzzo with their tanks, including this one. As long as my sons come home."

"How close is the line to Santa Cecilia?" Maddalena asked.

"Closer than before," Claudio said. "But who cares? We're here."

Carolina was shaking her head. "Nobody in Italy cares enough," Carolina said. "That's why we're losing. I'm the only one who sees things the way they should be. We could have kept all our towns safe. If we Italians were more organized, if we didn't give up so quickly, if we weren't so scared, if we'd trusted Hitler more—"

"Since when are you the expert?" said Celestina, laughing. "I can't follow any of it."

"This country will be the same no matter who's waving his big arms around," said Chiara. "Germans or Italians or Americans. What does it matter anyway, if you don't have your brothers? Think with your heart, Carolina, for once."

"We'll get Maurizio and Giacomo back, Mamma," said Teresa. She took her mother's hand in hers. "One day they'll walk up to the door, both of them, like we always said."

"I think we can win with the Germans *and* they'll come back," Carolina said. "What do you think of that?" She pushed past Teresa into the middle of the radio room and stood with her hands on her hips. It was the most she'd said in weeks.

"But it's not *very* close to Santa Cecilia?" Maddalena asked, ignoring whatever Carolina and her mother were arguing about. "Are they near there now, the Americans? Protecting it?"

"What's amazing is how little you understand,"

said Claudio. "There aren't even mice left in Santa Cecilia."

"The Leones are still there," Teresa said. "The mother's too sick to leave."

"*Gesù mio*," said Chiara. "First that woman scares off a husband, now she kills her only son."

This is my chance, thought Maddalena. She clenched her fist and said, "I think it's almost sweet, the way Vito Leone takes care of his mother. Some other son would just leave and forget. Don't you think?" It seemed everyone was staring at her, but it was only Zia Zabrina. Maddalena blushed and clenched her fist tighter.

"Look at you," said her aunt. "Who's this man? Is this Massimo Leone's son?"

Suddenly Chiara was laughing, a sound Maddalena hadn't heard in months. "Yes, but I wouldn't call him a man. More like a clown."

"He can tell very funny jokes, that's true," Maddalena said, so quietly that it was almost under her breath. "A little like a clown. But he's very polite. Carolina thinks so, too. It's not just me."

"He was a month from the draft," Aristide told his sister. "A month! Before the surrender. The silliest boy you'd ever met, nothing like his father at all. He'd come in the store and just stand there like a sheep chewing."

Maddalena couldn't listen. She turned to Carolina, and begged with her eyes for help. "I think he's almost cute," Carolina finally said, "when the light hits him right."

The twins and Zia Zabrina giggled. "Who's cuter, do you think? Vito Leone or Toto Volpe?" Celestina asked. "It's not much of a contest, but I think Toto. He has very thick hair."

"They're all too young for me," said Teresa. "I like for a man to look like a man."

"I don't like this kind of talk," Chiara said. "Not even a little bit. It's talk like this that gets girls in trouble."

"She's right," Claudio said. "Just because we're not in the village doesn't mean you can act like a *cafone*."

The room was quiet. The radio began repeating the same news of the Volturno.

"You're no fun, Chiara," Zia Zabrina said. "I don't see the harm in what these girls are saying. What else are they supposed to talk about in a war?" She lit up a cigarette and winked at Maddalena.

"I'm sorry," said Chiara, sternly, her eyes fixed on Zabrina. "You don't know a girl got killed because of this. We won't talk about how." She made the sign of the cross.

"Killed? For talking about boys? That's crazy—" Zabrina began, then stopped when she saw her brother's face. In a second, she started again: "I don't think it's ever wrong to talk. You don't know how beautiful it is to have people to talk to, unless you don't have them anymore. The signora who brings me cigarettes, every week we sit down in this room for hours, and she's got the best stories!

She didn't come for two weeks, and I was pulling my hair out, missing her, but then you came, and all I want to do now is talk and smoke and hear you talk, and smoke and talk some more—"

"God help us," said Chiara.

It was raining. It rained all night, and for the rest of the week and through the middle of November. Zia Zabrina kept talking, and it soon became a race to see who could get away from her fastest. In the meantime, mudslides buried what was left of the vineyards. Claudio stood for hours the first day, ankle-deep in the sludge behind the house, his arms folded into his chest, staring at his vines floating on the mud. When he came inside, he smashed his fist into the door. After that, he took to reading and spent most of his time in the radio room with one of Zabrina's books on his lap, half-listening to the news when it came on. When Claudio had noticed them, Zia Zabrina said, "My cousin brought those books a long time ago and told me, if you really want to understand the world, this is what you read. I've never touched them." Claudio hadn't heard of the writers—Virgil, Homer, and Ovid—but after the mudslides they became his best friends. He never again mentioned making wine.

In the meantime, Maddalena hid in her bedroom closet and finally wrote her letter to Vito. She told him she'd spoken sweetly about him to her family, what great things she told them about him at her own great risk. It would take time—years, maybe—but she'd keep telling them little things, and one day her mother and father would wake up and fall in love with him as surely as she had. She read over the letter many times, sealed it, addressed it, and waited a week for a sunny day to stand by the road.

As she pressed the letter into a friendly looking woman's hand—her name was Olga, she learned, a mother of six traveling with her family to the coast—Maddalena looked twice over her shoulder. No one was watching. She gave the woman a few lire and begged her to keep herself and the letter safe, and not to forget to post it when she passed through Teramo. It was early December, and Olga and her family were among the few travelers still escaping into the mountains. If Maddalena had waited a week more, the road would have been empty and covered in a foot of snow. Now there was at least a chance that Vito would get the letter before Christmas.

CHAPTER 12

Vito woke to the familiar sound of gunfire. He'd fallen into a deep sleep in the middle of the afternoon, and now another day had gone by without a letter from Maddalena. He slid out of bed and crawled along the cold hallway floor in the dark toward his mother, careful to keep his head below the line of sight from the front windows. He used to feel each string of gunshots as though they were lodging in his chest, but now, after almost six months of it, he barely winced. The sudden *ratatat-ratatat* was as common as a spurt of rain. The sound of breaking glass that had once followed the gunshots had been replaced with silence, every window on the main street shattered. So far only the Dragos had been bombed, and the tanks had twice made the turnoff onto his street before turning around. The other houses in Santa Cecilia stood as solid as ever, though their stone walls were spray-painted with swastikas and cratered by bullets and their gardens trampled and wooden fences torn down.

Only once had Vito tried to see the soldiers up close. Late one November afternoon, he'd sneaked into the upstairs of the Piccinelli house, hidden beneath the front windows, and peeked up between the flashes of light. All he'd caught was the back end of a tank. He wanted to keep looking, but the longer he crouched there on the floor, among Chiara's smashed blue dishes and Aristide's large family table, the more terrified he became that he'd die there from a bullet in the head, and that Maddalena would come home and find his rotted body stinking up her house. So he lay flat on the floor and tried to sleep through the noise.

He'd come to know the Piccinellis' home as well as his own. He'd wandered through every room, opening drawers and inspecting whatever remained. He found letters from relatives in Rome and Sardinia piled at the bottom of the front stairs, and stacked them neatly on the dining table. Sometimes he took his lunch there—two or three olives, a potato—and ate, clinking invisible glasses with Aristide and Claudio and discussing the state of the war. He held to his face dresses he thought were Maddalena's. He found the notes and maps to Zabrina's that Chiara had left for Maurizio and Giacomo and copied down the directions. One day, he told himself, I'll surprise Maddalena there.

At his real home, it seemed his mother was getting better. The winter was the coldest they could remember and all she could eat were nuts and potatoes, but unlike Vito, somehow she maintained her weight. Her son had grown so weak that the simple crawl across the house made his muscles ache. His growling stomach kept him awake at night, when he lay shivering under every blanket he could find in his house and the Piccinellis' and every other family's in the village. He'd raided all the empty rooms in Santa Cecilia, but no one had left anything of value—not a scrap of food or a radio or an envelope of lire hidden under the mattress.

Some days, without warning, the old Concetta Leone would appear—the calm, loving woman who spoke normally and unafraid. Though at those times she had little memory of what had happened over the past few months, he always believed that the spell—or whatever was attacking her mind—had completely broken. But after a few hours of talking, when he told her about the future and described the beautiful life he'd have with her and Maddalena after the war, the spell always took hold again. She screamed in pain and claimed her bones were breaking. She convinced herself that soldiers were gathered outside the door about to knock it down and shoot them both. When Vito talked about the past, memories of his father and sisters and the nonna who slept in the crib, she stayed calm longer; after a while, this was all Vito let himself say to her.

He watched her now. She slept peacefully on her back, her mouth open and her arms flung above her head. Sleet tapped on the window above her like handfuls of pebbles. Vito grabbed one of her blankets, wrapped it around him, and recalled what he'd been thinking of when he'd fallen asleep a few hours before. He'd been trying to come up with a plan to make money after the war. He'd live with his Zio Gabriello in Naples for a while and learn to be a tailor. Or maybe he'd beg Renato Puzo, who had no sons, to let him work in his *tabaccheria*. If no other chance came, he'd drag his mother—wasn't she looking stronger? wasn't the color coming back into her cheeks?—to Philadelphia, find work there, and return to Santa Cecilia a rich man. In that moment, though the tanks rumbled on the other side of the village and he faced another night of total darkness and lonely, restless sleep, everything seemed possible. Then he heard the loud screech of the buzzer.

His mother stirred but didn't wake. A good sign, Vito thought. A sign of health! He sank to the floor and walked on his knees to peer out the window. The road had brought all kinds of people since September 8: runaway Italian Partisans, old ladies desperate for food, entire families rushing to beat the sun to safer towns. A few had come to the door to beg or ask about distant relations. Once a week or so, on no particular schedule, the bus to Avezzano came through, half full with stray soldiers and burn victims and refugees who could afford the fare and—Vito jumped to his feet—bags of mail.

He saw a man in a dark, fur-hooded jacket trudge through the melting snow—away from his front door. It wasn't Ganzo, who was long gone, but he did carry a bag strapped to his back. Vito watched him hurry down the street and duck behind the church.

Vito ran down the stairs. There on the landing lay the letter the fur-hooded man had slid under the door. He grabbed it. It was postmarked in

Teramo on December 16, 1943—three months ago.

Inside were two full pages of a girl's loopy handwritten words, which he took in all at once. He couldn't finish one sentence before skipping ahead to the next, then the last, then the middle, then the greeting, then the end again. Maddalena had addressed him "*caro mio*" and signed her name "*con affetto.*" She'd told her parents beautiful things about him; she was safe, though lonely, with only her silly aunt to talk to. She had nightmares about Luciana. Her mother and Carolina seemed far away, though they lived in the same house; Vito seemed far away, because he was. And she missed him. "My body is here in the country," she wrote, "but my mind and heart are dancing with you in Santa Cecilia." Vito rubbed his eyes, then banged his fist against the wooden door. He blamed Mussolini and Carolina and his mother all at once for keeping him from her. He sat on the stairs and read the letter over and over, slowly, until the sun set completely and he could no longer see in the dark.

Nowhere in her letter did Maddalena ask Vito to write back. She wrote only of the days and years after the war, when the world would "start again" and they'd be older and smarter. "We'll get married," she promised, "and live the way God and our families want us to." Before this could happen, though, her older sisters had to find husbands, and her parents had to "fall in love" with Vito the way she had. Until that day, Vito had to be patient and stay safe and follow the rules.

Vito read these words carefully and thought only, I have to see her. Whatever she said about patience and safety made no sense in a war. It was March, the end of winter, and the snow was melting steadily. His mother seemed stronger. He still couldn't leave her alone, but surely she could walk a few hours a day in April, when the air was warmer and the ground dry. The letter gave him new energy. He had directions and a map. He'd drag their blankets and food behind them in a cart, and let his mother sleep whenever she needed. They'd beg families along the way to take them in for a night. So what if it took them a month to reach the farm? When they arrived there, the Piccinellis would praise his bravery. To protect Maddalena, Vito would make the excuse that he and his mother were on their way to relatives in the north, and heard about the Piccinelli farm from locals they'd met on the road.

As Vito dreamed up excuses, twenty-six thousand tons of bombs fell on the towns around him, on the roads and bridges from Anzio to Cassino and the hills north of Rome—but not in Santa Cecilia. Vito had grown accustomed to the planes storming low over the village, but they were coming more often now. "The Allies are everywhere," the bus driver told him one day in the piazza. "They're squeezing out the Germans." But then a soldier in the front seat told them that the air raids were exaggerated, that the Germans "still have this country by the balls." Vito didn't know whom to believe or which would be worse. But he'd get to Teramo no matter what.

In early April, after a week of warm days, Vito woke his mother at dawn and told her they had to leave. "It's very dangerous here," he said. "This mountain is next to be bombed."

She gripped the sides of the bed. "Here? Now?" Then she let go. "*Dio*, Vito, let them do it. What do I care if I die? I'm half dead anyway."

"Get up," Vito said, and pulled her off the bed. "There's no time for talk like that. Are you warm enough?" He guided her arms into her winter coat, then wrapped her in two of the blankets from her bed. He pulled a wool hat down over her ears. "You can walk for a little while. If you get tired, we'll stop."

"Where are we going?" she asked.

"I got a letter from Babbo," he lied again. "He knows a family north of Teramo with an extra room. He's protecting us, even from across the ocean."

"He's a good man."

"Sure," Vito said.

The morning air was pleasant and cool. They walked for almost three hours, stopping to rest only twice. Vito pulled the cart with his right hand and held his mother's hand with his left. The roads were dusty and nearly empty except for a few old men on donkeys. Near noon they ate from a chestnut tree, then slept under it for another hour. They drank water and a little wine from jugs Vito stored in the cart. Concetta told stories Vito heard a hundred times: how fat she'd been when she met her husband, how she'd never thought he'd choose her. "Keep talking," Vito said. "I like hearing your voice."

By evening, they'd traveled farther than Vito ever dreamed they'd reach the first day. They found an abandoned house near Celano, where Vito piled clothing and sheets on the stone floor. He fell asleep immediately beside his mother, and was awakened by the warm sun through the windows.

"I'm proud of you," Vito told his mother, though they got a late start on the second day and she walked more slowly. He held her around the waist to keep her steady. "You're a strong woman."

"My body is strong," she said. "It's my head that goes sometimes. But with you taking care of me, it feels clear."

"Whatever it is," Vito said, "you're making me very happy."

As they climbed the high mountains of the central Apennines, heading northeast, the road grew steeper. They stopped just a half hour after they began and sat on rocks, looking down on the clusters of *paese* in the valley. The roofs and walls of some of the houses had caved in; others stood untouched. Most of the villages were quiet and empty, with only the occasional carriage lumbering down a street. Vito had never seen this much of the world at once. He lay his head on his mother's shoulder and shifted close to her for warmth. She wrapped her arm around his back.

He thought a moment, then said, "Do you know where we might stop in a few days?"

She held him tighter. "No," she said. "Tell me about this house your father found us."

"Not that," he said. "Before that. The Piccinellis'." He had to prepare her—and rid himself of the guilt he'd been carrying. "I think they have a farm not far from here. We can stay with them and eat a good meal. How nice will that be? Like a little bit of home."

"No," she said, before he could finish. She looked at him. "You think I'm going to beg from Aristide Piccinelli? Not after what he said about you."

"That was a hundred years ago," Vito said, with a laugh. "Everything's different now. Let me explain." He pulled out Maddalena's letter from his pocket and handed it to her. "Read it," he said. "She told them all good things about me. About you, too, I'm sure. They'll be happy to see us."

She shook her head. "Please, Vito." She mouthed Maddalena's words as she read the letter, shuffling the pages against the wind gusting up from the valley. Then she handed it back. "Listen to me. It's too soon. You have to protect yourself. She doesn't want you there. There's no invitation in this letter."

"I read it," he said. "I know what's best." He stood up. "What does she know? She's just a girl. She's scared. It took three months for this to get to me. I'm sure she's written more since then, probably telling me to come."

"You're just like your father," Concetta said. "But I'm saying to you: I won't go to that house. Not for me. For you. You want them to see me like this? Like a vagabond? God knows what they thought of me before. Wait until the war ends. I'll be better then. I'll invite them to the house, cook them a feast like a good mother."

"We're halfway there," Vito said. "We're not turning around."

"We don't have to," Concetta said. "We'll go straight to the house in Teramo." She squeezed his hand. "Maybe there I'll clean up." She smiled up at him.

Vito rubbed his face and stared up at the icy mountain. The road became very steep before it disappeared around the peak. His mother's voice shook as she spoke, whether from cold or frustration he couldn't tell. He grabbed a rock and heaved it at the trees below. "Leave me alone," he said, and stood with his back to her.

From the west, up the road they'd just walked, came two men. The taller one wore a long gray coat and carried some sort of bundle over his shoulder. The other one, short and light-haired, was dressed in a formal suit jacket and thick brown pants torn at the knee. Both wore hats and army boots and walked slowly. As they got closer, the tall one raised his hand in a friendly wave. *"Italiani?"* he asked.

"Si," Vito said. *"Certo."*

Concetta turned around. "Who's that?"

"How should I know?" Vito said. He folded his arms.

"My head hurts," she said. "I want to go back to that house. I have to rest."

"We'll see."

"I have the zigzags in my eyes," she went on.

The men stopped in front of Vito. Their faces were smudged with dirt, and they smelled. He'd seen these kinds of soldiers for months, wandering through Santa Cecilia like ghosts. None of them had turned out to be Buccio.

They took off their hats, and the dark-haired one said his name was Marino Covelli. His friend was Karl, a German—"a friendly one," he assured Vito—who spoke little Italian.

"We get by on my German," said Marino.

Vito introduced himself and his mother, and Marino squatted to take her hand. "Good morning, Signora Leone. How are you today?"

"Sick," she said. "I have to sleep."

"She's fine," Vito said. "A little tired from the trip."

"Where are you going?" he asked.

"North" was all Vito wanted to say. His cart, he remembered, was full of food and wine and clothes, and these two men were bigger than he and could easily take everything.

"My family is north, too," Marino said. "Verona. But it's too dangerous to go there. My friend and I are looking for a place to live, and work, and wait out the war. Do you know of anything around here? And if you could, do you have a few lire to help us out?"

Vito shook his head. "There's an empty house down the road," he said. "Empty houses everywhere. Nowhere to work, though."

Karl tapped Marino's side and said something in German.

"He wants me to tell you we rescued Mussolini," Marino said, smiling. "To convince you we're good soldiers, not criminals. He's as desperate to get back to Frankfurt as I am to get home to Verona."

Vito had never heard of Frankfurt and didn't know what to believe about Mussolini. Marino moved closer to him, and Vito stepped back. His heart was racing. As if reading his thoughts, his mother grabbed him around his legs and said, "I'm afraid, Vito. My mouth is burning. Get me out of here, please."

"Maybe we can help with your mother," Marino said. "And you pay us back."

"I don't have anything," Vito said.

"What's wrong with her?" Marino asked.

"Not now, Mamma," Vito said, as he reached under her armpits and tried to lift her. "It's her head," he explained. "I'm sorry. You see I can't help you. You should go on ahead before it gets dark. There are many kind families in this area."

"It's only an hour past dawn," said Marino. He moved closer still. "We have all day. You tell me you don't have anything in those bags for us?"

Vito stopped. The other man, Karl, squatted beside the cart and reached into the sack of food. He looked at Vito and smiled.

"It's just nuts and some rotten potatoes," Vito said. "Please. You can get that anywhere. Please. Look at my mother. She needs it. I'll share with you. Just don't take it all—"

It was then that Marino's fist struck him. Vito fell, and his head slammed against the ground. After a moment of blindness, he saw the blurry figures of the two men running up the mountain, dragging the cart behind them. They looked back once. Blood drizzled from Vito's nose into his mouth. His mother was screaming. The sound echoed and looped into the valley.

Vito's first thought was that his mother wouldn't make it back to Santa Cecilia alive. His second was that he didn't care. His third was that he no longer had the directions to Teramo, and would have to wait years to see Maddalena now. His fourth was that he'd never tell her about any of this: his stupid attempt to visit her, the man who knocked him down in one punch, the lies he told his sick mother. As Concetta reached for him, he lay motionless on his back, staring at the blue sky, wishing he could close his eyes and wake up in the house he never should have left.

CHAPTER 13

The road through Zia Zabrina's no longer brought friendly families. Instead, foreign-looking bearded men came, some in uniform and some in rags, freezing and soaked with rain. Maddalena watched them from her window, her second letter to Vito safe and unsendable in her pocket. They walked right up to Zabrina's front door and begged for work. They didn't stay after Aristide said sadly, "We can't help you." They limped and spat, and their breath smelled of liquor. They told stories of finally making it home and finding only a pile of rocks.

Every day Chiara expected one of these men to be Maurizio or Giacomo. She held on to the hope that they'd escape the Russian front and find their way to the farm. She didn't know what else they could do after Italy switched sides: Run across the line? Turn around and start shooting? It made no sense to her, and no one could explain it. So she waited. She spent the afternoons at the front window, rosary beads clicking between her fingers. When a man, any man, approached the house, she half rose and pressed the beads to her chest. If he wore an Italian uniform, she prayed aloud and leaned into the glass. Maddalena and Teresa would stand on either side of her, holding her hands and waiting for her to realize that the man was too short, or had too long a nose, to be either of her sons.

A week into May of 1944, a carriage arrived at Zabrina's farm. It was pulled by an old, skinny mule, which sputtered and brayed so loudly that everyone in the house hurried to the window to see.

"*Dio!* Who's here?" Chiara exclaimed. She stood up and folded her arms over her stomach.

Zabrina and her friend Vincenza, the woman who brought the cigarettes, hurried out the front door so fast to greet the carriage that they nearly slipped on the mud. It was difficult to see the faces of the drivers through the glare, and yet Teresa called out, "Mamma, look! Do you see who it is? It's Maurizio!" She pointed, then slapped Chiara's arm again and again with the back of her hand. "Do you see the dark-haired one? Do you see?"

"What?" Chiara said. She opened her eyes wide and leaned in closer to the window. She was breathing hard. "Maurizio? That's him?"

The man wore an Italian soldier's uniform. He stood with his back to them for a moment. Aristide, motionless, watched Zabrina and Vincenza shake hands first with him, then the other man, a blond. Zabrina kissed them both. The best Maddalena could tell, the soldier was the same height as

Maurizio, with broader shoulders and muscles more defined against his shirt. His profile seemed familiar.

"My son!" said Chiara. "My son is a man!" There were tears in her eyes. She turned to her husband. "Look at him!"

"I told you it would be like this, Mamma!" Teresa said. "Oh, Mamma!" She jumped up and down. "Didn't I? Didn't I say he'd walk up to the house like it was any other day?"

The soldier faced the window and gave a hesitant wave. He shaded his eyes and squinted at the five women and two men frozen behind the glass.

Whoever he was, Maddalena saw now, he wasn't her brother. His face was similar, but not the same. He could be a cousin, but he was not Maurizio. She swallowed, afraid to speak, and laid her head against her mother's shoulder.

"That's not Maurizio," Carolina said matter-of-factly. "Anyone can see that."

"Of course it is!" said Teresa. No one moved. The man came closer, whispering and smiling into Zabrina's ear as if escorting her into a restaurant. Chiara lowered her head, whether in thanks or disappointment, Maddalena couldn't tell. The blond walked alone behind the others.

The front door opened and crashed against the wall. "Piccinelli!" Zabrina called, though they stood right in front of her in a tight pack in the radio room, which had no wall to separate it from the hallway. "Visitors!"

The two men stood next to Zabrina with their hands clasped behind their backs, shifting their weight from foot to foot. The blond stared at the floor. The soldier glanced at each woman until she noticed, then quickly turned his eyes away.

"Chiara, this is Sebastiano Belfiore, from Verona," Zabrina said, a big smile on her face. "I've kept him a secret for an entire month, but no more!"

"It's a pleasure, Signora," this Sebastiano said. He smiled, took her hands into his, and kissed both her cheeks.

"Yes," she said. Her face was pale. She stared at him and wouldn't release his hands.

"Are you not feeling well, Signora?" Vincenza asked.

"No," Aristide said. "No." He placed his own hands over Chiara's and pulled them from Sebastiano's. "You have to forgive us," he said to the young man. "You look very much like our son, who's still fighting the war. In Russia. We haven't heard from him in a long time."

"I'm so sorry," Sebastiano said. He bowed respectfully to Chiara. "I'm sure your boy will be home soon," he said. "Look how safe I turned out. This whole mess is almost over, and what you hear over the radio, especially about Russia, is very exaggerated."

She nodded, her eyes still fixed on his face.

"So these are the girls!" Zabrina said. She nudged Sebastiano toward them.

"Were you *in* Russia?" Carolina asked.

"No," he said, to the floor. "I'm sorry."

Maddalena watched how each of her sisters accepted his kiss. Teresa smiled shyly, as if his lips tickled her cheeks; Celestina's face was as red as a tomato, her mouth a wide, toothy grin. Carolina, in her filthy dress, looked expressionless over Sebastiano's shoulders at the crowd of people watching her. He seemed almost tired by the time he reached Maddalena, and his kiss no more interesting than the one he gave Claudio.

The other man's name, said Sebastiano, was Konrad Bauer. He wore civilian clothes. Up close, his hair was more white than blond, the skin around his eyes and fingertips a faded pink. Maybe he was an albino, Maddalena thought, like a boy she used to sometimes see on trips through Broccostella. The boy's family pretended he looked the same as everyone else, but he had the same see-through skin as this Konrad. Carolina had called him the human light bulb. He was not even twenty when he died, and even then his family insisted that he was as normal as any other boy.

Konrad stood slightly hunched over, as if his head weighed too much. He was shorter than Sebastiano, but twice as big in the arms, though both men had more muscles than Maddalena had ever seen close up. She thought of Vito, who used to pull on the fabric his shirtsleeves and say sadly, "I could fit a loaf of bread in here!" The buttons on Konrad's shirt strained the fabric, ready to snap.

Vincenza explained that these boys had been

working on her farm for the past month. "There isn't much to do right now," she said, "but come summer and fall, we'll need all the hands we can get. And my husband—he felt for them."

"We're so grateful for their kindness," Sebastiano said. "Most people slammed their doors in our faces before they even heard our story."

"You'll stay for lunch," said Zabrina. "I've heard the story through Vincenza. Now I want my family to hear it. What do you think, Chiara? We could use the entertainment."

"*Certo*," Chiara said, after a moment's thought. "We don't have much to offer, but—"

"We have plenty," said Zabrina.

"We don't want to be any trouble," Sebastiano said.

"It's no trouble," Aristide said, and led the men to the radio room.

While the men drank wine, the women crowded into the kitchen. Teresa and Chiara huddled in the corner in front of the fire, stoking the wood. "We can barely feed ourselves, and now we have these three?" Chiara said quietly.

"Vincenza had the boys bring fresh zucchini and corn," Zabrina said, overhearing. "She's outside getting them now. And we have potatoes and peppers and figs. It's plenty."

"That's not a meal," Chiara said. "What kind of people will they think we are?"

"I'm sure they're happy just to be here, Mamma," said Carolina.

Zabrina grinned, and walked over to Teresa. "They look poor now, *carina*, but that Sebastiano—let me tell you—his family owns a big hotel in Verona. He showed me the pictures." She tugged on Teresa's sleeve. "And he's handsome, wouldn't you say?"

Everyone stopped and stared at them. "He looks like my brother," Teresa said.

"You're the oldest," Zabrina said. "By a few minutes, at least, right? But if you don't like him, you have three sisters who might."

"What noise you're making, Zabrina," Chiara said. "We have food to cook."

"Food isn't the point!" Zabrina said. "Stop worrying about lunch and listen to me! Sebastiano is hard-working, a good young man. He writes letters to his mother and father twice a week. Vincenza has only known him a month, but already she and Emidio call him 'son.' They don't want him to leave."

"You don't know anything about him, or his parents," Chiara said, "except what he's told the woman who brings your cigarettes. How can we judge him without his family?"

"He's very honest," Zabrina said. "You can tell. I'm just saying let him come around. See for yourself. That's all I'm suggesting."

"He could be my brother!" Teresa repeated.

The men were telling jokes in the other room. Their voices rose to a laugh and chairs slid across the floor.

Zabrina laughed and lightly pinched Teresa's hip. "Don't talk nonsense," she said. "What harm can they bring, Chiara? Let them come around. You see? Even in war there's love. Even here."

"What about the other one?" Carolina asked.

"Konrad?" said Zabrina. "I don't trust Germans, especially the men. But he's Sebastiano's best friend. Wait until you hear: they helped rescue Mussolini. That's the story no one would listen to."

Maddalena stood in front of Teresa in their bedroom, rubbing her sister's face with a damp cloth. She was in charge of making her look beautiful. Celestina made good soup but had no talent for beauty; Carolina didn't even offer to help. Chiara had to finish lunch with Zabrina. And so the job had fallen to the youngest.

"You're ripping my skin off," Teresa said. "I don't see the point of this."

By order of their mother, Maddalena had polished Teresa's shoes and steamed her best clean dress, a fancy blue linen. She set the rag on the table and straightened the seams at her shoulders. "You saw what happened to Mamma's face when Zabrina was talking," she said. "You bring weddings into the conversation, and she forgets about Maurizio and Giacomo. That's the point."

"That won't last," said Teresa. "And it's not a very good reason to get married."

"So just pretend," Maddalena said. "Mamma doesn't do enough for you to just pretend?"

"I'm ready to be a wife," Teresa said. "I'm almost twenty-four years old. But I'm not ready *today*. This isn't how it happens, is it? A man shows up at the door, and *boom!*"

"I think this is exactly how it happens." Maddalena smiled. "In my books, all the husbands are found like this." She stood behind her sister and brushed lint from the back of her dress. She wasn't sure she could ask Teresa this, but when the lint was gone, she took a chance. "Back in Santa Cecilia, was there anyone, I don't know, *for* you?"

"No one who might not come back," Teresa said right away, as if they talked intimately all the time. "I don't know where he is or where his family went. Ezio. You know."

Maddalena didn't know. It was part of her sister's secret life, which she and Carolina didn't share. Whenever Maddalena or Carolina came near them, the twins stopped giggling or walked out of earshot. Maddalena knew Ezio, the butcher's son, only from the shop. Whenever she saw him, inside the store or out, he was wearing a bloodstained apron and carrying a cleaver. He'd left for Russia more than two years ago.

"Were you in love with Ezio?" Maddalena asked.

"Love?" Teresa said. "I guess so. He never sang to me from the street, if that's what you mean. It was no great romance. We made plans, though, before he left."

"You'd want to marry him, then, instead of Sebastiano?"

"Who is this Sebastiano?" said Teresa. "Of course I'd want to marry Ezio instead. But maybe I say that only because he's not here. It's easy to love somebody, and think about having his babies and cleaning his house, when he's not in front of your face every day. In the village, I wasn't sure about him; he smelled of meat and acted very serious. He loved cow livers as much as he loved me, I think. Now that he might be dead, I think of him and see a light all around him. He seems perfect in my head: sweet and decent, a man of honor, you know? But I can't wait for him if someone else comes along. That was the plan we made."

They were sitting on the edge of the bed. Maddalena's feet dangled above the floor. The sooner Teresa married, the sooner *she* could marry. "I think I'd do it now, if I could," Maddalena said. "If Mamma said it was all right—"

"You?" Teresa said. "Married?" She laughed. "You're still a baby! And for you, Babbo—and Mamma especially—it won't be easy. Not a butcher's son, or a war refugee, even if he did rescue Mussolini!" She rolled her eyes.

"What do you mean?" Maddalena asked. "What makes me different from you, when it comes to who I marry?"

"Don't play innocent, Maddalena," Teresa said. "I'm not Celestina, who doesn't see anything, or

Carolina, who sees only what she wants. You know you're the favorite."

Maddalena shook her head.

"It's all right. I'm not jealous. None of us are jealous, for some reason, though maybe we should be. As long as you admit it."

"I have nothing to admit," Maddalena said.

"It's easy to see what will happen to the older Piccinelli girls," said Teresa. She looped a strand of Maddalena's hair around her finger. "Celestina will get married when she's forty, after a lot of trying; he'll be a widower, with four kids already. Carolina will marry a man three feet tall, with a squeaky voice and big ears." She laughed. "He'll buy all her food for her in the mornings and maybe even have her babies for her, too."

"He won't have a choice!" Maddalena said.

"Me, I'll marry someone kind and ordinary, and take care of him and his mother, take care of everyone until they die. It's already happening." She put her arm around Maddalena's shoulder. "But you, no one can guess. Maybe because you're still young, but it's more because you're different. You're the only one of us who's like Mamma, more of a Roman than a Santa Ceciliese."

"I thought Carolina was the one like Mamma," said Maddalena.

"She thinks she is," Teresa said. "But it's you who'll live the life Mamma couldn't lead."

"What do you mean?" Maddalena asked. "What kind of life?"

Teresa stood up. "Does my skin look yellow to you?" she asked, and leaned close to the mirror. "When this war's over, someone's going to buy me expensive makeup."

Maddalena watched her, and made a decision. It felt like the wrong time, but she didn't know when she'd get a chance like this again. "I think I might be in love already," she said.

Teresa turned to her. "What?" she said. "Not with Sebastiano?"

"No," Maddalena said. She looked at her feet. "Don't tell anyone, all right? Only Carolina knows. When we were in the village, Vito Leone used to—"

Teresa covered her mouth. "I knew it! Celestina thought I was crazy." She stepped closer to her. "Keep talking."

"We used to meet and talk, that's all. I used to make fun of him the way everybody else did. But I know him now. He's not as silly as people think, and he's very sweet, like I keep trying to say even though nobody hears me."

Teresa bit her lip and smiled.

"I don't want to love him, Teresa, especially when I think about Mamma and Babbo. I can't go against them. Every time I think of how they'll look at me if they find out, it makes me sick to my stomach. So I try sometimes to forget about him. But then I remember how good he was to me and how well he takes care of his mother, and I feel guilty and I think, What if he dies in the village all alone? What if my thinking about him is what's keeping him alive? I sent him one letter, but none since the winter because I have no way to get it mailed. I have three hidden in the closet. And I made promises to him—"

"We have to talk about this," Teresa said, and yet she seemed to lose interest. She patted Maddalena on the shoulder. "Really. This is big news."

They heard their mother in the next room, asking for them.

Maddalena's face felt hot. "I'm sorry," she said. "It's your turn, not mine."

"Yes," Teresa said, all smiles again. "It could be." She put her hand on her chest and looked at her reflection in the mirror. "Everything could change for me now, whether I want it to or not."

"You look beautiful," Maddalena said. And she did. Her black hair was as thick as their mother's and fell naturally on her shoulders. Her face was plain, her eyes dark and friendly. She didn't have the Piccinelli nose; Celestina, the joke went, had gotten it twice. She was taller than Maddalena, and her chest more full. Because she was the eldest, the good jewelry glittered around her neck and wrists.

Teresa opened the door to the hallway, then closed it and spun around. "He doesn't look like Maurizio, does he?" she asked. Her smile was shy. She had perfect teeth.

"Of course not," Maddalena said. "This whole family's cracked in the head."

* * *

At dinner, Zabrina kept pinching Sebastiano's arm to get him to pay attention. Wasn't he supposed to try to impress the family? Maddalena wondered. Did he even know what the old ladies had planned for him? He didn't say much. When he did, he kept his eyes lowered and puffed out his lower lip just slightly. It was hard to tell if he was bored, embarrassed, or just very tired.

When they liked someone, Chiara and Aristide couldn't stop talking. They told stories from their childhood, asked questions to which they already knew the answers, and, to break even the briefest silence, offered whatever bit of food lay between them. This is what they did with Sebastiano. Because he was a soldier and somehow brought Maurizio back, they decided almost immediately that he was at least worthy of Teresa's consideration. Maddalena, watching this happen, worried that it would not be the same for Vito: that he'd blush and slouch and stutter through his first dinner at the Piccinelli table, and her parents would ignore him and rush in silence through the meal.

Though it was months from Christmas, Chiara described the holidays she'd spent in Rome as a young girl: the crowds pushing her through Piazza Navona on the twenty-fourth, her fear, not that she'd be trampled, but that her new dress would be wrinkled for the next day's big dinner at her zia's villa. She spoke fast, each word hurrying to keep up with the next. "It wasn't even cold," she said. "We didn't have to wear coats. Just scarves around our necks."

"That's impossible!" Aristide said. "That can't possibly be true!"

They smiled across the table at each other like two people falling in love.

"There was a fence in front of the Nativity at St. Peter's," Chiara went on. "The fence was twice as high as me, with spaces between the wood where kids could look through to see the manger and the animals and the Virgin and the hay. I didn't ask him to, but all of a sudden my zio lifted me up high over the fence, set me down on the other side, and pushed me on my *culo* toward the manger. I used to love to kiss the Baby's toes at our church, but to me this Jesus at St. Peter's, He was the Real One. 'Run!' my zio said. 'Go and kiss Him!' He laughed and clapped his hands."

Zabrina was grinning. When Chiara took a long breath, she saw her chance. She took Sebastiano's hand and said, "I think it's time for your story."

His head jerked up. "Me?" he said. "Now?"

"It will help with our digestion," she said.

They waited while Sebastiano rubbed the side of his stubbled face with his palm. Konrad looked at each of them one by one, as if trying to figure out why no one was talking. Sebastiano had tried to keep up the translations for him, but stopped after the first of Chiara's Christmas tales.

"Signora has told you that Konrad and I helped

rescue Mussolini," Sebastiano began. He smiled out of a corner of his mouth and played with the napkin in front of him. "And it's true: Without us protecting him, he'd have never made it out of Italy alive. We were both soldiers, Konrad on the German side, me for the Italians. I was stationed with about twenty other Italians at the Campo Imperatore Hotel in the Gran Sasso, on guard at the door of the room where Il Duce was hiding and making phone calls all over the world. The farther down the hall you stood, the better off you were if the Allies came shooting, but they put me third for reasons I don't know. I was never very lucky."

He looked quickly around the table.

"We spent all our time waiting, allowed to do nothing but stare at the wall in front of us and hear Il Duce bang his fists in his room. He came out a few times to talk to us, to give us big speeches about how we were the protectors of Italy's future and the future of the world, that he was the key to it all, and that heaven would reward us if we gave our lives to him. The man next to me was almost crying, he was so proud. But I felt nothing. I'd stopped believing in Mussolini a long time before, just as I'd stopped believing in La Befana when I saw that all she meant was extra house cleaning for my mother. You reach a certain age, and you see that one person can't change the world, certainly not you, and not even Hitler." He took a sip of his wine. "Anyway, on September tenth—we marked every hour of every day—six SS gliders passed over the hotel, and we knew something was about to happen. It was Hitler's men surveying the territory, planning to rescue Mussolini before the Allies could find him. We'd already moved him all over the country in the days after the surrender, from Rome to Ponza to La Maddalena and finally to the Gran Sasso. But we had no orders to move him again."

"La Maddalena?" Maddalena asked. "Where's that?"

"It's an island next to Sardinia," said Carolina. "They didn't name it after you, though; don't get too excited."

"I didn't think that," she said.

"So we were on alert," Sebastiano continued. "We barely slept. As I said, there were only twenty of us altogether, not much to protect the most important man in Italy, and they kept switching us around to different posts in the building, maybe so we wouldn't get bored. Two days later, the SS planes came again. It was the middle of the afternoon, and I was stationed with a dozen other men at the front door of the hotel. We watched them fly in low, aiming to land on the meadow down the hill from the hotel, where we'd been allowed to stretch out and relax the first few days we'd arrived. As the gliders got closer, though, they must have seen that the meadow was full of rocks, so they quickly lifted their noses"—here Sebastiano grabbed an imaginary steering wheel and cocked his head toward the ceiling—"and flew right for us in the hotel. Instead of running, *stronzi* that we were, we ducked under the window, ready to let the plane crush the glass and stone against us. But they were better fliers than we thought, and managed to crash land just a few yards from the hotel, in a big cloud of dust that made a rain sound on the windows. In seconds the Germans were banging down the front door."

"This gives me the shivers," said Zabrina, rubbing her arms, "to hear of men so brave."

"We didn't try very hard to block them, I have to say. They took us quickly. Most of us believed more in the Germans than in our own men. You don't know the confusion in the Italian army before the Germans came to teach us; we knew very well how to smoke and eat and maybe clean our uniforms, but that was all. We could barely march until Hitler's men showed us. So after we saw these soldiers survive their plane crash, we almost kissed them when they walked through the door. They could take whatever they wanted!"

"They would anyway," said Aristide.

"They marched straight for Il Duce's room as if they knew right where it was. Our commander ordered us not to resist, so we stood in the hall, just watching them. Then all of a sudden here comes Benito in his black coat and hat marching out of his room toward me, white hair puffing out from his head, his face watermelon red. There were Germans on all sides of him, carrying his suitcases, knocking everyone out of the way."

"It must have been an honor to have lived in the same house with him," Teresa said. "The rest of us only hear his voice or see him as a speck on a balcony. I would have loved to kiss his hand."

"You're very sweet and trusting, Signorina," he said, "As you should be. But I'm sorry to disappoint you and say I felt no honor. He's a man like anyone else; he's just louder about it. And now this whole country is in a deep hole because of his loud talking. If I could have sat down with him, I would have told him how he's ruined Italy forever."

"You're right," Teresa said. "When I think about it, he's not who everyone thought he was, was he?"

Maddalena looked knowingly at Carolina. It was never hard to convince Teresa of anything, but it had never been this easy, either.

"What about Konrad?" Carolina asked.

When he heard his name, Konrad turned to her, raised his glass, and drank.

"I'll tell you," said Sebastiano. "The first SS planes, the ones that crashed, couldn't fly again. Other planes behind them learned from the first ones' mistakes and landed right, and it was into one of these that the soldiers stuffed Mussolini and his luggage." He started laughing. "The glider wasn't built for three men and one man's junk. It was too heavy in the middle, like a pregnant woman, as it tried to lift off the plateau, and we all stood with our hands on our heads, wondering if it would make it. But it did. It wobbled over the mountains on its way to Rome, with all of us, Italians, Germans, standing around watching, thinking, What are we supposed to do now? Where do we go? The war wasn't over; there was still fighting for us somewhere; but not here or now, in the middle of nowhere. I heard someone say, 'Benito got to go home. Why not his men?' and that person was me."

"You were right," Aristide said.

If it were her father at that hotel, Maddalena thought, he'd have returned to his family a long time before. The day the trucks came for Maurizio and Giacomo, the women had screamed and cried—it took two men to pull Chiara from Giacomo—but Aristide had stayed calm. "Don't give up your life for anyone," he'd said, when he hugged them good-bye. "Anyone." They'd looked at him as though he were crazy. They believed in Hitler and the master race, that Italy could get back the glory it had lost. For weeks they'd been telling people, "We'll make the world listen!" They didn't think their father knew about anything except selling flour and candy.

"When I turned back for the hotel, I had no plans to stay a soldier," Sebastiano was saying now, mostly to Teresa. She nodded so hard at every word he said that a ringlet of hair kept flopping in front of her face. "I'd done enough.

I was ready to just keep walking. I'd walk until I saw my mother's face, and only at that moment would I stop. Then I stepped right onto this man's big boots." He laughed, and turned toward the German. "*Jetzt spreche ich über dich.*"

Konrad waved and smiled wide, as if he'd just noticed him.

"I told him, 'I'm talking about you now,'" Sebastiano said. "He doesn't get to be included much. I knew German from my father, who did business in Verona with merchants from Berlin. When I stepped on Konrad's shoes, I said, *'Entschuldigung,'* excuse me, and asked him in his own language if he'd been one of the soldiers in the glider that crashed. He shook his head. He said he'd arrived on the seventh one, and that Mussolini was in the air before he'd even landed. 'Not much use for you, then,' I joked. 'No,' he said. It was very windy and we had to talk with our hands in front of our faces. Soldiers were running up and down the plateau, guiding the last fleet of planes onto the rockless parts of the land. Then Konrad spoke the words I'd just told myself: 'The war's no good anymore,' he said. 'We should all go home.' He looked at me nervously, and I knew then that he would help me, that we would leave the Gran Sasso together."

"And now here you are!" Zabrina said.

"If one of you were a woman," said Carolina, "we'd call that a love story."

Chiara pinched her arm, hard enough to make

her jump. "Pay no attention to her, Signore," she said. "Her one joy in life is to say the wrong thing."

"But she's not wrong," Sebastiano said. "It *is* a love story." He paused, and took a long drink of wine. There was much shifting in seats. "We were in love with *life*."

"Yes!" said Zabrina. "With *life*."

"We were young men," he said. "We still are, you know, in age at least. What business does a young man have with fighting and death, with starving in the woods? It's foolishness, from here to here!" He raised one hand from chest to forehead. "If every man listened to his heart, there'd be no one to fight Hitler's war for him. No Italians, that's for sure. The Germans, we're not too sure about—they have anger in their blood, I think, and they want everything to change. But not Konrad. He loves family, loves women and good cooking and the fresh air of the country. He likes things simple, the way they used to be. I think he must be a little bit Italian somewhere in his blood. *Nicht war, Konrad? Du bist ein bischen italienisch?*"

"Jawohl," Konrad said. *"Besonders für die Mädchen."*

"What did he say?" Carolina asked.

"He said yes, he is a little Italian," Sebastiano said, "especially for the cooking."

There was an empty platter between him and Carolina. "Here you go, then," Carolina said. She pushed the platter toward him and smiled.

He seemed confused at first, then grabbed his fork and pretended to eat.

Maddalena was sure Sebastiano had translated wrong. Why else did Konrad not get the joke? No one else seemed to notice. Her mother was too happy to have this ghost of Maurizio to talk to, and Aristide was busy deciding whether he was good enough for his eldest daughter; Teresa was already looking at Sebastiano through a white veil; Celestina was probably wondering if Vincenza had any more men hidden in her carriage; Claudio flew far above them in the air over the Gran Sasso, letting one of those gliders speed him to the war as quickly as it could. As for Carolina, she'd turned Konrad into that soldier who'd waltzed with her on the street in Santa Cecilia. Zia Zabrina had been right after all: Here, to a smelly farm in the middle of nowhere, came love—for everyone but Maddalena.

"Did you ever make it to Verona?" she asked.

"No, Signorina," he said. "Too dangerous. Between the rain and the armies always changing course, there were no safe roads. It's that way still, which is why your babbo keeps you here at your zia's. Konrad and I didn't even know how to escape the Imperatore, but we knew we had to do it sooner instead of later. In the middle of that rescue night, while the other soldiers played cards on Mussolini's desk, we took our chance. There were no guards, and we walked out the back door of the hotel like paid-up guests. For weeks we walked from village to village, hiding in empty houses and begging. It wasn't easy. Hunger makes you crazy, you know; it makes you do things you never thought you'd do."

"What things?" Carolina asked.

"I can't talk about that," Sebastiano said sadly. "I'd have to tell you of despair and darkness in the heart, and there's no place for that at this table tonight. I'm here to honor Signora Vincenza, who, when all hope was lost, after a winter in hell, saved Konrad and me. We may have rescued Mussolini, but Vincenza and her husband rescued us." He raised his glass to Vincenza and motioned for Konrad to do the same.

"I could never have children," Vincenza said. "These last few months, with these two boys in the house, it's as if I have a family for the first time."

"Life is nothing without children," Chiara said.

Maybe Sebastiano could post one of her letters, Maddalena thought. He seemed kind enough, and now that Teresa knew about Vito, she could ask him.

"When are you planning to go back to Verona?" Aristide asked.

"It's still too dangerous," Sebastiano said. "The Allies are everywhere. Nobody knows whose side to be on, so everyone's an enemy. I've sent letters to my mother, tried to disguise them as much as I could so no one will find me. It's my only hope that she knows I'm safe. That's all I can wish for. I risked my life to defect, Signore—the army's marching up and down the mountains looking for people like me, I've seen them. I'm not going to risk it again until the war is over."

"That's very smart," Teresa said.

"You can stay as long as you like," Vincenza said.

"What I hope is that your mother received your letter," Chiara said. "If I had one word from my sons in Russia, anything at all that said they were alive, I'd be dancing right now instead of sitting here."

"You'll be dancing soon, Signora Piccinelli," said Sebastiano. "I'm sure of it."

Long past midnight, Vincenza left with the men, promising to bring them back as soon as she could. As the family stood waving at the carriage from the window, Carolina made the joke that this year La Befana had come exactly four months late—to the day—and brought Teresa a husband.

CHAPTER 14

Vito found his mother lying on her side and knew by the smell that she'd dirtied the bed again. Her eyes were closed. She wore a sheer white summer dress, ruffled at the wrists and neck.

The sheets and the back of her dress were stained and wet. "Goddamn it," Vito said. He pressed his palms against his temples. "Open your eyes. I know you're awake."

She pulled her knees in closer to her stomach. "I'm sorry," she said, and turned her face against the sheet.

These sheets, the last of the clean linens in the house, had come from his bed. A trip to the river, even during the day, would have been too risky, so he'd spent the first three weeks of May scrubbing each of his mother's dirty sheets as hard as he could with rainwater or water from the spring. But he couldn't get them completely clean. A large spot, darker in color and keeping its odor, always remained no matter how hard he pounded it against a rock. Once, desperate, he'd tried to rid the smell with smoke from a small fire he made in the yard, but the fabric had come too close to the flames and caught fire, leaving him with one fewer set and the fear that the smoke would lead the Allies (or Germans, or whoever the enemy was now) to him. After that, he gave his mother the bed linens his sisters had left behind, then the thin blankets and tablecloths, and finally his own sheets. He didn't want her to sleep on anything that wasn't purely clean, but now that was all they had left.

He kept a large bucket of water and rags ready in the corner. He laid one of the rags over his right wrist, and kneeled beside the bed. "Stand up," he said.

"In the morning," she said. She was breathing hard. "Can't we do this in the morning?"

"You know we have to do it now," he said. He squeezed her hands and pulled her gently to him, lifting her from the mattress as he stood. "There." He wrapped his left arm around her shoulders and held her steady. They stood side by side, her head even with the top of his arm. Her legs were shaking. "The bucket is where it always is," he said. He turned his head halfway to look at her eyes. She had closed them so tightly that they blended into her face, forming a thin line of lash where the pupils ought to be.

"I'm sorry, *figlio mio*," she said. "You shouldn't have to do this."

"I've heard that before," said Vito. With his thumb he rubbed the smudge of tears beneath her eyes. "Just promise me you'll try to feel better, all right?"

She nodded and unclenched her eyelids.

"Okay," Vito said.

He turned his face away and waited while her dress fell to the floor. She lifted her leg to step out of it, but the movement made her wince and she had to pause before trying it again. When she'd finally freed herself of the dress, Vito kicked it toward the bucket. Then she removed her underwear, bending her knees and pushing the cloth over her ankle with her other foot. After she'd got the underwear off and into her hand, she stood up straight again and tossed it into the bucket.

"Good," Vito said.

Without speaking, still facing the opposite wall, Vito took his left arm from around her shoulders. She wobbled a little. He walked behind her, gripped her right shoulder with his right hand and steadied her body. She reached her hand up to take his, and Vito fixed his eyes over his mother's head on the sprig of dried flowers hooked to the opposite wall. He didn't look down. He took the rag into his left hand and scrubbed her lower back. He slid the cloth into the crack of her *culo*, unable to see what he was cleaning, but trying to cover all the skin she couldn't reach. He bent lower, held his breath, and quickly cleaned between her legs, careful not to press too hard. Then he tossed the rag into the bucket.

"Okay," he said, standing up. He wiped the

sweat from his forehead with the back of his wrist. "Okay." He pulled the sheet from the bed with one hand. He folded it over and over until it formed a thick square with the dirty part buried in the middle. That, too, he tossed in the bucket. From the bureau he took a pair of clean underpants and a dress, which he'd prepared the last time she'd done this. He'd hoped he wouldn't have to use them, but now, his head still turned away, he knelt and guided her legs into the thick white panties. When they reached her knees, she was able to grab them and pull them to her hips. He pulled open the neck of the dress and slipped it over her head.

When she was fully dressed, Vito looked her in the eye at last. Her face was pale but not afraid. The dress he'd picked had bright flowers embroidered across the chest. He pulled strands of her thin hair away from her eyes and patted them against her scalp. "That's better," he said.

"I don't want to know what I look like," she said.

"You look fine."

He walked her over to the chair in the corner of the room. An inch of the dress dragged along the floor and trailed dust. She'd shrunk since she wore it last. After each step, she took a long breath and Vito waited until she nodded before he made her take another. She'd been like this since their failed trip to the Piccinelli farm. She'd had fevers and rashes. In the meantime, he'd written Maddalena a passionate letter he was too afraid to mail, and waited for word from her that never came.

He sat on the edge of the mattress, facing his mother. "Do you understand what you've done?" he asked. "What you keep doing?" His hands were folded in his lap.

"Yes," she said, chewing on her fingers. "I'm sorry. I'm so sorry."

"What did you do?" he asked.

"Don't make me say it," she said.

"Okay," said Vito. "So you're here now, in this house with me? You're in Santa Cecilia with your son, Vito, right?"

"Where else would I be?" she said. She looked at him, confused.

He shrugged. Last week he'd been Massimo, his father, late from a morning trip to Avezzano. Most of the time he was the Italian man who'd struck him across the face and left him by the side of the road. Sometimes he was a German soldier looking for Vito Leone, and she was screaming, "He's not here! He's dead already!" Unless he heard her call his name, Vito entered her room only twice a day to make sure she was still breathing and to try to make her eat.

He considered going to the river now to wash the pile of half-dirty linens he kept downstairs, but was too afraid to leave the house. The bus driver, his only source of news, had just told him the unbelievable: Rome had fallen to the Allies. He'd barely stopped in the piazza to tell him, then hurried off to Avezzano in his empty bus. Vito tried to put it out of his mind. He thought maybe he'd scale the gorge in the dark, drag the bag of clothes behind him in a sack, and get to the river that way. He didn't know what the river water could do to clean fabric that the spring water could not. Was it that the current moved rapidly? Why had God made him so stupid? He didn't understand how the laundry worked, something every eight-year-old girl knew. What he did understand was that it was wrong for his mother to sleep on that brown spot.

"I have clean sheets for you," he finally said.

She stared at him, her face blank.

The few times Vito had been to the gorge in the dark, he'd gone with Buccio and they'd had to hold hands to make sure they could find each other. If something happened to him there now, who would find him? How would his mother survive now that the region was exploding?

"They're like new," Vito continued. "I scrubbed them good. It took a long time, but I finally got them white." He stood, opened one of her bureau drawers, and pulled out the cleanest of the sheets. He stepped back and held it up a few yards from his mother, whose eyes were bad even before. To be safe, he flipped the sheet front to back many times so she couldn't look at it for too long and notice the spot. He smiled through the show, then started to fit the sheet on the mattress.

"A good wife," Concetta said. "That's my son! That's what I've made!"

"What?" said Vito, bent over the bed. He unbuttoned the mattress and reached inside to rearrange the cornhusks. The bed had become flattened over the year since the surrender, and needed constant fluffing up. He shook his head. "I do what I have to do."

"God will punish me for this," she said, not listening. "Aristide Piccinelli told me that!" She looked at the ceiling. "You think this is sick, Vito, what you see now? This is nothing."

"You'll get better," Vito said. "You have to rest and let your head cool, that's all. The trip wasn't good for you. It was my mistake to make you walk so much. But you look a little better tonight than yesterday. Better than a few minutes ago! Maybe tomorrow you can even cook me something."

"This is nothing," she said again. She swayed in her chair. "This is not sick."

"Keep thinking like that and you'll make it worse," Vito said. "I know nothing makes sense now, Mamma. But once the war's over, everything will be normal again, even you." He walked over and crouched beside her. "Then you won't have to worry about anything. You, me, and Maddalena will play cards and take long walks. Even if you're still a little sick, Dr. Fabiano will be back to help."

She shook her head. "Look at you," she said. "What kind of man are you? That girl won't marry you anymore, if she ever would. And it's all my fault."

"You have to stop saying that," Vito said. "You hear me? I told you before. You have to stop saying that or I won't listen to you. I won't take care of you anymore."

"But it's true," she said.

Vito heard the distant roar of planes. "Get up," he said. He reached under her arms and lifted her, though she wasn't ready.

"Not so hard," she said.

As he dragged her to the bed, with her legs limp and the soles of her feet turned up, the noise outside grew louder. He laid her down. "Go to sleep," he said. "I'm done talking to you. Tomorrow you wake up and cook."

"Tomorrow I'll be dead," she said.

Vito walked to the bureau and blew out the candle, which was quivering from the vibration of the planes. They flew directly overhead. Vito looked at the ceiling, his heart pounding. Then the explosion came.

It knocked Vito down and sent a shower of pebbles against the front windows of the house. He gripped the bureau for balance, then crawled over to his mother. He grabbed her by the waist, pulled her onto the floor, and pushed her under the bed. She was crying. "Quiet," Vito said.

They lay there together as the house shook and swayed. Vito closed his eyes and waited for the ceiling to cave in and crush them. More explosions came, one after the other, from the direction of the Piccinelli store and the olive grove and the farms farther down the mountain. The roar of the planes was so loud that Vito felt his head was about to burst. He covered his ears and rolled onto his stomach, calling "Maddalena" into the dust and dirt on the floor, as his mother screamed and stomped her feet and pushed up on the bed frame for air.

CHAPTER 15

Maddalena's Christmas began a few hours before dawn on the 24th, when she woke to find only one sister in her bed. Her eyes adjusted and she saw it was Celestina, spread out over the space Teresa and Carolina had left. With her arm over Maddalena's chest, her back arched, and her hair fanned out around her head, she looked like an Arabian princess from one of the movies Maddalena had seen in Avezzano.

As best she could tell in the moonlight, no one was sleeping on the floor or huddled in the corner. The only sound was the sleet crackling against the window. Maddalena sat up, sure she was missing some holiday surprise. She listened more closely, but there were not even whispers or movements in other rooms of the house.

She slid under Celestina's arm and let it flop onto the bed. Instantly, her sister stretched to fill the new space, and the snoring began.

There was no one in the hallway or the kitchen. Only Claudio was in the radio room, asleep on the *divano* with his mouth open. A book rested facedown on his chest. Maddalena drew the curtains to look outside, but there was no movement in the yard in front of the house. It was then that she heard the back door open and close. She walked quickly to it, and found Teresa shaking the snow off her boots.

"What's going on?" Maddalena asked.

Teresa squatted and sopped water from the floor with a towel. "Quiet!" she whispered. "Go back to the room."

"Are you coming?"

"Yes, yes, just go back. Don't make any noise."

Maddalena waited inside the bedroom doorway. Teresa entered barefoot, on her tiptoes, her hair a mess, carrying the balled-up towel. She knelt beside the bed, opened the mattress, and stuffed the towel inside it.

"So now you know," she said, shivering. "We figured you'd wake up sooner or later." She grabbed the top blanket from over Celestina, wrapped herself in it, and stood looking out the window.

"Know what?"

"I'm freezing to death," she said. "I've had a fever for a month, and no one's noticed. I'll never be normal again."

"So get in bed."

Every night, they took turns ironing the sheets directly on the mattress. When the sheets were hot enough, as close as possible to catching fire, they'd quickly slide beneath them. Last night it had been so cold that the sheets had cooled by the time Maddalena set the iron aside and climbed in.

"I don't understand her," Teresa said, not moving from the window. "It's nothing you can see with your eyes, but it's something. I can feel it."

"Who?"

"She doesn't know what she's doing with Konrad. It's a big game to her. If you ask me, what she says to him and the way she acts, it's not right. You're smarter with your Vito."

"He's here now? Konrad?"

"They come at night," Teresa said. "The two of them, mine and hers. We wanted to tell you. They've been here twice, sometimes three times a week since August. They tie the horse to a tree in the woods, and we meet them in the barn after everyone goes to sleep. Those times they've showed up in the morning, for a visit?" Maddalena nodded. "Well, really they spent all night in the barn."

Every time they showed up, Chiara ran around as if it were a holiday and made them drink whiskey to get warm. In the afternoon they took naps, or Konrad gave them a little German lesson, before they headed back to Vincenza's.

"The last thing they want to do is sit around with Babbo and Mamma all day, talking like monkeys, after they've stayed up with us all night," Teresa said. "So sometimes they just sneak back to Vincenza's farm before dawn. When they get there, they don't even remember the trip, they're so tired."

"Vincenza knows they do this?" Maddalena asked.

"It was her idea!" Teresa said. "Hers and Zia's, the two romantics." She walked over to Maddalena's side of the bed and got in beside her. "If you ask me, the two of them are in love, too."

"With Sebastiano?"

"With each other."

"And now Carolina and Konrad," Maddalena thought aloud.

"I'm trying not to say." Teresa drew her body close, pressing her sweaty forehead against Maddalena's neck. Celestina twisted and snorted but didn't wake. "If I say too much, I'll make it true." She was still shivering. "I will say this, though: My little sister's learning German very fast."

"What's he doing with her?" Maddalena asked. "You can't let her get in trouble. You want her to be another Luciana? That was in a barn, too."

"Pretty baby," said Teresa. "Don't you think I told her that? What she said was, 'I don't have the luxury to be in love with him, Teresa,' and I thought, what's that supposed to mean?" She was lying facedown on the mattress, which made her voice garbled. "I tell her, how can you love someone when all you can say to him is 'Barn. Hay. Cold.' Oh, and 'Cigarette, please!'"

"You're not doing it right," said Maddalena. "It's not about love. She wants an adventure. He'll get her to run off with him and leave all of us. And that's not the worst that could happen. She's alone with him now, with both of them?"

Teresa shrugged and turned onto her other side. "I couldn't stay in the cold one more second." She lay quiet for a while, then said sleepily, "Think about it, Maddalena. That man out there will be my husband." She reached her hand back and laid it on her sister's arm. "Teresa Piccinelli's going to have a husband, and his name is Sebastiano Belfiore."

"What do you do in that barn all night?"

"We'll have a baby a year later," Teresa said. "As soon as the war's over. And I'm not even scared. Not even a little bit. I want it to be tomorrow. His family could be drunks or in jail, and I wouldn't care. I'd marry him no matter what."

"Go to sleep," Maddalena said, but Teresa had already drifted off. She climbed over her, grabbed a coat and boots from the hall, and followed two sets of slushy tracks to the barn. How had she not noticed them before? Did they run out and cover them up in the middle of the day? The wet snow coated her face and made everything blurry, but she could see a pale orange glow in one of the barn windows in the distance.

She stood under the overhang at the side window, which was just low enough to peek through if she stood tall. She saw Carolina and Konrad sitting and sharing a blanket. They passed a cigarette back and forth and made gestures over the smoke. Across from them, Sebastiano sat on a large upturned bucket, his elbows on his knees and his chin in his hands. After a few minutes of watching lips move, Maddalena walked around the barn and pushed through the front door.

She caught Sebastiano in mid-rise, about to run and hide. "*Porco Dio!*" he said. "You scared us to death!"

Carolina started laughing. Maddalena hadn't heard that expression since her brothers left, and even they had used it only when they were so angry they couldn't help themselves.

"I came to keep you company," Maddalena said, trying to sound relaxed.

"To watch over me, you mean," said Carolina. "Did Teresa make you policeman?"

Maddalena ignored her. She knelt and held her gloved hands over the candle. "Doesn't do much good, does it?"

"No," said Sebastiano. "But there's only a few hours until morning. Before you know it, we'll be sitting inside by the fire, Mamma Piccinelli feeding us soup." He lifted his blanket. "Come under?" he said.

Maddalena straightened. "I don't think so," she said. "I'll share with Carolina."

"Carolina's already sharing," Carolina said. "Why do you think I'm out here? I can get warm with you any night."

"Take it all for yourself if you want," Sebastiano said. He rose and handed her the blanket. "I can't watch a girl freeze."

It was too cold to think. Maddalena grabbed the blanket, wrapped it around her, and found a place on the hay as close to Carolina as she could get. "What were you talking about?" she asked.

No one answered.

"*Konrad spricht Deutsch,*" Carolina finally said. "*Er lehrt mir.*"

Maddalena turned to Sebastiano for a translation. He was hugging his arms tightly into his chest. "German lesson," he said.

"*Gib Sebastiano die Decke!*" said Carolina.

Konrad clapped, and kissed her on the lips. "*Wunderbar!*" he said.

"Give him the blanket!" Carolina repeated in Italian. "When did you get so rude?"

Maddalena looked toward the house, as if she could see Teresa through the walls. "All right," she said.

Sebastiano slid closer to her until their legs met. She pulled the covers over them.

"See. It's not so bad," he said. He put one hand on her knee. This close, she could see the few tiny scars on his cheeks. They looked like the dents in the wood of her kitchen table. "So, you know a lot of German now," she said to Carolina.

"I do," she said. "A little English, too. You don't have to say it like it's an ugly thing."

"Did I say ugly?"

"Don't pretend, Maddalena. You're not good at it."

"I was just saying what I noticed."

"Fine," said Carolina, rolling her eyes. "Notice something else."

Sebastiano looked amused. "I have two sisters," he said. "They fight all day, so loud you'd think they were killing each other; then when they have to leave each other, they start crying."

"We don't fight," said Maddalena.

"We never have," Carolina agreed. "And we never will, either. We shouldn't."

Maddalena smiled at her, though she wanted to take her by the ear and drag her back to bed. What if Babbo found them all together, or Teresa saw her sitting under a blanket with her *fidanzato's* hand on her knee? Carolina hadn't learned anything, no matter how much she preached. She'd let this Konrad sweet-talk her, and before she knew it she'd . . .

"I mailed your letter," Sebastiano said to Maddalena. He squeezed her thigh. "Don't worry. I didn't read it."

"Thank you," she said.

Since spring, Maddalena had given Sebastiano three long letters to send to Vito. Teresa did the talking for her, and even gave him a little more than the price of postage for his trouble. In the second letter, Maddalena had told Vito he could write to her at Vincenza's address.

"Nothing for me from Santa Cecilia?" Maddalena asked, trying to sound as though it didn't matter. It had been four months since she'd given Vito the new address, and still no word.

"I'm so sorry, *bella*," Sebastiano said. "But you have to think: your letters may never have even made it to the village."

"In a way, that's what I'm hoping," Maddalena said. "Otherwise I'd have heard from him."

"I want to see this Santa Cecilia someday," Sebastiano said. "I want to see the fancy store Zabrina tells me about, and the expensive Roman furniture. She tells me the Piccinellis live like kings."

"And we've told you our zia's head is in the clouds," Carolina said. "But you'll see for yourself, someday. If no one's bombed us off the mountain."

Maddalena was shaking, as much from worry as cold. She thought of Ganzo, or whoever was delivering the mail, tossing her letters on the pile of stones that was once the Leone house; of Vito and his mother lying dead underneath. She couldn't bear to think that he'd died without knowing for sure that she still loved him, that somewhere in the Teramo mountains beautiful words were being spoken about him.

"You're not warm yet?" Sebastiano asked, and rubbed Maddalena's arms in a rapid motion.

"I'm fine," she said. Carolina was looking at her.

"Don't think the worst, *piccolina*," Carolina said. "Vito Leone will live forever. I have a feeling. He seems like the type. If you want to worry about something, worry about Mamma and Babbo when they find out. You'll wish he was dead."

Sebastiano laughed. "This is the silly one, right?" he said. "Teresa told me about him. 'More like a girl than a husband,' she said. But can he be so bad if Maddalena loves him?"

"No," Maddalena said.

"It's not him so much," Carolina said. "It's his whole story: his mother, his father and sisters. One is worse than the next. Maddalena can think whatever she wants now, but when we go back everything will be different."

"I'm still here," Maddalena said. "I can hear what you're saying. Vito and I are going to have a perfect life, right in Santa Cecilia. We believe in the old expression: Never go so far from home that you can't hear the church bell ringing. You should believe it, too."

Konrad had been listening closely. It seemed while they were talking that he followed every word, yet, when they stopped, his only reaction was a nod. He must have learned some Italian by now, Maddalena thought, unless he wasn't trying. Maybe he was just stupid.

"Teresa will have to move far away," said Carolina.

"That's Teresa," Maddalena said.

Sebastiano described the town of Verona; the little street where his father managed the Albergo Belfiore; the colors shimmering on Lake Garda in the winter. "Your sister went back to the house not even an hour ago," he said, "and I miss her already."

"She was sick," Maddalena said. "All this time you make her sit out in the cold—"

"She's not so sick when she's with him," said Carolina. "Believe me. She's just lazy. She'd rather sleep. She thinks, 'I'll have Sebastiano for sixty years. I can wait until the ground thaws to kiss him.' But I don't have the luxury. I have to get my kisses when I can."

She grabbed Konrad by the ear, pulled him closer, and pressed her lips against his. "*Ich liebe dich*," she said.

"*Und ich liebe dich*," he said back.

Maddalena glared at them. "Come inside with me," she said to Carolina. "I don't want to see that." She tried to stand, but Sebastiano held her down.

"A girl pretty as you," he said to her, "I'd think you'd be more of a romantic."

"I am," Maddalena said. "But I follow the rules."

"Sneaking around the store and the butcher shop?" Carolina said.

"After that," Maddalena said. "I learned my lesson. I thought you did, too."

"How about the secret letters?" Carolina said. "Or do you have an explanation for that, too?"

"I do—"

"Everybody has an explanation," Carolina went on, not waiting for her sister's. "Claudio discovers books instead of running away to fight; now that the women are safe here, Maddalena, why doesn't he go? And why can't Babbo take the carriage back to the village once—just once—to see if our house is standing? And look at Mamma, the worst of all. What happened to that girl in her portrait? She looks back on her life, and the best thing she can remember is some time she kissed God's plastic toe."

"So you do have the luxury with Konrad," said Sebastiano. "You just don't take it. This is very interesting. My sister used to talk about the New Women of Italy, this idea that women can work in jobs with men and stay single and even fight in the war."

"What does that have to do with anything?" Carolina said. "I'm just saying, even I have an explanation for not doing what I want to do, and I hate it!"

"Teresa's doing what she wants," Sebastiano said, "even though she's afraid to move so far from her family, to a city she doesn't know. So you can do the same: Let Konrad take you to a new and exciting country." When he translated this for Konrad, he clapped his hands together and hugged Carolina tighter.

"Teresa hasn't moved yet," Carolina said. "Ask me again when she does." She turned to Maddalena. "I'll tell you something else. Luciana Campini had a better life in nineteen years than either of us will have in eighty. She did in her barn in Broccostella what I want to do in this one—and what you wanted to do in Vito's house."

"Stop showing off," said Maddalena. "We're not the kind of girls you make us sound like."

"I'm not sure anymore," she said.

Maddalena remembered lying on the couch under Vito, the whiteness of his skinny chest and arms as he lifted his body after kissing her breasts, his knee between her legs stretching the fabric of her skirt. She'd been scared, but she knew that whatever she said—stop or go, leave or stay, sing or dance—he'd do; whatever she wanted or didn't want from him, he'd be kind enough to give. She'd been too afraid to make love, so she didn't; instead she let him heal her legs and keep her warm. She was scared still, and grateful that she wouldn't have to worry about it again until the night of her wedding.

She broke free of Sebastiano and stood up. "Please come back with me, Carolina. We have a lot of cooking to do today. You can see Konrad in the morning."

Carolina had her eyes closed and her arms around the German. "No," she said. "The cooking can wait."

"It's not right," Maddalena said.

"What did you say?"

"That afternoon with Vito," Maddalena said, "the first time I rode the bike? You remember? You protected me. Now it's my turn."

"You needed it," Carolina said. "I don't. You were young—and still are. I'll be twenty next year." She rested her head on Konrad's shoulder and looked at her. "And you can't compare this man to Vito."

"This isn't about Vito," Maddalena said. Her face flushed, and she held back tears. "You said we shouldn't fight."

Carolina got up and stepped over the candle to Maddalena. She held her close and said, "You don't have to worry, *piccolina*. Honestly. I'm smarter than Luciana, remember? I know what I'm doing."

Maddalena nodded. "I couldn't live without you," she said.

"You won't have to," Carolina said, and gave her one quick kiss on the lips.

Maddalena left the three of them in the barn and walked back through the snow to her two other sisters. The sky was lightening in the east, turning the world an iron gray. Later that morning, Sebastiano and Konrad arrived with a basket of fruit and flowers for Christmas Eve dinner, and everyone made a fuss. Carolina yawned through the cleaning of the fish, then slept until it was time to fry and eat them. They took the carriages to midnight mass at the church of San Giovanni in Frattoli, and afterward drank wine and played hours of *tombola* and *bestia* for money. At New Year's, there were fireworks at Vincenza's farm; at La Befana a gold bracelet for Teresa from Sebastiano. That the bracelet had been stolen on the road from the Imperatore many months before, no one knew; that Sebastiano had pocketed Maddalena's stamp money, no one suspected. There was too much promise in the new year—1945, a nice solid number, half a decade away from half a century—to be suspicious; and there was too much need for love to question it, especially when it appeared out of nowhere, flashed its dark eyes, and stayed.

CHAPTER 16

Vito's Christmas was another cold, bleak day in a month of cold, bleak days, as Santa Cecilia froze over for another winter. He walked alone over the rubble of the ruined church and kneeled for a few minutes before the untouched altar. Icicles had formed on the statues; a fine gray dust covered the parts of the floor still sheltered by a ceiling. Don Paolo had taken the valuables with him, the tabernacle and gold monstrance and any offerings left in the boxes, but left the cross. It hung securely on the back wall. Vito stared at the wide white eyes and the red feet and hands, and wished Jesus a happy birthday. He thanked Him for the protection He'd given him and his mother. He asked Him to give him a sign that Maddalena was safe, as he hadn't received one single letter from her since the first, now almost a year ago. He started to cry, buried his head in his hands, and begged Him to end the fighting. It had been quiet on the ground in the village since the summer, but he feared every one of the hundreds of planes that flew past every day. Without a radio, and with only little help from half-aware travelers, Vito couldn't know that the Allies had taken central Italy and tried to force the Germans out, and that these Germans were now sneaking through the little Apennine towns. Vito saw them one afternoon from the wall of the gorge, and wasn't sure what to make of them: They were running in a line up a hill toward Frosinone, waving their guns in the air.

Vito spent the rest of Christmas Day as he spent most other days, looking onto the main road from the Piccinelli dining room and running out to greet the few people who seemed friendly or whom he thought he recognized. He waited for Buccio or Maurizio or Giacomo, but none of them came. The letter of passion he'd written Maddalena a year ago and been too afraid to mail, the one that described the shape of her body and reminded her of the afternoons they'd spent behind the butcher shop and the night on his sofa in the dark, he carried with him in his pocket.

Near evening, as Vito walked back to his house to fix his mother a holiday dinner of chestnuts and dried meat he'd been storing in the Piccinellis' basement, he spotted a young woman cresting the hill toward him. The wind kicked up and blew her shawl from her shoulders. She picked up the shawl in mid-step and continued quickly toward him, shaking dirt from it and cursing. She pulled a small wagon loaded with newspapers and two small cloth suitcases. A little boy, maybe seven years old, walked beside her, tugging at the bottom of her dress.

"This isn't Broccostella, is it?" she asked Vito, breathing hard.

"No," Vito said. "You have about three miles." He pointed down the road toward the olive grove. "You see the tops of those trees? Where they end, that's Broccostella."

She looked angrily at him. "I wanted to get there tonight." Her face was round and very white, like a sheep's, but not unpretty.

"You're on the right road," Vito said. "But you'll never make it before dark. There's a hole the size of a house in the road ahead, and the curfew—"

The boy kept tugging, and she interrupted Vito with, "What is it, Francesco?"

He looked up at her and stuck his thumb in his mouth. His eyes were blue and watery.

"What?" she repeated. She turned to Vito. "My little cousin," she said. "I wanted to get him to his mother's in Broccostella before Christmas. If he didn't walk so slowly, we'd be there now. We'd have our feet in front of her fireplace." She tugged on the boy's arm. "Wouldn't we?"

"You're sure she's there?" said Vito. "Broccostella's empty."

"She's waiting for us," she said. "Anna Rossi is her name." She pulled her cart closer and looked down at the boy. Their shoes were thin planks of cardboard tied around their feet with string. Then she started on, without thanking him.

"You won't make it to Broccostella tonight," Vito called after her. He knew the Rossis, a wealthy family with one daughter a few years older than he. He hadn't heard that she'd married.

The woman kept walking, dragging the boy and the cart with her. Vito ran to her and said, "It's not safe!"

"We can go through the bushes," she said. "We're small and don't make noise. They can't hear us over the tanks."

"There are twenty houses in this village you can sleep in," Vito said, almost laughing. "Look around. You can just walk in!" He swung his arm toward the row of shattered windows and broken-down doors along the main street.

The woman stopped and looked, as if for the first time, at where she was. It was getting dark fast. She bit her sheep lips. "You can wait one more day, can't you?" she asked the boy. "The day after Christmas is just as good."

He buried his head in her skirt.

"If I have my choice," she said, "then tell me which house is best."

They were a few feet from Maddalena's. He hesitated a moment, then pointed and said, "That one." They walked to the house and looked through the store window. Barrels lay upturned or in pieces on the floor; the shelves had been cut up and burned for warmth first by the soldiers, then by Vito himself. Vito could have chosen any house; there was even time to hurry to his own street, where it was safer, but instead he held the woman's hips and pushed her through the Piccinellis' window. "The beds are upstairs," he said.

He helped the boy into the woman's arms. The moment she had him, she hurried across the room and up into the house without turning around. He called, "Signorina!" but her only response was loud clomping on the stairs. He stood in the window, his head resting on the grainy cement casing, and stared into the empty room he'd seen a thousand times. "Good luck to you," he said. Then he went home through the dark to his mother.

He set the food on a plate and took it to her room, and they ate their Christmas meal together on her bed. It took ten minutes. When it was over, she lay back down and slept. In his room, Vito arranged the sweaters and pants and dishcloths he now used as blankets. He saved Maddalena's shirt, the one she'd worn that first night she came to his house, for the top layer. He pulled the shirt up to his chin and tried to sleep, worrying now that he'd let two strange people into the house of the girl he loved.

The next day, the Festa di San Stefano, Vito peeked through the door at his mother sleeping quietly, then ran down to the main road to see if the woman and the boy were still at the Piccinellis'. A thin sleet was falling and had coated the trees with a layer of silver ice. His tracks in the slush were the first in the village. The air smelled like burning leaves, as it always did in the morning, but he was so hungry that even that aroma made his mouth moisten with spit. He snapped off an icicle from a tree just to chew on something and dangled it from his lips like a cigarette.

He pretended his breath was real smoke, that he hadn't finished in a week the half carton of cigarettes he'd meant to give Buccio before he left. He was holding the icicle between his thumb and forefinger, blowing out a puff of white, when the sound of voices stopped him.

He ducked behind the corner house, which faced the spring and marked the turnoff onto the main street, to listen more closely. The voices were coming from the direction of the olive grove and Broccostella. He stood with his back against the wall, not sure whether to run home or stay and listen to words he didn't understand. After a few minutes the voices stopped. He slid along the side of the house and peeked around the front, where he saw five or six uniformed soldiers—American or German, he couldn't tell—gathered in front of the Piccinelli house. Two sat on the ground near the low window, smoking for real. They wore hard round hats and guns slung over their shoulders; they were tossing a small object, some sort of ball, back and forth. When one soldier opened his mouth to drink in the sleet, his friend caught him off-balance and kneed him in the *culo*. He staggered and fell, and they all belched out deep laughs.

Vito's first instinct was to run home. Then he remembered the woman and the boy. He knew well enough how to get to the Piccinellis' from the back, so he walked carefully and listened at every step for voices coming closer. He held his breath when he got to the Castellanis'. He heard the soldiers clearly now—they were only a few feet away—and he knew that if they were facing his direction, they could see him run across the empty space between the two houses. So he walked far behind to the chestnut trees that jutted from the mountain. The ground was rocky and slippery here, and more than once he fell and soaked his pants in the slush. By the time he reached the back of the Piccinellis', icy water was dripping from his cuffs.

He climbed to one of the second-floor windows, using the grooves of mortar between the stones as hand- and footholds. His left shoe slipped off, then his right, and he found it easier to climb barefoot, though his toes were numb from the cold. He thought he smelled food but told himself it was only his mind playing tricks. When he reached the window of Aristide and Chiara's room, he saw only the wardrobe and the stripped bed. The other rooms were dark. He smelled food more strongly, and guessed that the soldiers were cooking something out front.

He jumped down and started up the wall toward the girls' bedroom window. His fingers were scraped white from gripping the stone, and his upper arms quivered. Sleet pelted his head and ran in cold trickles down his back. When he reached the second floor, he saw the blurry figure of the woman. She sat with Francesco in her lap, her arms wrapped tightly around him, her hair undone and falling over his head and eyes. Vito tapped on the glass with his knuckle, but they didn't hear him. He nearly slipped and fell to the ground. Then he stopped and listened, and when the soldiers' voices grew louder he knocked hard on the glass with his forehead.

The woman jerked her head up. She saw Vito and bit her lip in what looked more like fear than relief. She motioned to the front of the house with her head and Vito nodded: *Yes, I know they're there*. The boy looked up and waved, opening and closing his fingers as if squeezing a toy. The woman slid him off her lap, crawled over to the window, and kneeled on the floor in front of it. She turned the crank and the glass plates opened away from her, scraping Vito's knuckles. He used the rest of his strength to pull his torso up and dump himself into the room.

His head smacked against the floor. "Are you all right?" he whispered, as if he hadn't hurt himself. When he sat up, the room was spinning.

"Some house you brought us to," she said, but then suddenly she was hugging him. She pressed her fingers against the back of his neck, her chest rising and falling with her heavy breathing.

Vito lifted his chin from her shoulder. "Shh," he said, "don't talk so loud." He stopped to listen. He tried to shrug her from his shoulder, but she stayed locked onto him. "What's happening out there?"

"They've been here since you left last night," she said. "Germans. I can't wait anymore. We've been trapped, terrified, because of you. First they walked around downstairs, looking for food, I think. Then they came upstairs to sleep, and we hid in this closet all night with them in the room."

"*Gesù mio*," Vito said. He whispered to her, "You're an Italian woman alone. You can't let them see you."

She let go of him. "Don't you think I know that?"

"You have to keep hiding," he said.

"They're standing outside in the cold," she said. "Like idiots. I can hear when they come in."

"Why do I smell food?" Vito said. "Am I going crazy?"

"They're cooking," the woman said. "They have all the food in the world, you know. And cigarettes and dry clothes and liquor. They're a marching hotel."

"I'm starving," Francesco said. His face was so pale it looked blue.

"He's sick," the woman said. "He's been sick since the day he was born, the poor angel, but now it's worse. I gave him all the food I had." She smoothed his hair with her fingertips. "I didn't have much for him, but now I have nothing."

"They're cooking meat," Vito said.

"Of course," she said. "I tried to get some. It

took me an hour to walk two feet to the kitchen. I was trying to make no noise at all. I heard someone in there singing to himself, and I came back."

Vito stood up and looked through the doorway. "There's someone guarding it?" he whispered. "Don't talk so loud!"

"I think he left," she said. "I haven't heard any singing for a while." She sat on her knees. He could feel her watching him.

"You have to get back in there," he said, and pointed to the wardrobe.

"It's so tight we can barely breathe," she said. "I found this, though." She unbuttoned her coat and Vito recognized Maddalena's pink-and-blue shawl, the one she'd worn that first day on his bike. "It's not pretty, but now I've got two. It keeps me warm."

"You can't wear that," Vito said. He stepped closer to her. "It's not yours." He reached out and took the material between his fingers, remembering how the shawl kept slipping off Maddalena's pale shoulders. He lifted it to his face and smelled wood and smoke, all traces of Maddalena gone.

The woman looked at him. "What the hell are you doing?"

"Take it off," Vito said. He pulled on it.

"What, is it yours?" she said. "It's a rag. It was covered in dust, wrapped around a painting of some lady who thinks she's the Virgin Mary."

"It belongs to the youngest girl in this house," Vito said. "She—" he stopped.

"She what?"

"She's my *fidanzata*," he said.

"Really?" the woman said. "That's not her in the painting, is it?"

"What painting?" Vito asked.

She opened the wardrobe and took out the portrait of Chiara Piccinelli. The frame was cracked, the canvas torn diagonally from corner to corner, through her neck.

"This is her mother."

"Well, I sat on her," said the woman. "By accident." She saw his face and said, "Oh, I'm sorry. Your mother-in-law." She giggled.

He slid the painting under the bed. "I'll fix it," he said. "Now get back in."

"I have to eat," she said. "Then I have to get out of here." She pulled her coat back over the shawl. "You know, if you're quick, you can get some of the food. For yourself and for us."

"No," Vito said.

"Soldiers aren't very smart," she said. "They have bullets for brains."

"I'm not very smart, either," Vito said, then wished he hadn't. For all this woman knew, he was the genius of Italy. Why keep acting like the same old Vito Leone? "I am famous, though, as an expert thief," he lied.

"See?" the woman said. "You *are* smart. I could tell right away."

"They'll leave soon," Vito said.

"How do you know?" she asked. "If they do go,

you know there won't even be bones left for us to chew on."

Vito peered out the door toward the kitchen. Shadows from the fire flickered on the wall. "I have my mother," he whispered over his shoulder. He avoided the woman's eyes, pointing vaguely out the back window. "If something happens to me—"

She bit her lip again, the same scared way as before.

"The smart thing to do is to go out the downstairs door in the back," Vito said, "and I'll take you to where I live. It's very safe there. I have a little dried meat left."

"You're talking a little dried meat when there's cooked meat two rooms away?" the woman said. "But no, you go back through the cold and snow to your mamma. Do you see this boy's face? It's scaring me. He needs hot food now."

"Then *you* get it," Vito said.

"Me?" she said. She pointed to her chest. "You'd send a girl? I thought you said you were a good thief."

"No," he said. "I don't know." How quickly the new Vito, the smart one, had disappeared. "I don't know what I'm saying. I mean, it's too dangerous for anybody."

"How old are you?" the woman asked.

"Nineteen," Vito said. "Why?"

"Nothing happens to a nineteen-year-old boy in a village," said the woman. "Out there, yes, in Russia or Albania. But not here."

"That's not true," Vito said. "Did you see across the street? This very road—" In the middle of his sentence the woman picked up the boy and walked him over to the corner of the room, by the window Vito had fallen through.

"Stay here, Francesco," she said to him. "Don't move until I come back. I can't wait all day for this man to feed you."

"No," he said. "You can't." He stopped her with his hand at her shoulder. "I'll go."

She slid back toward the wall. "I don't hear them now."

"Maybe I'll go," he said. He was shaking, his clothes wet and cold. "But before I decide, you have to do two things."

"What?"

"One: Take off that shawl and leave it where you found it," he said.

"Fine," she said. "I'll put back the sacred shroud before I leave. What else?"

"Tell me your name. I want to know who I'm risking my life for," he said.

"That's easy," she said, quietly. "Filomena Vitale." Her body softened with every syllable, like one of his bike tires when he let the air out. Saying her name made her shrink in front of him and seem younger, no more than twenty. He looked more closely at her face. She could even be his age, though she had a body Buccio would have gone crazy for: wide hips and a large chest. Her face grew innocent and blank.

"All right, Filomena," he said. It was the name of his father's mother, who'd died a year before he left for America. There were plenty of girls with that name, but to him it always sounded old and powdery. "And what about Francesco? Is he really your cousin?"

"That's three questions," she said. "Haven't you decided yet?"

"No," Vito said.

"He's not my son, if that's what you're asking," she said. "I'm who I said I am. I take care of him, the same as you'll take care of me, right?"

"Maybe," he said. He rubbed his forehead to think some more, and it was at that moment that she started kissing him.

The boy giggled. Vito reached his arm around Filomena's back and pulled her against him, as if by instinct. He didn't know what he was doing; he knew only, instantly, that he could do whatever he wanted with this girl and it wouldn't matter. She was probably a *puttana* anyway. Her tongue slid along and under his.

She kissed differently from Maddalena. She used her tongue as if she were digging food out from between his teeth, while Maddalena let it lie there for Vito to prod and tickle. This new way unnerved him, and so as Filomena's tongue darted in and out between his lips, he imagined it was Maddalena's: that she'd surprised him with a trip across country and made it home, and was so happy to see him that she couldn't control the muscles in her mouth.

What he did like was the heat it made: the girl's cheek and chin against his, her hand slipping between the buttons of his shirt, beneath his undershirt, to rub his cold skin until his entire body flooded warm. Filomena ran her hand over his stomach, up around his ribs to his chest, and down to his *uccello*—which no hand but his had ever touched.

He reached inside her dress. She arched her neck as he carefully followed the same path she'd taken: stomach, breasts, between the legs. He pressed his palm against her bristly hair and his fingers into the folds of skin. He pressed harder, amazed at the very fact of it, until he heard her say "softer," and he had to open his eyes and remember there was a girl attached.

"I'm sorry," he said.

"It's all right."

Vito leaned her against the wall near the door. "Are you more comfortable like this?" he asked. Something overtook him. He forgot about the boy. Let him watch—he was too young to remember, anyway.

"Sure," she said.

He traced lines up and down her back with his fingertips, then under the lip of her thick underwear. Her skin was coldest here. She slid farther down the wall—to give him more room, he thought—and soon he was holding her against it and his hands were pulling down her underwear. He didn't know what to do next. She had her arms wrapped around his neck, her legs on either side of his waist, and her middle pressed against his.

"Yes?" he said.

"Yes," she said. She looked directly into his eyes, with passion, her forehead sweating, like a woman in a movie. "But first you get me the food."

He blinked. "You're still hungry?" he said, and let her legs slide to the ground.

"I need to eat first," she said, "or I might faint." She kept her eyes on him. "This takes a lot out of a woman. Do you know? Have you ever been with a woman before?"

It would be stupid—suicide, even—to try to steal this food. Someday people would say "We always knew Vito Leone had no sense, but to walk into the soldiers' guns for a piece of trash?" He thought for a moment. "The deal is: if I get food now, then we . . ." He made little circles in the air with his open hand.

"*Si*," she whispered, and pulled him to her by his belt.

He went to the door and listened for the soldiers. There was no movement downstairs or singing in the kitchen. If they were asleep downstairs, it was likely a drunken sleep, the deepest and hardest to wake from. He put one bare foot slowly in front of the other, not looking back at Filomena, and stepped out into the hall. The floors creaked, but more quietly than if he'd had shoes on. If it got bad, he could run down the stairs and tear through the back door. He could scramble down the outside wall and lose any soldier in the woods he knew so well, zigzag around trees if they started to shoot.

He stood outside the door to the kitchen, his cheek against the scratchy wall, but heard nothing. The shadows of the flames danced over his face. They don't expect anyone, he thought; they think they've scared off every Italian from Naples to Milan. He inched his head past the door frame and saw an old, stubbly-bearded soldier asleep in a chair in the corner, a brown leather-bound book against his chest. He wore a thick fur coat over his uniform and one of those hard gray hats. The skin under his eyes was blotchy and wrinkled. Shards of glass and pieces of terra-cotta dishes and pots were strewn on the floor around him.

As Vito took one long step forward, the man stirred and sank deeper into his chair. If he woke, Vito would hit him in the head before he knew what was going on.

He grabbed two sharp pieces of terra-cotta from the floor and held one in each hand. In the kettle over the dying fire he found a half-eaten thick, white gravy, flecked with brown. The slop smelled like meat, but Vito had never in his life seen meat like this. Was there milk in it? Who'd cook meat with milk? He dipped his finger in and licked something so salty that it burned up all the spit in his mouth. He used one of the terra-cotta pieces to scoop some up, leaving enough in the kettle for at least this one soldier. When he tried to swirl the gravy around to make it look like no one had touched it, it stuck to the broken dish like plaster.

The house was silent, though he thought he could hear Filomena breathing as he crept back to the bedroom. With every step, he imagined a soldier jumping out behind him.

When he was face to face with her again, he held out the bowl triumphantly with his right hand. With his left he hid the bulge in his pants. "Here," he said. He smiled and breathed deeply.

Without a word, Filomena took the bowl with both hands, lifted it to her mouth, and sucked the gravy from the sharp edge.

"Be careful," said Vito. "You'll get cut."

She kept her mouth on the bowl, rotating it and swallowing fast. The cream stuck to her chin and under her nose. She kept licking her lips. When she'd downed half—more than half, from where Vito stood—she handed the bowl to the boy, who'd run up to her the moment Vito returned. He smelled the gravy, pinched his nose with two fingers, and licked the bowl clean. "Disgusting, isn't it?" Filomena said to him, and smiled. "A pig's dinner."

Vito looked at her. Her dress was twisted around her waist, and she kept her legs slightly apart. A glob of gravy stuck out like a pimple from the end of her nose. "I'd think you would have let the boy eat first," he said.

"I'm hungry, too," she said. "And I have to take care of myself, don't I? So I can take care of him?"

She looked at the boy, suddenly worried. "You got enough, right?"

He nodded.

"Still," said Vito.

"You would have given him the whole bowl, wouldn't you?" she said. "I could tell by the way you talked about your *fidanzata* and your mamma. I knew you'd bring back enough for both of us."

"I'm not such a saint," Vito said.

"Of course you're not," said Filomena. "And I'm not such a *puttana*." She smiled, leaned in, and grabbed between his legs. "If I were, I'd keep my promise."

Francesco giggled again, and Vito stepped back. "You're teaching that boy well," Vito said. "Get him back to his mother, at least, where he belongs."

"I'm trying," said Filomena. "You think I want him?" She rolled her eyes. "Anna Rossi comes to us this big"—she clasped her hands at arm's length from her stomach—"and lives with us and eats our food for a month. She dumps him out on the floor in the morning, and by the afternoon she's on the road back home."

"You're not her cousin?" Vito asked.

"You don't know how the world works, do you? Why would he be with his cousin and not his mother?"

"You're Anna Rossi, then?" Vito said.

"*Gesù mio*," she said, rolling her eyes again. "I worked in an orphanage. In Terni, with my mamma and nonna. I helped take care of this little boy and all the others. When the war started, people came for the others, but no one came for him."

"She got lost, maybe," Francesco said. "Maybe she's waiting for me."

"They were going to keep him, Mamma and Nonna. Then a bomb hit our house in the middle of the afternoon, and killed them both." She looked him in the eye. "I have no one in the world anymore. I'm an orphan myself. I want to get out of Italy, but I'm no monster. I have to give this boy a home first. Whoever's in Broccostella, that's who I'll leave him with."

"There's no one there," Vito said, lowering his voice. "I'm sure the Rossis are gone—"

"You can't say that," she said. She stepped behind the boy, bent down, and clasped him to her chest. "Someone in Broccostella will take him. I could have dropped him on a street corner in Terni, you know. But I didn't."

"I guess you're the saint, then," Vito said, rolling his eyes. "Take off the shawl. Now, please. I'm taking it with me."

She let go of the boy and slowly, like a striptease, removed the top shawl. Vito grabbed Maddalena's and pulled it off. Filomena stood there for a long moment, holding the first shawl at her hip, her neck and shoulders bare.

He folded the shawl in quarters. Maddalena's letter was in his pocket. As best she could, she'd promised him love; this Filomena could offer only her body. No one would blame him if he forced her to keep her promise, wiped that smirk from her face with rough kisses. He was a man, and men knew the difference between the kind of girl you marry and the kind you have on the side. Buccio had told him as much. He considered this. Then he said, "Take care of the boy," and walked away before he could change his mind.

He put his leg through the window. He climbed down the wall into the snow and found his shoes buried in the slush. When he looked up, no one was watching him.

The fingerful of gravy had made Vito hungry, but there was no food in his house. He brought up some dry branches from downstairs, built a small fire, and warmed his numbed feet. All he could think was, Vito, you're as dumb as they say you are.

Whenever he used to put off his chores—bringing in firewood, weeding the little garden, or studying his lessons—his father would repeat his favorite expression: "The man with time shouldn't wait for time." It drove Vito crazy, this stupid Santa Ceciliese saying. He used to mumble it in funny voices as he dragged his schoolbooks to his bedroom. Now he knew what his father meant. He had a woman all to himself in a room, with all the time in the world to spend with her, and what did he do? He left her there, waiting for a different time and a different woman, not sure either would ever come. When Maddalena returned, she'd bring the same family she'd left with: the sister who hated him, the father who'd called him a half man, the mother who turned up her Roman nose to every village boy. If he were smart, he'd find a way to get to America, to find his father and a job that brought in money. Then when the war ended he could take the boat back and show up in Santa Cecilia with his pockets full, and no one could say he didn't deserve Maddalena Piccinelli. But this was just a daydream. He'd tried to leave once already and couldn't get ten miles down the road.

When he could finally feel his toes, he put out the fire and walked back into the cold to the outhouse. He stood behind it, his back against the warped wooden planks he'd helped his father nail together. He unzipped his pants, closed his eyes, and found Filomena. He imagined what might have happened if she hadn't tricked him, if the boy weren't there, or the Germans. He had her up against that wall again, then—no: She became Maddalena, flushed and sweaty from her cross-country trip, the war and her family far away, the house all to themselves. Then suddenly it switched again: summertime, a bed with sheets, hours in the sunlight through the window; Maddalena throwing her head back, him climbing on top of her, spreading her legs with his knees.

Vito slid down the length of the shed, working himself faster, then let go. The seat of his pants dipped into the slush.

Immediately afterward he felt scared, as if he'd

been watched. He felt the shame of Maddalena's innocent eyes on him. He stood up, looked right and left and back again, then looped his belt back around his pants. He was shaking in the cold. No one was around, only the birds flying in circles above the trees.

He went straight to his room, without checking on his mother, and fell asleep. When he woke, sometime in late afternoon, it was to the sound of her gasping for breath and banging her fist against the wall. He turned over and covered his ears with Maddalena's shawl and shirt. His life would never change. "Shut up!" he yelled into the mattress. He decided to let her suffer and scream, and not go help her. But he was not strong enough. He listened to "Vito, please! Please, Vito!" over and over until he couldn't stand it anymore.

He stood at the door, watching her thrash around in her bed. "Mamma," he said. "It's all right. I'm here."

"It's nothing!" she yelled in her strangled voice. "Leave me alone, Vito! Get out!"

"First you call me, then tell me to get out," he said. "What am I supposed to do?"

"Get out!" she said.

He stopped when he saw the sheets. "Goddamn you!" he said. She was crying. He grabbed her hand mirror from the dresser and threw it against the floor. "Clean it up yourself!"

He couldn't stay in this house. It was almost dark, but he walked down the hill to the main road. He kept to the side of the street and ducked in and out of the trees. It was warmer than earlier, the air thick with mist, the town quiet. The slush had melted into pools of muddy water. Vito splashed through them, feeling like the last man on Earth, like the grass and the flooded streets and the mountains and square white houses were his alone.

He peeked around the corner house, as he'd done earlier, but he couldn't see far through the fog. It hung just above his head, like a ceiling that stretched from Santa Cecilia to the end of the world. He walked hunched over to avoid it. The ground felt steady, the tanks far away and the soldiers surely gone, but still he took careful steps and stopped to listen for voices or throbbing engines. He passed the beheaded lion statues of the Castellani house, keeping his eyes straight ahead.

When he put his hands on the windowsill at the back of the Piccinelli house and started to lift himself up, the stone felt warm. He looked at his palms and rubbed them against his cheeks. The smoke in the air smelled different. He stepped back into the road, nearly tripping over a thick metal pipe, and saw through the fog that the outside of the second floor was streaked with soot. Thin trails of black smoke curled from the top of the smashed front windows. Vito stood and stared as if paralyzed: one hand over his mouth, the other on top of his head. He'd seen lots of fires in the village, at least one a year for as long as he could remember, and helped put them out. His first instinct was to run inside and stamp out the flames with a broom or the soles of his shoes. He breathed deep. "Think first," he told himself.

He took it all in at once: the smoke from the upper windows floated out in a trickle, too slow for a new fire; the front of the house was already soot-covered, which meant that the electrical wires had already burned through; if anything inside were burning strongly, there'd be more smoke. He relaxed. The fire was almost out. Whenever it had started, enough time had gone by for Filomena and the boy to either escape or burn to death, and either way, Vito could do nothing about it.

To be safe, he grabbed a copper pot from inside the store, filled it with wet snow, and carried it up the stairs to the kitchen. As he'd guessed, the wires had charred; they drooped down the side of the wall, hissing and popping tiny sparks.

"Filomena!" he called. "Francesco!" No one answered.

The soldier's chair was gone, probably stolen for firewood. On the floor lay the flaming sacred heart of Jesus, the only scrap left of the painting of Him that had hung above the doorway. Vito slipped it into his pocket, thinking it some sort of miracle that it didn't burn. He'd save it and show his mother, then give it to Maddalena or her mother. He checked the pot that held the last of the Germans' gravy: a thin, scorched layer clung to the bottom.

He walked to the bedroom, waited a moment at the door, and prepared himself for the worst: the girl tied to the bed, shot or stabbed, the boy's body slumped on the floor. But the room was empty. There was the bed and the heavy wardrobe and, thrown in the corner, the terra-cotta shard they'd used for a plate. The fire had not spread this far.

He checked the other bedroom. Whoever had set the fire had done it quickly and not very well. Only the wires and the curtains and half of the wooden door to the terrace had burned. The rest of the front of the house, though, they'd tried hard to ruin. They'd split the big table down the middle with some sort of ax and hacked the legs off both pieces. They'd thrown the blue dishes from the china cabinet to the floor. For all Vito knew, Filomena and Francesco had taken a match to the drapes just for fun, after the Germans left. They'd laughed about it as they trudged through the slush toward Broccostella.

Vito sat on the floor, resting his elbow on an upturned chair and his head in his hand. He waited for his heart to stop pounding. He coughed on the black smoke. He heard gunfire starting in some other village, soon to reach his. He should go home, but the thought of his mother made him want to start smashing things again. Instead he crawled onto a long plank of the table and lay across it.

He closed his eyes. How many more days would he have to live this way? He'd have been better off in the war; at least when he got back, he'd have something to show. He'd be a hero and collect government checks for the rest of his life. Just yesterday he'd thanked God that he'd missed the war, but maybe this was worse: living through it without any way to change it. God had kept him from the fighting, but He'd made him suffer for his safety.

After a while, an idea came to him. He sat up quickly on the table and looked around the house as if for the first time. He jumped up and walked in and out of the rooms again, stopping in each to study the furniture. Some pieces had been broken apart; others—the bureau, the cabinet—were dented and filled with bullets. Only the back bedrooms seemed untouched.

He'd fix it up, all of it—the soot on the white stone front, the drapes, the wires. He'd learn how. He'd teach himself. Or he'd ask men who came through town to help in exchange for—something. He'd steal paint and tools from Ganzo's house; he'd remove a picture of his sisters and use the frame for the burning heart; he'd sweep every inch of the second floor and wash the walls and stand the partitions in the store aisles back up. If the Germans—or Filomena or anyone—wrecked it again, he'd start over. Then when the Piccinellis came home, in a year or a month or five years, they'd open their arms and thank him. Even Carolina. Even Aristide and Chiara. They'd look at him, amazed, and say, "You want our daughter? She's yours."

THE PROCESSION

CHAPTER 17

For weeks after the war ended, there were parties all over Teramo. It was as if food—roasted pigs, ricotta, eggplant, veal—had come home with the soldiers, had been liberated with the rest of the world. The spring was bringing new life, not only to the crops, but to the people who tended them. Any sense that Italy had chosen wrong both in siding with Hitler and breaking with him; that it had turned its back on Mussolini in fear and surrendered its place at the top of the world to the Allies; that it had badly lost a war it had been fighting, one way or another, for close to ten years, seemed to matter little to these Abruzzese. All that mattered was that the war was over. Bands played in the streets, fireworks sparkled from the sides of the mountains, weddings were thrown every weekend in the little church near Zabrina's farm. Soldiers wore their uniforms instead of suits; brides wore the dresses they'd been sewing since their *fidanzati* left. The Piccinellis celebrated with the people of Frattoli and Teramo and the towns all around them, though secretly they resented how little the war had touched them. No bombs had dropped here. No one but soldiers had been forced to leave their homes. Not one of them had seen his neighbor pulled from a pile of rubble.

"I don't see what everyone's so sad about," Celestina said, on a May morning at the height of the new happiness. She was standing with her family at the edge of the road in the center piazza of Frattoli, watching the last procession before they were to leave for Santa Cecilia. Today, a band zigzagged through the streets from the church to the fountain in the town square; a group of ladies followed behind, carrying pink and yellow flowers in elaborate arrangements. Tomorrow, Vincenza's carriage would take her, her husband, Konrad, and Sebastiano north to Verona. Sebastiano would introduce his family to the two people who saved his life, spend a week or so in his old house, then go to Santa Cecilia and marry Teresa in the town where she was born. The other carriages, one borrowed from Vincenza, would head southeast, over the Gran Sasso and through Abruzzo, and take the Piccinellis home.

In their two years in Frattoli, the Piccinellis had almost gotten used to the thin air and the dry fields and the animals, to Zabrina's endless talking. Now they feared that the world they'd left behind no longer existed. They could have gone back much sooner—the roads were safe by mid-April, and Aristide knew it; he could have ridden ahead and checked on the house—but they had put it off. Chiara folded and refolded the laundry. Claudio copied passages from Virgil onto sheets of unlined paper. Carolina took long walks and arrived home sweaty and late for meals. Maddalena dreamed of Vito alive, then woke to the real chance that she'd find only his grave when she returned.

Only Celestina was unworried. She stood at the edge of the crowd with her arms out, shouting, "Good-bye, Frattoli!" She waved back at the soldiers who marched in the parade. Now that Teresa was a month from marriage, the sister next in line was eager to pick her own husband from the flood of young men surely on their way home to the village.

Carolina stood beside Konrad, fidgeting. She'd look at him, half-smile, look at the ground; then he'd do the same. Next to her, Teresa gripped Sebastiano's arm with one hand and sobbed into a handkerchief with the other. Vincenza and Zabrina clapped to the rhythm of the band.

Maddalena wore a sleeveless dress for the first time that year, enjoying the moist, sweet air on her arms and taking in, with the music and the display of beaded dresses and the prayers for peace on Earth, the sense of hope that had brought them all here.

As the priest mounted the platform, two soldiers with guns strapped to their chests came toward the line of Picinellis, who were about to bow their heads. The soldiers' faces were serious, even as Celestina winked at them and whispered good afternoon. They ignored her and stood directly in front of the family with their elbows at their sides. Heads began to turn away from the priest, who'd just begun his greeting. The soldiers looked first at Aristide, then Claudio. When their eyes met Sebastiano's and Konrad's, they immediately reached for them. One grabbed and held Sebastiano's arm, the other Konrad's. The one who grabbed Sebastiano pushed Teresa aside with the butt of his gun.

"What is this?" said Sebastiano. He looked first at Teresa, then at the expressionless Konrad.

The crowd started to back away and suddenly the Picinellis were in the center of a circle, with the townspeople on all sides staring and whispering. Another group of soldiers, younger and unarmed, gathered at the edge of the fountain to watch over the scene. The priest stopped talking for a moment, looked over, then began again.

The soldier holding Sebastiano whistled, and two young men in dirty brown shirts hurried over. Their faces were tanned and rough, and they wore torn leather shoes. Maddalena guessed they were farmers. Two women, carrying three crying babies on their hips, followed behind them.

Maddalena took Carolina's hand in hers. She watched Claudio hide behind their mother, then slip into the crowd and turn himself into one of the staring townspeople.

"You're making a mistake," Sebastiano said to the soldier. He repeated this to Teresa, then Aristide. Then he shrugged his free shoulder. "No,

I guess he's not," he said with a grin. "My name is Sebastiano Belfiore, from Verona. It's true: I was at the Campo Imperatore. I left the army, but I'd served my country—" It wasn't until he saw the two farmers that his grin fell.

"What's this about?" Aristide asked. He walked up to the soldier. "I can tell you—"

"*Zitto!*" said the soldier. He held both of Sebastiano's arms behind his back now, and pushed him toward the two farmers. The other soldier did the same with Konrad. "These are the ones?" he asked.

At this point, the priest had given up on his speech, and the band was pushing through the crowd, their instruments above their heads. Vincenza started to cry, and Zabrina put her arms around her shoulders. Teresa's eyes were wild. She stood motionless.

"They are," one of the farmers said. "Ask my wife. Ask my brother. Ask anyone in this town. They'll tell you. I described them a hundred times. Now I see their faces in front of me again. They came to my house, begging. I told them we couldn't help. The tall one punched me in the face, knocked out two of my teeth." He pulled one side of his mouth open with his index finger and spun around to show the townspeople. "The blond one, the dirty German, ran inside and threw my wife on the ground. My wife who had a baby two months later! They took everything in the house. We didn't have much, but they took everything."

The crowd was quiet as he talked, then grew loud. They moved in closer and shook their fists and yelled for the soldiers to take this trash to the jail in Teramo.

Konrad shook his head and looked back and forth from Sebastiano to the man.

"You have the wrong men," Sebastiano said. He craned his neck to find Vincenza. "Tell them, Signora. Tell them what kind of men we are."

Vincenza stepped forward, rubbing her eyes with a handkerchief. She explained that the men had come to her house about a year ago, and that they'd never given her any trouble. They'd helped on the farm. "We don't have much, either," she said. "But nothing is missing. They're like our sons." She pointed to the farmer. "This man must be wrong. Why would they steal from him and stay so well with us?"

"Listen to her," Aristide said to the soldier. "She's telling the truth."

"Don't believe these people!" someone called from the crowd. "They're not from here! We've never seen them before!"

Teresa searched Sebastiano's face for some sort of answer, but he looked at her blankly. All Konrad communicated to Carolina was the flush of red on the back of his neck and the tips of his ears.

"I saw it with my own eyes," the farmer went on. The townspeople swelled with his every word. "Why would I lie? I don't want anything back. I want them in jail! I'll come to the trial and testify, and so will my wife!"

"Your family is in very big trouble," the soldier said to Aristide. And soon the men of Frattoli, shoulder to shoulder with the gunless soldiers, had pushed back the women in the crowd and formed a tight circle around them. "If you've been helping these men—"

"We didn't help them."

It took a moment to realize that this was Carolina talking.

She let go of Maddalena's hand, stepped forward, and reached into a pocket on the inside of her dress. She pulled out first a gold bracelet, then a ring with a shiny red gem. She held it up in her palm like a communion wafer.

"Where did you get those?" Chiara asked.

Everyone was looking at her. "Konrad," she said. She pointed to him and the crowd grew loud again. Over the noise, she said, in a voice like a little girl's, "I didn't want them, but he slipped them to me in our house. He was trying to be romantic, but it scared me, and I couldn't understand him when he talked. I knew they were probably stolen, but I was too afraid to tell anybody. I'm so sorry I kept them, Mamma, but I didn't know what else to do." She turned to the soldier and the two farmers. She wore an expression of naive blankness that Maddalena had never seen on her before. "We don't really know these men," she continued. "We don't know what they wanted to do to our family."

Teresa slipped her hands behind her back. When they came back around, her own gold bracelet was missing from her wrist.

"That's his mother's jewelry!" Sebastiano tried to explain, but no one listened to him. The soldiers had heard enough. They took the ring and bracelet from Carolina, showed them to the farmer, and though he didn't recognize them they gave them to him anyway. There was applause when he slipped the ring onto his wife's finger, and she held it up to the light over the head of her screaming baby.

As the soldiers carried Sebastiano off, he turned to see his *fidanzata* one last time. "I was really a soldier!" he called over the throngs of people.

They spit on him and Konrad and shouted "*traditore*" and "*disgraziato*." The priest had fought his way back up to the platform and started his speech from the beginning.

"I never lied to you, Teresa!" Sebastiano said. He thrashed his head back to meet her eyes. "We did rescue Mussolini!"

The crowd laughed and booed. Someone kicked Konrad in the leg. Chiara wrapped her arms around Teresa's neck and shoulders, as if to keep her from running after him.

"I was going straight, Teresa!" Sebastiano was saying, already just a head bobbing among the heads of the Frattolese. His voice faded as they led him toward other end of the town. "I was going straight for you!"

* * *

That afternoon, the Piccinellis went home to the wide silver tray of empty *spumante* glasses Zabrina had set out earlier. She had planned a celebration for the evening, a farewell toast before a good night's rest before two safe trips. She'd prepared a speech about love and luck and the beauty of making a marriage in the middle of a war. She'd asked Claudio for a poem she could copy down from one his books, and folded it into a card for Teresa. Now, as her brother's family finished their packing in silence, she cleared the tray and glasses and split the bottle of *spumante* with Vincenza in the kitchen.

Teresa and Celestina had gone immediately to the barn without entering the house, and no one followed them. Carolina and Maddalena locked themselves in their bedroom, where Carolina stood with her forehead pressed against her arm, the way she'd stood the night Luciana died. Maddalena sat on the bed beside her, and though she wanted to speak—to ask questions, to offer whatever comfort or prayers she could—she let her sister be.

After a while, with the house silent and the sun setting over the barn, Carolina lifted her head, turned around, and banged her fist on the bureau. What was left there, Zabrina's little mirrors, statues of Mary and Saint Anne, jewelry boxes painted in peeling gold leaf, jumped up and clinked back down on the wood.

"This is an unfair life," Carolina said.

Maddalena nodded.

"I couldn't do it," Carolina said. "After all that, after all those nights in the barn and all the kissing, after the thousand times I told him 'I love you,' I couldn't do it." She looked at her. "We were going to sneak away, Maddalena. Two nights ago. I was ready. I'd packed everything. I had a long letter to you, already written. I knew Konrad was a thief, but I believed him when he told me why he did it: that they had to survive; that after they found Vincenza, they didn't have to steal anymore and now it was all in the past. He'd be going home to Germany to rebuild his country, and I'd be with him. We weren't going to wait for Teresa and Sebastiano because we didn't want anyone to stop us." Here she made a fist again, then unclenched it. "But when it came time, I couldn't do it. I couldn't leave you, or Santa Cecilia, as much as I hate it! I couldn't leave Mamma. I couldn't even leave Claudio. Konrad was in the barn ready, and I was in here under the covers with my arms around you and Celestina, terrified to give you up."

"It's all right," Maddalena said, suddenly so relieved that she grabbed Carolina around the waist, buried her head in her lap, and forgot to be surprised. "You did the right thing. Didn't you find that out today?"

"I'm an idiot," Carolina said. "That's what I found out today. I heard that farmer's story and saw his wife with those babies, and for the first time I knew what kind of man Konrad was. It made me afraid for all the time I'd spent alone with him. But

I didn't decide not to go with him two nights ago because of that, because he was dangerous; I didn't go because I was too much of a baby to leave my family. Do you understand? Do you see how I'm an idiot twice over?"

"I don't see that," Maddalena said. "All I see is that it's finished now. That's all that matters. In the morning we're going back to Santa Cecilia, where no one knows the story, and you'll never have to think about it again."

"I'll end up at home," Carolina said, "taking care of Mamma for the rest of my life. One girl always does. There's always one who doesn't marry. I used to think it would be Celestina, but I tell you now, it'll be me, and Mamma and I will tear each other's hair out."

"That won't happen," Maddalena said. She smiled at her, but Carolina's face was serious.

"Teresa hates me now," Carolina said. She paced in front of the window. "We became friends, you know? For the first time. She didn't know about any of the stealing. Sebastiano told her he borrowed money from Vincenza to buy that Christmas bracelet. I believe everything else he ever said to her was true: all the love, all the war stories. He was trying to change, maybe, like he said. But how could I let her marry him, Maddalena, after I heard what he did to that farmer?"

"You couldn't," said Maddalena. She kept to her place on the edge of the bed, where she'd once sat with Teresa and made her beautiful for the man now locked in a Teramo jail. "Think about it this way: You saved her, Carolina."

Still, Carolina folded her arms and stared out the window. Maddalena watched her. Every few minutes—remembering, maybe, some kindness of Konrad's or Sebastiano's head arching in the crowd to tell Teresa he loved her—she shook her head and closed her eyes.

It wasn't until the middle of the night, as Maddalena lay awake in bed with all three of her sleeping sisters, that a new fear finally reached her: all the stamp money she'd given that thief, all those letters he'd never sent.

Aristide had spent many hours arranging the bags in the two carriages it would take to get back to Santa Cecilia. Vincenza's was an open wagon, with thickly spoked metal wheels and a roof they could pull up if it rained. This morning the air was clear and crisp, though, and they'd have no trouble with rain. He walked around the front of the carriage, patted the horse, and scratched her neck until she stretched and neighed. He rubbed his eyes, looked over to his sister waiting on her porch, and said, "It's time to go."

There was little conversation on the road. Maddalena sat beside Carolina. Claudio guided the horse. In front of them, Aristide rode with Chiara and the twins in Vincenza's carriage. Zabrina had waved to them, promising to visit in the next year somehow, now that there was no longer a wedding to rush for. It seemed strange to Maddalena to plan anything again, even something a year off. It seemed a temptation of fate to expect people to show up when you wanted them.

She was sweating, though the air was cool and she wore nothing over her sundress. The world did not look the same as it had two years ago. Every other house along the road was crumbled. The forests where they'd slept on the way to the farm were now acres of burned trees sticking their twisted black limbs up from the dirt. But the fighting had stopped, and no more Italian sons would die, so people sang happy songs as they put their houses back together. They waved at the Piccinellis from their sunken roofs and invited them over for wine and *frittate*; they asked Claudio and Aristide to help them lift parts of a wall off their furniture.

The first night of their two-day trip, they slept in an abandoned house near Collarmele. One of its walls was missing, but the roof was stable and there was enough room on the floors to spread blankets. "Just think," Celestina said, as she wadded one of her old skirts into a pillow, "when we wake up tomorrow, it will be the day we come home."

"Yes, just think," said Carolina.

Maddalena couldn't sleep. Her legs ached from the hours in the carriage, and her scalp felt as if it were on fire. She prayed, as she did every night, that Vito was safe and that her house was standing. She prayed he didn't hate her for sending only one letter, if her suspicions about Sebastiano were true. She prayed that her brothers were waiting for them, playing bocce in the piazza with the old men.

It rained the next morning and soaked the clothes and blankets in the uncovered carriage. By the afternoon the skies were clear. The closer the Piccinellis got to Santa Cecilia, the worse the world looked: the grass flattened by tanks, the villagers singing less and working harder. Scraps of uniforms hung from tree branches. At one turn in the road, someone had arranged animal bones to spell out "*Grazie, Il Duce.*" It made Maddalena shiver. Planes still flew overhead, waking her from whatever restless sleep she fell into, but they seemed almost friendly now, as they, too, were on their way home.

They passed through Broccostella, where the villagers looked up at them sadly, nodded in recognition, then went back to work on their houses. The tunnel of trees leading out of the town and into Santa Cecilia seemed to sag. At the entrance sign, still proudly announcing their tiny village, Aristide's carriage stopped. Claudio pulled up alongside him. Though it was almost summer, the leaves on the olive trees were thin and the ground a mess of muddy patches. In the center of the hill, a crater the size of a tank had been half filled in with dirt and rocks a different color from the rest. Maddalena could hear her mother and the twins sobbing from the next carriage, but she and Carolina kept calm. Claudio was talking to himself:

"It's not as bad as I thought, so far," he said, and kept on about how he'd expected one big pile of rubble and cats crawling in and out of the holes and women screaming; he kept talking as the carriages started up again and they passed the bombed-out barber shop and the sunken porch of the Al Di Là. Most of the houses had not been touched, but even those looked strange: weeds grew through the cracks in front, gardens overgrew into the street, and statues lay on their sides.

"Piccinelli!" their old friends called from their windows.

Farmers and shepherds walked alongside the carriages, their faces caked with dirt. "Welcome home," they said, and shrugged.

Celestina and Aristide waved to their neighbors and asked after the health of their families, but the rest of the Piccinellis kept quiet. They fixed their eyes ahead as they turned the bend in the road.

Then, there it was—unless they were dreaming—their house and store more perfect and lovely than when they'd left. Not only was it standing, but the outside of it gleamed white and the front door grate was polished black. The glass in every window had been replaced. Even the soot from the window in the Grotto had been wiped clean.

"Giacomo!" Chiara called out. "Maurizio!" She leaned over the carriage door. "My sons are home!"

"I don't believe my eyes," said Celestina. She looked around her in all directions. Fulvio Drago's house was still a mass of rubble; the Castellanis' was black with soot, the heads of their precious lions cracked off and lying faceup in the grass; the Puzos' was a mess of purple and green weeds, some of which were growing through the glassless second-story windows.

"They wanted to surprise us!" Chiara said, as she pushed on the door of the carriage with her leg. "Let me out, Aristide!" She called again, "Giacomo! Maurizio!"

Then Guglierma Lunga appeared on her terrace. She leaned over, yelled, "Piccinelli!" and waved. They turned to her.

"Saint Christopher told me you'd be back today," the old woman said. "I was waiting for you. Ask me anything. I can tell you who's dead and who's not, and who's still missing."

"Why is our house so nice?" Celestina asked.

Guglierma shook her head. "It's no miracle," she said. She poked her cane through the bars of the railing. "God didn't reach down and spare you and leave the rest of us to suffer. Believe me or not, you have Vito Leone to thank for your beautiful house."

"Vito Leone?" Aristide said. "I don't understand."

"Where's Giacomo?" Chiara said. "Where's Maurizio?"

"Who?"

"My brothers!" said Claudio.

"Oh," said Guglierma. "I already forgot them." She rattled the bars with her cane. "I'm sorry, but that's not a good sign. The saints don't mention them anymore."

"They're not back?" Aristide asked. "They didn't do this?" He had tears in his eyes. "Don't lie to me, Signora. This better not be one of your games."

"Why would I lie?"

"It's for Maddalena," Carolina said, half under her breath. "All this—" She opened her arm toward the house and spoke louder. "It's one big kiss of love from Vito Leone."

"Is he crazy?" said Chiara.

Maddalena's head was spinning. "Is he alive?"

"His ghost didn't do this, *principessa*," Guglierma said.

They walked through their house as if in a new country. Every wall, inside and out, was newly painted. Dishes had been glued together and stacked and displayed in the china cabinet. The dining chairs had been recarved, the table repaired, the floors swept. Vito had even scraped the burned parts from the kettle, and left a framed picture of the Sacred Heart on the counter next to a bowl of dried chestnuts. He'd washed and folded Maddalena's shawl and left it on her bed.

He'd put the store back together, too, righting the aisles and mending the barrels. As Maddalena watched a dazzled Claudio shake his head in admiration, as she walked through the rooms of what was now a house as good as new—no, better—she felt the life she wanted stretch out before her. It had become more than a possibility. Her father put his hand on her shoulder and said, "Look how you saved us."

Still dazed, the family gathered on the terrace. The carriages stood, fully packed, in front of the store below them. They walked in circles around one another, like pigeons. "What does it mean?" Celestina kept asking.

"If only it were my Giacomo, or Maurizio," Chiara said. She'd been sobbing since the moment Guglierma took them away from her again.

"Be grateful," said Aristide.

"I am grateful," Chiara said. She wrung her handkerchief between her fingers. "But it's too much—it's not right. The boy's wrong in the head. What does he want? Money? I don't like when people do things for me; I don't like the obligation. I don't trust anyone anymore."

"Grateful," Aristide said, more forcefully. "If God could hear you—"

"I don't think he wants money," said Teresa. She spoke slowly and without emotion. "Listen to Carolina."

"He wants Maddalena."

"It can't be," Chiara said. "He's more crazy than I thought. Who told him he could come into our house? How did he get in? To think: while we were away, he was walking through our rooms. It's scary."

"It's romantic," said Celestina.

Maddalena knew enough to keep her mouth

shut. One by one, the families who'd already returned to Santa Cecilia appeared below her on the street. They'd gotten word that the Piccinellis were back, and now they brought wine and cheese and cookies sprinkled with precious sugar. Aristide invited them up, and soon they crowded the terrace, talking so fast that their words spilled into each other. They described the ruined church, which the Piccinellis hadn't yet seen; they whispered about the determination of Vito Leone. Ada Lupo, who'd grown plump, was there; and Fiorella, who talked about Luciana as if she were just another girl who hadn't yet come back from the retreat. "Can't you just hear her when she finds out what Vito did?" she said. Teresa and Celestina huddled in the corner with a few of their snobby friends, one of whom carried a baby. The friends gossiped about the soldiers who were still missing. When Maddalena heard that Buccio was among them and that no one had heard from him for months, she felt almost grateful. Buccio would be lucky, she thought, if he never returned.

But she couldn't concentrate on much of anything people were saying. She kept looking down at the street, over to the piazza in the direction where Vito would soon come. She thought of slipping down the back stairs through the woods to his house, but she didn't have the courage.

After a while, as the sun was setting and the families began to leave, he appeared. He stood alone near the butcher shop. His hands were in his pockets. It had to be him. She grabbed the railing and watched him walk up the street.

Even from this distance and in the twilight, he looked bigger than she remembered. His shirt, a green one she'd seen many times, fit more tightly around his arms and chest. He walked slowly, looking back and forth from the ground to her; he was smiling but seemed afraid to come closer. She had the urge to throw her arms around him, to kiss his lips and every inch of his face and neck and chest. She was, for the first time, and in spite of what everyone said about him now and over the years, proud of him.

"Vito Leone!" she heard Claudio call. He and Aristide were in the street, unpacking the carriage. Everyone on the terrace turned around and watched Claudio approach him and hold out his hand. "It's true what we hear?" Claudio said. "You did all this?"

Vito nodded. He glanced up at Maddalena, then back to Claudio. Aristide walked up and offered his hand, as well. The men leaned in close and said something Maddalena and the others on the terrace couldn't hear. Then they started laughing, and Claudio clapped Vito on the back.

Carolina came up behind Maddalena. "This is either the smartest or the stupidest thing he's ever done," she said.

"I thought he was dead," Maddalena said. She covered her mouth with her hand. "And now he's not. I don't care what the rest of it means."

The men looked up from the street. Vito waved and blew the sisters a kiss. He fixed his eyes on Maddalena, who waved back and managed to call out a weak "thank you." It was all she could say in front of this audience. When she got him alone, when she could look at him up close and feel his heart beat and the strength of his chest against hers, she'd find the right words to convince him how grateful she was.

CHAPTER 18

Maddalena waited on the church steps for the procession to start. She wore the pale green chiffon dress her mother had sewn over the last month, and a hat with a matching silk ribbon tied under her chin. It was long past noon. The crowd that lined the streets of the village were fanning themselves. Maddalena was about to ask Carolina what was taking so long, when she felt a tug on her sleeve.

"*Buongiorno, bella,*" Vito said. He, too, had on his best clothes: a pair of light-colored pants that seemed new, shiny shoes, a pin-striped vest. He'd slicked his hair back. Before Maddalena could respond, he whispered, "I have something important to tell you."

He asked her to meet him in their new secret place down the hill behind the church. He'd tell her the important news there, the minute the procession ended. "Don't be late," he said; then he nodded at Carolina and disappeared down the steps.

It was the Festa di Sant'Anna, the third weekend in July, when Santa Cecilia threw Our Lady of Mothers a big party. Saint Cecilia herself didn't get this much fuss—her feast day fell in late November, when it was much too cold to parade in sleeveless dresses and dance past midnight. Her village had hosted this festival for Saint Anne every year as far back as anyone could remember, long before the church was built in Cecilia's name and through two wars since.

Every village had its own traditions, but in Maddalena's mind, Santa Cecilia's were the best. Their rose petals arranged on the streets in the shapes of hearts and crosses seemed to grow naturally from the dirt. Their statue of Saint Anne—rescued by Don Paolo when he fled after the surrender—was the most finely carved of all the statues Maddalena had seen. The saint's eyes, humanly sad, seemed to follow her as she marched beside her in the procession. Each house was decorated with the family's nicest bedspread, hung from the front windows like a colorful painting. The gold stitching sparkled in the sunlight.

When the procession finally started, though, and Maddalena followed little Don Paolo through the village with the other girls, she had to struggle to keep up her sense of joy. As much as she tried to ignore it, the world around her had changed, and kept changing as she marched. The church had caved in on one side. Evelina Drago, who'd moved in with her sister in the next town, had laid her bedspread over the wall that had fallen on old Fulvio. In the olive grove, lily petals were spread over the crater to transform it into a pale yellow sun.

Yes, plenty of young men still lined the road

and climbed the wall that overlooked the gorge to spot the pretty girls. They whispered to their friends and smoked and pointed, and the brave ones ran up to the girls they liked, to try to reserve a dance for later. But this year, most of these men wore soldiers' uniforms instead of suits. They had bandages wrapped around their heads or arms, and some had stopped speaking altogether.

One of these soldiers—Maddalena could hardly bear to look at him—was Buccio Vattilana. He'd shown up a week ago, in a pack of rough-looking soldiers on their way to Rome. He'd grown a beard so thick it hid his mouth. No longer chubby, he stood now on crutches in his sagging uniform. He watched Maddalena pass, seeming to look through her, his face expressionless. A torn piece of fabric hung where his left leg used to be. The Campinis had arranged themselves on the other side of the road, facing him. They no longer acknowledged any Vattilana and never mentioned Luciana to anyone. The loss of Buccio's leg was not punishment enough, they said, for what he'd done.

Every Sunday, Maddalena and Carolina had laid flowers at Luciana's corner of the Campini crypt and cleaned the dirt from the grooved letters of her name. For the baby, who never got a name or a space for them to clean, they took one flower from Luciana's bouquet and threaded it through the grate. They crossed themselves and prayed for their souls.

Maddalena thanked God for reaching His hand down to shield her. He'd spared her for reasons she didn't understand and wasn't sure she deserved. Not only did she survive a war, she was now celebrating in a new dress, waving to people in the piazza of her home village. After the celebration, she'd meet the man who loved her, and they'd kiss in a clearing under the pine trees until it was time to go dancing. Her parents didn't love Vito yet—Sebastiano had made them more suspicious than ever, they'd told her—but she forced herself to believe they simply wanted her to wait until she was older and her sisters had found husbands.

She was walking behind Celestina, who carried a basket of flowers. Her sister's legs were smooth and tanned under her powder-blue skirt, her elbows locked at her sides; she walked carefully, afraid to trip in front of any man who might consider her for his wife. She'd almost made them late, begging Carolina to convince her that the hair she'd spent all morning pinning up didn't make her nose look too big—though, sadly, it did. Celestina was not ugly, even with the nose; she was just plain, with a face like a statue's scrubbed of its sharp edges. Carolina and Teresa marched beside her, hands folded across their chests, eyeing the men darkly and mouthing the words to the Latin chants. Watching them, Maddalena worried that maybe someone a long time ago had put a curse on the girls of Santa Cecilia that made them unlucky in love; she asked God to spare her from this, too, then apologized to Him for asking too much.

Maddalena took Carolina's hand as they passed

the store and smiled up at their mother, who was waving from the terrace. If this were another year, she and Carolina would have been whispering and giggling, but they hardly talked anymore. Maddalena would mention something important—Vito, Fiorella, the sadness that followed Teresa like a cloud—and Carolina would shrug and say it didn't matter. But since Konrad, Carolina went along with Maddalena's secret meetings. She even spoke kindly to Vito when she saw him in the store. Whatever war the two of them had been fighting, she seemed too tired to keep up.

"I'll say you went to Ada's," Carolina said, after the procession ended. "But don't be long. Everyone knows Ada's not that interesting."

Maddalena found Vito sitting on the grass, rolling a cigarette. She didn't like him to smoke when they were together, so he quickly stuffed it in his pocket. "How beautiful you look," he said, and opened his arms out for her to step into.

Of all the changes that had happened in Santa Cecilia since Maddalena left, the change in Vito surprised her the most. He'd helped every family, not just hers, repair their house. He stayed up late, drinking and playing cards with the soldiers who made it back from the war and their fathers and grandfathers. When these men came to the store, they made fun of him for never winning any card games, but not the same way they'd made fun of him before. Instead of silly, they called him unlucky, a young man whom God left behind and was trying to win back. Vito had grown taller, his voice deeper. He'd chipped a tooth, and it stuck out as sharp as a fang, making him look almost tough.

Maddalena untied the ribbon under her chin, pulled off her hat, and tossed it onto a dry branch. She felt again the miracle of Vito's muscles around her waist. He kissed her on the mouth, pressed himself against her, and reached into her dress until she stepped back. "Vito," she said.

This roughness, as new a part of him as the strong arms, both thrilled and frightened her.

"I'm sorry," he said.

"You have something to tell me," she said.

"Yes." He kissed her again. He shifted his feet. He held her at her shoulders and looked her in the eye. "I've been writing to my Zio Gabriello," he began. "In Naples. The tailor. The one who taught my father. He's old now, and doesn't get much business, but he tells me that if I leave here and go, to Naples, he'll teach me the trade. And then I'll have a job, a good one, and make enough money for both of us."

"Leave here?" Maddalena said. It was all she heard. "For how long?"

"That's the one thing," he said. He kept his eyes fixed on hers. "Years," he said.

"Years?"

"This is what I learned, Maddalena," he said. He tried to pull her down to sit on the grass, but she resisted.

"My dress," she said.

"I have no life here without a trade," he said. "During the war, nothing made sense. After the war, everything's clear. I'm not smart enough for a government job, but I know I'm smart enough to be a tailor. I'm good with my hands—everybody says so. And I thought, I'd visit you every week if I could, then move back to Santa Cecilia when I'm done. I'll set up a shop in my house downstairs, like your store, like my father had. And by then, your sisters will be married, and your mother will stop staring at me like I'm about to punch her in the face, and everything will be perfect."

"She doesn't stare—" Maddalena started to say, then stopped. Vito was smiling at her.

The week after her family returned to the village, her parents had taken chickens and ricotta and a tray of cookies to Vito's house to thank him, and promised him and his mother free groceries for the next five years. They said he'd always have a place at their dinner table, if he wanted it. Chiara had even taken Concetta an expensive gold necklace. But the visit was short, and afterward they'd sat on their terrace above the store and made fun of the Leone house and hoped the Piccinellis were now done with that family forever.

"I'm smart enough to see that what I did for your family wasn't enough," he said, then whispered, "especially with what happened to Teresa. I still have to prove myself. You're sweet not to tell me, but I know I still have far to go. If I didn't, you'd be my wife already."

The night Chiara had given Concetta the necklace, she'd led Maddalena by the hand into her bedroom and closed the door. She sat Maddalena on the bed, stood in front of her, and told her, with a waving finger and anger in her voice, that she and Aristide would never allow Maddalena to marry Vito Leone. Maddalena was too precious, she'd explained, and too beautiful and smart to waste on him. What he'd done to the house seemed done out of kindness—and that was how they had to treat it on the outside—but it was anything but kind. It was arrogant. He was trying to force the Piccinellis into something, and no matter what the village gossips said, they were never going to let him do it. Sebastiano had taught them something, Chiara said, and they wouldn't make the same mistake twice.

Maddalena had listened quietly to her mother and pretended to go along. "I understand," she'd said, then spent the last month praying to God to put love for Vito in her mother's heart. She tried to protect Vito from even knowing the prayer was needed, but he seemed to know all along.

"What about your mother?" Maddalena asked now.

"Listen to how well it works out," Vito said. "I help a family with their house; they check on my mother as much as she needs. That's my payment for all the work I've done here. They take turns. And now that the war's over, the nuns will come more often."

Maddalena rubbed her eyes, trying to hide the welling tears. Just as her life started to settle, here came this new disturbance. "This doesn't sound like you," she said. "You said you'd stay here forever. Now you're leaving for years, and maybe you'll find some other girl in Naples."

Vito covered her mouth. He smiled at her. "Ssh," he said. "I don't want any of this plan. What I want is to stay here and marry you and work in your store. But I can't. And my waiting around will only make it worse. I thought of this when I was waiting for more of your letters, and when they never came I thought, You have to make your own life, Vito. So I'm going to Naples, Maddalena. It's not so far, and it's not for me, it's for us."

"You've already decided, then?" she said. "You're not telling me to ask what I think. You're just telling me."

The band started up on the other side of the village—a crash of drums and horns and guitar, then the first notes of "Incantatella." They'd play through dinner for the customers at the Al Di Là, who had to eat on the left side of the front porch now that the right side had sunk into the street. Vito took Madalena's hand and tried to swing it to the rhythm, but she kept it limp.

"This is good news!" he said. "This is how we'll be together for real. No more meeting in the bushes. No more secrets. In a few years, we'll dance in the piazza in front of everyone. There's only one other way we can do it, and I know you won't like it."

"What?" Maddalena said.

"We go to Naples together," he said. He lowered his head. "We run away, get married there, live with my zio."

"No," she said immediately, without a thought. She saw herself alone in a little apartment in Naples, no family around her but this old Gabriello, whom she'd never met. Vito would be sewing in the next room, hunched over yards of fabric in his lap. She'd heard Naples was dirty and the people vulgar, that the war had ruined anything beautiful there. If Teresa had gone to Verona, she'd at least have had Sebastiano's sisters and parents around her, and the shimmering lake, and could take a train to Santa Cecilia whenever she wanted. If Maddalena moved to Naples against her parents' wishes, they'd slam the door in her face if she tried to come back.

"I didn't think so," Vito said.

"It's all too much," Maddalena said, though the second plan made the first almost welcome. She reached for her hat and tied it back on. "You won't leave soon, right?"

"After Ferragosto," he said, and started back through the trees. "Maybe even two months."

She shook her head. "I've barely been home two months," she said, but he was already far ahead of her, rushing to hear the music. "It's not fair."

Just before the road, he turned and waited for her to catch up. He untangled a twig from her hair, wiped her eyes with his handkerchief, and promised that this was the best idea he'd ever had. Then they separated: she toward the road, he behind the church, so as not to be seen coming from the darkening woods together.

The band began the evening's festivities at sunset by leading the people of ten villages in the tarantella. The wooden platform wobbled beneath their instruments and the armies of kids who raced across it to appear for a few seconds onstage. Colored lights illuminated the trees from the spring to the bend, and the circle of the piazza had become a dance floor. Vito rested his elbow on his new friend Claudio's shoulder and felt lucky. He'd never loved the Festa di Sant'Anna the way he did tonight.

He remembered his last Festa, before the war broke out, when he and Buccio had hidden under the platform, trying to look up the girls' dresses. They'd seen nothing but a few white flashes of underwear. They'd suffered through the entire holiday in tight suits, sweating and mumbling Latin words they didn't understand, pretending to admire the laundry hanging from the windows. Only the midnight fireworks had thrilled them. They'd claimed a place on the wall of the gorge and watched the colors explode for what seemed like hours. The finale was their favorite: the bursts of white light followed by chest-shaking booms, what Buccio had called "thunder and lightning bombs." They'd lain back and closed their eyes and imagined the mountains falling over.

Since then, Buccio had seen real bombs, and bullets rip through the chests of men a foot away. He'd seen his own leg cut off and thrown in a bag, and the grave of his *fidanzata* and unborn child. He'd become a drunk. He could barely stand on solid ground during the procession, let alone a crumbling narrow wall over a thousand-foot drop. Vito watched him now, as the band played "Facetta Nera." He took a few staggering steps, then passed out on one of the Castellanis' lions. His father, never far behind him, quickly pulled him off and dragged him away.

"Are you going to bid?" Claudio was asking.

It was almost nine o'clock, and the old ladies were gathering in front of the platform to assemble a pile of rags into a giant headdress. The men waved their lire, trying to win a chance to wear the disguise. Once the winner put it on, he had one full song to dance around the circle and brush up against the girls. The headdress had a scary face drawn onto it this year: a wide mouth with crooked teeth, a mass of multicolored shirtsleeves for hair, and hollow, egg-shape eyes.

"You think I should?" Vito asked.

Claudio shrugged. "It's a stupid peasant tradition that makes no sense. You pay all this money, you knock into a few giggling girls, and it's over. Then they start the bidding again. I ask you, why pay a fortune to be the first one if they're going to do it again as soon as the song's over? Why not wait until the end, when most of the men have played already and it's cheaper?"

"So you won't bid?" Vito said with a grin.

"Of course I'll bid," Claudio said. "How else can I touch those bodies?" From his pocket he pulled a wad of money wedged in a silver clip.

Vito scanned the crowd: the girls in their sundresses rubbing their arms, the men counting and pooling their bills, Maddalena in a pack with Carolina and Ada and Fiorella. Her hair, unpinned and freed from the hat, lifted and fell onto her bare shoulders as she talked. This was the first year he was old enough to wear the mask.

He carried a hundred lire, nearly all he had to his name. The rest of the country and most of the world had come alive again, and still his father had sent no money or letters since Christmas the year before. Most of what Vito had saved he'd used to fix up the Piccinelli house, to buy paint and wire and glue and pay strangers who helped him. But the Piccinelli grocery was now his kitchen—meat, pasta, candy, all his for the taking—and until now, what else had he needed money for?

So many people filled the street that it was hard to tell who was bidding. The leader of the band stood at the end of the stage, pointing to men on both sides. The crowd grew quiet between bids, then gasped and giggled and whispered whenever someone bid higher. When the price reached twenty, Claudio waved his hand. Someone buried in the crowd raised him. Vito tried thirty, but the same person beat him, too.

"Who's over there?" Claudio asked. He craned his neck, but all he could see was an arm sticking out from a pack of people. He bid again. The man immediately raised it.

"Your turn," Claudio said to Vito.

"How much do you have?" Vito asked.

"I'm going to tell you?" Claudio said.

Vito noticed Maddalena watching them. He waved his hand to increase the bid once more and she smiled. No one challenged him right away, and he assumed he'd won.

But then the bandleader called again on the invisible man. The crowd swayed to get a look at him. The musicians stomped in place on the stage, making a rumbling sound. Dr. Fabiano's nephew started a run of bids with the stranger, whom the crowd now parted to reveal. As best Vito could tell in the torchlight, he was an older man, thirty at least, with short, dark hair. He wore a suit with the jacket sleeves rolled up. No one was talking to him, only staring and pointing and turning to whisper to someone else. He looked familiar, but not enough to place him.

"Well?" Claudio asked Vito.

"It's too much money," Vito said.

"But it's an honor to be the first of the night," Claudio said. "It's prestige!"

"*Vaffanculo*, you and your prestige," Vito said,

smiling. "I'll wait until later. Maybe I'll go twice."

But Maddalena kept glancing in Vito's direction. Carolina lifted her chin at him. He took a breath. "One hundred lire," he shouted to the bandleader.

The crowd clapped. The drummer struck his cymbal. From the roof of his shop, the butcher called down, "Good man!" and held his cupped hands over one shoulder, then the other, a sign of victory.

Then: "I double that." The stranger waved a handful of bills at the bandleader and walked over to the old women. He was taller than Vito but seemed no bigger.

"What a night for the church!" the bandleader said. "Am I right, Don Paolo? Can you spend all this money?"

"If only it were enough," Don Paolo said, shaking his head. "With all my hungry ones, ten times a hundred won't save them."

No one paid him any attention.

"Come on, Vito!" the crowd was shouting. "Dig deep!"

He'd bid everything he had and was too proud to borrow from Claudio. If only this were two years from now! he thought. He turned toward Maddalena, pulled out his pockets, and threw up his hands. "Next time," he mouthed.

"No one?" the bandleader said. The crowd quieted. "Do we finish with two hundred lire, then? The highest bid I've ever seen in this town?" Everyone was looking at Vito.

"I'm done, Signore," he called toward the stage. "The well is dry. For now."

"All right, then! We have a winner!" Everyone clapped, and the band played a few notes of *allegria*. "What's your name, Signore?"

"Antonio Grasso," he said, and bowed three times, once toward each section of the crowd, like a senator.

"So that's him," said Claudio. He folded his arms. "The great flower-picker."

"He's back?" Vito asked.

Antonio kneeled on the ground as one of the old ladies fitted the giant mask over his head. She steadied him and helped him up, and he stood still for a moment, staring everyone down through those oval eyes. He shook his head, hard, and made a growling noise. The hair of sleeves spun out around him. The girls, squealing with every shake and growl, took their places around the edge of the dance floor as the music started.

"Don't you live in this town, Vito? It's not so big you can't follow what's going on. He's been here for a week, staying with his aunt in Broccostella—your old teacher, Signora Grasso."

"I know who the Grassos are," Vito said. They were a rich family who'd lived near Dr. Fabiano when Vito was little, then moved to America not long after his father and sisters. Signore Grasso had opened a *tabaccheria* in Santa Cecilia, then a bakery, and though they both failed, he still had enough money to take his wife and kids across the ocean. Antonio was five or six years older than Vito, and they'd never played together or even spoken, as far as he could remember. Now he looked older than twenty-six. "What do you mean, the great flower-picker?"

"He's here for a wife," Claudio said. "All week he's been inviting himself to the house of every single girl in the village. He wants a bride from the old country to take back to the new. He'll be at our house soon enough."

Vito looked at him.

"For the twins, or Carolina, God help him," Claudio said. He slapped his back. "Don't worry about it. You should be happy! The sooner they get married, the sooner you have a chance with Maddalena." He turned Vito toward the dance floor. "Now watch him. See which girls he bumps into most, and maybe we can tell which flower he'll pick. I bet Ernesto Drago five lire he'd pick the fattest one."

Antonio hopped around the piazza, whirling his head to brush the sleeves against the circle of girls. He kept growling. He got on all fours like a dog and crawled toward a pretty girl from another town. Vito shook his head. You weren't supposed to jump up and down as though your feet were on fire, or make like some rabid animal. The costume was funnier if you danced in it elegantly and slid gently up to the girls you found beautiful.

The crowd clapped to Antonio's one song and watched him knock into not only Ada, Fiorella,

Clara, Carolina, Celestina, and Maddalena, but every girl in the ring. He had no taste, no understanding of the tradition, Vito thought. He went from girl to girl like a charging bull, with no dance steps in between. Instead of booing, though, the crowd cheered and laughed and chanted "Antonio! Antonio!" as the band began the final chorus:

> *O bella piccinina*
> You're such a little scamp!
> Blushing pink at that boy over there,
> Sweetly whispering a phrase,
> Winking in your red hair—
> You say hello, and then you go.

Antonio approached a girl Vito at first only half-recognized. She stood just outside the circle, by the corner near the side of the stage, clapping off-rhythm as if very tired. She wore a peasant's dress, as gray and heavy as a sack, and the shawl she had on the day he'd met her on her way to Broccostella. She was staring at Vito even as Antonio slammed into her and nearly knocked her down. He looked closer, but then the circle broke and the song finished and she was gone.

Had Filomena come looking for him? What did she want? Vito hurried toward where she'd stood, keeping one eye on Maddalena and the other searching faces for the *puttana* who'd probably set the Piccinellis' house on fire. He had Filomena to thank, in a way, for his change of luck, since without her he'd have had less to fix up—but that's not what he'd say if he found her. He'd warn her to keep her mouth shut and pretend they'd never met.

He wasted an hour looking. By the time he got to put the costume on, for thirty lire, the excitement had died down, and many of the girls had gone home to private parties thrown by their families. Maddalena and her sisters had waited, though, and when he'd elegantly crossed the dusty dance floor to the romantic tune of "Serenata Celèste," they seemed happy to see him coming.

He turned and arched his back against Carolina's shoulder, thinking maybe the girl wasn't Filomena at all but her ghost, come back to haunt the places she'd traveled. She might have been killed by soldiers on her way to Broccostella and could be looking for Vito to apologize. Her face did seem pale, her hair limp and unkempt, her eyes glowing, when he'd seen her across the piazza.

He brushed against Maddalena six times, Teresa and Carolina and Celestina twice, and Fiorella once, just to make her feel better. He'd followed the silly tradition the right way: with class, like a man, and when Maddalena threw her arms around him at the end, in front of everyone, it seemed he'd beaten Antonio Grasso after all.

CHAPTER 19

The next day, close to noon, Vito took his mother to the store. They walked slowly down the aisles, her head bobbing, his hand on her back to hold her up. They passed other customers: Signora Drago, inspecting whatever she touched and holding it close to her ears, two salesmen on their way to Frosinone, and Antonio Grasso sifting through bags of candy. He wore shiny black shoes and the same ash-colored suit as the night before. His hair was slicked back with a little too much grease, showing off a square forehead and dark eyes deep in thought over which color sweets to buy. When he noticed Vito, he nodded and whistled a tune.

Vito put a jar of *conserva*, two onions, four ounces of sugar, and six tomatoes on the counter in front of Maddalena. He pressed a bill and some coins into his mother's right hand. Though the groceries were free, his pride made him pay at least a little bit each time.

"Give the money to Signorina Piccinelli," he said.

It was very quiet. Behind Maddalena, Aristide

stood bent over a table, rolling pasta into long, flat strips. He sprinkled flour on the table and ignored the customers.

Concetta reached out carefully. Her arm was swaying. She bit her lip as one coin slipped from between her fingers and clanked against the counter. Maddalena grabbed it, and took the rest from her hand. *"Brava!"* she said. "*Grazie*, Signora!" She put the money in the drawer and recorded the items in her black book.

Vito kissed the top of his mother's head.

"I have to tell you, you look very nice today," Maddalena said. "That's a beautiful scarf." She rubbed the sheer golden fabric between her fingers.

Concetta's lips cracked into a smile. She kept her arm outstretched until Vito eased it down to her side. Staring at Maddalena, she said, "Sandra?"

"No, Sandra is in America," Vito said. "This is Maddalena."

Concetta reached up again, and Maddalena bent over as she laid her hands on her face. "*Cara* Sandra," she said. *"Cara."*

"No, Mamma," said Vito.

"It's all right," Maddalena said.

Vito shook his head. "It's no use," he said. "I thought today was one of her good days."

Antonio got in line behind them, crinkling a cellophane bag of caramels tied with a red ribbon. "*Buongiorno*, Signora Leone," he said.

"She won't remember you," Vito said. "She barely recognizes me."

"She's a wonderful woman," Antonio said, and kissed her hand. She straightened her back and smiled. "She was always kind to me. I used to come to your house to visit your sisters."

"Bello," she said, and patted Antonio's cheek.

"The Leones are all good people," Antonio said. "I see your father every once in a while in Philadelphia."

"I know," Vito said. "It's another Santa Cecilia over there."

Antonio laughed. He laid his hand, like a priest, on Vito's shoulder. He was maybe a head taller. "No, it's nothing like Santa Cecilia," he said, shaking his head. "Nothing at all. Some of the same people maybe, chasing one another across the ocean, but a whole other world altogether."

"I'm sure," Vito said.

"How is Signore Leone?" Maddalena asked Antonio. "Vito never talks about him."

Vito looked at her. He'd told her many times that whatever went on in America didn't matter. His father had abandoned him and his mother, and until he came back, he was as good as dead. Maddalena wanted to hear that he was rich, that his sisters were married to successful Americans, so she could tell her parents they could brag about at least half of Vito's family.

"Very well," Antonio said. "He gets more sewing business than he can take. Long hours, of course, and hell on a man's fingers, but it's good money. You never see Massimo Leone or his beautiful daughters without a needle and thread in their hands."

Vito helped his mother sit down on an upturned bucket by the door. "Rest for a minute," he said, and walked back to the counter. "If I could ask you, please, Antonio," he said quietly, "not to mention my father and sisters in front of her. It makes her very upset. I try to make her forget they're even alive, and just hearing their names—"

Antonio handed Maddalena money for the candy. "I apologize," he said to Vito. "I'm so sorry. There was no way I could know."

"Of course not," Vito said.

"But they'll be back soon, I understand, Signore Leone and his daughters."

"They will?" Maddalena asked. She closed the drawer.

"They will?" said Vito.

"For the wedding," Antonio said. "I'm told the two of you deserve my happy congratulations." He lifted the bag like a champagne glass. *"Auguri!"*

Aristide stopped his roller. He straightened up, turned around, and came toward them, wiping his hands on his apron. "Who's saying that?" he said. He glared at Vito.

"Not me!" Vito said.

"She's still a girl," Aristide said. He kept his eyes on Vito. "Watch yourself, *vaglio*."

"Oh, Signore, I'm sorry," said Antonio. "I'm all wrong today. No one talks about your daughter, except to say how beautiful she is."

Aristide turned back to the dough.

Antonio looked at his watch. It had a thick gold band. He wore cufflinks and a silk tie with diamond patterns, and his face was newly shaven. A man born with his shirt on, went the old expression.

"How long are you in the village?" Maddalena asked him.

"As long as it takes," he said, and winked. "You know I'm coming to your house for dinner in two nights, yes?"

"I do," Maddalena said.

"We're looking forward to it," Aristide said.

"I hope I don't keep saying the wrong thing," Antonio said.

"I'm sure you won't," said Maddalena. They smiled at each other as she straightened the bow on the bag.

Vito wanted to grab the man's face and rip the joy from it. "Who are your lucky hosts tonight?" he asked.

"*La famiglia* Lupo," Antonio said. "Do you think Signorina Ada will like these sweets?"

Maddalena nodded. "I can almost guarantee it," she said.

"Wish me luck, then," he said, and headed for the door.

"Oh yes, good luck," said Vito, but Antonio had already pushed through the door into the street, without a good-bye to Concetta. She sat quietly on the bucket, eyes closed, rubbing her hands together.

"The great flower-picker," Vito said to Maddalena. "What a *stronzo*."

Aristide turned around. "I told you to watch yourself."

"Excuse me, Signore," said Vito. "But I have to speak my mind. My father wrote to me about him a few years ago. I wasn't sure if it was the same man, but then I went and found the letter, and there was his name, Antonio Grasso, as plain as the nose on my face. My father said he saw him on the street in Philadelphia. 'Come for dinner,' my father says. Antonio says, 'Okay,' and Babbo and my sisters spend a lot of money on a lamb for him and his family, and they come—all ten of them!—and they eat the whole thing, without blinking. No problem. A year later? My father was still waiting to be invited to his house."

"If that's true," said Aristide, "I'm sure there's a good reason."

"Yes, that he's a *stronzo*," Vito said, quietly. "I was planning to come to dinner Thursday myself. Is there room at the table?"

Aristide didn't answer right away. "Of course."

On her bucket, Signora Leone was snoring. "You'd better take her home," Maddalena said. "We'll see you Thursday." She smiled.

"Of course," he said.

As he walked his mother down the main street, he felt the stares of people from their windows. He half-expected Filomena to jump out from behind a tree. Antonio walked far ahead of them, slowly, swinging his bag of caramels like an incense burner. Vito didn't trust him. Yes, he could easily pick Carolina or Celestina, and bring Vito that much closer to marrying Maddalena. But who would stop him from picking the youngest, the most beautiful, if he wanted her?

That night, Vito wrote a long letter to his father. He asked him to tell him all he knew about Antonio, and how well the Grasso family lived in America. At the end of the letter, he demanded money—a lot of money—because he deserved and needed it, and could no longer afford to wait two years to earn it.

CHAPTER 20

The Piccinellis' table had been moved into the center of the room, covered with a fancy white cloth, and set for nine. On each plate, a slice of bright orange melon sweated under a blanket of prosciutto. Maddalena stood in the doorway to the kitchen, wearing an embroidered blue dress and her mother's expensive rouge. Her hair was pinned back and held with silver clips. The first one ready, she was now supposed to tend to the kettle while her sisters and mother dressed.

Through a little window crowded with plants, she watched Antonio Grasso on the terrace, drinking wine with her father. They slouched in their chairs and drank from the good wineglasses. Aristide had asked Antonio to come at seven-thirty, a half hour before dinner usually started.

Someone was climbing the creaky back stairs from the store. "It's you!" she said, when she saw Vito.

"Who else?" Vito said. "The great Antonio Grasso has already come, and everyone else lives here." He knocked over an empty glass with his elbow, and it chinked against a candlestick. He held it up to the light. "Not chipped," he said. "Claudio let me in."

"You're early," Maddalena said. "I'm surprised. Everyone's still getting ready. You don't know how loud it is back there!"

"Ah yes, all the excited girls!" Vito said. "All wondering, will he or won't he pick a Piccinelli flower."

"Celestina's going crazy," said Maddalena. "She made us keep the hot rollers in twice as long, even though she kept saying, 'I smell smoke! Do you smell smoke?' " She smiled. "I'm so nervous for her, Vito. She's already in love, just from watching Antonio at the Festa. That's all it took. That and all his money."

Vito took a big sip of wine and stepped closer to her. "Do you see what I see?" he asked. He looked around the room.

Maddalena shook her head.

"We are, at this moment, alone together in the Piccinelli house."

Maddalena looked again through the window. Her father was leaning in to talk to Antonio, his back to her. "It's a miracle," she said, and wrapped her arms around him. "We should start a new holiday. July twenty-eight: The Festa of the Empty House."

And they stood there kissing, to the music of the women whispering in the back rooms.

When they heard Claudio pull down the storefront door, Maddalena said, "We don't have much longer."

"We never do," he said. "You know what I was

thinking? Antonio can take all the flowers, but I have the gold."

She laughed. She was nervous. "I'm sorry," she said, and touched his sleeve. "I'm not making fun of you. When did you come up with that?"

"Just now," he said. "To tell you what a rich man I am, that's all. It wasn't supposed to be a joke."

They jumped apart when the terrace door opened, though Aristide barely noticed them. "Where is everybody?" he said. He nodded at Vito. Just as Maddalena was about to answer, he said, "Who cares! Let's sit down. I'm at the head. Antonio, you next to me. Chiara!" he called. "We're inside!"

Antonio bowed to Maddalena. "It's very nice to see you, Signorina," he said. He turned to Vito and shook his hand, holding his other on top of it. "And you, Vito. How is your mother?"

His American accent gave his words a kind of thickness, as if they were spoken through a funnel. Maddalena hadn't noticed it before. He lit a brown cigarette, not waiting for an answer from Vito, and flicked the match out the front window. He sat back in his chair as Aristide poured the wine. Before he drank it, he held the rim of the glass to his nose. *"Perfetto!"* he said.

"Is it not like I told you?" said Aristide. "It's some of the last from my father's vineyard, now gone forever. We drink this only on special occasions."

Maddalena was about to excuse herself when her father said, "Come sit here next to me. You're not working tonight."

She sat across from Antonio and motioned to Vito to sit beside her. It was nearly dark outside, but the breeze through the windows was still warm and fluttered the lacy tips of the tablecloth.

Antonio's cigarette smoke curled in the air and unraveled into a cloud around Maddalena's head. It smelled like tree bark. She laid her fingers flat on the edge of the table and smiled politely at him.

"So when are you going to get yourself to America, Vito?" Antonio asked.

Maddalena looked down. Vito reached for the wine.

"There's no other place," Antonio said to Maddalena. "Italy, I was just telling your father, is finished."

"Finished," her father said, with a wave of his hand.

"Well, maybe I'll get it started again," Vito said. "I think you should see Venice and Florence and Naples before you give up on this country."

"I've seen all of those," Antonio said. "Venice is Venice, of course, and water doesn't burn the last time I checked. But Florence is a pile of rocks now, and even before the war, anything great in Italy was great a thousand years ago. Not anymore."

"Everything in America is great, you're saying," Vito said.

"No, but it's the future, *ragazzo*. This is the past. I would think your father—such a good man, the best tailor in Philadelphia!—would want you to know that, to see it, at least." He shrugged. "It's true, though; the trip is very expensive."

Vito's neck reddened. "Expensive or not," he said, "it doesn't interest me."

When the women came in, everyone stood up. Claudio appeared and took the seat across from Vito. Chiara stood between Carolina and Celestina, with Teresa behind them, staring at the ceiling. Antonio took Celestina's hand and kissed it. "It is my special honor to see you again," he said.

She managed only a mumbled, "*Grazie*, you too."

Carolina scowled as Antonio repeated the same gesture and greeting for her mother and Teresa. "Smile!" Maddalena mouthed to her when Antonio turned his back, but Carolina just rolled her eyes. When Antonio finally got to her, she tilted her head to the side and said, "So many honors in one day, Antonio."

"Carolina knows, of course," said Aristide quickly, "that young women call guests Signore when they're older."

Carolina looked at Antonio. "How old are you?" she asked.

"Twenty-six."

"Well, the twins are twenty-six, too, and Mamma, well, Mamma is twice that and more, I'm sorry to say." She took his hand again. "So, since *they* don't call you Antonio, I'll make up for the years myself. I called you Antonio when you were fourteen and I was nine, right? When I caught you stealing from our chestnut trees?"

"I think we should eat," Claudio said.

"Call me whatever you want," said Antonio. He patted her hand and made his way back to his seat.

Teresa sat next to Claudio, and Carolina next to her. Chiara remained standing. The usual arrangement, men at one end of the table, women at the other, was a jumble.

Just as they'd started to enjoy Celestina's *pasta ceci* soup, served by Teresa and Chiara, Aristide said, "Let's hear more about your new country."

"Oh yes!" said Celestina. "Tell us everything!"

"First let me say how delicious this soup is, Signorina," he said to Celestina. "Better than my mother's."

"I told you," said Aristide.

"In America," Antonio began, "everyone has a little bit of green around their house. It's not like Italy, where you have all green or nothing, and where it's nothing it's just dry and brown. Over there, people have a little bit of every color in their house, and they *move*. They leave these houses once in a while! They take trips to New York City with the tall gray buildings (you try to look up at them, and you fall over) and Washington, where all the buildings are white. There are dances every night of the week where I live—dances on wide wooden floors, to instruments you've never heard before—and all the Italian people live together and know each other by name.

That's how I know Signore Leone, and Vito's lovely sisters."

If they were so lovely, Maddalena thought, why didn't you marry one of them? They were the right age, and though she barely remembered Sandra and Silvia, she'd never heard anyone speak ill of them.

"My father was not poor, you know, in Santa Cecilia," Antonio said. "He didn't have to worry too much about money. He saved, and he helped give this man"—he pointed to Aristide—"a lot of business. The Grassos lived liked princes here, but in America, with two bakeries and a restaurant, we live like kings! I tell you, over there we're all fat! Thank God for the Irish food and the seasickness on the boat on the way here, or you couldn't have fit me through the door."

"Is that how your father describes it in his letters, Vito?" Carolina asked.

Vito shook his head. "No." He turned to Maddalena. "To him, it's not so great all the time."

"I'll tell you what's great," Antonio went on. "There's a street right near where we live, called Market Street. It's wider than three of Santa Cecilia's roads together and paved smooth with black tar, not muddy and full of holes like here. And it's crowded with cars morning to night. There are tall trees on either side of this road that grow pink flowers in the springtime, and when the wind blows, the trees cover everything, the cars and the men's hats and the grass, in bright petals.

And on each block—it just goes and goes!—there are twenty stores: some for ladies, some for men, everything you need! Ten groceries, gold and diamond jewelry, and restaurants with music and stone tables on the sidewalk. Does this village even know what a sidewalk is?"

Maddalena shook her head.

"I've seen them in Avezzano," Celestina said. "They're spectacular!"

Antonio turned to her. "Yes," he said, narrowing his eyes. "The nighttime is the spectacle, though. What we get in Santa Cecilia once a year at the Festa, they get every night from April to October. The streets are closed to the cars. Policemen in blue uniforms stand at both ends to keep them away, and the road becomes a dancing party. They lay down smooth wood floors on the street, so you can dance better. All the stores stay open until late, and the bands play on each corner—famous bands, ones you hear on the radio, not old men with big bellies—and women walk up and down with their *fidanzati* to show off the dresses and furs they bought that afternoon. It's like Rome used to be ten years ago." He turned toward the kitchen, where Chiara was busy clanging pots, and spoke louder. "I remember Rome like a dream, and now Rome . . . well, Rome is across the water."

"If I were a young man again!" Aristide said. "The life I'd live! Do you hear me, Chiara?" He shook his head and poured more wine.

She ran in from the kitchen. "What? What did I miss?"

It sounded beautiful, Maddalena thought: one long Festa di Sant'Anna, broken up with big dinners and trips to the city. Celestina looked more nervous than interested; Carolina had her arms folded, as suspicious as a cop; but Maddalena was moving through these pictures Antonio painted.

Vito pushed his chair closer to hers and rested his hand on her knee. Her hand found his and squeezed it. She wanted him to take her to America someday, after he'd made money and they were older and could take their children. If his father had made enough as a tailor to take himself and two daughters there, then Vito could do the same.

Later, Maddalena sat peeling an apple and listening closely to Antonio's story about the red, white, and blue parades on the Fourth of July when Carolina stood up from the table, downed her shot of sambuca, wiped her mouth, and said, "Excuse me."

Aristide's hand went to Maddalena's leg to hold her down. Vito's hand still rested on the other side. She pushed them both off, smiled at Vito, gave her father a look that said, I'll take care of her, and followed Carolina out to the terrace.

It was cold now. The candles Aristide and Antonio had lit earlier had burned down. A man was walking the street singing "Tu Scèndi da le Stèlle," though Christmas was still half a year away. Carolina stood in the far corner of the terrace, pulling pins from her hair.

"What's the matter with you?" said Maddalena. "You didn't say a word at dinner. You should be inside."

"Celestina I can see," Carolina said. She threw the pins onto the street, where they clinked like little bells. "They're the same age, and it's time for her." She shook her head. "But not you. When there's four of us, why should you get everything, and us nothing?"

"Would you speak quieter, please? The window is open."

"Do you think I care?" said Carolina, louder than before. "Do you think it matters to me?" Maddalena walked toward her, but Carolina held her at arm's length. "I don't want you to say anything sweet, okay? For once in your life, don't act so nice."

"You think I want Antonio Grasso? With Vito sitting next to me?"

"That's not the point. The point is he wants you, and that he doesn't try to hide it, and that Babbo and Mamma, and even poor Vito, just let him talk and talk, and don't ever—not once—try to say 'Carolina has wanted to see another country all her life' or 'Carolina learned a little English from a soldier in Teramo.' It's never Carolina! Even tonight, it was the nice blue dress for you and the good make-up for Celestina—just in *case* he liked her better, but there was never a chance of that, was there? And what do I get? I have to do my own hair and fight for a place at the mirror at the last minute." She folded her arms and her eyes filled with tears. "Did anyone ever think, even for a second, that he'd pick me? Did you, as my sister, did you even once think he would?"

"You don't want me to be nice? All right, I will be honest and tell you that maybe if you tried to be more respectful to people, to not be always so difficult to talk to, then maybe—"

"To be like you is what you're saying," said Carolina. "To be nice on the outside all the time, but on the inside making all kinds of dirty plans in secret and thinking the worst about people—"

"When do I do that?" Chairs were moving in the dining room, and the singing man—it was Buccio, drunk again—was getting closer. Maddalena pointed to him. "You're thinking as straight as he is now."

"You're terrible to Vito. Do you even know how terrible? How much do you care, really care, about him? Honestly? With your heart? You say you love him, but if you really do, why don't you stand up to Mamma when she tells you he's not good enough? Why do you come crying to me, saying maybe one day she'll change her mind, but do nothing to help? That's what I would do. And so I see how you are. All those meetings with Vito I keep secret for you; and the night Luciana died when you snuck over to his house because you thought maybe you'd lost him for real, and you had to put him back on your leash. I'm the only one who sees it—too many things to even remember—but who can I tell?"

"Will you let me talk?" Maddalena asked.

"I'm tired of your talking."

"When did you start hating me so much?" Maddalena said. "How do you hide it? I could never hate you like this." She didn't let her respond. "I told you about Vito's plan to learn a trade. He knows I'll wait for him. All I do, Carolina—you know this—all I ever do is try to make everybody happy at the same time, to keep everyone together: Mamma and Babbo with me, me with Vito. I don't think that's a crime. It's the only thing in the world I'm sure about."

"That's the difference between you and me. Between me and everyone in this family. I want to fight—with a man, with you, with everyone! But I want to do it on the outside, not the inside, like I did with Konrad. I want a man who'll say, 'You want to call me Antonio? Okay then, I'll call you *strega*.'"

"I don't think that man is Antonio Grasso. And I don't think you know me, or anyone, as well as you say."

"I'll never find out what kind of man Antonio Grasso is," said Carolina. She folded her arms. "As for you, I know that since we were little, I've hated this place, and you've loved it more than the birds, more than the drunks! I thought at least we'd suffer here together, and get to be old ladies yelling at people from this terrace. I gave up Konrad for that. Maybe I started to hate you then, that day in the bedroom after they took him away, when you were so happy I hadn't left you. In the carriage on the way back from Zabrina's I wanted to scream. And now you'll be going for good, to a place I dream about, and leaving me here to rot."

"I'm not going anywhere," Maddalena said. "Where do you get these ideas? I haven't done anything. No one's said anything!" She shook her fists in front of her. Her face was burning, and she felt a dizziness like those first staggering steps after rolling down a hill. "Even if Antonio chooses me, which he won't—he's almost ten years older than me, Carolina—how do you know I'll go? That Mamma and Babbo will let me? How do you know I won't run away with Vito and live in Naples like he wants me to?"

"Because Naples is wrong and Vito is wrong, and you know it." Carolina turned her back to her. "You'll do what Mamma and Babbo tell you. You always have. And you know what? For once they'll be right. Antonio can give you what Vito never will. You heard him tonight. That's the best life anyone could wish for, and that life will never come to Santa Cecilia. Or Naples. When Antonio picks you, you'll say yes—because you should, and because, under all that love for Vito, you want to."

"I don't understand you." Maddalena stepped away, staring at the mistied crisscross straps on the back of her dress. The skin beneath them, pressed through the diamond shapes, looked red and itchy. She wanted to undo the straps and rub her back with oil and salt, to soothe them as Vito had done to her legs; she wanted to tell Carolina that her life could be easy if only she let it. Instead, she said, "You're breaking my heart."

The muscles in Carolina's back tightened. "That's two of us, then," she said. She turned and looked toward the dining room. "Soon to be three."

"I can't do anything about that. I can't choose who Antonio Grasso falls in love with."

The door opened and Teresa appeared in an apron, squinting to see them in the dark. "Are you finished?" she asked. "I can't keep banging the pots in there forever."

Carolina wiped her eyes and walked over to her. She took her gently by the arm. "I want to tell you this, Teresa," she said. "I'm so sorry about what happened in Frattoli. I'm sorry I did what I did without asking you first."

Teresa rubbed her palms on the apron. "Carolina," she said. "Every time you apologize you make it worse. I told you I don't think about it anymore. I pretend it never happened."

"Carolina's not good at that," Maddalena said.

"We're having a discussion," Carolina told Teresa. "I want to know what you think about it."

"All right," said Teresa.

"If a girl had to choose between Antonio Grasso and Vito Leone for a husband, who should she pick?"

"That's what you're arguing about?" Teresa asked.

They waited for her answer.

"I noticed it, the way Antonio talked only to you, Maddalena." She took her hand. "Celestina has no idea, I think. She thinks she's making an impression."

"Maybe she is!" said Maddalena. "You can't read his mind."

"Vito is a very good man," Teresa said, "and tries so hard, but you know the answer to Carolina's question. Everyone knows it—even Vito, probably. No one would blame you if you picked Antonio instead."

"What did I tell you?" said Carolina.

"You're both dreaming." Maddalena pulled her hand from Teresa's. "According to you, my love counts for nothing."

"You're eighteen," said Teresa. "When I was eighteen, I'd have ripped my heart out for Ezio DiDeo. Can you see me with him now? A butcher's son with meat in his fingernails?"

At least Ezio isn't a thief and a liar, Maddalena wanted to say. But she couldn't take any more of this. She pushed past them into the dining room, where Antonio sat with his elbow on the table and his head in his hand, listening to Celestina. He winked at her. Vito and Claudio had moved to the other end of the table and brought out a deck of cards.

"Want to play?" Vito asked, as she started to clear the dishes.

"No, *grazie*," she said. Then she rushed to the kitchen to hide her face.

THE CAR

CHAPTER 21

The good lace tablecloth was stained with more than two weeks' worth of wine, and Maddalena had run out of clean dresses. Aristide took money from the strongbox to buy American cigarettes for Antonio's many visits, and Chiara worried that all her dishes tasted alike. Carolina kept quiet around Antonio; she spoke mainly to the twins. Vito came twice more before Ferragosto, the August holiday, began, and each time sat with Claudio and paid little attention to Antonio's stories. Sometimes Antonio brought food, a lamb, a roasted pig, from his Zio Domenico in Broccostella, who'd promised to join them as soon as he could.

"Do you think he's talking to Babbo about me right now?" Celestina asked Chiara, the same question she always asked. It was two nights before Ferragosto, and the men were on the terrace drinking espresso with sambuca and playing *bestia* in the torchlight. "These big meals are making me fat."

Maddalena scrubbed the pot with a wire brush. She felt Carolina's eyes on her.

"You know how many girls there are in Santa Cecilia and Broccostella together?" Chiara said. "He's even gone to Pescosolido a few times."

"But he's had his dinner here every night for two weeks," Celestina said. "You can't tell me that doesn't mean something."

"It means he's having lunch somewhere else."

"No," said Celestina. "He's at home here with me, I can tell. He likes my cooking."

"But when will we know for sure?" said Carolina. "I'm getting tired. And if we're going to have a wedding, we need to plan."

"Stay calm," said Chiara. "There's plenty of time."

"It doesn't take long," Carolina said. "We fix up Teresa's dress; we talk to Don Paolo for ten minutes; we tell the Al Di Là to cook us a feast. What's left?"

"Stop, Carolina," Maddalena said. "You'll curse it."

"I want Zia Zabrina to come with Signora Vincenza," Celestina said. With Teresa out of the room, she talked more freely about weddings. "I want them to meet Antonio."

Chiara put her arms around her. "Listen, *cara mia*," she said. "You can't predict what a man will do. If you get your hopes up too high and he changes his mind, think how sad you'll be. Just try to put it out of your head."

"Think what marrying him would mean," Maddalena said. She picked up the pot and hung it from a hook in the wall. "You talk like it's a party in the next town, but if it happens, you'll never see us again. Never! America's not Naples, Celestina. It might as well be the moon."

"The trip is long, yes," Celestina said, "but Antonio has money. I can come back for Christmas every year if I want. And Antonio can pay for you to visit me over there. You forget what a difference money makes."

Maddalena shook her head.

"I'm surprised, Maddalena," Celestina said. She stopped and looked at her, and her eyes grew heavy. "To tell you the truth, I didn't think you'd miss me."

The men were making a lot of noise outside. Aristide coughed, still learning to smoke American cigarettes. Someone was banging on the table hard enough for the sound to echo into the kitchen.

"Of course I'd miss you," Maddalena said, and accepted Celestina's arms around her.

The store was busy the next morning, but Maddalena was happy to work. Claudio had taken the older girls shopping in Frosinone before most of the stores shut down for the holiday, and it felt good to keep her mind busy with something other than wedding talk and avoiding Carolina. Maddalena and Aristide worked well together, especially with so many customers. And it would only get better. Tomorrow, vacationers from all over Italy would arrive in Santa Cecilia and the villages around it to spend two weeks in the fresh mountain air.

Vito had hovered at the counter for a while in the morning, trying to get a moment alone with her. He came back in the late afternoon, but the crowd was just as bad. Some tourists had come early, and they lingered in the store asking about the quality of the nuts and olives and pasta they sold. Killing time was all there was to do in Santa Cecilia during Ferragosto.

Just before seven, the last customer strolled out the door. Since her sisters were away, it was now Maddalena's job to help her mother with dinner. First she needed to lock the store and pull the grate down, and for that she needed her father, who'd left over an hour ago without saying when he'd be back. She called for him upstairs, but no one answered. She checked behind the house, where he kept his tools, and looked up and down the street, but she found only Buccio. He walked by her, singing the old sad song "Goodbye Maria, and Take the Moon Away," and didn't respond when she asked if he'd seen either of her parents.

It was getting dark, and one by one the windows on her street lit up. "Mamma!" she called up the stairs, but again no one answered. She couldn't leave the store. After pacing back and forth in the Grotto, she gave up and rested her head on the counter, hungry and tired from the rushing around. She yawned. The church bell rang the hour.

By eight o'clock, Maddalena was near tears. She

propped a chair against the door of the store and searched all the rooms of the house. Everything was in place, but no one was home. No food had been prepared. The lights had not been turned on. She ran back down, took the chair from the door, and stood outside with her hands on her hips, waiting, desperate enough to ask Guglierma Lunga what had become of her family. Wind rushed through the open windows of the store, rattling the stacks of newspaper and sending the top sheets flying around the aisles. She leaned against the outside wall and folded her arms across her chest for warmth.

She was about to run to Vito's house for help when she heard the sputtering of an engine. A car was speeding toward her from the direction of the olive grove. Cars came more often since the war had ended, and now the bus to Avezzano came twice a day, but it still shocked her to hear that angry engine and see something move so fast up her little street.

The car slowed and flashed its lights as it neared. It stopped in front of the store. Her father jumped out from the backseat.

"What are you doing?" Maddalena asked. She shaded her eyes. "Where is everybody? Whose car is this?"

Aristide kissed her forehead, then pointed to the car as if that would explain. It was not unlike the one that brought news, except the front was taller and wider than the back. It seemed to sit up like a dog. She couldn't see the driver. Her mother, in the flowered hat and gloves Maddalena hadn't seen since Easter three years ago, peeked out from the backseat and smiled. She held her purse tightly to her chest.

Then Antonio Grasso stepped out, grinning, from the passenger seat, and came toward her. A man she didn't recognize waved to her like an old friend from behind the wheel.

"We're going to a restaurant," Aristide said. "In Avezzano."

"A restaurant?" said Maddalena. "Who?"

"All of us," he said.

"What about the others?"

He didn't answer. Maddalena glanced at her dress. "I don't look right," she said.

"I told you to wear something nice today," Aristide said.

"Because you said we might be busy," Maddalena said. "And we were. My dress is stained."

Antonio took her hand and kissed it. "It doesn't matter," he said. "You look beautiful as you are." Before she could argue, he led her around the car and opened the rear door. She slid in over the warm leather seats beside her mother.

"Be good," Chiara mouthed to her.

"This is my Zio Domenico," Antonio said, when everyone was in. "The uncle I've talked so much about during our many wonderful meals. The car belongs to him."

The man turned around and offered his hand

to Maddalena. His face was long and droopy-chinned. "It's an honor," he said.

In seconds they had reversed direction and were speeding toward the olive grove. Domenico pushed and pulled on the long pole that came up from the floor, and everyone lurched forward as the engine popped. It wasn't until Maddalena's head banged the roof that she knew for sure she wasn't dreaming.

They drove out of the village, down the hill past the entrance sign and through the tunnel of trees. It was here that she'd first felt Vito's strong hands, and the dust smoking up around the car reminded her of that day. He was probably in his kitchen now, she thought, cooking dinner for his mother. Later he'd come to her house for espresso and find the rooms empty. He'd worry. She wanted to get a message to him but didn't know how or what she'd say.

The car broke through the trees, the dust settled, and they rolled along the paved road, with fields on both sides and the sun an orange sliver on the edge of the mountains. Domenico swerved to dodge ditches and rocks, but when he hit them, the car bounced and threw Maddalena against the roof again. She rested her head on her mother's lap. Chiara stroked her hair and tapped her fingers on her back as if it were a piano.

"Slow down, will you, Zio!" Antonio said. He turned and smiled at Maddalena. "Is this your first time in a car?"

"It is," Aristide said, when she didn't answer.

This was nothing more than Antonio showing off, she told herself, and by accident it happened to be the day her sisters were away. Otherwise they'd be here too, squeezed in beside her. She pictured them in Frosinone, walking down the streets arm-in-arm, stopping for a *gelato* in a bar with tuxedoed waiters. "How's everyone else going to eat?" she managed to ask her mother.

She stopped stroking her hair. "You worry about the wrong things," she said. "They'll be fine."

Maddalena sat up when they drove through Broccostella, a town twice the size of Santa Cecilia but with half as many people. Domenico honked three times at a mule blocking the center of the street, but it didn't move to let him pass. The rider whipped it as hard as he could, then shrugged his shoulders and called out, "What can I do?" He pulled out a loaf of bread from the basket he was carrying and waved it at them. "With my apologies?" he asked.

"Stupid *Italiani!*" Antonio said. He shook his open hand at the man. "You know how long it would take to get from Santa Cecilia to Avezzano in the States? Ten minutes! There are lines in the road, and lights, and the only animals are squirrels—and you can run over those if you have to."

Chiara put a gloved hand to her mouth and laughed.

* * *

Maddalena had not been in Avezzano in over five years. It was the largest city she'd ever seen, and the wide piazzas and buildings—some over ten stories high—again amazed her. There seemed to be a fountain on every corner. The roads were paved but steep, lit every few blocks by gas lamps. The car rolled backward a little on one of the steepest hills before reaching the top. All of the Avezzani were dressed up and rushing around, even though it was dinnertime and most of the stores had closed.

In the center of town was a marble sculpture Maddalena had fallen in love with, even though it gave her nightmares. She'd stood in front of it five years ago, thirteen years old but still feeling like a child, and stared at the three men struggling to break free of one long, fat snake slithering between their legs and around their necks. The man in the middle had curly hair that stuck out far from his head, like a crown, and every inch of his face was stretched with pain. She remembered looking at his open, screaming mouth, at his rolled-back eyeballs, and imagining that the snake was coming for her next, about to lick her ankles.

They were approaching Avezzano *centro* when Antonio said, "Up here is where the bombs hit. Thanks to the speed of the Italian government, it looks the same now as it did three years ago." Maddalena craned her neck to look out the window as Domenico pulled over. "We can get out and look," Antonio said. "We're a little early for our reservation."

They stood looking at the dirt hole that used to be a square, bigger than the entire olive grove. Around the edges, someone had arranged a row of boulders to mark where people shouldn't cross. Half a building slumped in the center of the hole, its belly of rooms exposed. Facing the building on the other side, close to where Domenico had parked, stood the ruins of Maddalena's statue: its square marble base and, above it, the legs of the three men. Their bodies had been blown off at the waist; their arms and torsos were scattered in the grass below. Their heads stared up from the ground at what remained of them.

"It's a tragedy," Antonio said. "I used to try and draw this statue when I was a boy. I would sit in front of it for hours while my father did business in town, but I could never get it right."

Maddalena leaned forward over the line of boulders, toward a chunk of hand that pointed up from the ground.

"Don't try it, Signorina," said Antonio, smiling. "There's a policeman watching over every piece of that statue that's left." He nodded toward someone over by the fallen trees. "Zio tells me they're planning to rebuild it one day, and I say, what are they waiting for? Can't they at least gather up the broken parts and put them in the mayor's house? But the Italians have no sense."

Maddalena looked at him.

"If there's one sad thing about life in America,"

he said, "it's how fast you forget your childhood, a little each day, with nothing to remind you." He put his hand on her shoulder. "Don't worry, though. Somehow I'll take a piece of that statue with me. I might have to come back here in the middle of the night, dressed in black, but I'll get it."

The restaurant was called Paradiso. The host, a thin, red-cheeked man in a bow tie, was expecting them, and led them to a table by the window in front of a shelf of bright flowers. As they were about to sit, Chiara pinched Maddalena's leg and said, "Come with me." She asked the host, "Is your bathroom inside or outside?"

"Inside, of course," the man said. He walked them to the other side of the restaurant, through a long maze of bare stone walls.

Chiara pulled Maddalena into the room with her. It was cold and barely big enough for one, and the flimsy door didn't quite reach the ground. A dirty white toilet sat against the wall.

"It's time to tell you," Chiara said.

"*Now* it's time?"

Maddalena held the sleeve of her dress over her nose and stood cheek to cheek with her mother, pressed close to avoid touching the toilet or the door.

"Calm down and listen to me," Chiara said.

"What choice do I have?"

"Good, because this is already decided," said

Chiara. "All of it. Antonio has picked you as the girl he wants to marry."

Maddalena straightened her back against the door, though she feared the weight might crack it. "Too bad for him," she said. "Tell him to pick again."

"This is not a joke," Chiara said. "There was never a choice for him. He wanted you always, the minute he saw you all grown up at the Festa. He has a lot of money, Maddalena, and he's promised us he'll give you everything you could possibly want: a big house, a car like the one today, a good family to watch over you. This isn't like Sebastiano. We know his mother and father; we know what kind of man he is. He even heard about your impressions and said he could put you into an acting school in Philadelphia, if you'd like that."

Maddalena shook her head, as heat flashed through her body. No, that's not what she would like. She squirmed to grab the door handle, but her mother blocked her arm. "I'm as good as engaged to Vito, and you tell me to marry another man?" Maddalena said. "What kind of girl does that make me?"

"A smart one," Chiara said. She looked at her. "No one cares more about what people think than I do. They'll say you were smart enough to know that Vito is nothing and Antonio is something. You believe that already, not only because I'm telling you now. I know you, *figlia mia*."

"Why does everyone think they know me, when

they don't?" said Maddalena. "You don't know that I love Vito and can never love Antonio. It's as simple as that."

"Listen to me," Chiara said. "When I moved to Santa Cecilia, I was an eighteen-year-old girl, just like you. I was in love with your father because he was handsome and quiet and wore a velvet hat and came to my house all the time smiling. My mother and father were dead. They had no way to tell me I was making a mistake marrying a man who would never leave the mountains. Do you notice that the only time we leave Santa Cecilia, Maddalena, is to go to a place even sadder—with dead grapes and your silly aunt and that farm wife with the cigarettes? In some ways I was lucky with your father—I won't lie to you. He's been kind to me. He's never hurt me. If he's taken other women, he hasn't bragged about it like every other man in the town. But there were a hundred men as good as that in Rome, and fifty of them could have built a villa for a wife and family! That's what you don't know when you're eighteen, Maddalena: that there are plenty of good men in the world, and love is easy to feel for any one of them who takes care of you."

"Vito can take care of me," Maddalena said.

"How?"

"He's going to Naples. He's going to learn to be a tailor. He has it all planned."

"Like his father?" Chiara said.

Maddalena stared at her. "Yes."

"Look where he ended up," Chiara said. "You see? If you want the good life, you go to America. I can't have it anymore; I'm too old and unlucky; but I want it for you. Why wait twenty years for Vito when Antonio is ready now?"

"It won't be twenty years," Maddalena said. "If you give him a chance—"

"He never had a chance," her mother said. "I tried to tell you many times. He could fix every house in Santa Cecilia and he wouldn't have a chance with you. For any other girl in the village, he's more than good enough. He's probably the best in this town now, I give him that: for Carolina or Celestina, he's perfect. Carolina and Vito are the same age; they belong together anyway. He'd marry one of them, I think, if we asked him. For men, too, one woman's as good as the next. Except you." She stroked her hair. "If you could have heard how Antonio talked about you."

"This is crazy," Maddalena said. "I won't do it! I don't even know him. You can't make me marry somebody I don't want to marry."

"You're right," her mother said. "But I can say this: If you marry Vito Leone, you won't be our daughter anymore. It's because we love you, *carissima*. You should never have even thought of him."

Maddalena was crying. The inside of her body felt hollow, as if whatever was in her—heart, bones, blood—had spilled out onto the floor of the bathroom.

"You know the old saying," Chiara said. "'Who loves you makes you cry; who doesn't, makes you laugh.' Do you remember your nonna used to say that?"

"It's a stupid saying."

"You think so now," she said. "But remember: Your father and I, we love you more than anyone ever will, more than your sisters and your friends and Antonio and Vito put together, more than your own children will. That's why we're doing this. You can cry all you want, but if you don't marry Antonio, if you marry Vito instead, you can never come back to our house. We'll slam the door in your face."

"That doesn't sound like love to me," Maddalena said.

"We'll make it easy for you," Chiara said. "You won't have to do any of the hard parts. Claudio is telling your sisters now, in Frosinone. We'll talk to Vito, and his lunatic mother if we have to, when the time comes, when you're already gone. You'll never have to face him after he knows. Until then, we'll keep it a secret. And you'll forget about him sooner than you can imagine. You're not stupid, Maddalena. You knew this could happen."

"Carolina told me, but I didn't believe her," she said. She grabbed her hair at the roots, made two fists, and pulled. "Oh, God, how can you do this?"

Chiara held her hand over her mouth. "Don't let them hear you."

Maddalena pried her hand off. "You've been planning this from the beginning. You let us talk and talk."

Chiara stared at her.

"Babbo loves Vito," Maddalena said. "He doesn't think he's nothing."

"He does now," said Chiara. "The two of us are alike, Maddalena, you and I, but your father is different. He's spent his life in the store, and he thinks good people are the ones who are nice to him, even if they don't pay him. But he's spent a lot of time with Antonio now, and with Domenico, and he sees that the Grassos are like us: We don't belong in a town with three streets."

"It's not true," said Maddalena. "Nothing you're saying is true."

Chiara pulled her close and held her head down against her chest. The fabric of her dress, the most expensive she owned, felt soft on Maddalena's cheek. She cried into it to muffle the sound.

"How can I want you to leave me?" Chiara said. "You think this is your sacrifice, but it's not. It's mine. You're my beautiful Maddalena—my life! You were born in my house, and you were special from the first minute, always more special than the others. You knew that, too, right? Mothers don't love their children the same."

Someone knocked on the bathroom door.

"And after you're gone," Chiara went on, "don't you think I'll suffer? I'll still be alive, yes; I'll cook and clean and stand in church every week with your sisters, and when they marry I'll sew their dresses. But my heart will be half dead. And still I tell you: You have to go."

Maddalena grabbed her as tightly as she could, imagining the other world, the one Antonio belonged to. She tried to think of the places he'd described, but all she could see was a wide black road with strange people walking quickly toward her, speaking words she didn't understand. She'd have Antonio beside her, but she'd be alone. Her head felt heavy, and her mother's hands moving up and down her back, pressing against her spine, were making her dizzy.

They stood that way while the person on the other side of the door kept banging, until Chiara finally opened it and they stepped out of the tiny room. The woman outside was old and heavy, with puffy hair and a fat nose and a flower pinned to her dress. "It's about time," she said, and pushed in past them.

Chiara walked Maddalena back through the maze and the crowded restaurant to the table. Antonio and her father and Domenico stood when they approached. They all had bowls of steaming soup. She could smell the orange blossoms on the windowsill. Around her, plates were clinking and people chattering and throwing up their hands. Her mother sat her beside Antonio.

"Are you all right, *tesoro*?" he asked.

She couldn't look at him. She didn't know what

she had the courage to do. She watched her mother nod for her.

"She'll be fine," said Aristide.

Antonio shifted closer and put one arm over Maddalena's shoulders. With his free hand, he picked up her spoon, dipped it into her soup bowl, and held it to his mouth. He blew on it until it cooled. He pressed the spoon between her lips, and she sipped the broth.

CHAPTER 22

On his way to the Al Di Là, Vito kept swerving to avoid tourists. They swarmed from every direction, up the hill from the olive grove, down the steep road at the spring, through the woods behind Dr. Fabiano's house. They'd arrived in cars and buses, carrying bags of fruit and wearing wide-brimmed hats; they spoke muddy dialects, asking for the nearest hotel (Broccostella) or a fine restaurant (Avezzano). The city people flashed money when you pretended not to understand. Many hadn't seen their relatives in Santa Cecilia since before the war; they stood under balconies and screamed up, "I'm here! I'm here! Come get your zia!"

The tourists had kept the Piccinellis rich during the past two weeks of the Ferragosto, but all they'd done for Vito was make Maddalena too busy to see him. The store was crowded from dawn to sunset with people buying twice as much food as usual for their unexpected relatives, and tourists making up for it with gifts for the people they imposed on. The Piccinellis started selling maps and American magazines and expensive skin lotion popular with northerners. Aristide and Claudio made two or three trips a week to Avezzano to restock the shelves. The girls worked through the *riposo* and after dinner to bake cookies and tie them into bags, fill sausage casings, and organize the receipts. Vito tried to talk to Maddalena and arrange a meeting in their new spot behind the church, but she treated him as though he were invisible. Since the holiday had begun, she seemed rushed and distracted, so nervous that five minutes with her felt like five hours. Her father kept her upstairs, away from the loud and demanding customers, and told Vito she was too busy to see him.

And yet when Vito had offered to help with the extra work, Aristide had refused. "It would take too long to show you," he'd said, as he stacked empty boxes in the Grotto. "Wait until after the holiday, when everything's calmer, and I'll train you myself."

In the meantime, Zio Gabriello had written to Vito to confirm his apprenticeship. He could leave whenever he wanted, the night the holiday ended, if he chose. All he had to do was pack. Instead he sat for hours, as he was doing now, at the same table under the same red umbrella at the Al Di Là, smoking and making conversation with strangers. He watched people go in and out of the Piccinelli store across the street, nervous that one of them might be Filomena. But he hadn't seen her again since the Festa, and felt more relieved with each day that passed without her reappearance.

He watched Maddalena stand alone on the terrace. She rested her elbows on the railing and rubbed her face. She folded her arms and stared at the clouds, over her shoulders the shawl Filomena had tried to steal. After a few minutes, her mother came and pulled her back inside. How easily he could lose her, he thought, if she learned of Filomena; how easily one little mistake could erase all the good things he'd done.

Though the weather was perfect, dry and warm, windless, Vito longed for the turn of September in a few days, for the chilly evenings with all the tourists gone. Soon he could sit in peace again with Maddalena on her terrace and sneak kisses when Claudio or Carolina went inside to grab a sweater. He'd get a few nights like that this year, and then, one morning in the middle of the month, he'd have to leave.

"There you are!"

This was Buccio's voice, rising at him from the street. He was rushing, weaving between donkeys and carts and honking cars. "I was just at your house," he called, and vaulted himself with his crutches up the café stairs two at a time.

"I'm always here," Vito said, as he kissed his cheek. "You look good, *vaglio*."

Buccio's eyes were clear and his hair neatly combed. He'd shaved his beard to a thin stubble. "*Grazie*," he said, as a waiter appeared with a glass of wine.

"A little early, isn't it?" said Vito.

"I have news," Buccio said, unsmiling. He drank the full glass in one gulp and motioned to the waiter for another. "Bad news. Maybe you know it already."

"Know what?"

He lowered his head and thought for a moment. He looked over at the Piccinelli store. The waiter arrived with two more glasses. Buccio downed one and said, "Grasso picked your flower. Maddalena."

Vito rolled his eyes. "You're drunk."

"I swear to you I'm not," Buccio said. "I heard it from Ernesto Drago this morning. He comes to our house for coffee. I overheard him tell my father that Aristide himself told him, and told him not to tell anybody, that it was a big secret. They're like women, those two, gossiping every morning. Usually I'm asleep, but today I woke up early for some reason. Fate, maybe."

"They must have meant Celestina," Vito said. He stood up, then sat back down, his eyes fixed on the house across the street.

"I heard 'Maddalena,'" Buccio said. "Very clear. The names are as different as the girls."

"Who wouldn't pick her?" Vito said. "He's not blind. But Maddalena doesn't even like him enough to eat dinner with. She wants him for Celestina, but just because of the money." As he spoke, the past two weeks rushed back at him: how little he'd seen Maddalena, all the card games Claudio had refused.

"Drink," Buccio said. He handed Vito the other glass of wine.

"I don't need it," Vito said.

"You have to find out what's going on," Buccio said. "If she's lying to you, I'll—"

"She's not lying," he said.

"Girls are worse than men these days," Buccio said. "Maybe she wants the money for herself. If she does, it's not right. I'll tear her house down if she does this to you." He leaned in closer. "I have grenades, you know."

Vito stood up again, this time for good. "It won't happen," he said. "Hold on to your bombs, Buccio. You don't know her like I do." He slammed the chair into the table.

"I'm sorry," Buccio said.

Vito walked quickly down the stairs into the street, trying to steady himself as he nodded and smiled at the tourists. He peered into the window of the Piccinelli store and saw only Claudio and his father behind the counter. He walked around to the front door and pressed the buzzer.

Carolina's voice. "Who is it?"

"Vito," he said. He looked through the bars of the grate at the solid wood door.

Silence. Then, "Yes?"

"Could I see Maddalena, please?"

More silence. He grabbed and shook the bars. He'd spent a week in this very spot painting and polishing them, scraping rust from the wrought iron leaves.

"I'm sorry, she's sleeping," Carolina finally said, louder than before. Then, in a whisper: "Come to the back. Don't let anyone see you."

Vito stepped into the street. The second-story windows were dark and the terrace empty. He walked through the narrow space between the Piccinelli and Castellani houses. He'd said good-bye to Maddalena in the dark here over two years ago, afraid he'd never see her again, while a few doors away Luciana Campini was dying.

Maddalena came through the door barefoot, and stood between an old carriage wheel and the back wall. Her hair was undone and looked greasy. She wore a plain blue dress that hung unevenly on her shoulders. "Here we are again," she said. "Hiding in the woods."

"Are you all right?"

"I'm sick," she said. She was shaking, and her voice sounded scared. "We're all sick."

"You should wear shoes, then," he said. He reached for her, but she kept her arms crossed tightly over her chest. "I don't care if I catch it," he said. "I want to hold you. I haven't seen you in so long."

"It's been two weeks," she said. "It's like being in jail. Carolina let me out for a minute, but then I have to go back. She's the only one who's not sick." Her face was pale and blotchy, and two little pimples had formed on her chin.

"I have a question," he said, stepping closer. "Do you know who Antonio Grasso wants to marry?"

Her eyes searched his for a moment, as if for an answer, then looked down. "No," she said. "I don't know anything."

"It's not Celestina," Vito said.

"It's not?" Maddalena said, still looking down.

He stepped closer to her. "Buccio told me he wants to marry you. If that were true, would you tell me?"

"How am I supposed to know what he wants?" she said. "How am I supposed to know anything?"

"You're yelling at me," Vito said. "Your face is white. Buccio's hearing gossip about you. I'm not stupid."

"I'm sick—"

"If you want to marry this great Antonio, tell me!" he said. He threw up his hands and told her this little lie: "If it's true, I'll go away. I won't bother you anymore."

Her eyes met his again, and this time they were full of tears. "I don't love him," she said. "I don't want to marry him. I'm telling you the truth, Vito. Maybe he wants to, I don't know, but I don't want to leave here. Or leave you. Don't believe anything else people tell you, no matter what." She unclasped her arms from her chest and locked them around his. "Promise me you won't believe them."

"Okay," Vito said as he held her, but she kept crying.

"Do you promise?" she said.

"Yes, yes," he said. "It's okay, calm down. I promise." Her forehead felt sweaty and hot against his shoulder, and she gripped him so tightly and with such desperation that he became afraid.

Carolina had been watching them through the glass design in the door. As soon as Vito noticed her, she came outside and tried to pull Maddalena away. "You have a fever," she said.

But Maddalena wouldn't let go. She dug her nails into Vito's back and sobbed into his shirt. He had to raise his arms above his head to prove to her sister that he was not the one keeping her there.

Vito went to see Buccio's father, but the old man told him that he could do better than listen to gossip from a drunk. What the Piccinellis did, he said, was none of his business. Ernesto Drago said the same. He asked at the Al Di Là, in line at the spring, at the *tabaccheria* and the barbershop, but everyone told him he was crazy, that he'd proved himself to the Piccinellis. "If you want to ruin it," said Signora Puzo, "keep acting like a jealous little lovesick girl."

No one had seen Antonio Grasso for weeks, not since the start of Ferragosto. Vito went to Broccostella to find his Zio Domenico, but no one answered the door. He waited outside the man's house for hours, until the last lights on the street went out, and he had to ride his bike back to Santa Cecilia in darkness.

Maddalena's fever had not been a lie. It had

spread in the days since he'd seen her, and scared off most of the tourists. They packed themselves into the buses and cars that had brought them a week and a half before. There was fear of tuberculosis, though no one had died and Guglierma Lunga was the only one who insisted it had come. Dr. Fabiano went from house to house with his oldest son, his apprentice, close behind. The Picinelli house became a fortress, with the girls quarantined inside and Claudio working the store. The streets grew as empty as they'd been during the war, and Vito refused to leave for Naples, or even pack or ask around for a carriage to rent, until he was sure everyone he loved was safe.

It was hard to tell if his mother's fever was the same it had always been or if this was the new sickness. Neither Fabiano was much help. Vito changed the damp cloth on her forehead five times a day and wandered the rooms of the house, waiting for something to happen. Then, on the first Friday in September, it did.

From his window, Vito saw a girl walking alone on the left side of the road toward his house. She kept her head down, but he recognized her immediately. She had the same stringy hair he'd seen at the Festa and the layers of raglike clothes and the thin legs. He watched her approach his house, stop, shade her eyes, and look up at him in the window. He ran down the stairs.

"What are you doing here?" he said, when he faced her.

"*Buongiorno* to you, too," she said. "I'm hungry."

Her sheep face, sad-looking but still somehow pretty, was smudged with dirt. She'd tied a piece of bright green and white fabric, which seemed to be torn from an Italian flag, over her head.

"How do you know where I live?"

"It's not a big town," she said, laughing. "I asked one person. Do you have any food?" She laid her hand on his stomach and squeezed the muscles in his arms. "You look like you get enough now. Give me something, please. I can pay you."

"I heard that before," he said. Though there was no one on the road, he pulled her inside.

She sat on the stairs with her knees apart. She untied the flag, tucked her hair behind her ears, and removed one of her many raggy blouses. "I saw our house," she said. "Remember our house? The pretty one's not your wife yet, is she?"

"She doesn't live there anymore," Vito said. "Her family moved away."

"You're not a very good liar," she said.

"Tell me you didn't ask them about me," he said.

She straightened her sleeves. "Maybe I did," she said. "Maybe I stopped in the store and asked the handsome young man behind the counter, and he told me all about you."

"What did he say? Did he ask how you knew me?"

"Give me some food and I'll tell you," she said.

I'll never get rid of this woman, Vito thought. You even think about making a mistake and the punishment keeps showing up for the rest of your life.

He led Filomena upstairs to the sofa. He went to his mother's room to tell her he had company and not to be afraid if she heard voices, then to the kitchen for the plate of dried salami and olives he'd set aside for his own lunch. He took it to Filomena, who stuffed it all in her mouth without a word.

"Well?" he said.

"The handsome boy said nothing," she said. "He wasn't the one I asked. It was this old lady, down the street from the store." She started laughing. "See how smart I am?"

"Yes, fine," he said. "Now get out of my house. I can get the police to put you in a room with all the other prostitutes."

"Don't you want to talk?" she said. She stretched out on the cushions. "You used to be so kind. You used to climb buildings for me. Don't you wonder what happened to our little boy?"

He'd forgotten about Francesco. "What? You ate him, too?"

"I loved that little *bastardo*," she said, her face serious. "You think I have no heart, but I do. I took him halfway across Italy because I loved him. And I stayed with him until the end."

"The end?"

She stared at him, tears forming in her eyes. "Fever," she said. "Some kind of terrible fever, like the one in this village now. We made it to his mother's house in Broccostella, but there was no one there, so we waited in the barn through the winter. We ate dirt, I tell you—worms! I almost came back to you, but there were too many soldiers around, and then the bombs started. Francesco was coughing up blood, and his skin was on fire. One morning he didn't wake up. His body was as stiff as a tree trunk. I dug his grave myself, and made a cross on the ground out of little stones. In the spring a few people came back to the town, and I gave them a message for Anna Rossi. I said, 'Tell that *puttana* if she wants her little boy, she can look for him in her yard.' I said. 'Tell her he died waiting for her, that all he ever wanted from his little life was to see the face of his Mamma.' Then I went to live in Avezzano, with some other New Women of Italy."

He wasn't sure he believed her, but he said, "I'm sorry about Francesco. He's innocent. But why did the New Woman of Italy have to destory the house?"

"I don't know what you mean," she said.

"I went to find you," said Vito. "The day after I risked my life for you. I wanted to check on Francesco, but you were gone. The house was on fire, and all the furniture upside down."

"Germans," she said, and shrugged. She looked at him sadly. "That's what they do. They had a station outside Avezzano. Before they left, they bombed it to the sky."

He looked at her closely. "Okay," he said, waving his arms. "I don't care. It doesn't even matter now."

"It must have mattered to your *fidanzata* with the shawl," she said. "Is she some kind of witch or something, with that hair? I bet she wasn't too happy to see her house wrecked."

"She's not a witch," Vito said. "She's the opposite."

"An angel?" said Filomena. "What a romantic you are." She slid her foot along Vito's leg, from his ankle to his knee. "Angels are very pure."

He pushed her away. It was early afternoon, the *riposo* taking hold of an already sleeping village, and Vito was tired.

"Imagine how upset your angel would be if she knew what you did with me," she said. "In her own house."

"Almost did," he said.

"That's not how I remember it," she said. She put a finger to her temple and pretended to think.

Vito looked at her. She removed another blouse, leaving only a sheer white slip with silk buttons up the front. He could see the honey color of her breasts, and the dark nipples pressing against the material. She tossed the blouse on the cushion beside her.

"What do you want?" he said, rubbing his face. "Money? I don't have any. I just gave you all the food in the house."

"You had plenty of money at the Festa," she said. "I was cheering for you."

"Well, it's gone now," he said. He had five lire in his pocket, and eighty more in his room. He took out the five and held it in front of her. "I'll give you this, but only if you promise to leave this village right now, before nighttime, and not tell anyone you ever knew me."

She grabbed the money and stuffed it into one of her skirt pockets. "That man who outbid you. Maybe I should go see him. He'll have plenty to give."

"That's a good idea," Vito said. He stood up. "He's perfect for you. I can give you his address."

She was looking at the bulge in his pants. "Not only him," she said, and smiled. "I think you might love me just a little bit."

He sat back down. "This isn't love," he said.

"Just because you want to marry the angel," Filomena said, "doesn't make you one yourself. I bet you could find twenty lire in the house, if I let you spend them on me." She unbuttoned his pants and moved her hands around inside. It felt too good to stop her right away. He breathed hard and closed his eyes, and by the time he opened them, she'd stopped moving her hand and unfastened her silk buttons.

"I'll give you thirty lire," he said, and stepped away.

"I thought so."

"But only if you leave now," he said. He buttoned his pants. "And never come back."

She raised her eyebrows. "You're serious?"

"Yes," he said, thinking, I won't make another mistake, not when I'm this close.

"All this for the angel?" Filomena asked.

He walked over to the bureau and pulled out the money from the top drawer, where he kept his reserve. He held the bills in front of Filomena's face. "Just leave," he said.

She grabbed the money, stuffed it in her pocket, and wiped her hand on her skirt. "You're either very stupid or very smart," she said, quickly rebuttoning her slip. "But what do I care?"

It was nearly dark when a screeching sound woke him. Someone was holding down the outside buzzer and calling his name. He always felt drunk when he woke from his afternoon naps, his legs and neck sore and his vision blurry, but today was worse than usual.

"Run, Vito!" This was his mother, banging her fist on the door. "They'll get you."

He found his pants on the floor and slipped them on, then Maddalena's white shirt. The woman downstairs kept calling him, pressing the buzzer, and banging on the door.

He found Concetta with her back to the wall in the hallway, shaking. He grabbed a blanket from the sofa, wrapped it around her, and walked her back to her room. "No one wants to hurt me, okay?" he said. He helped her into bed. "The war is over, Mamma. It's a woman's voice, right? There are no women soldiers. It's probably someone who needs directions. But just in case, don't move from here. Not until I come back."

"Don't let them take you!" she said. She pushed the covers off her. "Guglierma warned me!"

"*Stupida!*" he said, and grabbed her arm. He held her down.

She looked at him. "I'm so scared."

The woman downstairs kept yelling.

"I have to go," he said, and kissed her quickly on the cheek. He slammed the door and ran to the stairs, calling out, "I'm here! I'm here!" On his way down, he slipped and jammed his toes on one of the steps. He was hopping on his good foot when he opened the front door and found Carolina, all dressed up in a hat and gloves.

"*Mannagia O!*" he said. "What's all the noise about?" He fell back onto the bottom stair and sat there, catching his breath. "I almost killed myself." He squeezed his foot and dug into the skin with his fingernail, picking out splinters.

She stared at him, serious behind the veil. This was a different Carolina, standing almost shyly in the doorway.

"Why are you trying to knock my house down?" He sopped up the blood on his foot with the bottom of his shirt. "Is your sister all right? Is the fever worse?"

"Already you know nothing," she said. She

looked over her shoulder, toward the church. "We don't have much time, Vito. You have to listen to me."

"What is it?" he said. "I don't like the look on your face."

She slumped against the doorway, pulled off her gloves, and smashed them into a ball. "Maddalena is fine," she said. "She's not going to die."

"Thank God," Vito said.

"She looks like death," Carolina said. "But make no mistake: She's not sick over you. She doesn't care about anyone. She didn't think twice about what she did. You know what she worried about? That she couldn't do it in Santa Cecilia. The church mattered more than the man!"

"What are you talking about?"

"I gave her the chance to tell you," Carolina said. "But she didn't take it, because she was too afraid. I should have told you myself two days ago, but I kept hoping she'd change her mind. And so I came here because I wanted her to see your face, Vito, as she was marrying Antonio Grasso. I didn't want her to leave this village without seeing what she did to you. But now that I'm in front of you, I don't want you to stop her. I don't want to give her the satisfaction of seeing you run after her."

Vito grabbed her at the shoulders. "What kind of trick is this? You coming to help me?"

"Oh, Vito," she said. She touched his arm. "You don't live in the world with the rest of us, do you? Don't you see that she doesn't deserve you? How much better than you she thinks she is, and always has, and how wrong she is? Antonio Grasso is her perfect match."

"Now I know you're making fun of me," he said. He dropped his arms. "This time the joke's not funny, not even a little bit. Why can't you just leave Maddalena and me alone, and find a husband for yourself? I hear there was a German in Teramo. Why don't you go to Germany and find him, and stay there?"

"It's not my joke," she said.

"I don't believe you."

"You know the worst part?" Carolina went on. "The worst part for me?" She moved away from the doorway, closer to the stairs. "I think I'm just as terrible as she is, that all the Piccinellis are the same. I let Maddalena keep thinking she was better than you, even after I realized it was the opposite, even after I knew the whole time—because I know her, Vito, better than anyone—that she'd hurt you." She looked at him and laid her head against his shoulder. "That first night Antonio Grasso came to dinner, I saw that she'd leave us alone here. It was like I was seeing the future."

"She loves me," Vito said. "Not him. She told me not to believe anyone who told me different."

"That might be true," Carolina said. "But so is this, Vito." She reached for his arm. "Whoever she loves, she's marrying Antonio Grasso."

He stared at her, and believed for the first time that she was serious. He pushed her arm out of the way and punched the wall. "When?" he asked, his face hot and tears forming.

"Right now," Carolina said. She touched his sleeve. "But please, Vito, I'm begging you, don't go after her. Let her think you don't care. Don't make her into one of those princesses from her books, with men chasing her up and down the street."

"Just tell me where she is."

She folded her arms. "You make yourself a peasant for her," she said.

"Tell me where she is!" he said.

"She's easy to find," said Carolina. She stepped away from him in her big, clumsy shoes. "Go to the church in Broccostella. Look for a woman in white. Call out 'Signora Grasso' and watch how fast she turns around. Watch all the money fly out of her dress. But please, Vito, don't let her see you. Because it's already over. Don't let her think you'd still love her after this."

He glared at her and, leaving her standing in the open doorway at the bottom of the stairs, ran to the backyard, grabbed his bike, and rode down the main street past the store, down the hill of the olive grove, under the canopy of trees. The world blurred around him as the sun set behind the mountains. His bad foot pumped the pedal and went numb.

The streets were a maze. He turned up a curve and nearly smacked into the grates of a *sartoria*. A group of men sitting on chairs in front of a house waved their hands at him and told him to slow down, that he was going to kill somebody.

He stopped in the middle of the central piazza and rubbed his face. He spun around to get his bearings and saw an old woman carrying a fistful of broccoli. He pointed to his left and asked, "Is this the road to the church?"

"You passed it," she said, and waved the broccoli in the direction he'd come. "It's easy to miss. Turn right at the road with the *sartoria*, and go up the hill."

The hill was very steep. He jumped off his bike, left it in the street, and ran up the cobblestones to the stairs of the church. He climbed them two and three at a time, winded and dizzy, and pulled open the heavy door. He ran through the vestibule and pulled open another set of doors.

The gray stone walls rose high around him. He took in the entire church at once, scanned the pews and the little caverns glowing with candles. It was empty.

He ran down the aisle to the altar, crushing flower petals underfoot. The image of Jesus, stained in glass and illuminated, held His hands out to welcome him. There was no marriage register on the table near the pulpit. The air was musty, as if no one had been inside for months.

Someone was moving in the rooms behind the altar. Vito found the door to the sacristy and knocked.

"Who's there?" said a man's voice.

"A visitor," Vito said. "Would you please come out?"

A priest opened the door. Vito vaguely recognized him from the Broccostella festivals but didn't know his name. He had heavy eyes and a wrinkled face. His mane of white hair stuck straight up in the back, and his shoes were untied. "I was just changing my clothes," he said. "What can I help you with, son?"

"I'm sorry, Father," Vito said, his heart pounding. "But the wedding here today—was there a wedding? Is there going to be a wedding?"

The priest looked at him closely. "I know you from somewhere," he said. "What's your name?"

"Vito Leone," he said. "From Santa Cecilia." He took a breath and thought a moment. "I'm a friend of Antonio Grasso's."

"Oh," said the priest. "What a shame, then. You missed it all."

Vito looked at him, then fell to his knees.

"My son," the priest said. He grabbed his arm to help him up, but Vito wouldn't move. "It's all right. I'm sure the Grassos will forgive you."

"The bride," Vito said, his hands over his face. "What was the bride's name?"

"Maddalena?" said the priest. "Beautiful girl. Young. But between you and me"—he squatted to look him in the eye—"too young. When the girl can't stop crying long enough to put the ring on, something's very wrong."

"That wasn't her name," Vito said. "Her name was Celestina."

"No, I don't think so," the priest said. "I'm sure I remember. Wait a second." He opened the door to the sacristy, and reached in to pull the register from a cabinet. He opened it up to the page and showed Vito the signature: a scrawled *Maddalena Piccinelli*, in the handwriting Vito recognized from the one letter she'd sent him.

Vito ran his fingers over her name, and Antonio's above it. Maddalena was here, in this church, on the dusty floor where he was now kneeling, and she was holding a pen and crying and signing this name with Antonio beside her, while he, Vito, was miles away in his bed. His bed was still there, and his mother, and Carolina; they'd always be there; but Maddalena was married to another man.

He kept his hand on the page, wanting to rip it out and crush it in his fist. He wanted to throw it at the priest's face and tear the gentle, understanding smile from his lips. He wanted to bury his face in the book and suffocate himself and never wake up.

"You're not well," the priest said, as Vito's fingers began to shake.

Vito didn't respond.

"Do you need me to stay with you, my son? Do you need God's help?" He closed his hand over Vito's finger and set the book on the floor. Candles flickered around them. "Listen, Vito, I think I know who you are," he said. "You're the one she wanted to marry. Am I right?"

Vito looked at him.

"A-ha!" the priest said. "I was right! I've always been a matchmaker." He patted Vito's hand. "I've known the Grasso family all my life. I could see how strangely they behaved. Everything fast, everything secret. It's not the right spirit for a wedding, I tried to tell them, but they ignored me. Take comfort in this, though: I've never seen a bride so angry in my life. If she could have punched Antonio, she would have."

"Where are they now?" Vito said. "You have to take me."

The priest smiled. "Oh, no," he said. "That I can't do. Stay here for a while and cool your head."

"Please help me," Vito said. "Please tell me where she is."

"You'll only embarrass yourself," the priest said. "And you'll only make it worse for her."

"No," Vito said. "I have to find her." He got to his feet and, without another word, ran down the aisle and pushed through the heavy doors into the night. His legs wobbled and tingled as he walked down the hill to his bike. He propped it up and looked around at the empty streets, the unfamiliar town, the families at their windows, eating, a woman carrying drinks on a tray to a table. He didn't interrupt them to ask how to get to Domenico Grasso's. He headed in the direction of the house as best he could remember it, taking the curves fast and low. He made it to one end of the town and realized the Grassos were at the other; he made it to the other end and staggered up and down the street, trying to recognize the house. When he finally found it, he banged on the door yelling, "Open up!" though he could see even then that the windows were dark. There was no one outside on the back terrace: no music, no dancing. Whatever party they held was not being thrown here.

So he rode back to Santa Cecilia the way he had come. Just before the entrance, he hit a thick tree root and his bike spun out from under him. He smacked his head on the ground and his elbow on a rock. He lay there a moment, with the wheels upturned and whirring a few yards away from him in the blackness and the warm blood trickling from his nose into his mouth. He sopped up the mess with his shirt and lay on his back, crying and grabbing at leaves.

He heard someone walking toward him and fumbled to get back on the bike. The front wheel was bent, and he had to stop to bang it straight with a rock. He approached his house and saw its front door closed, Carolina gone. It occurred to him for the first time that she had missed her sister's wedding for him, and though he tried to reconstruct some of what she'd said just two hours before, he could remember only the image of Maddalena with a wedding dress full of money.

He passed his house, unable to face his mother.

He rode behind the church to the cemetery and stopped near his nonna's grave. He got off the bike and, with little thought, lifted it above his head and threw it as hard as he could against a large stone crypt. The front wheel snapped off and spun into the air; the rest of the bike slid down the wall of the crypt intact and landed slumped but upright on the grass.

Vito left it there and felt his way among the trees, past the new secret meeting place and down to the hill that sloped to the gorge. A sharp pain shot through his arm, and the blood kept running from his nose. He'd never show this face to the liars of Santa Cecilia again, not for the rest of his life. They'd laugh at him and flood him with pity, and then behind the walls of their houses they'd whisper and tell his story over and over, the way they did with his mother. Whatever happened to her, or Carolina or Filomena, he didn't care; all that mattered was that Antonio Grasso had made a fool out of him and taken Maddalena away. She'd live the life he could never give her, not with the best tailoring business in Italy. She'd spend her days on wide streets with shops and cars and music; she'd spend her nights dancing—all on the other side of the world. There was no longer any use for him. He'd rot here, in the black woods, on the rocks jutting up from the river, and sooner or later he'd be forgotten.

CHAPTER 23

"You've never been to Genoa?" Domenico asked Maddalena.

"No," she said.

She crossed her leg over her knee on the warm leather and tried not to look at anyone. She straightened her shoulders and sucked in her stomach and folded her hands as if she were in church, locking in whatever might make her explode. If she let go, stopped fighting the urge to throw herself against the windows and scream, it would take her over; the world would close in, and she'd slide onto the floor, a crazy woman, an embarrassment.

"Florence?"

She shook her head.

And what would Antonio do? He'd try to comfort her, and she'd scream louder; he'd try to hold her and she'd bite his wrists. He'd call a doctor, who'd stick her with needles until she slept. He'd leave her in Italy and go back to America disgraced.

"A boat is a beautiful place for a honeymoon," said Domenico. "Have you ever been on a boat?"

"So many questions already, Zio?" Antonio said. "Let her leave her town first."

That's what she was doing: leaving Santa Cecilia, and Lazio, and Italy forever. She was in a car driving too close to the edge of the mountain road, circling in wide loops the pile of stone and trees on which she'd lived her life. With every curve, she sank lower toward the valleys, dipping farther down to the flat land, to the miles of farms lit in flashes by the headlights. A misty rain coated the car like sweat and spit on her when Antonio rolled down his window for air. They passed through nameless villages, if she could call them that, these blocks of five or six lonely houses barely clinging to the mountain, no store or church in sight, no carved wood signs to announce them.

Just an hour ago, she'd been in her family's store. While Claudio and Antonio loaded her bags into the trunk, her father had pulled her aside and told her not to think of them. He'd held both sides of her face and leaned in close. "Promise me," he'd said. "Forget us. If you can't, pretend a bomb hit us. We all died, but you survived. Make yourself believe there was never a Santa Cecilia at all."

She'd promised.

"You've cried enough," her mother had said. "Don't let Antonio see you. Be happy in front of him. Show him respect. When he's not around, you can go into your room and cry and miss us for a while if you have to. But you're married now, and Antonio is your family, not us. Soon enough you'll have your babies to think of, and you'll forget you ever lived here."

Maddalena had left Carolina in the street in front of the store, had watched her take off her hat and turn back into the house, but all through her wedding she'd kept hoping the door would open and her sister would join her at the altar. Afterward, Maddalena had not been able to eat any of the dinner the Grassos had served at the café outside Broccostella. She'd gone behind the kitchen and thrown up while Teresa, herself weak and feverish, held her forehead. It was Teresa and Carolina who'd told her to marry Antonio, and now they hated her for taking their word.

Maddalena had clung to her mother until her father pulled her away. He guided her out of the store into the cool September evening, his hand firm on her waist. Celestina waited by the back door of the car—Celestina who'd helped alter Teresa's wedding dress at the last minute so Maddalena could wear it, Celestina who'd expected all this fuss would be for her. When Maddalena saw her hold out her arms, she fell into them, grateful, sobbing, saying, "I'm sorry, I'm sorry"; but Celestina only patted her twice on the back, and stepped aside to let her pass.

Domenico was already in the driver's seat. Antonio opened the door, rolled down the window, and waited for Maddalena to step in. He kissed Chiara and said, "All I have now belongs to your daughter."

"*Grazie*," she said.

It was then that they'd heard a man yelling from the other end of the street. Domenico flicked on the headlights.

Buccio was hobbling toward them, large and ghostly in the flood of the lights. He stopped for a moment to shield his eyes. "Wait!" he called out. "Don't go anywhere!"

"Hurry," Aristide said, and nudged Maddalena toward the car. "Get in." She didn't move.

"It's just the drunk," Antonio said.

"Yes," Buccio said. "Just me." He walked directly to Maddalena and held out his right crutch. "*Strega!*" he said, and jabbed the crutch at her face. "*Puttana!* Who do you think you are?" he said. He spit on the ground. *"Strega! Puttana!"*

Claudio stepped in front of him, grabbed the crutch, and threw it over the car to the other side of the street. He punched Buccio in the face and watched him fall to the ground, then kicked him in his good leg. "Go," he said to Maddalena. "Go now!"

Aristide pushed her into the car. She slid across the backseat and covered her face.

Buccio lay on the grass. He started crying, and slurred the words, "I'll blow up your store." He pointed at Aristide. "Just watch me! *Boom!* No more Piccinellis! And no more Vito to fix it!"

"Shut up," Aristide said.

Maddalena took her mother's hand through the window as Domenico started the engine. "Tell

Carolina I'm sorry," she said to her. "Tell her to tell Vito, please. Tell everybody. Don't let them say those words about me."

Then the car pulled away, and Maddalena had screamed as her mother's hand was forced from hers. She'd turned and looked behind her at Buccio's leg sticking up from the yard. She'd had no time to hold in her mind the lights in the windows, the roof where every afternoon Fiorella took a sunbath, the street where she'd first seen Vito on his bike. And if Antonio were right, she'd forget them all a little more each day. Domenico drove slowly, honking his horn, and Maddalena watched her family wave, swinging their arms side to side and shaking white handkerchiefs in the taillights. She watched the people of her village lean out their windows in their shirtsleeves, smoking, waving the little red buds of their cigarettes at her as she passed.

"You should try to make it to Florence before you go," Domenico said now, as the car neared the station in Frosinone. He'd leave them here, and then Maddalena would spend her first night with her husband on the overnight train to Genoa.

"There's no time," said Antonio. "She doesn't want to see Florence anyway. There are more exciting cities to come. Am I right, *tesoro?*"

"Yes," she said, and swallowed whatever was rising in her throat.

THE BOAT

CHAPTER 24

Concetta narrowed her eyes at the shirt. Then she looked at Dr. Fabiano. "It's dirty," she said. "You want me to wash it?"

"This is Vito's shirt," Dr. Fabiano said. "There's no doubt, Signora. Don Martino in Broccostella saw him in it, blood and all. He hurt himself. On purpose." He lowered his voice. "He's dead."

Concetta threw her head back, laughing. "Really?" she said. "You should stay for some wine, Doctor. When Vito comes home, you can tell him that yourself."

"I know this is very hard," he said. He let out a long breath. "But Vito is not coming home, Concetta. Not tonight, not tomorrow. Not ever. You have to trust me; I see death all the time. I know it like your husband knows needles and thread."

"And I just saw Vito this morning," she said. She tried to stand. "He was in his bed, sleeping. He's so tall now, his feet hang over the edge. We sat for an hour last night and ate figs." Her hands were shaking. "Vito!" She called out again.

Again there was no answer. On the table was a plate with the skins of four figs.

Dr. Fabiano lifted Concetta, guided her across the hall to Vito's room, and pushed open the door, which had been left ajar. "Do you see him now?" he asked. "Is he sleeping on the bed?"

"Of course not," she said. "He's not home." Her body went limp.

"Listen," said the doctor, holding her. "Your son was very brave, as brave as a soldier, but sometimes sadness can take over. It can poison your mind, make you think things that aren't real. You know about that, don't you, Concetta?"

She nodded.

"He stayed and protected you the way the soldiers protected Italy. And when he had to, he became a man. Right in front of our eyes! He helped half the families in this village. He was very strong, very kind. That's how we'll remember him."

"He's getting married," she said.

The doctor sighed. He kneeled beside Concetta, now fully sunk to the floor. "He's with God now. Think of it this way: God is waiting for him with a brand-new silver bike, with a motor. He's saying, 'I'm sorry, Vito Leone, for the hard life I gave you.'"

He helped Concetta back to her bed. Before he left, he promised to visit, to send the nuns and Don Paolo. He said the village women would take care of her as long as she lived, and not to worry. Her son's body had not been found yet, but when it was they'd have some kind of funeral, in a week or so, as soon as a big enough space could be cleared in the church.

CHAPTER 25

It was a few hours past midnight, and the village was quiet. Carolina lay asleep on her bed, her two sisters beside her. When the hand came over her mouth, she woke immediately. Her eyes widened. Another hand held her body down as she thrashed.

"Don't scream," Vito whispered. "I'm not dead. I'm not a ghost. I didn't kill myself. Don't scream, don't scream."

She stared at him, her body stiff, then relaxed. He let her pry his hand off, and she backed up against the headboard. The bed wobbled and Teresa turned over but didn't wake.

"*Porco Dio!*" she said.

Vito smiled. He nodded, took Carolina's hand, and led her out through the hallway and down to the store.

When they were alone behind the counter, she folded her arms and said, "I knew you wouldn't kill yourself." The room was dark, her face barely visible. "I couldn't listen to the way people talked. I couldn't hear that someone threw himself off a cliff for Maddalena Piccinelli." She grabbed him at the waist, held him for a moment, then leaned in against his chest. "I'm glad I was right. I'm happy you're not dead."

"Thank you," Vito said. She felt heavier than Maddalena and Filomena. Those two were girls; this was how a woman his age felt. "I need your help."

"You didn't go to Genoa, did you?" she asked.

"Is that where he took her?" Vito said. "You're helping already. No. I didn't go there. I've been hiding in my house for more than a week." He looked down. "I couldn't come out. I couldn't face anybody."

After Maddalena's wedding, he told her, he'd ridden his bike around for hours, then stayed in the woods until almost dawn, thinking maybe he should kill himself, that killing himself would be the best punishment for her and all the Piccinellis. He'd taken off his bloody shirt and thrown it in the river. But then, just as he was about to leap onto the rocks, he got scared. He couldn't do it. So he sneaked home in shame. No one saw him. For three days he didn't eat. He was half dead anyway, broken down the middle. He told his mother he had a fever, and she managed to heat a kettle of broth. As his strength came back, he started to remember everything Carolina had told him.

"I called you a liar," he said to her now, "but you were the only one telling the truth."

She nodded.

"And then Dr. Fabiano came," Vito said.

He'd watched from his room as the doctor told his mother about the shirt and listened to him tell her how he'd split himself open on the sharp rocks out of grief and desperation. That no one had found his body, that it had only been a week, didn't matter; it made too much sense in the village and in the doctor's mind that Vito Leone would do such a ridiculous, romantic thing: It was his destiny to make a fool of himself, and now it was fact. When Dr. Fabiano had come toward his room, Vito had hidden under the bed.

"You're like a saint now," Carolina said. "Maybe they'll throw you a festa."

"The day after Fabiano, a letter came from my father," Vito said, talking rapidly to get the rest of the story out. "This is the important part. This is why I'm here."

"You're going to live with him," Carolina said. "That's it, right? So you can be close to her. You don't have to tell me, because I can guess." She looked down.

He shook his head.

"Take me with you," she said.

"Listen," he said. "You don't know as much as you think. I'm not going to America. I don't have to. I wrote to my father when Grasso came, because I was worried. I was right to be worried. I asked him for money, and for anything he could tell me about this man who was looking for a wife in our town. I was trying to protect Celestina, or you, but also I could see how he treated Maddalena. I thought maybe there was a chance he'd try to go for her. But of course my father's reply came too late to stop him." He reached into his pocket, pulled out the letter, and handed it to Carolina. "You can read it, but I'll tell you what it says. It says, 'Don't let Antonio Grasso marry any Piccinelli sisters, or anyone in Santa Cecilia who thinks he has money. He's a liar. He has no more money than I do, and six more people to feed in his house. The Grassos closed the restaurant and bakery because no one came, just like in the village.' "

"No!" said Carolina.

"He probably had just enough money for the trip back and forth," Vito said, "and for that one suit he wore. In America, everyone knows the Grassos are finished."

"It's not possible," Carolina said.

"It is," said Vito. He took the letter back and held it up to her face. "Read it."

"How do we find these men?" Carolina said. She turned away from him and walked in a circle, her hands on her hips. "First Sebastiano and Konrad, now Antonio. How stupid we are. They lie to us, one after the other, and we believe every word."

"It doesn't matter now," Vito said. He gripped the counter, full of energy. "You're going to help me fix it. Tell me how to get word to Maddalena, and I'll go rescue her myself."

"Rescue her?" Carolina said. "It's too late."

"She married him for the money," Vito said. "That was the only reason. Am I right? That's why your father forced her? It had to be."

Carolina thought a moment. Then she nodded.

"So if he lied about the money, she won't have to go with him. She'll have an excuse to come back here. I can *bring* her back here."

"She'll be disgraced," Carolina said. She shook her head. "Divorced. And everyone in Santa Cecilia hates her already for doing what she did."

"Who could hate her?" Vito said. "And even if they do, I never cared what people thought, even before, even when they loved her. That's not why I tried so hard, why I fixed up your house. And now"—he raised and shook his fists—"now your father will *beg* me to marry her. Do you see that? Do you see how I'll win, after all?" He grabbed the letter from Carolina's hands. "For once in his life, my father did something right. This is a letter of victory!"

"Calm down," Carolina said. She folded her arms again. One strap of her nightgown hung off her shoulder. "It's not as easy as you think, Vito. Where's your pride? After what she did to you? She took another man right under your nose, made you a *cornuto*, and now you want to go make nice with her and bring her back? Why? So she can spit in your face some more?"

"It won't be like that," he said. "She loves me. She told me. You know she does."

"I know that she did."

All the windows of the store were closed, and the air smelled stale. Vito grabbed a handful of walnuts from one of the barrels and chewed them. He planned to leave on the first bus that morning, and he hadn't eaten in hours. "Are you going to help me or not?" he said. "Will you tell me if they're in a hotel in Genoa, or does Antonio have family there?"

"She deserves what she got," Carolina said. "I won't tell you where she is—"

"Carolina—" he said, thinking, I should have woken the other sister.

"Unless you take me with you."

"Don't play games," Vito said. "If you don't tell me, I'll ask Teresa. Or I'll go to every hotel in Genoa. I picked you because I thought you'd make the least fuss."

"Me?"

He looked down. "Okay," he said. "Because I wanted to tell you I'm sorry. For the way I treated you when you came to find me. You were the only one—"

"Who told the truth; yes, I know," she interrupted. "And look at the good it did me." She moved closer to him. "But you never lied to anybody, either, Vito. I don't care about apologies. I'm serious about going, if you insist on it. I could get enough money for both of us."

In the rush, he'd forgotten it would take money. He had no idea how much a train to Genoa cost. He thought a moment. "Okay," he said. "But you have to be on my side. You can't go there and try to turn her against me. And she'll need you when she finds out."

"She will."

"Promise you'll be kind to her," he said.

"When I see her," Carolina said, "how could I not? I'm not a monster, Vito. Without her, my life here is empty. I gave up the man who loved me to stay here with her. Did she tell you that? That's why I couldn't speak to her after she told me she was going to marry Antonio: It wasn't what she did to you so much, but what she did to me. I'm a selfish person, I guess. But I'll fall in love with her again when I see her. I'll fall so hard I'll come back and live in the village with the two of you for the rest of my life."

"You know the name of the hotel?" Vito said.

"Yes," she said. "I'll tell you when we get to Frosinone. We'll send her a telegram from there."

"No, no telegrams," Vito said. He paced from the counter to the door, then back again. "I don't want Antonio to know we're coming. I've already thought of a plan. We wait outside the hotel, and when Antonio comes out we go in and surprise her. When he comes back, she's gone."

"The boat leaves tomorrow morning, Vito," Carolina said. "We have to send word before then, or by the time we get there she'll be . . ."

He stopped pacing. He looked at the ceiling and counted the hours, though he'd never been on a train before and had little sense of how often they ran or how far Genoa was or how they'd find the hotel when they got there. "Can we make it in a day?"

"I don't know," Carolina said. "But the telegram will. Then it will be up to her."

CHAPTER 26

The walls of Maddalena's room at the Albergo Corona were covered in blue paper and overlaid with a pattern of black velvet interconnected urn shapes. As Antonio moved inside her and she went numb, she'd look over his shoulder and feel herself skating on the curves of those urns, looping under the dresser, around the mirror, through the terrace windows, and out onto the twisting cobblestone streets. Every night of their two-week honeymoon, he had been trying to make a child. After he'd finish, he'd lie on top of her, rest his chin on his folded arms, and say, "It could be growing right now." Then he'd fall asleep, and she'd arch her back to slide him off onto his side of the bed.

She was the thinnest she'd ever been in her life. It had started with the fever in Santa Cecilia, and got worse after weeks of not eating. Antonio liked her thin. He'd rub her belly and tell her it made a little bowl when she lay flat on her back. "I could eat pasta from here," he'd say, and gently bite the skin above her navel. He'd pull off her nightgown and her underclothes and stare at her naked body, picking out bones and teaching her bits of dirty English.

"Now you are *nudo*," he'd say. "Now we make sex."

She didn't hate him. She felt nothing for him. He talked on about his family, a brother and a sister-in-law, a father and mother, and she listened patiently. He described the big green parks all over Philadelphia and the house with three floors where they'd be living. He promised to take her for drives along the river and sit with her on the banks to watch the moonlight on the water. He told her he knew she didn't love him yet, but that all of that would change sooner than she thought. "When you wake up in America," he said, "you'll thank God for making you Signora Grasso."

This morning, the day before the boat was to leave, Antonio went to the bank to secure the rest of their money. He took their passports and the hundreds of lire her parents had given as a wedding gift. Maddalena straightened up the room, though it was the maid's job, and tried to keep her mind and hands busy. She stood in her underclothes, rubbed her belly and hips, and pointed her toe at the full-length mirror to see the shape of her leg. It was long and slim, yes, but also pale and bony. Branchlike. She slipped on her gray suit and had to pin the skirt at her waist; the jacket fit her like a sack. She wore cold cream to keep her face from cracking.

Close to noon, there was a knock at the door.

"Signora Grasso," said a man's voice. "It's Signore Fosca." The hotel owner.

She wiped her eyes, checked her face in the mirror, and crossed the room. "Yes?" she said.

"A telegram for you, Signora."

She quickly unlatched the door. She'd received four telegrams already on this short honeymoon: three from her mother, one from Domenico Grasso. She kept her mother's pressed in an album she'd bought at a shop in Genoa.

This telegram was different: addressed only to her, post-marked from Frosinone. She thanked Signore Fosca, shut the door, and stared at the thick yellow square of paper as she walked to the terrace. In the light, she opened it and read:

> ANTONIO A LIAR. GRASSOS BROKE. COMING TO HOTEL TO BRING YOU HOME. WAIT FOR US MORNING OF 18 SEPT. VITO AND CAROLINA.

She read it twice more, put it down, then read it again and again, trying to understand it. Each time it asked more questions. What had Antonio lied about? It sounded like money—money would make sense; everyone seemed to lie about money—but how could the Grassos be broke with all they'd taken over? Who could be broke in a country with more jobs than men? Or was it worse? Was Antonio dangerous, another Sebastiano? If that were true, wouldn't they have warned her or sent the police?

She stuffed the telegram in her pocket and walked back into the room, suddenly aware that she was a woman alone in a strange northern city. Antonio Grasso was the only person she knew for a hundred miles. She held her stomach, where his baby could be growing. Was this some cruel trick of Vito's or Carolina's, or was it the truth? And if it was the truth, had Mamma and Babbo really sent them to take her home?

With no way of knowing when Antonio would return, Maddalena searched the drawer where he kept his money and bankbook and passport. But of course he'd taken all of these with him. She looked through his bags and in the pockets of his pants and jackets and read every scrap of paper: letters, receipts, train schedules, directions for touring Genoa on foot. There was a photo of twin babies in the arms of a young couple, who must be the brother and sister-in-law he'd bragged about on the train. She found nothing strange. His mother's letters, posted from Philadelphia, said she missed and loved her youngest son, and was happy he'd found such a good wife. They didn't mention poverty or hunger; they didn't mention money at all.

Maddalena quickly put Antonio's things back where she'd found them. She pulled the drapes across the terrace window and smoothed the wrinkles on the sheets. She didn't know what to think. Surely Carolina and Vito hated her now, yes, but enough to send false news like this? There must be some truth in the message. But how could she leave Antonio, even if he'd lied, even if he were the most terrible man on Earth, now that she'd married him and made love to him and let him give her a child?

She stood against the desk, gripping the edge behind her, and watched the door as if it were a wild animal. She waited for it to announce her fate: for Antonio to come through unaware of any threat, or Vito to arrive early and rescue her. And it occurred to her here—alone in the dark and dusty room of the *albergo*, with the fancy vases and stained-glass lampshades and shiny marble floors laughing at her—that she had the power to control none of it. Someone else would decide how this would end, just as someone else had decided the war and her chances with Vito and every detail of her marriage. That she played such a small part in her own life did not enrage her. Not now. Not yet.

"Another letter to your mother?" Antonio asked. He was crouched in front of the fire and stoking the logs Signore Fosca had just brought up. He wore only his suit pants and shirtsleeves, though the room had not yet warmed. It was late, their bags packed and their tickets paid for, and he had nothing to do but talk.

"Yes," said Maddalena. Every time he spoke, she slid her letter to Vito and Carolina beneath the one she was pretending to write to her mother.

He rubbed his hands in front of the fire and

said, "I hope there's at least a little happiness in it."

Maddalena kept writing. After a few moments she said, "Of course there is."

Antonio sat back on his heels. "You'll have good news to report soon, at least," he said. "The first grandchild always brings luck. Tell your mother we'll send photographs and even call her on the phone so she can hear him cry."

Maddalena looked up. "We can do that?"

"It takes planning, but yes," Antonio said. "My brother talked on the phone to Zio Domenico just last month. He had to go to Frosinone to take the call at a certain time, and they could only talk five minutes, but it worked. You will hear your mother's voice again, *tesoro*."

She put down her pen and tried to hold the tears back. "I don't think I knew that," she said.

He crawled over to her on the bed. She quickly moved her stack of paper onto the nightstand, keeping her unfinished letter hidden. He ran his finger down the length of her arm. He had a day's stubble on his face. "Your life won't be so terrible," he said. "I promise."

"I'm sorry," she said. "Don't pay any attention to me."

He moved in tighter and reached his left leg and arm over her. He kissed her neck and rubbed her hip with his knee. "You know what I was thinking?" he asked. "This is our last chance to make a baby in Italy."

"No, Antonio," she said immediately, without thinking. He drew back. It was the first time she'd refused him. "I mean"—she put her hand on his cheek—"I don't feel so well tonight. I think it's my nerves. My stomach's been upset all day."

"This could make you feel better," Antonio said. He pulled down a strap of her nightgown.

"I don't think so, Antonio," she said. She caught his hand. "Please."

There was fear in her voice. He stopped kissing her, turned away, and settled his head on his pillow. "Good night, then," he said coldly. "Turn off the light and sleep if you're sick."

"All right," she said.

But before she got the chance, he'd sat up again and grinned at her. "You said you were sick since the morning?" he said.

"Yes."

"You know what that means, don't you?"

She shook her head.

"It means a baby!" he said. "That's the first sign! With any luck, you'll be sick again tomorrow and the next day and the day after that." Then he grinned wider, kissed her on the cheek, switched off the lamp, and turned back to his pillow, all in one swift, continuous motion.

She let him think what he wanted. The truth was that she could not distinguish one sickness from another anymore. She had headaches every morning and felt feverish at night. Food tasted heavy and metallic no matter when she ate it or how it was prepared. Today she could blame it all on nerves, but how much of it might be pregnancy, she didn't know. She had no one to ask.

When she was sure Antonio was asleep, she turned the light back on and finished her letter. She sealed it in an envelope and tucked it in the inside pocket of the suit she'd already laid out for tomorrow. The rest of the night she lay awake on her back, stiff as a dead person, her hands clasped over her chest. She listened for any sign of Vito: footsteps in the hallway, a carriage on the street, her name called up to the terrace. She watched the morning light turn the drapes from black to gray to gold, and prayed she'd have no use for the letter, that it would be one more that Vito would never receive.

At eight-thirty, Signora Fosca delivered a tray with Maddalena and Antonio's farewell breakfast. She'd strewn flower petals on the plate that held the bread and chocolates. When Maddalena could not touch her food or even the espresso she normally craved, Antonio finished them and made a gleeful declaration: By the summer there'd be another Grasso born in Philadelphia. Boy or girl, he was happy, he said, but a boy he wanted most.

Maddalena couldn't keep her focus on any task for more than a moment. She paced around the room, arranging and rearranging the tiny vases and *ninnoli* that decorated the tables and bureaus. She took clothes out of her suitcase, unfolded them, then folded them more neatly. "You look terrible," Antonio said, when he caught her staring into the mirror. He came up behind her and closed his arms around her waist. He rested two hands on her belly. "But never so beautiful."

She smiled weakly. Next to his, her face looked pale and her eyes sunken. She'd chewed bits of skin from her lips, and the wine she'd drunk yesterday had stained them purple.

Shortly before noon, their carriage pulled up in front of the *albergo*. Their bags were on the street in a neat stack. Antonio led Maddalena out of the empty room, closed the door, and took her hand to guide her down the stairs. It was difficult to keep her balance. Antonio's shining face, the gold-leaf angels burnished along the staircase, the chandelier shimmering felt unreal to her, as if she were watching a movie with her face pressed to the screen. In the lobby, Antonio floated away to talk money with Signore Fosca, and left Maddalena with the signora.

Signora Fosca had been kind to Maddalena. She laughed at anything and reminded her of Fiorella's mother: short and round, with a tight bun of black hair. As was customary, Maddalena thanked her for her happy stay, and accepted her good wishes and promised to send a postcard from Philadelphia.

At the end of the conversation, just before Antonio came out of his meeting, Maddalena handed her letter to Signora Fosca. She described what Vito and Carolina looked like, and said they'd ask for the Grassos but might arrive too late to say goodbye. "It's very important that they get this letter," Maddalena said. "I beg you to remember. It's also very important that my husband not know about it."

Signora Fosca looked suspiciously at the envelope. "I don't think a wife should have secrets," she said. The kindness faded from her face.

Once an actress, Maddalena forced herself to summon her best Zia Zabrina: "Oh, it's nothing bad!" she said, with a bright smile. She leaned in and whispered, "It's for a romantic surprise, Signora, for later! Your help will mean much happiness for us."

"Well, that's a different story!"

From the carriage, Maddalena gave Signora Fosca a special wave. When the old lady winked back, she relaxed a little. Still, as the carriage turned the corner, away from the hotel and toward the water, she looked in every direction for Vito and Carolina. She imagined them running behind the carriage. She held the handle of the door, ready to jump out. But there were only strangers on the streets, rushing around on bikes and in cars and carriages. And there was only Antonio beside her, twisting his watch around his wrist, turning to her every few minutes to ask how she felt.

They approached the dock, and rows of ships and boats of all sizes came into view. Antonio pointed out the *SS Terra Mia*. "Have you ever in your life seen anything like that?" he asked.

Maddalena craned her neck to get a glimpse but felt so dizzy that she had to pull back or she'd be sick. Then the carriage stopped, and suddenly the driver was helping her out and she was on her feet on the wobbly dock. The ship rose like a mountain before her.

If you could pick up this ship and drop it on Santa Cecilia, it would crush her, legs and head and all. It would stretch from the spring to the tunnel of trees halfway to Broccostella and stand as tall as the cross on the church. Its lower half was painted black, its middle striped in alternating white and gray. Railings all along the top sloped upward to a statue of a large, winged animal. In the center of the ship stood white, windowed buildings as big as the houses in her village, with spirelike poles jutting up from their roofs. People were already crowded into the seats set up behind the railing and jostling for places to stand and wave. Maddalena could hear no individual voices, just an undulating roar from the deck, and distant foghorns and the slurping of waves on the shore.

She walked slowly. Antonio pulled a cart overloaded with their luggage. The bags teetered and sagged as he dodged other passengers. He had to stop every few yards to make sure it didn't topple completely. "God made mountains," he said, "but man made the *Terra Mia* with his own hands, big as a mountain!"

She pulled her coat tighter against the chilly morning and the wind off the waves. The coat was made of heavy wool, with fur around the collar and wrists, a gift from her mother on her wedding night. No, she had never seen anything like this boat—nothing so immense and loud. She didn't believe in it, though it sat just yards in front of her. It couldn't hold all these people with their heavy coats and bags and furniture. It couldn't just swallow her up and take her away.

Even as she stepped onto the deck, and the conductor checked and stamped her passport, she didn't believe the ship would keep her. Even as she followed Antonio down the many flights of stairs to their small, windowless room, she resisted the possibility.

He unbuttoned the collar of his shirt and wiped the sweat from his neck and forehead with a handkerchief. He sat on the edge of the creaky bed and smiled at her. "We're underwater now," he said, and let out a long breath. "And just in time. It's a miracle."

She nodded.

"We have to go up soon," he said, "but before we do . . ." He slid onto the floor and kneeled before their luggage. "I have a present for you." He reached into one of his smaller trunks and fumbled with a package wrapped in newspaper. He hid it behind his back and grinned wildly. Then the ship's horn sounded, and Maddalena shuddered.

People were rushing through the hallway outside their room.

Antonio stuffed the package into his coat pocket. "It's not much," he said, "but I'll save it. We don't have time now." He led her back into the corridor, through the waves of foreign-speaking men and grandmothers and screaming children. They moved in a tight mass up the narrow stairway, carried by the crowd, until they pushed through a steel door into the vast open air of the deck.

CHAPTER 27

Vito and Carolina arrived in Genoa in the early afternoon. At the train station, they paid a man to drive them to the Albergo Corona as fast as he could. The man's brother, a student from Perugia, had sat across from them on the train, and told him this was an "emergency of love."

An old man answered the door of the hotel. *"Buongiorno,"* Vito said. He tried to speak calmly. "Please, Signore. Maddalena Grasso. Can you tell her she has visitors?"

The man looked from Vito to Carolina and introduced himself as the owner of the hotel. When he didn't let them in right away, Vito realized how much like vagabonds they must appear. His face was flushed and sweaty, and he had to take breaths between his words. Carolina's hair was pulled back neatly, but came apart in high wisps at the pin behind her left ear. She had dirt stains on the sleeve of her dress. They both smelled of the crowded train.

"I'm sorry," Signore Fosca said. "Signore and Signora Grasso left two hours ago for the dock."

"No!" Vito said. "Please, Signore. This is her sister, Carolina Piccinelli. I am a good friend of Antonio's from the village. You have to tell us the truth. We sent a telegram. We have important news for them."

"I don't lie, Signore," he said. "They had a boat to catch. I'm sorry." He leaned on the door, about to close it.

"Did she get the telegram?" Vito tried to ask.

"Please, Signore," Carolina interrupted. She held the door. "Can you tell us what ship they're on? How to get there?"

A woman called "Marcello!" from inside the hotel. Signore Fosca turned to her. She came up to the door, opened it wider, and looked closely at Vito and Carolina. She thought for a moment. Then she said their names.

"Yes!" said Vito. "That's us! Is Maddalena with you?"

"Come in, come in," she said, and led Vito and Carolina into the lobby. She smiled, shrugged at Signore Fosca, and reached into her pocket. She pulled out an envelope. "My husband doesn't think I know what goes on under this roof, but I do. Signora Grasso left this for you. She didn't say which one, only that it was for a romantic surprise."

"It's for me, then," Vito said. He grabbed Carolina's hand and squeezed it. "I told you she'd wait for us." He took the envelope, thanked the old woman, and said, "You've saved her life, Signora."

"I hope you're right," said Carolina. She held one corner of the letter and followed along as Vito read it to himself. After a minute, she shook her head and looked up at him, but he kept reading.

Caro Vito e Carolina,

I'm writing this in a hurry in secret, with Antonio in the room, waiting for you to come and take me back. I'm waiting to forget there ever was an Antonio. But if you're reading this, it's already too late, and I'm afraid of what's happening to me instead. I'll wait for you as long as I can on the 18th, like you told me to, and if you don't come, I'll get on the boat with Antonio, who you said is a liar.

I forgive you if the telegram was a trick. I deserve worse punishment for what I did. But I hope you believe me when I say I never planned any of it, and I never loved Antonio. Mamma and Babbo didn't give me a choice. I didn't know what else to do but go along with them. Now it feels like the worst mistake of my life. I should have said no, and run away. I should have been a different person. But how could I? I loved you, Vito, but I didn't believe you could fix this.

Even now, I think as I write, I could leave. Antonio is sleeping. I could take some money and get to the station before he wakes up. I could move to Naples with Vito just as we planned, where no one knows us. It seems perfect in my head as I write it, until I think, how can you bring a girl like me to your Zio, Vito? How can you raise another man's baby and pass it off as your own? And so there is this trap, because I may be carrying a child. And the more I think I can change what I did, the more traps. The plans are twisted and wrong—me a married woman with a baby in a town where everyone judges me—and again I have no choice. If you don't come in time and tell me what to do, I'll go where Antonio takes me. Whatever kind of man he is, I'll trust God to protect me.

Pretend I died the day Antonio came, and you won't be far from the truth. When you remember me, think of the plays and the bike rides in the olive grove, the dancing in the Grotto and the Festa, and that I tried to do what was right, even when it made no sense.

The night before I left for Teramo, Vito, you said you wanted to scare me. You wanted me to think of your life sometimes, while I was safe and you were alone. Now I ask the same from you. You have your mother and Buccio. You both have your families and the village, and each other. Think of me with no mother or father, no friends and no one to love, no one who knew me when I was a girl.

If you know for sure Antonio is a liar, I beg you never to tell Mamma and Babbo. They have no reason to know. Don't tell them you tried to find me. Make up some excuse why you were gone. Tell them you ran away together, that you're in love. Maybe that will be the truth after all. Maybe God put us on this long and terrible road just to bring the two of you together, and get rid of me.

Vito, I told you once never to believe anyone who said I didn't love you. That is still true. Whatever was true in Santa Cecilia is still true. I'm waiting for you here. I keep hearing voices on the street. Why won't you come early, while Antonio is still asleep?

Vito turned the page over. There was nothing more, and no signature. He read the last part again, unable to lift his head. He felt the Foscas staring at him. Carolina had turned her face away. "What ship is she on?" he asked, his eyes still on her words.

"The *Terra Mia*," said the old man. "But it's been on the water already an hour now. The letter is not what you expected?"

"It could leave late," Vito said. He folded the paper and stuffed it in the pocket of his pants. "Ships leave late, don't they?" He headed to the door and opened it. Surely one of the hundred cars or carriages on the street could drop him at the dock. To his left he could see the glimmer of water between two buildings. "We're close enough to walk?" he asked Signore Fosca.

Before he could answer, Carolina said, "Let's go home, Vito. It's over."

"When we're this close!" he said. "Didn't you read the letter?"

"I read it," she said.

He held the door open, ready to slam it in the face of anyone who tried to stop him. "You can stay if you want," he said. "But I'm going. I didn't come all the way here to give up."

"What kind of surprise is this?" Signora Fosca said. "It doesn't sound very romantic to me."

"The dock's no more than a mile," said Signore Fosca. "Just follow the road north along the water. The *Terra Mia*'s double the size of every other ship."

Vito ran out of the *albergo* and turned left toward the shore. He found the road immediately. He passed rows of sails and small fishing boats and flocks of seabirds feasting on the decks. The noise of cars' and ships' horns, gulls squawking, the ocean in a roar, thrummed around him. Still he outpaced the horses and the slow-moving cars and kept his eyes on the larger ships gathered at the far end of the dock. He didn't know how he'd find Maddalena once he got there or what he'd say to convince her to come home. He had no answer to her questions. He couldn't promise that the village would show her compassion. All he had to free her from her traps was love, which seemed at once everything and nothing.

When he came upon the row of bigger ships, Vito slowed to a walk. He looked up and down the length of the coast. There were ships of all sizes, but not one twice the size of another. The crowd was walking toward him in packs. They wept and laughed and held each other as the wind whipped their hair against their faces. A few stopped to shield their eyes and gaze out over the ocean.

He asked one of the men a question, though as he spoke he could feel the answer crashing against him: "The *Terra Mia*, did it leave?"

"You can still see it!" the man said, without turning to him. "My brother Luigino is on it, the lucky *bastardo!*" He pointed to where Vito had been afraid to look. On the edge of the western horizon was a dark, unmoving mass, a blur just above the surface of the water. "I told him," the man said, "'In two years, when I get the money, look for me on your doorstep in New York City!' I have a plan . . ."

Vito shaded his eyes, but the ship did not come into focus. He'd rushed all his life for Maddalena Piccinelli—to finish his bike before spring, to drag himself and his sick mother halfway to Teramo during a war, to fix her house and learn a trade and stop her wedding and save her from a liar—and all that rushing had brought him to this. He could do nothing now but stand still and watch her disappear, as the miles of ocean multiplied between them.

The man stopped talking about his plan and faded into the crowd. Soon a new crowd made its way to the berth the *Terra Mia* had left empty. These were happier people, clapping their hands and shouting at the ship heading toward the shore. They waved and called out names, though it was still much too far off for them to be seen or heard. Vito couldn't bear it. He squinted, but he could no longer see even the blur of Maddalena's ship. He turned back toward the hotel.

And there was Carolina, a few yards away, standing against a wooden post. How long she'd been there he didn't know. As he approached her, she pulled her coat closed tighter and ticked her head up to get his attention. Her cheeks and ears and nose were pink, her hair completely undone in the wind. "No luck?" she asked.

She'd said it as a question, but that's not how he heard it. She'd made the words tender, like the breaking of sad news to someone she didn't wish to hurt. Her face grew softer. He let her hold him there against the post, with the crowd passing. She rested her head on his chest, and he cupped his hand over her ear to warm it.

He was afraid. He had no plan for the life that awaited him in the village. He'd go back tonight a dead man, and sooner or later he'd have to resurrect himself and explain and fight with Guglierma Lunga and the other gossips. He'd go back a *cornuto* without the pride to let the woman go or the courage to kill himself over her. Only Carolina—not Buccio or his mother or even Maddalena—knew the full story from beginning to end. And she lived a minute's walk from him in Santa Cecilia, where every day he'd see her on the terrace or in the store and she'd remind him of the way it all really happened, not the version he'd tell the others.

This scared him now, as he held Carolina on the dock. He still didn't trust her, this girl who'd thought him unworthy of Maddalena for so long, who'd only recently switched sides. He didn't know that he'd often turn to her for comfort, that she'd defend him to her family and everyone else who called him a fool. He didn't know she'd wait for him the many years it took to come back from Naples and convince himself he'd forgotten her sister. She'd stand beside him and his father and sisters in the summer of 1950, when they returned to bury Concetta in a crypt they'd pay cash for. And later that month, she'd hold him again as she held him today, with her arms locked around his back and her cheek against his chest. They'd stand in the shade of the chestnut trees behind his empty house, too old for the olive grove or the woods behind the spring. She'd tell him he'd find only misery in Philadelphia, and beg him not to follow his father there. And when he refused, she'd ask him just once—because as much as she loved him, she did have pride—to stay in Santa Cecilia and make her his wife.

CHAPTER 28

The sun had sunk into mid-sky behind Maddalena and nothing more remained of Italy, not even the distant lights or the birds that had hovered over them during the launch. She and Antonio gazed together at the vastness to the east. Only an old couple had stayed on deck with them, arguing over the saltiness of the meat in the sandwiches they'd packed. They drank from a jug of wine wrapped in straw, and after a while they started laughing; when Maddalena looked over, the man had put on the woman's flowered hat.

"You won't hate me forever," Antonio said.

"I don't hate you."

He shook his head. "When I come near you, you go white," he said. "You're afraid to put two words together to speak to me. If you did, you'd have seen by now that I'm a good man. Everyone in Philadelphia will tell you what a hard worker I am, how I take care of my family. Once, when my brother Mario broke his elbow—"

"Please don't say any more," Maddalena said. She kept her back to him. "It makes it worse, somehow."

"All right," he said. He stepped to her side and lifted her chin to look her in the face. "Can I at least give you my present now?"

She nodded. She felt the eyes of the old couple on her as Antonio took out the ball of newspaper from the side pocket of his coat and handed it to her. It was as heavy as stone, and as Maddalena unwrapped it she realized that's exactly what it was: a stone foot, or part of one—the big toe and the one beside it, attached to half a sole and heel, broken off in jagged edges at the ankle.

"You don't recognize it?" he asked.

"No!" she said. She held it at arm's length, as the wind whipped the newspaper into the sea. "It's horrible!"

"It's from Avezzano," he said, "from that statue you love." He lifted her hands to hold the foot in the sunlight. "I did just as I said. I sneaked into the park at night, in this black coat, and stole it for you. So you could have something from home to keep, something unexpected. I know it's not a gold necklace."

She brought it closer, turned it over and ran her fingers along the toenails. It was carved in fine detail, with little hairs etched between the joints. She wondered which of the three struggling men it belonged to, and what would happen when they put him back together and saw what was missing.

"You don't have to say anything," he said. He kissed her briefly on the lips, holding the foot between their waists. "I want to make you happy.

I will if you let me. This is just the beginning. Tell me how to make you feel better about me and I'll do it. I'll do anything."

She looked at him: his pleading face, the stubble on his cheek, his gray, bloodshot eyes. "Be honest with me, then," she said. "About the money, your family, everything. If I knew the truth, I'd feel—I don't know—safer. Right now all I feel is afraid. You're like a stranger to me."

"Please don't be afraid," Antonio said. He put his arm around her waist and pulled her closer. "I've told you the truth from the beginning, Maddalena. My life is an open book."

"So if someone said your family had no money," she said, "they'd be lying?"

"No money?" he said. He'd raised his voice, and the old couple gave him a look. "Of course that's a lie. Who told you that?"

"It doesn't matter," Maddalena said quietly. "I don't care about money. I just want to know. I don't want any surprises. This gift is the last surprise I want."

"We had a bakery," Antonio began. "And then it closed. We'll open another before Christmas. My father is a businessman, like yours. In business there are ups and downs. One month you're on top of the mountain, the next you're at the bottom, the next you're halfway up already. It's not like Santa Cecilia, with one grocery and one butcher shop and one *tabaccheria*. In America you have to compete with ten other places, and you can never rest. Not for one second. So right now the Grassos are climbing the mountain. Do you understand?"

"I think so."

"Someone told you a different story, though," he said. "I'm sure I know who. What else did this mystery person say about the Grassos of Philadelphia? I'd like to hear the lies being spread about us."

"It was just that one thing," she said.

"In America there's no time for gossip. You don't find old ladies like Guglierma Lunga making predictions from their balconies."

"It doesn't matter."

"A woman shouldn't even worry about money," Antonio went on. "That's what husbands are for. How many checks did your mother write in her life?"

"None," said Maddalena.

"I thought so," Antonio said. He dug out a cigarette from his inside pocket and lit it, cupping one hand to block the wind. "Please say you feel better now."

She nodded.

"No wonder you were afraid," he said, and smiled. "Believe me, I can afford a better gift than a chunk of rock. But if you get scared again, Maddalena, about anything, just remind yourself of this: You're the luckiest girl ever to come out of Santa Cecilia. How many of your friends will ever ride on a ship like this?" He spread his arms and leaned against the railing. "Right now you know only that one narrow world, but look around you. You couldn't take it all in if you tried. You'll live ten lives for every Carolina in Italy."

At her sister's name she covered her face and turned away, remembering the warning her mother had given her. She wouldn't let her husband see her cry.

"I promise you, *tesoro*," he said, "the biggest problem you'll have in life will be what to name your babies."

She chose to believe him, though he could give her nothing but his word. He was her only friend now, and whatever he offered she'd have to open her hands and take. She had no one else to protect her. As hard as she begged God to change her life—to undo the traps He'd set, to tear her love for Vito from her heart now that she could no longer use it—she knew He'd never take her back to that first day on the bike in Santa Cecilia. Every word Antonio spoke could be a lie, sweet romancing meant to calm her, but she wouldn't know for sure until she saw for herself.

Was she so different from any other bride? If you were a girl from Santa Cecilia, standing at this moment in the church beside a boy you'd known for twenty years, someone maybe who'd gone off to war and come back safely, would you know any better than Maddalena Piccinelli what waited for you in his house? Doesn't every wife learn a new language and forget little by little the one she spoke when she was young?

And so the closer Maddalena came to Antonio's country over the next thirteen days, the less afraid she became. She'd bear it no worse than her mother, who'd married for love, had borne life in the village she hated. When Maddalena hid her face from Antonio and cried, it was out of grief, not fear; because however much of the world he would show her, whatever new lives she would become part of, she'd never see the middles and ends of the ones she began with.

She will not see Fiorella sit up from her place on the roof in the middle of summer to wave to the soldier from Broccostella. She'll hurry to cover the sun blotches on her face with her mother's makeup, then walk slowly down the stairs to greet him. She won't hide her hand in her pocket, since this soldier, Bruno, has lost his arm. His face will be ruddy and kind, and he will have just worked up the courage to ask her name from Claudio Piccinelli, who is sweeping dirt from the doorway of the grocery across the street. Fiorella is the only girl who will have made him forget about the war.

Ada will not even pretend to be happy. She will ask her mother how a woman with missing fingers can snag a soldier, while she gets older and puts on weight. She will refuse to attend Fiorella's wedding and will instead make jokes about what limbs will be missing from their children. One night Ada's older sister will find her in the woods behind the church with her husband and beat her over the head with a thick branch. She'll die a month later in the house where she was born, her sister weeping beside her.

Maddalena will not be there to hold her mother when Maurizio returns, not long from now, in an army truck, brotherless. He will write to her, the sister he barely remembers, but he will not tell her of the hole he'd dug for Giacomo in some Russian field. He won't speak about it to anyone but Buccio, who will have heard the story again and again at the bar of the Al Di Là. Every night, Aristide and Signore Vattilana will come and lead their sons back to their own beds to sleep. It will be Maurizio, after all, not one of his sisters, who ends up at home unmarried.

The plans Ezio, the butcher's son, made with Teresa have stayed in his mind through the winters on the front, and the hope that she hadn't found someone else kept him from pointing his gun at himself. He will take his place at the counter the day he returns and wait for Teresa to stop in. If Maddalena could see Teresa now, taking a cleaver to the side of a pig in the back room of the shop, she would not recognize her; she wears a bloody apron and the smell lingers in her hair, but she is happy.

Dr. Fabiano's wife will leave him and, soon after, Celestina will come down with a terrible fever. She will lie in her bed, her skin glowing with sweat, her hair fanned out behind her over the pillows. The doctor will see her as if for the first time, and when the fever breaks he'll stretch out the conversation long enough to change the wet towel over her forehead and stay for dinner. Later she'll cook him soup because he has no wife to care for him, and with every trip to his house another of the twenty years between them will erase itself. They will live together unmarried, but no one in Santa Cecilia, not even Guglierma, will make a fuss. They are happy that the doctor's German wife has gone back where she came from, and that Celestina has stopped taking soup to every single man in the village.

For a year after it happens, no one will tell Maddalena what Vito and Carolina decided under the chestnut tree. Her mother's letters won't mention the party she threw for them in her house after the wedding, or the suit Vito made himself. Maddalena will be standing outside Massimo Leone's tailor shop on Market Street when he'll notice her and hurry to the door, thinking her a customer. She'll come in and look around, rub the fabric between her fingers, and ask the price of a black pinstripe for her husband. She won't give him her name. Her heart will race. Then she'll see the photograph taped above the sewing machine: Carolina and Vito kneeling in the church of Santa Cecilia, the statue of Mary behind them, her mother and father blurry but visible in the corner. They are smiling; Vito has a beard; Carolina carries a bouquet of white flowers and her hair is pulled back. Without thinking, Maddalena will touch their faces and bring two fingers to her lips. When Massimo asks what she is doing, she will run out of the store into the crowded Philadelphia street.

On the boat, the old couple had gathered their bags and disappeared, leaving only Maddalena and Antonio on the deck. It was too cold to stay outside much longer, but Maddalena did not want to go back to their underwater room. She asked to stay here for a while, alone, and Antonio agreed to come find her in a half hour.

"I'm fine here," she said.

Once he was gone, she closed her eyes and rested her forearms on the steel railing. She let her body go so numb and far away that she could no longer feel the wind against her face. She heard the churn of the motor and the waves splashing, but she was not on this enormous ship in the middle of the Atlantic; she was back in Santa Cecilia and knew nothing of husbands or war or money. The road from the spring to her house was the widest she'd ever travel; it could fit thirteen girls across, twenty if they stood close. She was not dreaming; she was slipping off her shoe and rubbing her calf while a boy spied on her from behind a tree; she was making up stories and futures in her head, then stumbling barefoot through the olive grove to reach the stage.

ACKNOWLEDGMENTS

I have been blessed with the unwavering support of family and friends throughout the writing of this book. I remain forever grateful for their loving words, deeds, prayers, and patience at every turn.

Special thanks to Michelle Chalfoun, an extraordinary reader, writer, and friend whose insight and faith were instrumental in this novel's creation. Thanks also to Eve Bridburg and Kristin Duisberg, for their (un)solicited pep talks and crucial feedback on early drafts.

What immense luck to have had the following mentors: Chuck Selvaggio, who noticed the green door; Liz Benedict, who told the truth; and Ralph Lombreglia, who pulled me back from the edge. I thank them for their encouragement and friendship.

Mary Evans is an agent of uncommon integrity and savvy—I sleep well knowing she's on my side. It has been a privilege to work with my editor, Antonia Fusco, whose wisdom, passion, and dedication sharpened this story and gave it life.

I am indebted to the Bread Loaf Writers' Conference, Grub Street, Inc., Carberry's in Arlington, and Algonquin Books—all of which feel like home.

My deepest gratitude I reserve for Michael Borum, who guided me through the everyday triumphs and setbacks with unflappable confidence and love. Best friend, patron, maker of innumerable sacrifices—he has shown me that the joys of life are not only reachable, but sustainable.